VIGILANTE

Kerry Wilkinson is something of an accidental author. His debut, *Locked In*, the first title in the detective Jessica Daniel series, was written as a challenge to himself but, after self-publishing, it became a UK Number One best-seller within three months of release. Kerry then went on to have more success with the second and third titles in the series, *Vigilante* and *The Woman in Black*. His new book, *Think of the Children*, will be available in both paperback and ebook soon.

Kerry has a degree in journalism and works for a national media company. He was born in Somerset but now lives in Lancashire.

For more information about Kerry and his books
visit his website: www.kerrywilkinson.com
or www.panmacmillan.com

By Kerry Wilkinson

LOCKED IN

VIGILANTE

THE WOMAN IN BLACK

KERRY WILKINSON

VIGILANTE

PAN BOOKS

First published by Kerry Wilkinson 2011

This edition published 2013 by Pan Books
an imprint of Pan Macmillan, a division of Macmillan Publishers Limited
Pan Macmillan, 20 New Wharf Road, London N1 9RR
Basingstoke and Oxford
Associated companies throughout the world
www.panmacmillan.com

ISBN 978-1-4472-2566-9

1 3 5 7 9 8 6 4 2

A CIP catalogue record for this book is available from the British Library.

Typeset by Ellipsis Digital Limited, Glasgow
Printed and bound by CPI Group (UK) Ltd, Croydon, CR0 4YY

Visit **www.panmacmillan.com** to read more about all our books
and to buy them. You will also find features, author interviews and
news of any author events, and you can sign up for e-newsletters
so that you're always first to hear about our new releases.

VIGILANTE

PROLOGUE

The man had deliberately worn soft-bottomed dark trainers and dug out some old black jogging pants and a navy-blue T-shirt. There wasn't a great amount of choice in his wardrobe but at least he had enough dark clothes. He was also grateful for the unseasonably dry weather. He didn't own a big thick jacket but, even if he did, it would have made him stand out.

He had quickly discovered following someone was not as easy as it appeared on television shows. It didn't help that he only had set times during the night where he could carry out work such as this. Wearing dark items made it a lot simpler and the fact the council couldn't be bothered fixing street lights was pretty much a godsend. The trainers were something he had overlooked at first. It seemed silly now but not only were they quiet to walk in, which was exactly what he needed, but they gave him a head-start if he did have to run for it. He had made a special effort in recent months to get himself into shape. At his age, he was never going to be an athlete but he had managed to lose a few pounds from his stomach and put on a bit of muscle in his shoulders and arms. Free access to the gym had helped and he was faster too. Each session would begin with running. It wasn't stamina he needed, just speed. He knew he wouldn't have to race over a distance if it came to it, he only had to sprint to safety.

A few test runs had helped, trailing random people after dark and learning not to be seen. There was no rush to get things done, it was all about waiting for an opportunity and not being caught. The targets on his list weren't going anywhere and one by one they would all be dealt with.

Hopefully tonight was the time when the first name would be scratched from that list.

The man looked up a few hundred yards ahead of him. The person he wanted was still with a couple of his friends but it looked as if they were finally saying their good-byes. Though he had made every effort to stay out of the illuminated areas, the three people ahead of him were standing under a street light. The man watched their cigarette smoke drift upwards and could hear their faint voices. He saw one of their hands go into a jean pocket and swiftly transfer a palmful of something to the man he himself was watching. The handover was so quick and assured, neither of them even bothered looking around. Why would they? They knew the chance of being caught was minimal and, even if they were, they would be back on the streets soon enough.

The person who had initiated the transfer shook hands with the third member of the group and then turned around, walking towards a nearby alleyway. Even from this distance, he could see the person walking away had his jeans slouched somewhere underneath his backside, his underwear sitting high above them. He shook his head from the shadows at the ridiculousness of this current fashion trend.

Now there were just two people left under the light, the man decided he could move closer. His step was gentle but he followed a deliberate path towards his target, stopping around fifty metres away and resting against a wall in a heavily shadowed area. He could hear the voices of the two remaining people clearly now. Their local accents jarred as they spoke in American slang as if they had been born in 1960s Harlem.

It wasn't the black or white issue that annoyed him, he was fairly colour-blind when it came to race, but young white men who were busy making other people's lives a misery and thought they lived in a ghetto really did wind him up. He saw the type all the time – those who listened to rap music and thought they were some tough gangster because of it.

Idiots.

The two people moved from under the street light and started to walk briskly in the direction of where the man knew they both lived. He had figured it might come down to two people together. He wasn't confident he could take down a pair at the same time at this stage, certainly not for his first piece of work, but he knew there was a pretty good chance they would split up soon enough to go their separate ways.

He had done his homework.

The man kept pace with them, carefully watching his step. On one of his practice runs, he had soon worked out it wasn't just a case of staying unseen; you had to watch where you walked too. As best he could in the gloom, he avoided any stones on his path that could have caused a noise and hurried after the two figures, determined not to lose sight of them. They crossed a road as he knew they would and then, finally, he saw them shaking hands and saying their goodbyes for the night. The man crouched behind a car, unconsciously holding his breath. He felt his heart rate rise, knowing he was a minute or two away from the moment he had spent the past few months preparing for. He moved his hand to the outside of his pocket and felt for the knife. It was still there and, even through the material of his clothes, felt slightly cool to touch as if it were waiting for his hand to warm the handle up.

Ahead of him, the second man turned to his left and walked through an archway that separated the blocks of flats on the estate. His shadow disappeared away from the lights and into the night. That left just the one.

The target turned around and started walking towards where his follower knew he lived. The man trailing him knew he would have to act in the next five hundred yards. He stood up from behind the car and began moving quickly behind the victim. It didn't matter if he was seen now. He held his hand in his pocket and quickened his pace, moving within thirty yards of the person he had been watching for the past hour.

"'Scuse me, mate . . .' he said. The man was careful not to speak too loudly. There were still flats and houses in this area and he didn't want to risk anyone hearing him.

The target turned around quickly, eyes wide and clearly surprised someone had got this close to him without being heard. 'What do you—?' the victim managed to say before he stepped back.

There was no distance between them now but the target was reeling, as anyone would if a stranger had moved so swiftly into their personal space.

Then it was over.

The knife had flashed quickly from the man's pocket and into the other person's neck. Again the homework had paid off. The killer knew it was important to go for somewhere around the Adam's apple first in order to prevent any kind of sound. The victim grabbed the man's wrist but it didn't matter as his hold was weak. The man with the knife pulled back as he heard the gurgle from the other person's throat and then stabbed twice more in quick succession, this time aiming for the heart.

It wasn't as clean as he had hoped for but the job was done. The piece of filth dead at his feet wouldn't be peddling drugs or carrying out random acts of violence any longer.

The killer wondered if he would get the credit he should be due for such a positive act.

1

The sun was just beginning to rise as Detective Sergeant
Jessica Daniel walked from her parked-up red K-reg Fiat
Punto towards the thin white tent which had been put up
around the crime scene. She had been told on the phone it
was a dead body so had a reasonable idea what to expect.
Given the particular area of Levenshulme in Manchester it
had been found in, it wasn't necessarily a surprise either.
The youths who lived here seemed to spend large parts of
their free time finding new and ingenious ways to hurt
either themselves or someone else who happened to look a
little different to them.

They rarely went as far as killing each other though.

It had still been dark when Jessica had taken the call to
come to see this particular body. Being a DS meant she
was only phoned if something serious had happened. Her
sleeping patterns hadn't been so great over the past year
or so anyway but it seemed pretty typical that some poor
guy had got himself stabbed on one of the few mornings
she had been fast asleep.

Jessica reached the front of the tent and saw one of the
Scene of Crime officers walking out wearing a white paper
suit. They had obviously been quick off the mark that
morning even though their department was notoriously

under-staffed and relied on volunteers to stay on top of Greater Manchester's policing needs.

Noticing a familiar face towards the back of the tent, Jessica walked around to join Detective Inspector Jack Cole. 'Bit early for all this, innit?' she said. Cole shrugged. 'Have you seen inside?' Jessica asked, nodding towards the tent.

'Yes, I got here about two minutes before the SOCO boys.'

DI Cole was Jessica's immediate superior. They had been promoted at the same time eighteen months ago. He had gone from DS to DI, with her bumped up from Detective Constable to her current DS position. DI Cole was well known in the station for not wanting to get his hands dirty and preferring to work from his desk. Some people saw that as a negative and, although Jessica had at first, it did enable her to get more involved in things. Despite that, he was loyal and one of the people she trusted the most at the station, even though she didn't really know much about him.

Jessica was in her early thirties but the fifteen or so years between her and Cole couldn't have been wider. She was still living in a flat with next to no savings and taking things as they came. He was settled with two kids and a wife he clearly adored but kept that side of his life completely separate from his professional career. She had never met his partner or children and, as far as she knew, neither had anyone else in the station. He was a normal, unassuming guy who you wouldn't look at twice if you didn't know he was a detective.

Jessica acknowledged Cole's reply with a nod and

moved around to the front of the tent. The white material was encircled by the standard police tape on a pavement, with marked police cars parked nearby shielding their position from easy view. A couple of uniformed officers milled around near to the vehicles. As the morning began to get lighter people had started to come out of their houses and flats to gawp at the police scene. Jessica noticed a couple of young teenagers in school uniform on the opposite side of the street. The schools had only gone back after the summer holidays a few days previously and, while it was still early in the morning, it wasn't necessarily a surprise to see kids out at this time, certainly not in this area. The bigger shock was the school uniform as the estate the body had been found on was one of the roughest in the neighbourhood and just getting the youths to school was an achievement, let alone in uniform.

Jessica ignored them and walked around the tape to the tent's entrance.

The Scene of Crime team's job was to make sure any suspicious incidents were catalogued. Bodies would be cautiously removed from a murder site, photographs taken and everything measured and carefully chronicled. Things like fingerprints would be checked for, as well as blood or hairs that might belong to the perpetrator. It was very specialist work and the team didn't like having their scenes trampled upon.

There were two people working around the site and Jessica recognised both of them. She didn't know their names but people got used to seeing each other due to the nature of their overlapping jobs. Some people got closer than others but the ins and outs of dead bodies had never appealed to Jessica. Although she felt the crime scenes sometimes helped clarify her thoughts, she was more than happy to read a report rather than see the gory parts for herself.

Despite this, seeing as she was there anyway, she asked to have a look.

The person in the white suit standing by the tent's opening was a woman a few years older than Jessica. 'I'd rather you didn't.'

'I won't touch anything. If the light's okay, I won't even go past the entrance.'

The relationship between the teams was awkward. Technically Jessica could walk in if she wanted but, if she contaminated a scene, it would be a very serious matter. That meant that CID and other officers, no matter how senior, often deferred to the wishes of the Scene of Crime team.

The woman eyed her up and then turned around, ducking slightly and looking back into the tent. Jessica often found that you were more likely to get what you wanted if you asked nicely in situations like this.

The person in the white suit stood back up and peered at Jessica. 'All right, fine. But stay around here, okay?' She indicated the tent's entrance and Jessica nodded, stepping forwards as the flap was held up for her.

Inside a separate lamp had been set up to illuminate the body but the gentle sunlight was now coming through the thin sides of the tent in any case. Jessica could see all she needed to pretty easily. A young man's body was slumped face-up on the pavement. His legs were straight out below him but one of his arms was bent towards his neck, the other limp by his side. He was wearing jeans and some sort of black sweatshirt. Even though the top was dark, Jessica could see an even murkier stain on the man's chest, matching a circle of deep red spread out on the ground. There was an obvious gash in the middle of his neck where he had likely been stabbed and another hole was just about visible in his chest. In total there were two, possibly three, knife wounds and a very dead victim.

Jessica stepped backwards and thanked the woman for holding the flap up for her. 'Have you found anything yet?' she asked.

The woman shrugged and gave a small smile. 'Bit hopeful, aren't you?'

'You never know.'

'There was something under a couple of his fingernails on the arm you see raised; he might have grabbed his attacker. There were a couple of other odds and ends but it will take a few days. It should be easy to identify him though. His face is fairly clear and it's not rained or anything to mess up the scene. We found this in his pocket too.' She used a rubber-gloved hand to delve into a plastic container on the floor, pulling out two sealed plastic pockets. One had a small bag containing what looked like cannabis, the other had a canvas money-holder in it.

'There's ID in the wallet,' the woman added. 'Do you want the name?'

'I know who it is.' Jessica said. The woman clearly

looked a bit confused, so Jessica continued. 'I reckon ninety-five per cent of the Greater Manchester Police force would recognise that angelic face.'

It was fair to say Craig Millar was well known to the local police. Even though Jessica hadn't had the pleasure of arresting him herself, he had a face most of the local officers would know straight away. Jessica didn't know his exact age but was confident he was in his early twenties. Off the top of her head, she reckoned he had a criminal record for drugs possession, actual bodily harm, common assault and a drunk and disorderly or two. If she checked his full file, she would be fairly certain of finding more on there and probably a few police cautions or on-the-spot fines thrown in for good measure too.

And that was just what he had been caught doing.

His friends would no doubt have similar records and owe hundreds of pounds in unpaid fines to the courts. Once young people like Craig Millar got caught in the cycle of criminality, it seemed to continue until they ended up permanently in prison or, if they really annoyed the wrong people, dead on a pavement somewhere. She wondered who he could have upset. Maybe he was dealing drugs in an area he shouldn't? Or back-chatting out of turn to someone a bit higher up the criminal scale than he was? Or perhaps it was a stupid drunken argument with a friend who wouldn't remember much about it the next day?

Jessica found herself shaking her head as she walked back towards Cole. He clearly saw it in her face. 'Recognise him then?' he asked. His head was at a slightly sideways angle and she found his face difficult to read.

'That Millar kid. You noticed him too then?'

'I couldn't remember his name but the face was familiar.'

'What do you reckon? Whoever it was didn't bother taking his wallet so it wasn't just a mugging.'

'Drugs? Fighting? Who knows? If you're sure of the name we should probably get the address and find out if he lives with anyone before word gets around here anyway.' Cole indicated behind him and Jessica could see faces at windows of the block of flats that backed onto the road, with other people passing by on the other side of the road trying to get a glimpse.

Jessica said she had confirmed the victim's name with the officer who had the wallet. 'Who called it in anyway?' she added.

'If you had twenty quid on you, who would you put it on?'

'What makes you think I don't have twenty quid on me?'

Cole smiled. 'Reynolds reckons you still owe him a tenner and never bring money to work just so you don't have to pay him back.'

DS Jason Reynolds was an officer Jessica shared an office with. She grinned back at the inspector and gave a small laugh. 'It's got to be a dog-walker who called us.'

'Bingo.'

'I reckon we need a new way of investigating things like this. In future, let's just assume the bloke out walking his dog did it and work backwards from there; it's the perfect alibi.'

Cole's smile widened. 'I'll call in for the victim's address. It will almost certainly be around here anyway.'

Cole got Craig Millar's last-known address by phoning their Longsight base. It was a flat somewhere nearby but neither of them knew exactly where the place was and, from the records, they weren't completely sure if the victim lived alone. According to their own files, there were other Millars associated with the address but unsurprisingly no one was on the electoral roll. Jessica knew that anything seeming slightly authoritative would be roundly shunned in this area and doubted there were too many accurate records of who lived with whom.

Jessica crossed the road and asked the two teenagers in school uniform for directions to the victim's address. She didn't give the exact flat number but asked where the block was. The pair pointed her in what she assumed was the right direction without much of a protest and she and Cole set off to find out who actually lived at Craig Millar's address.

They crossed back over the road and cut through an alleyway that separated one set of flats from another. Jessica thought the whole area seemed fairly depressing, even with the sun now up and shining. The estate was a mix of red-brick two-storey blocks of flats and small houses. Most of the area was administered by a housing association, with signs all around bearing the organisation's logo and strict instructions that 'Ball games are not permitted'. Jessica knew full well from various newspaper reports and word-of-mouth around the station that, even if the association got tough on ball games, they weren't so bothered about low-level drug dealing and other misdemeanours as long as rent was paid on time.

Everything looked the same and the small scraps of land that hadn't been built on had patchy, muddied grass, graffiti littering many fences and walls. They continued walking and Jessica noticed a run-down children's play park on the opposite side of the road from them. She could see a pair of swings had been wrapped around the top of the frame they hung from and guessed that much of the rest of the equipment was unusable or vandalised.

It was easy for the police to blame the people who lived here for making a mess of their own estate but Jessica knew well enough a cycle of poverty was hard to escape from. Kids would struggle to get jobs, so sat around bored and hung about in gangs. Then when they were mature enough to have children of their own, which wasn't that old for some of them, the cycle would start over. Even if you wanted to get out, you would be up against it. A place like this would have a reputation, so it was easy to get left behind when it came to funding for things like education or anything else that might aid social mobility.

It didn't help either if you had to live close to criminal scumbags who cared about no one but themselves.

Jessica and Cole followed the teenagers' instructions and soon came across the row of flats they were looking for. He pointed out that the ground-floor apartments all seemed to have even numbers, so they took the nearby stairs up to the first floor. The concrete entrance to the stairwell stank and Jessica avoided looking towards the back of the area where the bins were overflowing. The stairs opened out onto a full row of odd-numbered properties on their left and a wooden rail running the full length of the building on their right plus a hard stone floor underneath them. The first thing Jessica noticed was a bank of satellite dishes overhanging the rail. It seemed as if every property had wires running from their front door across the ceiling covering the walkway and back down to their own dish.

They made their way halfway along the row until they reached the door they were looking for. Jessica knocked and waited but it didn't feel very sturdy. Most modern properties had double-glazed entrances and windows but the whole rank of flats had old-fashioned wooden doors.

Jessica had grown to like working with DI Cole, although his coolness did sometimes unnerve her. When they ended up working together, he was the calm thoughtful one while she went in running her mouth off. She had spent the past year trying to calm those instant reactions but it was a work-in-progress. In most situations, there was a tacit agreement between the two of them that Jessica would take the lead when it came to talking to witnesses or suspects. It wasn't a tactic they had ever spoken about, more something that had happened.

There was no immediate answer so Jessica knocked again, louder the second time. This time, she heard a voice from inside but couldn't make out what was being said. It didn't sound too friendly. The door was wrenched open and a woman stood there in a light pink dressing gown.

She had greying brown hair and was scowling before Jessica had even bothered to get her identification out.

The flat's occupant rolled her eyes. 'What's he bloody done this time?'

2

It seemed a pretty fair assumption the woman was Craig's mum but Jessica asked the obvious question to make sure. 'Are you Craig Millar's mother?'

'Yes, come on. It's too early for all this. What's he done now?'

The woman didn't seem in a very good mood and had clearly only recently climbed out of bed. Jessica guessed this wasn't the first time Craig's mother had been woken up because her son had been up to no good. Usually officers would make an effort to make sure people were at ease before giving bad news. At the absolute least, they would get the person to sit down. Quite often someone from uniform would be specially trained and drafted in to do it. The 'training' actually entailed an afternoon of role-plays with someone paid a lot more than they were. Ultimately, all officers knew there was never a good way to deliver bad news. Not acting like an idiot was rule number one – it was mainly about common sense.

'I'm afraid I've got some bad news for you, Mrs Millar.'

The woman rolled her eyes and swore. 'I don't know how many times I've got to keep telling him. He's out on his arse this time. I've had enough. I don't want his brother getting involved in all this shite.' The woman nodded behind her as if to indicate towards another son, who was presumably in a different room. He certainly wasn't visible in the hallway.

'I'm afraid your son is dead, Mrs Millar.'

Someone would have to formally identify the body but, given the wallet with his name in it and the fact Jessica recognised him, there was little point in making the poor woman suffer any longer.

She shook her head, taking half a step back. 'He's what?'

Jessica put a hand on her shoulder. 'I'm afraid he's dead.'

Craig Millar's mother took the news surprisingly well. Jessica sensed it was something she had probably had in the back of her mind for a long time given the lengthy list of her son's crimes. She introduced herself as Denise Millar and invited them into her kitchen, offering Jessica and Cole seats at a round dining table. The inside of the house was well maintained. The hallway was clean and decorated with school photographs of Craig and another boy. The kitchen was small but as tidy as the hallway. The table was at the centre of it, with worktops running the length of the room's sides. Apart from the door they had come through, there was another leading towards what looked like the living room.

Denise explained that her other son Jamie was still asleep. He had finished his GCSEs a few months ago but didn't want to stay on at school and hadn't managed to find a job. 'I just didn't want him going the same way as Craig,' his mother said.

The woman carried on as if nothing had happened,

making the three of them a cup of tea. Neither Jessica nor Cole had said they wanted one but Denise had made one for them in any case. As she sat sipping from her mug, she asked the officers how it happened. Jessica replied that they wouldn't be sure for a few days but it looked as if her son had been attacked.

Denise nodded as if it was the most natural thing in the world. 'He wasn't always bad,' she insisted. 'He got in with the wrong people at the wrong time. I knew some of the things he got up to but he was my son. I couldn't just kick him out. There was nowhere for him to go. He promised me he wouldn't bring any of *it* home with him but I don't know what he got up to outside of here.'

Jessica realised the 'it' could mean anything but didn't think it was worth pushing the point at that exact time. 'Do you know anyone who might want to hurt him?' she asked.

The woman snorted and put the mug down on the table. 'Christ. You tell me. He'd only been back out of prison for a few weeks. I didn't want to get involved with anything he did. I stopped asking for rent because I didn't want to be associated with wherever he got his money from.'

Jessica didn't know he had been in prison quite so recently. She wasn't surprised but there was a wide range of community punishments people like Craig Millar seemed to end up on that kept them out of jail.

'What was he in for?'

'Some assault or something, he was on remand. It

didn't go to court in the end so they let him out. He told me he didn't do it but then he always said that.'

'Do you know who he was out with last night?'

'No, I'd never remember the names anyway. I've got two kids with one always in trouble and a father that pissed off years ago. It all blurs into one in the end.'

Jessica nodded as Mrs Millar picked up her mug and took it over to the sink, washing it up. Jessica made a token gesture to sip some of the three-quarters of a mug she had left. 'Would Jamie know any of the names?' she asked.

Mrs Millar had her back to them but Jessica saw her freeze momentarily before turning around. 'He better not.'

'Could you ask him anyway?'

She met Jessica's eyes. The look told her that Jamie probably did know who his older brother had been out with but that his mother still hoped he was innocent and unaffected by the trouble Craig had consistently been in.

'I'll get him up and you can ask.'

Denise returned to the hallway and they heard her knocking on a door, then two muffled voices speaking. A few moments later she came back into the kitchen, her son trailing behind her. From what his mum had said, Jamie was sixteen years old but looked a little younger. He was pasty and skinny, while only wearing a pair of boxer shorts. He had what would be spiky brown hair when styled but for now it jutted out at random angles. His mother must have told him about his brother because there were tears in his eyes, although he was clearly trying hard to force them back.

He sat in the chair his mum had been in and she went through the other door into the living room. Jessica guessed she didn't want to hear whatever her youngest son might have to say but legally they couldn't speak to a child without their guardian present. Cole realised the problem so followed after Mrs Millar.

It was the two of them left at the table. 'Are you Jamie?' Jessica asked.

'Yeah.' The boy wouldn't meet her eyes and didn't look up from the table.

'I want to ask you a question or two if that's okay?'

'Fine.'

Cole and Mrs Millar returned and stood in the doorway. Jessica's colleague nodded to indicate he had told the mother why they needed her back. 'Okay, Jamie. I only really need to ask you two things. First, do you know of anyone who might want to hurt your brother?'

'No.' The reply was short and Jamie didn't look up from the spot on the table.

'Do you know who he would have been out with last night?'

Jamie finally glanced up from the table over to his mother in the doorway. She was looking at the floor herself. 'Maybe.'

'If you know their names, we can look into it if you're not sure. No one has to know it came from you.'

Jamie nodded slowly to himself as if weighing up his options. 'There's this guy Kev who he hangs around with, then Kev's brother Phil.'

'Do you know their last names or where they live?'

'Wright. Kev and Phil Wright. They live at opposite ends of the estate.' Jamie didn't know the exact addresses but had given them enough information so they could find out for themselves. If the Wright brothers were anything like Craig, the police would have plenty in their records.

They had all the information they could realistically need for now. Jessica told Denise they could arrange for a uniformed officer to come around if she wanted. The woman shook her head and Jessica said she would be asked to do a formal identification at some point in the near future. The woman shrugged and Jessica took out a card, turning it over and writing her mobile phone number on it, before handing it over.

'Call me if you want to talk,' she said.

Usually, she would leave a card for professional reasons if anyone remembered anything further relating to the case. In this instance, she thought the woman might simply need someone to talk to. There would be a family liaison officer appointed, as was the case in any killing, but Jessica genuinely felt for her.

'Poor woman,' Cole said softly as they walked out of the flat back towards the stairs. Jessica didn't reply but she was thinking the exact same thing. Craig Millar was clearly a right piece of work. He might have brought plenty of misery to the people he dealt drugs to but he had surely brought no greater unhappiness than to his own mother.

*

Another call to the station had established that Kevin and Phillip Wright did indeed share lengthy criminal records in common with Craig Millar. Jessica asked the officer she spoke with to read her the highlights of Craig's run-ins with the law too. She had remembered most of his record pretty well but there was a handling stolen goods she hadn't known about. She also checked why he had been in prison. As his mother had said, he had been remanded on suspicion of grievous bodily harm but charges were dropped by the Crown Prosecution Service because potential witnesses hadn't cooperated and the victim didn't want to give evidence in court. With someone who had a record like Craig, likely a well-known figure on the estate, it was no surprise that people stopped cooperating with the law. No one wanted to be seen as a grass, even if they'd had their face smashed in.

Kevin and Phillip, meanwhile, had two separate addresses but both were on the estate where Craig Millar's body had been found. Neither of them were necessarily suspects but they were apparently the last people to see Craig alive and would be arrested and taken to the station to be interviewed under caution.

Jessica and Cole made their way back to the murder site where the Scene of Crime team looked as if they were finishing up. Jessica went with one of the uniformed officers in a marked car to arrest Kevin, Cole going with a different officer in another car to pick up Phillip. They would both be spoken to separately. It was only a short journey and Jessica sat in the front of the car as the uniformed officer drove. Jessica knew the constable's first name was Jonny but didn't really know him.

They made small talk as Jonny weaved around the parked cars. 'One less for us to worry about,' he said, clearly talking about the body of Craig Millar. Jessica had never really been one of the laddish types at the station. Some of the females were and the gender boundaries had certainly blurred in recent times compared to the kind of stories some of the older officers would tell.

If there were any doubts as to her attitude regarding catching Craig Millar's killer, they had disappeared as Jessica sat with his mother. Regardless of what her son was like, his mum deserved the truth. Jessica didn't reply to Jonny's jibe. She just nodded.

Jonny clearly took her silence with the intent it was meant – she was his superior after all – pulling the car up outside a row of flats that looked almost identical to the one Jessica had just left. Kevin Wright's apartment was on the ground floor. The two of them went to the front door and Jessica rang the bell before knocking loudly. She was ready to start hammering for a second time when the door opened.

A man stood in the door in his underwear, smoking a cigarette. He had a shaven head and was fairly well built with broad shoulders and tattoos across his chest. 'Oh for f—' he started before Jessica interrupted him.

'Are you Kevin Wright?'

'Yeah, look, I ain't done nothing wrong, okay?' he said. There was a hint of aggression in his voice but he sounded more exasperated than anything else.

Jessica gave the standard caution she had given to people hundreds of times over.

Kevin interrupted her throughout. 'Craig? He's dead? What? I didn't do it.' Jessica would hate to admit it but she already believed him.

The interviews with both Kevin and Phil had thrown up very little of use. Jessica hadn't really thought they would. The fact both men had been picked up in their own flats the morning after the killing was a fairly safe sign neither of them had done it. If they had stabbed their friend, it was unlikely they would have hung around for the police to come knocking the next day. Their records showed they were clearly thugs but they were not idiots.

They shared the same solicitor. Jessica knew him well as one of the cheaper ones from the centre of the city. He was a frequent visitor to the station and an apparent favourite of the low-lifes who lived in the area. That meant they had to be spoken to one at a time, so Jessica handled both interviews with Cole. Each brother was clearly stunned that Craig had been killed the night before and Jessica believed most of their respective stories with both versions matching up fairly well. They each said they had spent the previous evening with Craig but insisted they had just been playing computer games at Phil's house, before spending the early hours hanging around chatting on the streets. There were very minor discrepancies around exact timings and Jessica strongly suspected there was a decent chance they had been up to no good while out and about but ultimately there was nothing they could hold either of them for in relation to the murder itself. Phil said he had left the group first and Kevin conceded he was probably the last person to see Craig alive. Both claimed they knew nothing about the death, with Kevin especially vociferous. Jessica had no reason to doubt them.

The forensics team would currently be working on Craig's body and the autopsy results would be released in a day or two. Given their lengthy records, Kevin and Phil's DNA profiles would both be stored in the National Database but new fingerprints and samples would be taken. The police were entitled to take a mouth swab on arrest and that would be sent off to update the database. Seeing as they had spent the evening together, there was every chance the DNA of the two brothers would appear on Craig's body, so linking them to him wouldn't necessarily prove anything untoward.

Neither of them said they had seen anything out of the ordinary and both claimed they didn't know anyone who would want to harm Craig. That last part sounded particularly ridiculous given the list of people he must have wronged at some point. Jessica was fully aware not much would happen until those initial forensics results came back. Both of the brothers' flats would be searched on the off-chance the murder weapon was found. Jessica thought they may well find drugs or *a* weapon but she didn't believe either of them was a killer.

For now the team would get cracking on a list of people who had a grievance with the victim. Starting with a suspects list of zero was always a big problem. Beginning with a list that would comfortably reach double figures was barely a better result.

Jessica would leave compiling that list to someone else – seniority did have its advantages and she knew just the man for the job: Detective Constable David Rowlands.

3

Jessica found Rowlands sitting in the canteen with DC Carrie Jones. Jessica outranked both of them but had great relationships with the pair of constables. Rowlands was cocky and frequently bragged about his female conquests but, underneath all that, Jessica saw him almost as an annoying younger brother who was there for her amusement. She was an only child, so didn't really know what it was actually like to have a sibling.

Fifteen months ago, Jessica had been involved in the first big case of her career. A complicated trail of murders had ultimately led back to her best friend Caroline's boyfriend, Randall, who had tried to kill Jessica. She had caught him and he was now secured in a hospital having been deemed unfit to stand trial. He hadn't spoken a word to anyone since being arrested.

It had been a tough year back at work for Jessica. Given her injuries, both physical and mental, she had been granted leave but wanted to quickly return to the job. Any officers hurt in the line of duty were obliged to undergo counselling sessions and Jessica had gone along with everything asked of her. It had been the support of the two DCs that had really helped her get her mind back on the job.

For one, Rowlands continued to poke fun at her, even

when other officers were going out of their way not to say anything that could accidentally upset her. It was that normality which helped her as much as any formal counselling.

Her friendship with Carrie was something that had grown enormously since her return to work. Before they had just been colleagues but now they were firm pals. It was a bitter-sweet friendship however as it had most likely grown because Jessica and Caroline had drifted further and further apart since the incidents of last year. It wasn't that they had fallen out but they had become different people. They had been friends for all of their adult lives but had gone from living together and talking every day to simply not speaking and seemingly having very little in common. At the time, Caroline had been planning to move in with Randall but, following his arrest, she had ended up moving out of the flat she and Jessica shared and settling into a place on her own.

The two constables were sitting opposite each other at a table with four seats. Jessica sat next to Carrie, who wasn't eating but cradling a mug of tea, pulling out the chair with a scrape. Both were in their late twenties, although Rowlands was due to turn thirty in a few months – a source of much amusement to Jessica.

'Is that a new wrinkle around your eye, Dave?' she asked with a grin.

The man looked up from the food he was eating. 'Hardee-har-har. You do know you'll always be those few years older than me, don't you?'

'Yeah, but I look younger. No greys either,' Jessica

replied, holding out a few strands of her long dark-blonde hair as if to illustrate her point.

Rowlands was eating some sort of spaghetti concoction but put his fork down and touched his own spiky dark hair. 'I don't have any grey hairs.'

'Only 'cos you dye it,' chipped in Carrie with a wink to Jessica. DC Jones had a strong Welsh accent. She was short and slim with light blonde hair and a cackling laugh that carried across rooms. Jessica always marvelled at how even her laugh sounded as if it had an accent. She was the type of person that, due to her slight frame, was easily underestimated by people who didn't know her. She was incredibly sharp though and Jessica liked her a lot.

'Oh aye. Female union again, is it?'

Jessica and the other woman laughed together. 'I've got a job for you actually,' Jessica said when things had settled down.

Dave had now finished eating and was fiddling with something stuck between his teeth. 'It's something you don't want to do, isn't it?'

'You're very perceptive in your old age.'

'Go on then.'

'The body we found this morning, Craig Millar, he will have annoyed a fair few people . . .' The constable rolled his eyes, guessing where the request was heading as Jessica continued. 'We've got a few uniforms on his estate knocking on doors but you know what it's like around there, people won't want to be seen talking to us. I want you to put together a file of people who may have had it in for him. It'll be a big list.'

Rowlands sighed. 'Didn't you bring in two brothers this morning?'

'Yeah. Their flats are being searched as we speak but I'm not convinced we'll get anything linking them to the actual killing.'

'When are you expecting results from the scene?'

'Dunno. Maybe tomorrow for the initial bits? It depends how busy they are with other stuff and what they found.'

'When do you want the list by?'

'Tomorrow's briefing. We'll go over it then and divide it up among officers so we can start ruling people out.' He scowled back at her. 'You've gotta be careful screwing your face up like that at your age, Dave. It'll only add more wrinkles.'

'Yeah, yeah.' Rowlands slid his chair back and stood up. 'I guess I'm going to have to go get on with this ubiquitous list then.'

Jessica looked at her colleague with a look of bewilderment on her face, while Carrie gave a small laugh. 'A *what* list?' Jessica said.

'Ubiquitous. I figured it's about time someone around here tried to raise the standard of conversation.' He was grinning, clearly joking.

'Can you even spell it?' Carrie asked.

'Did you get into a fight with a dictionary or something?' Jessica added.

'I figure at least one of us should be well-read.'

'The only thing you're well-read in is mucky magazines

and pizza menus,' Jessica snorted. Carrie laughed loudly, the familiar accent clear.

'You look like you're pretty good at reading pizza menus yourself,' Dave replied with a laugh of his own, patting his stomach and pointing at Jessica. He turned around and strolled off still chuckling before anyone could say anything back.

Jessica was mock-outraged and the other woman was clearly trying not to laugh. 'Cheeky bastard,' Jessica said.

In the same way that Rowlands wasn't really going grey or wrinkly, Jessica knew she wasn't getting fat. It was banter that got them through the days. Jessica turned to face Carrie more directly. 'So how's this new bloke of yours then?' she asked.

The two had forged a good friendship that had been littered with the Welsh detective's various disasters with boyfriends.

Since an encounter she regretted with one of Randall's friends and the way things had turned out with Randall himself, Jessica hadn't had anything that might even begin to count as a boyfriend. Not that she was bothered; the job was what drove her at the moment.

Just recently, it seemed as if Carrie had settled on someone she actually liked. Jessica could tell because, whereas before they would hold regular wine-fuelled inquests into disastrous dates, her friend had stayed pretty quiet about the latest man in her life.

'He's okay,' she replied with a small smile, slightly more quietly than usual.

'Still don't want to talk about him, then?' Jessica didn't

really mind. Her friend would open up when she was ready.

'Nope.'

'So what else is going on? Still having problems with the house?'

While a lot of police officers rented places while they were young because they could be moved around or apply for posts with other forces, Carrie's father was insistent that renting was throwing money away. Because of that, her parents put up the money for a deposit on a two-bedroom house where she lived on her own a few minutes' walk away from the Longsight station. Jessica had stopped over the odd night in the spare room after they had gone out together or following team drinks in the station's local pub. It was in a great area for getting to and from work but not in a terrific place considering the neighbours.

It wasn't as rough as the estate where Craig Millar had been killed but it wasn't too much better. The fact the locals knew she was a police officer just made things worse for her. Bricks had been put through her windows twice in the past year and, while targeting a law-enforcement officer would be an aggravating factor if someone was arrested for the damage, no one had been found.

'It's not been too bad. That Mills guy is back out of prison.'

'How long was he in this time?'

'Not long. His girlfriend didn't want to give evidence in the end and they dropped the charges.'

'Did you really think she would?'

'No. It's always the way, isn't it? Boyfriend smashes up

his girlfriend's face. She calls us when she wants protection then changes her mind the next day. At least it got him out of the area for a few weeks.'

John Mills was somebody else very well known to the local police officers. He was in his fifties but had a long record of being in and out of custody for various, usually violent, offences. He also happened to live half-a-dozen doors down from Jones after buying two houses and converting them into one much bigger property. A few months ago, Carrie had conducted some research in her own time and shown Jessica that crime rates on the estate where she lived directly correlated to whether Mills was in prison. When he was on the outside, he would have a network of low-level drug dealers working for him and things like burglary rates would go up without fail. It was hard to pin very much on him directly, though. There were always middle men to take the fall, with Mills set up as a legitimate businessman, owning a nightclub in the city centre. It was almost certainly where he laundered money but proving that was something far beyond either of their expertise.

Jessica nodded and the woman continued.

'She visited him every day. She still stayed at his house and I'd see her driving off to the prison for visiting hours when I wasn't here. You could still see the bruises on her face. The Crown were relying on her to give evidence but she was spending each day going to check on the guy who beat her up. It's ridiculous.'

Jessica couldn't disagree but knew from experience it often happened in instances of domestic violence. So many cases fell apart before they reached trial. Given his violent record, Mills would have been denied bail due to the likelihood of interfering with the one witness but that witness was happily visiting him each day in jail. The system was farcical.

'Does he actually cause you any direct problems?'

'Of course not. He wouldn't dare put himself on the line like that. If he really wanted to get at me, he'd have someone unconnected do it.'

'That's how cowards operate.'

Carrie had said nothing at first. There was no specific reason why Mills would target her, other than his hatred of the police. He wasn't stupid and wouldn't risk his empire crumbling just for a cheap laugh at the expense of a detective who lived nearby.

'He still stares . . .' DC Jones said quietly. 'Every time I walk past or anything like that. You can see him in the window or if he's outside. He stares and watches until I've shut my front door.' She didn't sound scared but there was something in her voice. Mills obviously intimidated her.

Jessica had seen the man herself. He was perma-tanned with cropped hair, big muscles and an imposing physique two or three times the size of hers. There was no law against watching someone but the intimidation of her friend was hard to accept. They just had to hope the Serious Crime Division, a department Jessica had had issues with in the past, would pull their fingers out and nail him for something.

'Are you coming out on Friday night then?' Carrie asked, changing the subject.

'I don't know, maybe. You always get the idiots out at the weekend. What do you reckon about that midweek pub quiz Dave's always going on about?'

'Yeah, we should go sometime. It sounds like a laugh. We'll find out how *ubiquitous* his knowledge is.' Jessica met her eye and both women laughed.

'The problem is he reckons there's karaoke afterwards,' Jessica said.

'So?'

'Do you know "karaoke" is the Japanese word for "arsehole"?'

'Is it?'

'No but it should be.' Jessica smiled but, from the look on Carrie's face, she wasn't convinced her friend had got the joke. 'Right, back to work,' she added, scraping her chair backwards and standing up. 'Have you got much on?'

'No, I might go give Dave a hand before he has a proper strop or tries to rope in one of the blondes from uniform to help him out.'

Jessica smiled, knowing full well that was almost certainly the type of thing Dave would be doing at that exact minute.

'I've got some paperwork and bits to go over,' Jessica said. 'I want to try to get it out of the way before Craig Millar's test results come back. I'm hoping it'll be simple but I'm not going to hold my breath.'

The constable looked at Jessica, squinting slightly with her head held at a sympathetic tilt. 'Are you going to be all right?'

Jessica hadn't dealt with a murder case since Randall. She knew what her friend was really asking. 'I'm fine.'

'You don't have to do it all on your own.'

Jessica had missed an opportunity to get help with that case and had almost paid for it with her life.

'I know.'

There were a few moments of silence before DC Jones lifted the mood by standing up and bounding past Jessica towards the exit. 'Good. Let me know about Friday, yeah?'

After an uneventful two days, Jessica wasn't in a great mood and still regretting her choice of accommodation. Caroline had moved out of the apartment she shared with Jessica in the Hulme area of Manchester a few weeks after Randall had been arrested and now had her own place at Salford Quays. Jessica had visited a few times and it was very nice but the atmosphere was always awkward between them. They had gone from being able to chat about everything and anything night after night to having nothing to say.

Rent prices in Manchester very much related to the quality of the area you wanted to live in. There were plenty of cheap apartments if you were happy to reside somewhere like Craig Millar did. The road they lived on in Hulme hadn't been too bad but Jessica had opted for a newer one-bedroom flat in the Didsbury district when she moved. She could have afforded to stay in the old one if she'd wanted but, having nearly been choked to death on her own bed, that was never going to be something she was happy with.

The new flat was in quite a respectable area but there was a distinct lack of decent takeaways. There were a few but they weren't as downmarket and full of grease as the ones Jessica preferred back near her old flat. Perhaps the best part was that her neighbours were nothing like Carrie's. If anything, Jessica herself was the blight on the area, given the age and state of the car she owned. Her flat was part of a block of six newly built three-storey town-houses that were all converted into apartments. Jessica lived on the middle floor of one and didn't really know her immediate neighbours, other than faces to say 'hi' to. Everyone pretty much kept themselves to themselves.

Jessica liked the flat itself but it was mornings like this that made her wish she had stayed closer to the station. Technically it was a fifteen-minute drive from where she lived to Longsight. Given the traffic lights and sheer amount of vehicles piling into the city centre, it rarely took her less than half an hour on a weekday.

In the time since Craig Millar's body had been found they still only had some very basic information back from the forensics team. Essentially, there was confirmation of the victim's identity and that he had been killed by either the second or third of the three stab wounds.

Jessica stomped into the station through the front entrance in a mood because of the traffic. She started to head down a corridor towards her office but the desk sergeant caught her eye and called her over. 'I've got a phone number for you,' he said, offering her a Post-it note.

'Whose?'

'Someone at Bradford Park.'

The location referred to one of the force's main bases, where GMP's forensics team was located.

'What did they want?'

'Dunno. To talk to either you or Jack – whoever got in first.'

Jessica took the paper, on which was written a number and the name 'Adam Compton'. She went through a set of double doors down a hallway the short distance to the office she shared with Reynolds. He wasn't in and she walked over to her half of the room, sitting down after navigating a few piles of paper she had left on the floor the night before.

She dialled the number and a male voice answered on the third ring. 'Is that Adam?'

'Yes, who's speaking please?'

His accent definitely wasn't local. It sounded southern but she couldn't place it. 'It's Detective Sergeant Jessica Daniel from Longsight. You left me a note to call you.'

'Yeah, yeah,' came the voice from the other end of the line. From the undercurrent of noise, it sounded as if he were doing something in the background. 'Did someone tell you we found some blood scrapings under the fingernail of Craig Millar?'

'I heard yesterday. Did you get a match?'

'Well, sort of . . .'

'How do you mean, "sort of"?'

'According to the National Database, the blood belongs to someone called "Donald McKenna".'

'Isn't that a good thing?'

'Perhaps. Our records could be out of date but, according to the system, Donald McKenna is currently serving life in Manchester Prison.'

4

Adam Compton told Jessica his boss would be re-checking all samples and everything would be compared for a second time to the main National DNA Database. He did say that they had never had a false match as far as he was aware.

'Very rarely something can be missed or contaminated but I've never known the system simply throw up a wrong name,' he said.

Jessica gave him her mobile number and told him to call as soon as the second set of results came back. She checked their own files – likely the same one the forensics team would have access to – which also confirmed Donald McKenna was in prison. After that, she went to tell Cole about the phone call. He had arrived a few minutes after her and went to pass on the update to the detective chief inspector, who was based on the floor up from them. Jessica got back on the phone, this time to the prison to ask a question that most times wouldn't need asking: whether or not an inmate was actually on the premises.

Whoever had answered her call in the first instance had clearly thought she was winding them up but Jessica had eventually managed to be passed through to one of the wardens who worked on the wing McKenna was housed on. He also seemed a little confused by Jessica's question but took her phone number and called her back five minutes later to assure her he had walked to McKenna's cell and personally seen him there. With the obvious matter out of the way, Jessica had to arrange going to interview the prisoner.

Talking to inmates in relation to other crimes they hadn't yet been convicted of wasn't entirely dissimilar to the process if they weren't locked up. It was made easier by the fact you didn't need to go out to find someone but a prisoner would still be entitled to legal representation, would still have to be cautioned and could potentially be tried for a crime in a court like any other person. In instances such as that, the jury wouldn't necessarily be told the defendant was a current prisoner so they couldn't risk being prejudiced. Jessica arranged to interview McKenna at lunchtime, with someone from the prison helping to sort out a solicitor.

Her mind was already buzzing. The prison that had been rebuilt on the old Strangeways site was definitely not the type of place you could just walk in and out of. During the years she had been in the force, she had visited there on a couple of occasions for various reasons. It was a Category A, maximum-security establishment for some of the most dangerous prisoners in the region. Without even visiting McKenna or viewing his cell, Jessica was pretty sure there was no real way he could have got out of his room, escaped the wing, found a way off the premises, murdered Craig Millar and then gone back again with no one noticing.

And that was before they could come up with anything approaching a motive.

That said, she never would have guessed her best friend's boyfriend could have got himself into locked houses and murdered four people either. With those memories constantly in the back of her mind, she wouldn't be ruling anything out, no matter how improbable.

Jessica went to wait in Cole's office. She didn't fancy a conversation with the DCI and was slightly surprised to find Cole already back downstairs.

'That didn't take long,' she said.

'I think he's busy with some other stuff. Did you sort out the prison?'

'Yeah. Surprise, surprise, our man is actually there.'

'Do you reckon it's just a forensics mess-up?'

'Probably but it's not really like them. Maybe this Adam guy is new or something? Either way, while we're waiting for them to re-check everything, we may as well go have a word with Mr McKenna. If the results *are* correct, we're either going to have to look at him being out of the prison somehow or someone having access to his blood.'

The fact it was blood not hair that had been found under Craig Millar's nails complicated the issue. It seemed obvious to Jessica that hairs could be obtained easier than blood, so if someone was trying to fix up Donald McKenna they were going about it the hard way.

'Was it Strangeways Craig Millar was on remand at?' Cole asked.

'Yes. He and McKenna would have been in at the same

time but it's a massive place. It doesn't mean they knew each other.'

'True but it is a connection.'

Jessica knew he was right but it was circumstantial at best. She printed herself off a hard copy of the prisoner's criminal record to go over as Cole drove to the prison. She wasn't a big fan of his careful style of driving and figured a bit of not-so-light reading would keep her occupied.

The jail was based just outside of the centre of the city, only a few hundred yards away from the main indoor arena where gigs, boxing matches and comedy shows took place. In a recently designed city, its location would be odd given it was so central but it was nearly a century and a half old and, at least in terms of where it was placed, belonged to another age.

McKenna's record was extensive and perhaps the only thing he had going for him was that he hadn't actually murdered anyone yet – or at least hadn't been convicted of anything quite that serious. He did have quite the record though. He was fifty-two years old and had spent almost twenty years of his life in prison for various offences. The crime he was currently residing at Her Majesty's pleasure for was an armed robbery four years ago. He and another career criminal had held up a post office with sawn-off shotguns and escaped with a few thousand pounds. The money had been tracked back to them after they started spending it and both had been given life sentences. From reading his record it seemed pretty clear he was a thug but he didn't seem like a criminal master-mind to Jessica.

She gave Cole the rundown as he drove. 'What else has he got?' the inspector asked.

'Burglary when he was a teenager, a couple of serious assaults, threatening behaviour, a few drunk and disorderlies. Some thefts and a few other bits and pieces.'

'No drugs?'

'Surprisingly not.'

They parked at the prison and made their way into the front office where they would be frisked and have to go through the metal detectors. The man working in the area seemed overly keen to make friends. He introduced himself as Dennis and shook both of their hands. The name strip on his jumper read 'Doherty'.

'The governor is coming down to take you through,' he said, indicating some seats. 'You can sit there. He should only be a few minutes.'

Jessica thought Dennis Doherty was a slightly odd man. He had a scar across the left side of his face running from his jaw to his ear but it wasn't that which made him stand out. She couldn't quite place it. It wasn't that she regularly hung around prisons but, from her experience, a lot of the people who worked in places like this were overly officious and distant for obvious reasons. Dennis checked their credentials, as would have been expected, but then sat next to them and made small talk.

He was the person who had taken Jessica's call that morning and apologised for not passing her on quicker. 'I couldn't really understand what you were asking,' he said.

'No worries,' Jessica replied, trying not to get into a conversation with him.

The phone rang at the other end of reception and Dennis went back to take the call.

'I reckon you've got an admirer there,' Cole said with a smile, nodding towards the man's back.

Jessica shook her head. 'Blimey, it's all downhill from here if that's the case. He's old enough to be my dad.' She figured it really was time to re-evaluate her life if the harmless flirting of an older man was enough to get the alarm bells ringing. In the old days, she'd have told him where to go.

Soon enough a man she assumed was the governor breezed in through the back door. Dennis had turned around at the sound of the door but the entrant nodded to him, making his way straight towards Jessica and Cole.

They both stood up to acknowledge him and he offered his hand for them to shake. 'Good afternoon. I'm Christopher Gallagher, the governor here.'

He was a thick-set man somewhere around six feet tall with white swept-back hair and a tightly cropped beard of the same colour. He looked as if he were approaching retirement age and was wearing a light grey suit that was struggling to hold in his bulging stomach. They both shook his hand and DI Cole introduced the pair of them.

'I'm not sure I'm clear why you're here,' the governor said. 'I know you want to talk to one of our inmates in relation to a current investigation . . .' He was obviously fishing for information. They weren't obliged to tell him any more than that. Given the bizarre nature of the crime, they had agreed that no other details should be given to him at that point. They couldn't really storm into the prison accusing the governor of being negligent in letting a prisoner escape, especially when the inmate was apparently sitting in his cell.

'That's correct,' said Cole, without elaborating any further.

The governor waited for a few moments, obviously wanting to be told more but it was pretty clear DI Cole wasn't going to give him extra details. There was an awkward silence broken by the clearly peeved prison boss. 'Right, well, if you want to follow me this way . . .'

HMP Manchester had been almost completely rebuilt and renamed after a riot in 1990. The locals still called it Strangeways but the older Victorian buildings had either been knocked down as part of the construction or seriously damaged by fire during the protests. Jessica had visited a few prisons and, even though this was for the more serious offenders, its conditions were far better than some of the other places she had seen.

Most prisons had their own interview rooms for situations exactly like this. Sometimes officers would speak to prisoners in the regular visiting room but that only occurred if they weren't suspected directly of a new crime. The governor brought them across a yard and through lots of sets of locking doors. He didn't say a word throughout the entire journey, leading them down a host of identical-looking murky yellow corridors and up a flight of steel stairs before stopping outside a heavy metal door and holding it open for them. 'We've set some recording equipment up for you.'

It was hard to label Donald McKenna as a full suspect

given the fact he was incarcerated. But, assuming the second test came back as the first had done, his DNA *had* been found at a murder scene, which would take some explaining. As such, he would be cautioned and the interview would have to be recorded.

The two officers entered the room. 'This is nicer than our place,' Jessica said after the governor had left them alone, referring to Longsight station's own interview room.

Cole started making sure the equipment was working correctly. The recording decks seemed to be newer and more reliable than the equipment they had back at the station.

The inspector finished getting things ready and they both sat in silence waiting for their prisoner to arrive. A few minutes later, the door opened again and a man in a suit followed by another male in handcuffs entered. Jessica could see prison guards hovering around the door as it was shut behind them.

The suited man introduced himself as Donald Mc-Kenna's solicitor. Jessica vaguely recognised his face but couldn't place where from. A lot of people's features from the legal profession's defence and duty teams blended into one when you saw them so regularly. McKenna was dressed in regular prison attire. He had dark trainers, dark tracksuit bottoms and a sweatshirt which looked as if it were being worn over a T-shirt. Jessica thought he was in pretty decent shape for a man in his fifties. Like most inmates, his dark hair was cut short and he definitely looked younger than he was. He must work out, given the way his muscled shoulders were stretching his top.

Jessica was pretty good at judging how a suspect would react in an interview by the way they held themselves when they first sat in front of her. Some would try to be intimidating, especially as she was female. They would lean forwards and glare at her, almost inviting her to make them angry. A lot of the younger ones, the cocky gang members who still thought being arrested was cool, would slouch back in their seat, legs splayed wide and stare at the floor answering 'no comment' to every question. Every now and then, you would get someone who was genuinely scared, either because they were innocent or because they were guilty but terrified of what might happen to them. They would often fidget in the seat, looking to their solicitor for advice and talk far too quickly.

But McKenna was seated in a way Jessica had never seen before; he was simply relaxed, as if lounging at home watching television or in his local pub with a pint. His wrists were handcuffed but he had interlinked his fingers and put them on the table between them. He was looking at her but not in an intimidating way, he was smiling. It wasn't even a menacing gaze; he genuinely seemed pleased to be talking to them. Jessica could deal with aggression and thugs who thought they were big-time but a person being nice was something she wasn't used to.

Cole formally cautioned the suspect and briefly explained why they were there. The solicitor looked on unbelievingly at the two of them, shaking his head. After her superior had finished speaking, he moved his chair backwards away from the table a few inches.

She never really planned out how she was going to

tackle an interview, instead trusting her instincts. Something about Donald McKenna unnerved her though. He was still smiling and had gone from watching Cole speak to looking at her expectantly.

Jessica felt off-guard and ended up asking the one question she hadn't planned to, the one that made her sound stupid. To compound things, she asked it first and instantly felt ridiculous as soon as the words came out of her mouth. 'So, Mr McKenna, how did you get out?'

She sensed Cole shuffling nervously slightly behind her but he said nothing. The man's solicitor instantly started to interrupt but the suspect nodded along, lifting his hands from the table as if to indicate he was happy to answer. 'It's okay.'

His solicitor stopped speaking and the prisoner looked directly at Jessica again. He was still smiling but his light blue eyes had no menace in them. 'Detective, I really have no wish to escape the punishment I have been given. I sinned and I deserve to pay the price for that.'

It was definitely not the answer Jessica expected and she was aware he hadn't really addressed the question. The prisoner's words were clear, his local accent diminished. 'Can you explain how your blood happened to end up underneath the fingernail of a man who had been stabbed to death?'

'I'm afraid I cannot.'

'Where were you three nights ago?'

The inmate could have laughed at her but didn't. 'I was in my cell reading until lights out and then I would have been sleeping.'

'Do you have a cell to yourself?'

'At the moment, yes.'

If the second set of results came back positive, they would return to have a proper look at the area the prisoner was housed in. For now, they were on a fishing expedition. 'Do you know a man called Craig Millar? Until very recently he was on remand in this prison.'

'I'm afraid I don't have a great memory for names.'

Jessica took a photo from an envelope she had been carrying and slid it across the table. 'This is the man who was killed. Does his face ring a bell?'

McKenna picked up the image with his cuffed hands and studied it, narrowing his eyes as if to make clear he was concentrating. 'I don't believe I know him. We may well have moved in different circles. This is a large establishment.'

Jessica nodded and took the photo back, unsure if she believed him. 'Do you know anyone who might want to implicate you in a crime?'

He sighed slightly. 'I've wronged many people. I wouldn't blame any of them for wanting vengeance.'

A thought struck Jessica and she realised she had been a bit slow to understand the significance in the man's choice of words. 'Are you religious, Mr McKenna?'

The solicitor went to speak again but the inmate talked over him. 'I believe the Lord Jesus Christ died to forgive the sins I committed. There isn't a day that goes by where I don't regret the things I did and praise God he sent us his son so that I might one day enjoy the gifts of heaven.'

There was a silence after he had spoken. Jessica realised

why his demeanour had surprised her. Unlike a lot of criminals, he genuinely was sorry and, more importantly, he wasn't bitter about being locked up. Religious services were held in prisons and there was a chaplain on offer for people to speak to. Some inmates did 'find God' when they were inside and, while there was a possibility McKenna was faking his conversion as prisoners were given benefits for good behaviour, she had a feeling he was being genuine.

Jessica went to ask another question but McKenna spoke before she had a chance. 'You may ask how a man can walk from an institution such as this but the Lord Jesus walked on water and turned water to wine. If it is His will, a miracle is but the batting of an eyelid.'

5

There hadn't been much more they could ask after that.
Was Donald McKenna implying God had transported him
out of prison for some sort of higher calling? Even if he
was, Jessica wasn't entirely sure the Old Testament-style
eye-for-an-eye stuff would extend to killing some trouble-
maker who lived on a Manchester housing estate. There
were surely bigger issues in the world that needed ad-
dressing first? She thought it was an odd thing to say
though. Was McKenna really playing a game with them?

The governor, probably chastened by their refusal to
give him much in the way of details, hadn't returned to
talk to them. They had been led back to reception by one
of the guards and the prisoner returned to his cell. Jessica
tried to walk behind Cole through the front office on their
way out in order to not have to engage with Dennis. She
feared he would offer her his number or something similar
and, even though her superior was a fairly straight guy, he
did have a sense of humour when he wanted to. There was
no way Jessica could risk something that embarrassing
getting around the station.

They were walking to the car when Jessica heard her
phone ringing. She wasn't a technophobe as such but had
never really got her head around everything her phone
could do. She could use the phone and text messages and

the Internet was easy enough but she thought smart-phones were just one step towards robots taking over. She took the ringing device out of her pocket and fumbled with the screen before putting it to her ear. The conversation was fairly short and Jessica felt her mood nosedive further.

'All right?' Cole asked, clearly noticing her displeasure.

'The new test results are back. It's definitely Donald McKenna's blood that was found.'

For a guy who usually held back his thoughts, even her superior looked annoyed. He sighed. 'Great. We're going to have to see the DCI and then come back here later or tomorrow.'

'Let's go to Bradford Park first. Best if we know what we're talking about before we have to plan what we're going to do next.'

The Bradford Park base was in the Clayton area very close to Manchester City's football stadium. It was an important part of the area's overall policing strategy and lots of money had been spent updating the facility in recent times. Not only was there a neighbourhood team on-site, which would deal with local enforcement, but there was a large number of administration workers based there too. They were not officers but employees of the police force who would deal with things such as Human Resources. The Serious Crime Division, who dealt with organised crime and terrorist threats, worked from there as well.

The reason for their visit was to talk to the forensics

staff who had been dealing with the blood samples taken from Craig Millar. There was a whole section of the building given over to scientists and other laboratory workers. People were trained to analyse everything from fingerprints to a computer's hard drive. It was very specialist, technical work but did create divisions between the departments. A lot of officers believed they were on the front line doing the serious labour, with television programmes glorifying the work being done from the safety of a lab. On the other hand, plenty of the forensics workers felt constantly under pressure to prioritise jobs for certain departments, while balancing budgets that included private work and, if they were a member of the Scene of Crime team, getting called out at all hours of the day and night. Both groups seemingly felt under-appreciated by the other.

To be fair to the scientists, it probably didn't help that their Bradford Park base was openly referred to as 'Geek Corner' and 'Virginville' by certain officers such as Rowlands.

Jessica and Cole were shown through to a waiting area where they were told someone would come to see them. On occasion, officers would be permitted into sterile zones and autopsy rooms but there was no real need at this point. Jessica thought the room they were shown to was actually quite attractive, brightly decorated with a royal-blue carpet. The chairs they were offered were low to the floor but the material was bright red and comfortable. The person who led them through said they would bring some tea without asking if they even wanted one.

It was a far cry from the waiting rooms in their station. Back there, you would be offered a metal and plastic hard-backed seat like the ones you found in a school and the only refreshment on offer would be dodgy-tasting tea from a machine.

Jessica was just getting comfy in the chair, fiddling with her phone, when a man pushed open a glass door into the room. He was wearing dark trousers and shoes with a laboratory coat over a shirt. He had shoulder-length black hair and looked as if he hadn't shaved for a few days. His stubble was dark and Jessica would have guessed he was around her age. As he came through the doorway, he tripped seemingly over nothing and Jessica giggled.

The poor guy looked embarrassed as he walked across the room towards them.

'Detectives Cole and Daniel?' The two officers stood up to shake hands with the man whose face had gone slightly red. 'I'm Adam Compton. I'm one of the team who did the blood work on the body of Craig Millar.'

The three of them sat around a glass table. Jessica started speaking but they were interrupted by the receptionist returning with mugs of tea, putting them on the table. After she had left, Jessica began. 'Mr Compton . . .'

'Adam.'

'Sorry, Adam. We just wanted to clarify a few things with you about the testing procedures. Obviously results like this aren't what we would usually get.'

Adam nodded along in agreement. 'How can I help you then?'

'The obvious question is: could the results be wrong?'

Jessica didn't want to sound as if she were accusing him of making a mistake but, given the fact Donald McKenna was very much behind bars, it was a question that had to be asked. She softened her tone as she spoke.

Adam sounded nervous. 'That was what we thought at first. My boss wasn't, erm, happy. He thought I had made an error cross-checking things with the database.'

'Okay,' Jessica said. 'We may as well go back to the start for completeness' sake. Can you talk us through the whole database procedure . . . and, er, feel free to talk to us as if we're complete idiots.'

She knew most of it but hearing it from someone who knew for sure would clarify things. Either way, she didn't want a stream of technobabble.

Adam's accent definitely wasn't local. Even face to face instead of over the phone, she couldn't place it. 'What happens is that every time you arrest someone, you take those mouth swabs, don't you?' Jessica nodded. 'Those swabs give us a sort of pattern that is unique to the individual it's taken from. They are stored by various companies but that pattern is kept in a database that all sorts of agencies have access to.'

'That's the National DNA Database, yes?'

'Yes, the NDNAD.'

'That sounds like some kind of STD.' Jessica laughed quietly at her own joke but neither Adam nor Cole joined in and she quickly stifled her giggles into a fake cough.

Adam continued. 'Say there's a crime scene where you find hairs or blood or something like that, the people who work at the scene try to get as clean a sample as possible . . .'

'How do you mean, "clean"?'

'For instance, if you touched it with your fingers, you could transfer your own profile onto what you were picking up, which would contaminate it.'

'Right.'

'So anyway, assuming the sample is clean we would analyse it to get whatever pattern we could from it. That would then be matched against the victim to see if it belonged to them. If it doesn't and there's a chance it could belong to whoever committed the crime, we instead . . .'

'. . . check the pattern against the database' Jessica said, finishing Adam's sentence.

The scientist smiled at her. 'Exactly, yes.'

Jessica thought he seemed a bit awkward, perhaps nervous. He was quite fidgety, almost as if his body constantly wanted to be somewhere else. He started to continue speaking but the receptionist returned, telling him he had a phone call. He apologised and said he would be right back.

Cole picked up his mug of tea and took a big gulp. 'I think you've got another admirer.'

Jessica laughed under her breath. 'Stop it . . .'

'Seriously. The poor guy can barely get his words out.'

'Maybe it's you he fancies? Perhaps he swings that way?'

Cole was still laughing as Adam returned, sitting back down. Jessica could see what her superior was talking about now. The scientist would glance up at her but not want to catch her eye, looking at the table while he spoke.

Jessica picked up where they left off. 'I'm guessing that from the blood you found under Craig Millar's fingernails, the profile of that matched back to Donald McKenna?'

'Yes.'

'So what happened then?'

'Then I got shouted at for getting things wrong.'

'Really?'

Adam looked a little embarrassed again. 'Sort of. Look, mistakes can sometimes be made in labs. If samples haven't been kept correctly or someone hasn't followed the procedures or so on, like I said, they can be corrupted.'

'But they weren't in this case?'

'We don't think so, no. If there's something that doesn't seem right, we go all the way back to the original sample and re-test that, rather than rely on the pattern stored in the database. It doesn't happen very often and usually takes days.'

'How come you got it so quickly then?'

'It only takes time because these samples are stored all over the country and it's only the actual database itself which can be accessed anywhere. Because Mr McKenna was someone local, it turned out we were storing his original swabs.'

'And it all matches?'

'Yes.'

Cole spoke. 'Is there any chance someone else could have the exact same, er, "pattern" that Donald McKenna does?'

'Theoretically, yes but not really. It's something like a one-in-a-billion chance of someone else having the same DNA profile. I guess there are six or seven billion people in the world so someone could but even that's very unlikely.'

Jessica hadn't checked for anything like birth certificates but had seen on their records that Donald McKenna had no known relatives. She felt she had to ask the question anyway. 'What about a brother or something like that?'

'You share half the same genes with your siblings or parents. What would happen then is we would see a partial match. Say for instance someone like Mr McKenna's brother had done something, we would get that partial match to Mr McKenna himself and know it was someone related to him by the first degree. If it was an uncle, we might get a second-degree match or third for a cousin or something.'

'It sounds simple.'

'It's not.'

'Okay, so you're saying it has to be *his* blood then and no one else's?'

'There is one other possibility. If you had an identical twin, you would share the same profile. It would have to be identical though, like you came from the same egg. Non-identical twins would show as first-degree matches like a regular brother or sister.'

Jessica looked at Cole, who spoke directly to her. 'Does he . . . ?'

'Nothing in the files I saw,' Jessica said. 'We'll have to check the birth records properly when we get back but, if he did have a twin, I can't believe it wouldn't be on our system.'

Cole nodded. Jessica looked back to Adam, who had been watching her and quickly moved his gaze as she turned. 'Okay, are there any other possibilities?' Jessica asked. 'Could someone plant evidence or anything like that?'

Adam puffed his cheeks out and blew through his teeth. 'Maybe but it's pretty hard. For one, if you had blood from Mr McKenna, you would have to keep it sterile in some way . . .'

'. . . so the blood didn't get contaminated.' Jessica finished his sentence again and inwardly kicked herself for doing so. Finishing each other's thoughts was what old married couples did.

Adam looked a little confused but didn't react. 'Exactly. If it wasn't kept properly, you would contaminate the blood you had taken and it would be useless. But, even if that's what had been done and you had kept it all clean, you would still be up against it because the crime scene would have to look right.'

Jessica knew exactly what he was talking about but let him continue. 'Maybe if it was hairs or something like that on a body or at a scene, someone could have placed them in a clever way but it wasn't hairs we found. There was blood which had mainly dried directly under the nail.'

He moved his hands up in front of his chest to illustrate his point. 'If someone was trying to stab you, you might try to grab their wrist to stop the blade. If you snatched hard enough, you could break the skin and that's how you would end up with someone's blood underneath your fingernails. That's exactly what it looks like; it's not as if there was loads of blood but you wouldn't expect there to be.'

'In other words, it would be pretty hard to fake getting dried blood under the victim's nails.'

'Right. Not impossible but you would have to really know what you were doing.'

Adam risked another look up from the table towards Jessica but looked away when he saw she was still watching him. She noticed he had deep brown eyes, the type which sometimes looked as if there was no separate pupil because they were so dark.

Jessica looked to Cole and widened her eyes as if to ask, 'Anything else?'

He took the hint and stood, offering his hand for Adam to shake. 'Thanks very much for your help, Mr Compton.' Jessica shook his hand too.

'Can I, er . . . do you mind if I give you my phone number?' Adam had clearly asked Jessica, not Cole. 'Just in case, y'know . . . if you want to check anything else or whatever? You don't have to . . .'

Jessica pulled her own mobile phone out and typed his details into it, ignoring the knowing smile she knew Cole would be giving her.

'You already gave me your number, so I can text you if need be?'

Jessica had forgotten she had given Adam her number over the phone. Technically it had been for professional purposes but she guessed the 'need be' could end up being some sort of invitation for a pint or something. Given the guy's nervous behaviour, she couldn't imagine he had ever asked a girl out in person.

'Okay,' she said. Adam turned and walked back towards the door, tripping over in the exact same spot as before. Jessica smiled and turned back to her colleague.

'I didn't say a word,' Cole said. He hadn't had to, his raised eyebrow said it all.

Back at the station, it was now pushing late afternoon and clocking-off time. Jessica wasn't too bothered by keeping to set hours and most of the team ended up working unpaid overtime as and when required. Jessica had gone over their records and, according to everything they had on file, Donald McKenna was an only child. He was born locally and she would send some poor constable out to check the register office's records but there was no reason to think there would be a mistake in the information she had access to. Names could sometimes be spelled wrong but she had never known an instance where an entire person was simply missing from a record.

From everything Adam had told them, Jessica could only see three possibilities. First, someone had access to the inmate's blood and somewhere to store it securely, plus the knowledge of how to plant it at a scene. Second, Donald McKenna had an identical twin, not just a brother or sister, who no one knew about. Third, the prisoner had simply walked unnoticed out of a maximum-security prison and stabbed someone to death before returning.

Regardless of which option was correct, it was going to take some figuring out.

6

The media hadn't bothered reporting the stabbing of Craig Millar in much detail. Some crimes were given more prominence than others when it came to running orders on news bulletins or the front pages of newspapers. Jessica always made a point to look for how her cases were being reported. It seemed clear that whoever was in charge of the various decisions relating to the importance of the story had decided a dead young man on an estate notorious for anti-social behaviour didn't rank too highly. Jessica sighed at the front-page story in the local paper about a soap star who was having a baby.

She was sitting on the corner of Rowlands's desk on the main floor of the station and held the paper up for him to see. 'Why are people interested in the contents of the uterus of whoever this person is?'

It was a rhetorical question she didn't really expect an answer to. She got one anyway.

'I'd pay *special* attention if it were me.'

Jessica rolled her eyes. 'You're a real charmer, Dave?'

He winked at her. 'So what do you want me to do with this list then?' he asked.

Jessica grinned. 'Well, you know you put together all those names of people who might have it in for Craig Millar? I want you to put together another list for people who could have it in for, or be associated with, Donald McKenna. Then I want you to check the lists with each other to see if anyone shows up twice.'

'You are joking?'

'I'll leave you this to keep you company.' Jessica dropped the paper on his lap, with the front-page photo of the soap star on top. 'Have fun.'

It was the day after her visits to see Donald McKenna and Adam Compton and Jessica knew she would definitely have to return to the prison. The governor would have to be put in the picture this time so Detective Superintendent William Aylesbury was going to make the initial contact and then Jessica and DI Cole would visit. DSI Aylesbury had been the DCI at Longsight up until six months ago. He had been the natural replacement when the previous incumbent had retired. Jessica hadn't really got on with the chief inspector until the last few months of his spell at the station where she had begun to understand the way he worked. His promotion meant he was no longer based at the same station as her because he had jurisdiction over multiple stations in the area and the local chief inspectors were answerable to him. Jessica had seen him once or twice since his elevation and he always said 'hello' to her.

Given the strange nature of the test results, it was felt someone far more senior than them should be the one who filled the governor in. No one was directly accusing him of a failure but he would be asked to double-check the security arrangements on the particular wing Donald McKenna was housed on. Coming from someone as senior as the DSI meant he couldn't complain. The key thing was, no one was accusing the prison of being negligent, they simply didn't know what had happened.

Having spoken to Rowlands, Jessica exited the main floor and headed to Cole's office. She found him typing on his keyboard. 'Is he ready for us yet?' Jessica flicked her eyes upwards, indicating the floor above and the DCI's office.

'Yes but he's not in a good mood. I don't think he liked having to make that call to Aylesbury earlier.'

'I think he's still pissed off at having to cross the border.'

Detective Chief Inspector John Farraday originally came from Yorkshire but had been asked to move to Manchester after Aylesbury had been promoted. Usually, there would have been an internal appointment from the local police force but DI Cole had only been promoted to his current position less than two years ago and was never in contention. There was no obvious choice in the other local stations so management had looked elsewhere for a suitable person.

To Jessica, it made absolutely no difference where someone came from; she treated people as she found them. To a few older members of the team, there was still some sort of bizarre cross-county resentment in relation to a Yorkshireman coming to Greater Manchester and telling them what to do. Before he started, a couple of the more experienced uniformed officers spoke about how 'tight' they expected the new appointment to be. It didn't help that Farraday himself didn't seem overly pleased at having to live in Manchester. In the past six months, Jessica must have heard him complain about the 'pissing rain' at least three times a week. Still, it did piss with rain at least three times a week, so he probably had a point.

Cole stood up from his desk and they both went up to the first floor. They walked past the windows of their boss's office and knocked on the door before being waved in. 'Cole. Daniel,' Farraday said. He greeted everyone by their surnames and Jessica had a sneaking suspicion it was because he couldn't remember their first names or titles.

Farraday was sitting in his chair doing something on his mobile phone. He was around six feet tall but seemed more imposing because of his large chest and shoulders. He was somewhere in his late forties but had only just begun to go grey. Jessica often thought he would have been an extremely good-looking guy when he was a little younger. He had a very symmetrical face and, although the wrinkles were building up with age, he still had a boyishness about him. That was until he spoke. The man had an enormous voice even when speaking at a regular volume, let alone when he shouted. His accent was thick and something he was obviously proud of.

The two officers sat and Farraday put his phone down and began.

'I've just finished speaking to the superintendent. From what he says, the prison governor is not happy whatsoever. He reckons we're telling him how to do his job. Personally, I think he probably needs to be told how to do his job but it wasn't my call to make. Either way, it's been cleared for you two to go back tomorrow. You can interview McKenna again and check whatever you want in his cell or wherever.'

He was drumming his fingers on the desk while he spoke. 'Based on whatever you come back with, someone's going to have to make a decision about what we do next. Do I think we'll be able to charge him? I doubt it. We'll have to get the CPS in or something.' Her boss had an incredibly irritating habit of asking himself a question and then answering it. Jessica wasn't sure if other people noticed it but every time he did it she had to battle not to clench her teeth in annoyance.

'Surely we can't charge him, can we?' Jessica asked.

Farraday glared at her. He didn't like being interrupted and clearly hadn't finished his train of thought.

'As I was *about to say*, I can't believe the CPS would be recommending charging McKenna, given the guy is behind bars. You'd have to have a complete set of morons on the jury to find him guilty.'

Jessica knew there were plenty of 'morons' just ready and waiting to sit on a jury but doubted any of them were crazy enough to find beyond reasonable doubt that someone behind bars had committed a crime on the outside.

'Given all that, we have to start looking into anyone that might connect Millar to McKenna.' Her boss stopped talking and leant back slightly in his chair, an invitation for either of them to speak. Jessica didn't want to point out she had already assigned Rowlands to look into anyone that connected the two men.

With Cole not looking as if he was going to speak, she

did get in first though. 'One of the constables was sent to the register office this morning and confirmed there was no twin registered alongside Donald McKenna. There's no obvious record of any other brother or sister born to his mother either.'

'Are his parents still alive?'

'There was no father's name on the birth certificate but the mother died years ago.'

Farraday shuffled in his chair, humming to himself. 'Any bright ideas?'

Jessica didn't have any. As far as she could tell, they were doing all they could. She looked at Cole, who looked as blank as she did.

'No, Sir,' Cole said.

'Are we bringing in the media?' Jessica asked.

'Do I think we should bring in the media? Not yet. We'll wait until after you've been back to the prison tomorrow.' He paused for a second. 'Anything else?' Neither of them answered.

'Right then. I'm off to the cricket.' Jessica looked queryingly at the man sitting next to her but Farraday filled them in before either had to ask. 'Lancashire–Yorkshire at Old Trafford. Last day of the County Championship season. Would have been there first-thing if it wasn't for having to deal with the super.'

Jessica didn't know what to say. If her boss wanted to go to the cricket, she guessed it was up to him. 'Is there anything specific you want us to be moving with then, Sir?' she asked.

'No. Just try to connect Millar and McKenna. It's only

some scumbag kid, isn't it? If it *is* McKenna, I hope he takes down a whole bunch more of these little shits with him.'

Farraday stood up to indicate the meeting was over and the other two officers followed his lead. Jessica went back to her office – Reynolds was again absent – and sat at her desk. There was something a little unnerving about her boss's tone at the end of their talk. There was a lot of black humour in police stations and people got away with saying the most outrageous things because there was no real malice behind it but it didn't sound as if he had been joking.

Jessica had consistently found the DCI hard to read since he started. In his first week in the job, some of the officers had decided to see how many references they could get to Yorkshire into conversations with him. Someone would slip the word 'whippet' into a morning briefing. One officer kept going on about 'Batley', a town in the county, for no obvious reason, while others spoke about 'tea' and 'Yorkshire pudding'. Instead of using the word 'you', half the team were calling each other 'thee'. Things were getting out of hand but he eventually clocked the game when one of the younger members of the team spoke about 'Geoffrey Boycott', a famous Yorkshire cricketer, and then burst out laughing.

It was all very childish but the chief inspector took it in the spirit it was meant and had even invited everyone who worked in the station to his new house for an introduction party of sorts. He owned a large property to the south of the city in a nice area. The fact he had saved up enough to buy a place such as that hadn't helped his 'tight' reputation around the station. Apparently he had grown-up children but no one had met them, although his wife came across well at the party. Jessica had gone but spent much of the evening hanging around with Carrie and Dave. Rowlands had been rather taken with one of the family photographs that centred on one of their boss's grown-up daughters. Some of the other officers had made a big joke out of subtly moving items around, even if it was just switching ornaments with each other. Their host had taken a fair ribbing over a framed photo of Headingley cricket ground he had hanging in his hallway.

As well as that gentler side, Jessica had also seen him bellowing at various officers for perceived misdemeanours. His voice travelled and if someone was in trouble, everyone knew about it. He could be direct and abrasive and Jessica had never figured out if that was a genuine mean streak or just something about his manner.

The noise that indicated a text message went off on Jessica's phone. She took it out of her pocket and skimmed through the messages, laughing to herself when she saw it was from Adam Compton.

'Just wondrin if u fancied a coffee or sumthing?'

Given his clumsiness the previous day, she had wondered if he might contact her for some reason other than a professional one at some point. It seemed typical of his awkwardness that he wasn't brave enough to ask her out for a proper drink. Coffee? No. Glass of wine? Maybe. He may have been a bit geeky but he wasn't a bad-looking guy and seemed nice enough. She thought of the ribbing she would get from Rowlands if he found out she was thinking about going out with someone from 'Virginville'.

She typed a message back, read it over three times to make sure there were no critical spelling errors or any possible way it could be misinterpreted and then sent it.

'Maybe. Bit busy at mo. Will call u at some point.'

Jessica figured she would leave him hanging for a while longer. She had only given him her number for work reasons after all.

She tapped away at her computer's keyboard and logged onto the internal computer system to search for a phone number. She had left Denise Millar her phone number and only half-expected a call but decided she would be pro-active and contact her again herself. It wasn't that Jessica believed she could add much more to the investigation, she just wanted to hear how the woman was. Farraday's lack of feeling had sharply contrasted in her mind with that of the young man's poor mother.

She dialled the number into the desk phone and it was answered on the second ring. 'Is that Mrs Millar?'

'Yes, who's this?'

'This is DS Jessica Daniel. I visited you a few days ago.'

The woman had sounded downbeat but the inflection in her voice raised slightly after Jessica had introduced herself. 'Have you got some news?'

'Not really. I'm sorry if I got your hopes up. I was just wondering how you and Jamie were coping?'

'Oh . . . right.' The woman sounded disappointed and Jessica instantly felt bad for inadvertently giving an impression she had something of any significance to say.

Mrs Millar continued speaking. 'We're as well as can be expected. It's hit Jamie hard. He's not been out since.'

'I just wanted to let you know we are working as hard as we can on this . . .'

Jessica didn't finish her sentence before the woman started speaking again. 'It wasn't even the main story on the local news. I know he wasn't an angel but you'd think someone would be interested? No reporter or anyone has even come to speak to me . . .'

She tailed off and Jessica felt awful. 'I'm sorry . . .'

'Oh, I know it's nothing to do with you. It's not your decision, is it? The girl you sent around has been nice enough. I felt a bit bad as there's no food in the house. I told her I was fine and that she should nick off.'

She was referring to the liaison officer who was assigned to the parents or close relatives of victims in serious cases.

'Is there anything I can do?' Jessica asked.

She could hear Craig Millar's mother taking a deep breath. 'Just find who did it.'

7

Ben Webb hunched over the snooker table to line up his shot. He could feel a slight fuzziness around his eyes as the day's beer intake was slowly beginning to take hold. He had been waiting for the feeling all evening as he knew he played a lot better when there were a few drinks inside him.

The lights above the table flickered slightly and Ben pulled back from his shot, scowling at the hanging set of lamps above him. He crouched back over to line it up again when the lights went out fully. Ben stood and turned to his friend at the other end of the table. He could only see a silhouette in the gloom. 'Hughesy, you wanna go have a word?'

The snooker club was empty apart from four men around one playing table. Two were sitting chatting to each other, the only light a small desk lamp on a round table between their chairs. Four drinks were on the table and one of the men picked his up to finish what was left. Ben and his friend Des Hughes were standing next to the snooker table itself. Five large playing tables were in darkness near to them and now their lights had gone out too. Apart from the lamp next to the chairs, the only illumination came from the bar next to the exit.

Des walked around the table and stomped up the two

steps that took him away from the playing area onto an area where people could sit and eat. There were no lights there either and Des cursed as he clipped a few of the chairs on his way over to the bar. His heavy boots clanged off the chair legs, his cries of anger echoing quietly around the empty space. As he approached the bar, he called out. 'Oi, Mario. What happened to the lights?'

An olive-skinned man with dark hair walked through a doorway from behind the bar and approached the front. The man wasn't very tall but he stood a couple of inches higher than Des. It would have been clear to any outsider who was more intimidating though. The person behind the bar was slight and, while Des wasn't particularly muscular, he had naturally bulging forearms and hunched forwards as he walked. He may have been short in stature but he made sure his posture showed he meant business – it had served him well over the years. The lights from above the bar glinted off Des's shaven head, the tattoos running down his arms prominent against the rest of his skin.

'My name's not . . .' the man behind the bar started to say.

'I don't give a fuck if your name's Mario, Luigi or any other dirty foreign muck. Turn those lights back on before I come back there and turn them on myself.' Des thumped his fist on the bar to show he wasn't joking and the other man took a step back.

'It was closing time twenty-five minutes ago . . .'

Des stared at him and narrowed his eyes. 'I'm not going to ask again.'

The person behind the bar gulped and gave a half-look behind him before nodding. His voice wavered slightly but he said: 'Okay, okay.' The man went back through the doorway behind the bar and Des heard a low cheer behind him. He turned around to see the lights flickering back on over their table and then turned back to the bar. The server was in front of him again.

'Give me a pint of this stuff too,' Des said, pointing to one of the pumps on the bar.

The man stammered as he replied. 'I . . . I can't. It's too late . . . My licence.'

Des slammed his fist down on the bar, harder this time. The pump handles shook and glasses rattled. 'Do you really want me to come back there?'

The man shook his head furiously. 'No, no. Please . . .'

'Right, well, you better get pouring then, hadn't you?'

The barman reached under the bar and pulled a glass out. Des grinned as he saw the man's hand shaking as the liquid flowed from the tap into the glass. He put the drink down on the bar and looked up at Des. 'Two pounds eighty please.'

Des looked at him incredulously, picking up the drink and turning around. 'You must be bloody joking,' he said, still walking.

Back at the table, Ben was re-lining up his shot. 'Hughesy, what do you reckon? Pink or blue?'

Des put his drink down on the table between the other two men and walked towards his friend. 'Blue. Just kiss off it and roll down for that final red. Piece of piss and fifty quid in the bag.'

Ben hunched back for his shot as Des took a step back. The other two men stood and took a step towards the table to watch. Ben pulled back the cue and pushed forwards.

He knew instantly he had missed.

The white ball did slip nicely off the blue and run down to set up the red but the coloured ball rattled off both jaws and rested over the centre pocket.

'Shit.' Ben clattered the bottom of the cue down onto the floor and looked up to see Des shaking his head.

'It's all right. These two still have to clear up,' Des said, not sounding entirely convincing. He walked over to the drinks table and picked up his full pint glass, taking a sip from the top and then looking over at the other two players. He narrowed his eyes and spoke menacingly. 'We'll see if pretty boy's got any balls now, won't we?'

Des and Ben's opponents looked at each other and then one of them reached out to take the cue from Ben. He settled over the table before comfortably potting the red and then turning around and sinking the black. His friend replaced the black ball as Ben nervously walked around the table. He was a similar build and shape to his friend – short and hunched – but without the menacing demeanour Des had. He scuffed his feet as he shuffled, carefully watching each shot.

The yellow, green and brown balls all followed into the pockets and the man with the cue settled down to line up the simple blue. On the side of the table were four twenty-pound notes and two tens. Before he could crouch properly over the table to take his shot, he moved the money to one side.

'Oi,' Ben said. 'You've not won yet.'

The man looked back at him. 'I was only moving it.'

Des was still by the drinks table, pint in hand. He mumbled something but none of the other three could hear exactly what it was. The man with the cue gently rolled the blue into the pocket, leaving himself on for a straight pink.

'Two more,' the man's friend said excitedly. Ben gritted his teeth but said nothing.

The pink was hammered straight into the centre of the pocket but the white rolled slightly past the spot where the black was situated. The man with the cue crouched over the cue ball then stood up again. 'Do you reckon it'll go?' he said to his friend.

'Probably. Just be careful not to pot the white.'

Des walked over to the table and nudged the man holding the cue with his hip. 'Tough shot that, sonny. Tough, tough shot. Fifty quid at stake too. There's a *lot* of pressure on this.'

Ben joined in. 'Aye. Not easy, that. Looks to me as if the white's going to go in if you take it on. Might be better just playing a safety? Lot of money at stake.' Des nodded along with his friend's assessment.

The man crouched over the table and set himself, pulling back the cue and softly hitting through the ball. The black rolled towards the table and bounced off both jaws before dropping. The white was heading for the centre pocket, gliding almost in slow motion, before colliding first with the top jaw, then the bottom, and rolling safely into the centre of the table.

'Yesssss!' The man dropped the cue onto the table and snatched up the handful of money.

'Get in,' his friend said, walking quickly around the table.

Des slammed his half-full glass on to the table, a few drops splashing out of the top and on to the playing surface. 'Double or quits?'

The two men were dividing up the cash. One of them turned back towards Des and Ben. 'Sorry, guys, we've gotta get back. I've got work tomorrow.'

Des picked the glass back up and downed the rest of the drink in one before throwing it on the floor where it smashed. The other two men had put their winnings in their respective pockets and turned to walk away when the shattering of the glass made them both turn around.

'Are you . . .' one of them went to say but Des cut them off.

'Do you really think you're going to walk out of here with my money?'

The two men looked at each other, suddenly realising their beaten opponents weren't having them on. 'Sorry, man,' the taller of the two replied. 'Maybe play another night, yeah? Win your money back then?'

Ben spoke next. 'Do we look like a pair of mugs to you?'

The two men were walking backwards but Ben and Des took a deliberate step forwards almost as one, Des picking the snooker cue up from the table. 'No . . . no . . .' one of the men stammered. 'Seriously, you can have your money back, it's okay.'

He motioned to reach into his pocket but Des reacted

too quickly. He swung the cue forwards with the force breaking the wood in two and the sickening sound of wood on skull echoing around the near-empty room. The second man stumbled backwards over a chair and Ben was on him in a flash.

From the bar area, the server's voice was shouting. 'Hey, stop . . .'

Des kicked the body on the ground and shouted over towards the barman. 'Do you want some too?' The man had lifted the hinged part of the bar and was halfway out from his position but stopped moving as Des shouted. He took a step backwards and turned away.

Des kicked the grounded man again as Ben took care of the second person. He shouted as his fists swung down on the man's face. 'Do. You. Think. I'm. A. Fucking. Mug?' Each word was punctuated by a swing of the fist but neither of the two grounded men fought back.

Des crouched over the first person, rifling through the man's pockets, taking a mobile phone, wallet and the cash before putting all the items into his own pockets. 'Oi, Webbo, leave him,' he shouted towards Ben. 'Don't wanna kill the prick.'

Ben's eyes were wide and raging but his friend's voice froze him. He stopped throwing punches and used the floored man's own shirt to wipe his bloodied knuckles on, then went through the victim's pockets, also removing a phone, wallet and cash.

The two men stood up and walked over towards the bar area. The only noise was their footsteps and the faint whimper of one of the men on the ground. Des made his way to the barman, who was now facing the two men, eyes bulging with terror.

Des tapped him firmly but with an open-hand on his cheek. 'So then, Mario, what happened in here tonight? Made a bit of a mess of the place, haven't you?'

The man whimpered. 'Please . . .'

'I asked you a question, Mario. What happened in here tonight?' He used his thumb and index finger to cup the man's face and forcibly turn it to face him.

'Nothing . . .'

'That's right, nothing. Now get that mop out and clean this place up.' Des released the man and turned back to Ben. 'Let's go.'

The two men banged open the double doors to leave the club and walked down the stone steps that led outside. They didn't say a word to each other as they exited the building into the night and started walking down the middle of the road.

It wasn't a long journey home but Des had enjoyed one of the best nights he'd had in ages. They walked for a few hundred yards until they reached a junction. Des moved over towards a street light and uttered a quiet, 'hey' to his friend to indicate for him to do the same.

He stood in a position where there was enough brightness from the lamp that he could see what he was doing but so he wasn't directly under it. 'Do you wanna take the phones?' he asked, pulling the mobile he had taken from the club out of his pocket and offering it to Ben. His friend took it and Des added: 'How much did he have in his pocket?'

Ben pulled the other man's wallet out from his own pocket, replacing it with the phone. 'I dunno, you take this and I'll . . .'

He stopped talking as they heard footsteps from the path next to them. There was a man about to walk past them, hands in pockets. Ben was going to wait for him to pass before finishing his sentence. He turned away slightly from the unwanted interrupter as they drew level but suddenly felt a huge pain in his neck. He thought he heard shouting but for some reason his eyes weren't focusing. He started to reach up to where the pain was coming from but felt himself falling backwards, still struggling to see clearly. All of a sudden there was a man's face in front of him. He thought he vaguely recognised the person's features but then he felt another burst of pain and all he could see was black.

8

Jessica went to the station the next morning with the intention of getting into a marked car with Cole and heading back to the prison. She walked to the detective inspector's office but saw he was on the phone. He looked up, seeing her in the doorway, and waved her into the room. She could only hear his half of the conversation and couldn't figure out what he was talking about.

After a few moments he hung up. 'Ready to set off?' Jessica asked.

'There might be a problem with that.'

'How do you mean? Was that the prison?'

'No. Someone from North Manchester.'

The GMP's regular forces were divided up into around a hundred areas, each served by their own neighbourhood station, but the CID departments' jurisdictions were much wider and separated into North, South, East, West and Metropolitan. Jessica worked for the Metropolitan branch, generally dealing with anything central. There were sometimes tensions between the five divisions, usually over who controlled certain areas, but nothing too serious. Metropolitan were often caught in the middle simply because geographically they were literally in the centre. Crimes could originate in the centre of the city but then there would be obvious links to cases that had begun to be worked on by one of the other branches. Occasionally it worked in reverse but not that often.

'Why were they calling here?'

'Someone up there actually has a brain.'

'That's the first I've heard of it.'

Cole gave a half-laugh. 'They'd read about Craig Millar's murder and the details had stuck with them.'

'Because of some case from the past?' Jessica's instant fear was that another situation she had just started to get her teeth into was going to be snatched away because of internal politics.

'No, far from it. Two fresh bodies were found last night. Some DC was writing up his notes and spotted that the way the pair were stabbed to death seemed very similar to how Craig Millar was killed. He was phoning me to see if things sounded familiar.'

'Did they?'

'One knife wound to the neck, two to the chest?'

'On both of them?'

'No, just one but it seems close enough. Then he told me the two names.'

'Go on.'

'Desmond Hughes and Benjamin Webb.'

'You're joking?' Jessica recognised the names as easily as she had Craig Millar's. Cole shook his head.

'So three of Manchester's most prolific criminals have been taken out within a week of each other?' Jessica added.

'Looks like it.'

Jessica shook her head in disbelief. 'Wow . . . so what's happening now?'

'The Scene of Crime boys have taken the bodies and I guess we're back waiting for test results again. If there's anything to directly connect our killer to theirs then we'll have something pretty serious on our hands.'

'It can't be a coincidence though, can it? Killed in a similar way and all three with lengthy records.'

'You wouldn't have thought so, would you? It would seem to rule the Wright brothers out too.' Kevin and Phil Wright had been bailed the previous week and weren't really considered suspects for Craig Millar's murder but hadn't been formally excluded either. If these new killings were confirmed as the work of the same person, it would make their involvement even more unlikely.

'What do you reckon, organised crime?'

Cole shook his head again. 'No way. It's not clinical enough. If it were something like that, it would either be far more brutal or there'd be a gun or something. Plus these three might be thugs and nuisances but they're hardly criminal masterminds, are they?'

Jessica nodded in agreement and breathed out heavily. 'Did the guy say if the Scene of Crime team found anything on the bodies?'

'Nope . . . but I guess you've got a little friend who could tell you.' Cole had a serious look on his face throughout their conversation but, with the last remark, he broke into a grin. 'What was his name, Adam?' he added mischievously.

Jessica felt herself blushing slightly. 'Something like that,' she said, trying to sound calm.

Cole went to tell Farraday about the development as

Jessica made her way into the office she shared with Reynolds. Her colleague was already there at his spotlessly clean desk, typing on the keyboard.

Reynolds had been in the job quite a while longer than her. He was black and heavily built but outwardly gentle with it. He was well known as a bit of a wind-up merchant but a really good detective. Jessica often used him as someone to bounce ideas off, even though they rarely worked together directly. He was currently investigating a case involving a string of assaults on students. His theory was that there was some sort of local gang initiation ritual linked to it all but it was difficult to get information either way. Often the students would be drunk or embarrassed, so trying to tie one thing to the other was hard.

She wanted some privacy for her call, so made a quick excuse and walked through to the canteen. Jessica found an empty table in the corner and took her phone out of her suit jacket's pocket. She hadn't contacted Adam since the text message and felt a bit awkward. Although she was phoning him for professional reasons, he would most likely ask her about that 'coffee'. Jessica hadn't been planning to give him a proper answer but figured she would have to come up with something. She pressed the screen to dial his number. It had barely rung once when he answered.

'Hello.'

'Adam?'

'Yeah, hi.' He sounded a little nervy but certainly enthusiastic.

'It's Detective Sergeant Jessica Daniel. Have you got a

couple of minutes?' She made sure she emphasised her title as if to point out it was a phone call relating to the job.

Adam didn't take the hint. 'Oh great. I'm quite busy but I can talk for a bit.'

'I understand you might have a couple of new arrivals to be working on?'

'Huh? Oh right . . . Are they yours?'

'They might be. Have you found anything?'

Adam's tone lowered as the penny dropped that Jessica was calling for business reasons. 'Sort of. My boss is on it now. I'm about to go through and help. There's all sorts on the bodies though. It looks like they've both been stabbed but one of them has blood on his knuckles too. It's going to take a bit of sorting out. I doubt you'll get any results today apart from formal IDs.'

'What do you mean, "blood on his knuckles"?'

'Just that. It looks like he's been fighting. It's hard to tell. I don't want to tell you something that might not be true.'

'Fair enough. Can you call me if you get anything?'

'Er, we're supposed to call it back through to the division it came from first.'

'I know but I'm asking you to call me.'

'All right.' There was an awkward pause broken by Adam. 'Did you get my text?'

He obviously knew she had.

'Yeah. It's pretty mad here at the moment though. I don't really drink coffee either.'

'Oh, right . . . '

Adam sounded disappointed and Jessica felt a little bad. She sighed silently to herself and took a deep breath. 'How are you fixed for Sunday evening?' she added.

Adam's response was instant, his words blending together as he spoke too quickly. 'Yeah, brilliant, that's great. I'll see you there.'

'Er, where? Do you want to sort out somewhere to meet?'

'Oh right, yes.'

'I'll text you something, okay?'

'Yeah, of course. Sorry, yeah. Sorry.'

Jessica hung up and giggled quietly to herself. He had given her something to start on though. She went back to her office and logged on to her computer to look at the details that had already been entered for Webb and Hughes. She saw the area the bodies had been found in and clicked through to check details of the previous evening's emergency calls. There were the usual things she would expect to see but then one particular log jumped out at her: an incident in a snooker club where two men had been assaulted. It was the only call that seemed serious enough to perhaps be linked to Webb and Hughes, given the area their bodies had been found in. If one of them had fresh blood on his knuckles, it would either be from something unreported – or the record she had in front of her. She wrote down the details and picked up the phone, knowing she would have to play a little internal politics herself.

It took a few calls but she eventually pulled together everything she would need for the rest of the day. The prison visit was definitely off for now, given they might have a new crime to ask McKenna about.

She went to find Cole to pass on the news and he was back in his office. 'Hey,' she said. 'What did the DCI say?'

'He didn't seem too fussed and reckoned it was two less troublemakers we were going to have to deal with.'

'I spoke to Ad ... the guy from the labs.' Jessica repeated the details Adam had told her and then the report from the snooker club. 'There are two men who were beaten up. Both are at North Manchester General Hospital. One is in intensive care but the other apparently looks a lot worse than he actually is. The local boys up there were going to talk to him this afternoon but now we are. I had to go through Northern CID but they didn't seem to be too bothered about handing the case over. I think they see it like the DCI does – two more criminals off the street.'

'How do you see it?'

'That three people have been murdered, possibly by the same person, possibly by Donald McKenna or someone connected to him.' Cole nodded but Jessica couldn't tell if it was because he agreed with her or because he was acknowledging what she said. 'The northern boys say that wallets and IDs belonging to the two snooker-club victims had been found on Hughes and Webb so I don't think there'll be much doubt where the blood on the knuckles came from. They're going to pass that on to the forensics team, which might speed things up a little.'

'I guess it shows Hughes and Webb weren't mugged either if phones and wallets were found on them,' Cole added.

'Exactly, just like Craig Millar.'

'Are you off to the hospital?'

'Yeah, aren't you coming?'

'No. Farraday wants me on some other bits for now. His exact words were, "scum killing scum isn't a priority today". He wants to wait for the test results to come back before we go back to the prison too.'

There wasn't much Jessica could add to that. She was still clear to go to the hospital but her boss's attitude was starting to wear her down.

She went through to the main floor and made her way over to Rowlands's desk. 'Oi, grey head. Get your coat, you've pulled,' she said, clipping him round the ear.

'I'm not *that* desperate,' he replied, swatting her hand away.

'Neither am I but we've got a hot date with an assault victim at the hospital.'

'Which hospital?'

'North Manchester.'

'That's miles away. You're not driving, are you?' Jessica's skills with a vehicle were widely questioned around the station. She would describe her driving as 'specialist', others used the word 'reckless'.

'Well, Detective Constable, you have two choices. One, you can come with me or two, there were two more bodies found last night that may or may not relate to our case. If you want, I can get you drawing up a list of names connected to those two and then cross-checking everything back with what you've already done.'

Rowlands stood up quickly. 'Fine, I'm coming but I

hope someone's checked the seatbelts. I don't trust your capricious driving.'

Jessica looked at him again, narrowing her eyes. '*Capricious?*'

'I told you, I'm raising the level of conversation around here.'

'Did the letters in your alphabet spaghetti spell that out last night or something?'

'Jealousy isn't your best trait, you know.'

Jessica and Rowlands spent the rest of the day putting the pieces together. First they had been to the hospital where they spoke to the only one of the two snooker-club victims who was capable of talking. He told them he had been hit over the top of his head with a snooker cue. There was a large gash and he had a black eye, plus two broken ribs where he said he had been kicked on the ground. He had got off lightly compared to his friend though. The second victim was on life-support in the intensive care ward. He had swelling to his brain and the doctors weren't sure if he would survive or not. Jessica had shown the man some mug shots and he had identified Webb and Hughes as the culprits.

'Are you going to arrest them?' he asked.

'It's a bit late for that,' Jessica replied before telling him of his attackers' fate.

The two had lengthy records with a slightly more serious edge to them than Craig Millar. Hughes had been in jail for possession of a firearm plus he had a string of assaults to his name. Webb didn't have the weapons charge but most of their records matched up. They clearly worked as a pair. Interestingly to Jessica, they had both only been released from prison in the past year, meaning all three victims – plus Donald McKenna – had been in the same jail at the same time.

After leaving the hospital, they had gone to the snooker club where the emergency call had come from. They spoke to the owner, who told how he had been terrorised the previous night. He said he was too scared to intervene in the assault but had at least given a full description to officers the night before. Samples had been taken from the club and sent through for analysis but the local police hadn't connected that incident to the two murders at the time. Jessica texted Adam just in case but felt pretty sure someone else would have already told the labs about the link.

The owner didn't know Hughes and Webb personally but said he recognised their faces from the club. They hadn't caused him trouble in the past but, given their records, Jessica thought they were an accident waiting to happen once alcohol was thrown into the mix.

It was becoming clear that the three victims' links to Donald McKenna would be extensive. At first Jessica had set Rowlands to look for direct connections between McKenna and Millar but the link seemed to be the prison itself.

They arrived back at the station late in the afternoon. Jessica typed up her notes from the day and then went through the lists Rowlands had compiled. The names that linked McKenna and Millar were simply other known criminals. Some of them would have no doubt been in prison at the same time as Hughes and Webb too, which would be something to start with. She checked through the computer records and narrowed the list further but none of the names jumped out at her. They were all petty troublemakers, each of them a nuisance, but no one who she would have bet had the inclination, let alone motive, to kill three people.

With links to organised crime also seeming unlikely, as Cole had pointed out, it meant their only firm connection was still Donald McKenna, a man behind bars.

Jessica shut the computer down and walked into the reception area in preparation to head out towards her car. She had stayed at Longsight for forty-five minutes longer than she needed to but it wasn't as if she had anything to rush home to. With dismay she saw the bright autumn day had given way to grey skies and drizzle and what little summer they'd had seemed to be over for another year. She stood in the doorway of the station looking across the fifty or so yards to her car. She hadn't brought an umbrella or coat to work in the morning, trusting the way the skies had looked when she left her flat earlier on. It was always a foolish assumption to make in Manchester but she never learned her lesson.

She fumbled around her pockets for her car keys and held them at the ready before ducking her head and making a run for it. Rowlands had pointed out to her a few months ago that the force had started hiring recruits that were younger than her car. It was red, rusty and unreliable and Jessica didn't really know why she hadn't upgraded to something better. She could afford it if she wanted to but there was something sentimental about the vehicle and she had resigned herself to keeping it until it literally fell apart.

Jessica thought remote central locking would have been nice as she tried to force the key into the car's lock and ended up accidentally scraping a bit more paint away from the area around the key hole. There were enough scuffs and scratches for her to not worry too much as she eventually fell onto the driver's seat and shut the door behind her.

It was only as she slammed the door that she realised her phone was ringing. Her wet fingers struggled with the screen more than usual but she just managed to say 'hello' before it rang off.

'Oh hi. It's Adam, Adam Compton. I didn't think you were going to answer.'

'No, I'm here. A bit wet but here.'

'It's raining out?'

'Yeah. Shock, hey?'

'Oh right. I've not been outside all day. Erm, look, I probably shouldn't be calling you yet because it's not official but we did find a few things.'

Jessica felt her heart rate suddenly go up. 'What?'

'It's early and nothing will be confirmed until tomorrow but we found a few hairs on the top that Ben Webb was wearing. There's nothing unusual about that but they're not his or Des Hughes's. I got your text but someone had already phoned through. We used those samples from the snooker club but they don't belong to either of the two victims who were beaten up.'

Jessica held back from interrupting, letting him say the exact words she knew he would. 'They are a direct match for Donald McKenna though.'

9

Adam went on to reiterate that things would need to be confirmed. They were going to request a new swab from Donald McKenna in prison. He added that nothing was final and that samples could degrade over time. McKenna's initial swabs could have been contaminated or could have simply not been stored correctly. They had been on file since he was sent to prison for the armed robbery four years earlier. Nothing would be official until new saliva was taken and then re-tested against everything they had. He said his boss would pass on the first results to someone at the station officially the next morning but request a media blackout until a full re-analysis was done. It was a bit late to stop the release of the murder victims' names but it would look bad for everyone if it was all linked back to a contaminated sample.

He drifted off into scientific speak she didn't really understand and then said it was going to take days but Jessica wasn't really listening. She knew it would all come back to confirm what she felt sure she knew; Donald McKenna had somehow been involved with the murder of three people.

She decided to rest on things that night. Adam had trusted her with information she *technically* shouldn't have yet and there didn't seem too much point in passing it on considering it would be phoned through the next morning anyway, albeit with the proviso that the testers wanted new samples.

The following day, there was definitely a different atmosphere in the station. Big crimes always created a buzz and, although Craig Millar's killing hadn't got people going, Jessica knew as soon as she walked in that news had broken about the latest DNA results. She didn't let on that she already knew as the desk sergeant directed her upstairs for a meeting with Farraday.

As soon as she started to walk past the windows of his office, she could see Cole already sitting inside chatting with their boss. She knocked as a courtesy but was waved straight in and took a seat next to Cole on the opposite side of the desk from Farraday. 'Daniel,' the DCI said to acknowledge her.

'Sir.' The chief inspector proceeded to tell her everything she had already been told by Adam the previous evening. She nodded along in all the right places. If Cole suspected she already knew the details, he said nothing.

The DCI finished by summing up where he saw everything standing. 'Daniel, I'm moving you up to take lead on this. I know it should really fall to Cole but so far it's only three arseholes we're better off without. There are other jobs to do around here. Take whoever you want to the prison today but then we'll have to wait until the Bradford Park lot have done their jobs. If any more bodies show up, we might have to look again. All right?'

'What are we telling the media, Sir?' Jessica asked.

'Not much. The press office stuck out the victims'

names yesterday. Do I think they'll put the pieces together and link it to the other killing? Not unless someone gives the game away. It's not as if they're the sharpest bunch of knives in the drawer, is it?'

Jessica grimaced at the question he had asked himself but wanted to laugh at his dig about the local reporters. With her last big case a journalist named Garry Ashford who worked for the *Manchester Morning Herald* had actually helped her figure out what was going on, albeit not directly. Still, she liked the description and would tell him the next time she saw him.

'What exactly do you want me to do at the prison, Sir?' She wouldn't normally have asked but, with them in limbo waiting for further test results, there was only so far they could push things.

'Talk to the governor, check McKenna's cell, put the shits up them all – that kind of thing. Talk to the wardens, one of them might be bent. Do I think someone there must know more than they're letting on? Maybe.'

It hadn't crossed Jessica's mind that someone who worked on the wings could have helped McKenna in some way. It still seemed far-fetched but it was something she would bear in mind now that Farraday had mentioned it. A warden or someone in a similar position would certainly have more chance at getting blood or hairs from the prisoner than someone on the outside if they wanted to frame him. If they were working together, it would be easier, although still difficult in technical terms. It didn't get her any closer to coming up with a motive.

The three of them held the morning briefing in the

main incident room in the basement of the Longsight station. It essentially consisted of them telling everyone what had been decided in the office. The chief inspector reminded them all of their responsibilities to not leak any details to the papers. Jessica made sure she caught Rowlands's eye. She hadn't been able to prove it at the time but she was as sure as she could be that he had been giving information to Garry Ashford at the time of Randall Anderson's killing spree. It wasn't malicious and had drastically enhanced one of his friend's careers but it still shouldn't have happened. Neither he nor the journalist had ever owned up to it but the reporter's knowledge of the police force's inner workings had certainly stopped appearing in the local paper since Jessica had challenged them. Rowlands wasn't keen to make eye contact and looked away.

After the briefing was finished, she motioned him over to one side. 'Fancy a trip to the prison?'

'You know how to show a guy a good time, don't you? Hospital one day, prison the next. Are we off to the cemetery tomorrow?'

'Are you seriously giving out dating advice?'

Rowlands winked at her. 'Word around the station is that you might be looking for some.'

Jessica didn't think Cole was the type to gossip and doubted it was him who had said anything about Adam but news travelled pretty quickly around a police station, especially if it involved officers' private lives.

She thought about asking how Rowlands knew but didn't think it really mattered. 'Why? Are you jealous?'

'Nah, you're a bit old for me.'

Jessica snorted. 'Only if you're talking about mental ages.'

On arrival at the prison, they had been greeted by another member of front-office staff who was slightly unnerving. The people who worked there had obviously been given some sort of briefing regarding the police visit and the man was keen to ask questions and try to show how efficient he was. Jessica did her best to ignore him as Rowlands pulled out his phone and had what was almost certainly a fake conversation. Jessica thought she would remember that trick for next time.

If it was a phoney talk, he didn't have to pretend for too long. They had called to confirm they were visiting after putting off their trip the day before and the governor had been pretty quick to meet them in the reception area. After the usual security checks, he took them through into the main arrivals yard. He told them the large concreted area was where the security vans first arrived. Inmates were either taken back to their blocks if they were already prisoners, or moved into a separate processing office if they were new arrivals.

The governor was outwardly far friendlier on their second visit but his tone definitely seemed forced and a tad over-enthusiastic. He talked them through the areas that had been rebuilt and showed them where the old parts of the establishment had been before the riots. He led them off to an area where he said executions used to take place. Jessica knew the basics but was surprised when he told them the last hangings took place in the 1960s. She wouldn't have guessed it was quite so recent.

He took them into the main prison area and pointed out the various wings. He mentioned a famous rock star and told them how he had spent six weeks in the prison a few years previously. He offered to show them the cell but Jessica decided that would be a step too far. The pleasantries were at least interesting but they were there on business. If the governor was annoyed at having his impromptu tour interrupted, then he didn't react, instead walking them through to the wing McKenna was kept on.

It was essentially a wide and long hallway, with cells that went up three storeys high. There was a big gap between the two sides with a couple of pool tables interspersed with a few other chairs in the middle of the hard grey floor. Jessica had been into a few prisons but rarely into the area where prisoners were actually housed. In terms of the actual cells, there wasn't much sign of the stereotypical vertical bars most people would picture. The main gates in and out of the wings themselves were barred across and needed to be unlocked but the actual cell doors were thick, heavy and made of metal. It wasn't as grim as she might have guessed but certainly wasn't as bright and new as the visiting areas always appeared.

'Everyone gets to spend twelve hours out of their cell between eight and eight,' the governor explained. 'There's a games area towards the bottom of the wing with more pool tables and so on. What we've done is move them all down there just for while you're here. It was a bit cramped so some of them are outside in the rec area. It will give you free access to walk into the cells. You do have to understand that the property they have in their rooms is their own, though. Some get very, er, funny about things being moved.'

Jessica understood. People in pretty much any situation would be annoyed by someone else shuffling their possessions around. In prison, those items would be much more valued simply because the inmates had so little.

The governor continued to speak as he walked them further on to the seemingly deserted wing. 'If you do want to talk to anyone else, it can be arranged. I'm not sure everyone would want to talk to the authorities but I doubt many would mind that much. Mr McKenna is in a cell next to the interview room and ready whenever you are.'

He was certainly going out of his way to accommodate them. The governor led them off to one side of the hall towards one of the cells. The rooms already had their doors all open. Rowlands asked why. 'Between eight in the morning and eight at night, doors have to be kept open. If someone is feeling ill or wants to sleep or something like that they can go to the medical area. It's for everyone's safety really. Say an incident did happen, the guards wouldn't be able to see anything or know something was wrong if the doors were closed.'

'What about after eight?' Jessica asked.

'The main lights stay on for about an hour and then are off until around seven the next morning. They can have small lamps in their cells if they want to read and pretty much everyone has a TV in the room. Ultimately we can't watch them twenty-four hours a day. It's extremely rare anything happens. Most of the rooms have two people in them and there's a degree of matching to try to ensure people get along. There's a separate wing for vulnerable prisoners but genuinely most people just want to do their time.'

'When I was here a few days ago, Donald McKenna said he had a cell to himself,' Jessica said.

'That's true. A lot of it comes down to how crowded we are. Sometimes every cell has two people in it and we have to use places like the vulnerable wing just to get everyone in. Either that or release inmates who don't have much left on their sentence. At the moment, we're not quite at capacity so there are some prisoners who get a cell to themselves.'

'How is that decided?' Rowlands asked.

'Each wing has a senior warden. There's no way I can oversee everyone all the time but everyone reports back to me. I leave decisions like that up to them. It should come down to behaviour and things like that. Sometimes it just falls to the more senior prisoners though. A lot of it works itself out.'

Given Farraday's suggestion that someone on the wing might have some sort of involvement, that last part stuck out to Jessica. Ending up in a cell by himself could well indicate some sort of preferential treatment. It was still a far cry from that to either helping McKenna get out of the prison or aiding him to carry out murders but it was something to bear in mind.

The governor pointed them to one of the open doors.

'It's that one there. Feel free to take your time. I'll wait here if you have anything to ask.'

Jessica entered the cell as Rowlands waited by the door. There wasn't an awful lot of space for the two of them to fit inside. There was a bunk bed immediately on her left and the room was only a little longer than the bed itself. On the opposite wall from the bed was a desk that ran most of the length of the wall. On it was a small portable TV, a Bible and some battered paperbacks. At the end was a small sink with a mirror and some toiletries above it. Opposite the sink, at the end of the bed and only just fitting into the space between the bed and the wall, was a metal toilet. She figured it was certainly made for a man; there was no toilet seat, just four raised pieces of plastic.

At the end of the thin aisle that separated the bed from the table, there was a solid-looking window at the top of the facing wall. The glass was misty and impossible to see out of and there were bars in front of it. It had only taken her a few seconds to look at the whole place. 'Anything?' asked Rowlands from the door.

'You can pretty much see everything I can, Dave.'

She felt stupid for doing it but tried wobbling the four bars that blocked the window. They didn't budge. She looked under the bed, where there was a pair of dark trainers but nothing else. She pushed and tapped the walls, almost as if she was surveying the place. She didn't know what she was looking for. It's not as though she expected there to be a gaping hole in the wall with 'tunnel' written over the top but she hadn't expected something so cramped either.

Jessica tried moving the toilet and the sink, just to see if they were loose from the wall but, aside from a slightly wobbly pipe under the sink, the actual units didn't shift at all.

Eventually after checking everything a second time, she went back to the doorway and Rowlands moved aside to let her out. 'You wanna have a look?' she asked.

'Not much point really, is there? As you said, I could pretty much see it all anyway.'

'Have you ever been here before?'

'We had this training day thing but not in the cells, no.'

'What do you reckon?'

'I'd feel sorry for someone sharing with me. After I've been to the toilet, you would *definitely* need more space than that to air it out.'

Jessica pulled a face at him. 'It's times like this when I wonder why you're single.'

'Through choice.'

'Yeah, theirs.'

The two of them walked back towards the governor. 'Did you see everything you needed to?' he asked.

'Not much to see, was there?' Jessica replied. 'Let's just say, for instance, that you *could* get out of that cell. Where would you end up?'

For just a moment, the governor grinned condescendingly at her and then quickly reverted back to his regular expression. Jessica knew he was about to talk down to her in the least patronising way he could manage, while secretly revelling in the moment.

'Well, let's say you removed the bars over the window

without a screwdriver, even though they are screwed into the solid stone wall and have been painted over. If you got those off and got through the window, which is five times as thick as regular glass and completely shatter-proof, you would still only end up on a patch of land that sits between two of the wings. You would actually be outside of the standard walkways, which would mean you would have to scale an eighteen-foot-high security fence with a roll of barbed wire at the top. Once you had managed that, you would still only be back on the permitted paths.'

Jessica could feel Rowlands shuffling from foot to foot next to her as the governor continued. 'Once you got to that path, assuming the patrols didn't see you, or the security cameras, either direction would simply lead you back to the main gates but only through two sets of double-locking doors whichever way you went. Because of that, you would have to scale another eighteen-foot-high fence on the other side of the path which would get you into the rec yard. You could get across the yard easily enough, though there are spotlights, but on the other side are a few more wire fences. The first one is hardened steel which encloses the area, then there is one outside that is eighteen feet high again and similar to the others. If you could get through all of that, you would be at the wall. That's twenty-four feet high and a yard thick, plus coated with an anti-vandal substance to prevent climbing. If you somehow got to the top of that and avoided being seen by the rooftop security, you could drop down the other side but it actually works out at a drop of around twenty-five feet, eight yards or so. Assuming you landed okay, I guess you'd be scot-free . . .'

He let the statement hang in the air and clearly didn't need to add anything more.

'Could you tunnel out?' Rowlands asked. Jessica was glad he had said it instead of her. The question sounded ridiculous.

'Well, I guess if you had something to dig with but even then it's around seventy yards in the straightest line from here to the wall. I don't know where you would get rid of all the dirt or how you would get out on the other side though.'

He had certainly made his point. Jessica then asked the question she had been worrying about. The governor had been perfectly nice, despite the undertone to his words, but she couldn't judge how he would react next. 'Can you trust all of your staff, Governor Gallagher?'

He was certainly taken aback by her directness. 'Sorry?'

Jessica repeated her question word for word. The man's eyes narrowed as he thought how he should respond. 'I'm not sure I like your tone . . .'

'I'm not sure I've liked yours either.'

For the first time that day both of them were being upfront with each other. Jessica wasn't going to be the one who gave way first.

'Your super left me his number, you know?'

'I didn't ask you about that.'

Governor Gallagher stared at her, his eyes thin as he struggled to control his anger. 'I trust my staff.'

'All of them?'

'*All* of them.'

As quickly as the mood had deteriorated, Jessica raised it by chirpily changing the subject. 'Right, that's good then. I think it's time to see Mr McKenna.'

10

Jessica didn't really know why she had tried so hard to wind the governor up. She could have asked nicely or apologised but pointed out it was something she had to ask about. She could even have just left it. Not only had she asked the question and pushed the issue, however, she'd really enjoyed it. Perhaps it was because of the delight he had taken in pointing out how hard it would be to escape or maybe it was because she simply wanted to see what his reaction would be? You could learn a lot about people from how they responded to direct accusations. Some people would shout and swear to try to show they were innocent. Others would evade the question. Some might start to sweat and stumble over their words. Governor Gallagher had not done any of that; he had just seethed with rage. Was that because he was *that* protective over his staff, or because of something else? Jessica wasn't sure but his reaction had been interesting.

On the way back off the wing, he took them through to a security booth which contained a bank of monitors linked to the cameras that seemingly watched the whole prison. It was perhaps one final way of showing them how ridiculous they were being. There were a few men and one woman in a small group towards the back of the room as they entered. They all had the same uniform on: dark shoes, dark trousers and a white shirt. Jessica could see each one also had heavy-looking bunches of keys attached to their waist. The governor signalled for one of the men to come over. He looked like the oldest of the group, somewhere in his fifties or so, Jessica would have guessed. He had wisps of hair around the tops of his ears and a few strands combed across his head but was mostly bald. His face had a reddish tinge which, from experience, Jessica knew was most likely the sign of a heavy drinker.

'Detectives, this is Senior Warden Lee Morgan. He is in charge of the wing you have just been on. I figured it was best if you spoke to him, if only for *completeness.*' The governor put special emphasis on that final word, as if to indicate they should finish whatever they were trying to because he would do his best to make life difficult for them if they wanted to come back.

Jessica introduced herself and DC Rowlands and they all shook hands. The warden talked them through his role and made a point of saying how much experience he had. He spewed out a few statistics to show how behaviour had improved on the wing since his promotion and then showed them the monitors for his area.

He talked a good game at least but Jessica felt she had already got into the governor's bad books that morning so might as well go for the double. She nodded and made approving noises throughout his talk but, as soon as he looked up to her for approval, she put the only question she thought worth asking. 'Why does Donald McKenna have a cell to himself?'

The warden spluttered slightly and started to repeat

something along the lines of what the governor had told them relating to capacities but Jessica cut him straight off. 'I understand that, Mr Morgan, but I'm talking specifically about Mr McKenna. Why does *he* have a cell to himself?'

'Er, well, Mr McKenna has consistently been one of the best-behaved inmates. Some of the other prisoners look up to him because of his religious beliefs and clean living, while others just respect his seniority.'

'Are there other people who have been here longer?' Jessica asked.

'Well . . . yes.'

'Are there other inmates who are religious?'

'Yeah . . .'

'Are most people well behaved?'

'Yes, of course.'

Jessica nodded slowly and let out a long, deliberate 'Hmm'. She let it hang and then, for the second time in a few minutes, drastically altered her tone.

In an upbeat, breezy voice she turned back to the governor who was hovering nearby. 'So, let's go see Mr McKenna.'

Governor Gallagher took the hint and started walking towards the door with the clear indication they should follow. Rowlands moved in behind him, with Jessica at the back. She was just about to exit the viewing area when Lee Morgan called after her. 'There's, er, nothing improper, y'know . . .'

Jessica heard him perfectly well but didn't even break stride.

The journey back through the prison to the interview

room had been another silent affair. Jessica figured that if Farraday had been serious about her 'putting the shits' up the prison staff, he would be pretty pleased. She also wondered if the governor would follow through with his mention of calling DSI Aylesbury. Ultimately, she hadn't outright accused anyone of doing anything untoward and if they chose to take her insinuations that way, it was up to them.

The governor led them up a flight of steps Jessica recognised and they were soon back by the interview room. He unlocked the door and let them in. 'McKenna is next door,' he said. 'Assuming it's okay with you, I'll tell them to bring him through in five minutes. Everything you need should already be here.'

Jessica had a quick look over the recording banks and nodded. 'Thanks very much for your assistance, Governor Gallagher. You've been enormously helpful.'

The governor clearly had little intention of keeping up the pretence of being civil any longer, grunting and walking backwards out of the room.

'He was very ingratiating,' Rowlands said after the room had cleared. Jessica simply looked at him. 'What?' he added.

'I am going to get to the bottom of where all these long words are coming from because I know – and you know – that you're simply not intelligent enough to know them off the top of your head.'

The two officers readied the room and a few moments later heard some clanging noises from the corridor. Just afterwards, the door opened again and Jessica felt a twinge of déjà vu as the same suited solicitor from a few days ago entered with a handcuffed Donald McKenna just behind him. They each seemed to be wearing the exact same clothing as from their previous meeting and sat in the same places. If it wasn't for Rowlands being present instead of Cole, it would have been almost an exact rerun of the setup from their first interview.

Jessica got the introductions out of the way and then asked her colleague for the set of two folders he had carried around all morning. From the first one, she took out a photo of Craig Millar. It was an enlarged copy of his regular mug shot, the most recent picture they had of him alive. She slid the photo face up across the table towards Donald McKenna.

'Do you know who this man is, Mr McKenna?'

He picked up the photo with his cuffed hands, studying it with a quizzical look as if trying to remember something. His solicitor motioned to look at it and McKenna angled it towards him. 'You asked me that before. I told you then – he sort of seems familiar but I can't say I know him.'

He handed the picture back and Jessica put it in the folder, pulling out a second photograph. 'What about this one?' She slid the second item face down across the table and McKenna picked it up. He turned the picture over and rocked back slightly, handing it to the solicitor.

The man in the suit instantly put it back on the table face down. 'Was that really necessary?' he asked.

Jessica picked the photograph up and turned it over. It showed Craig Millar's face close-up with a gaping, bloodied wound in his neck. 'Do you recognise that one, Mr McKenna?'

The solicitor went to speak again but his client simply said, 'No.'

Jessica nodded slightly and took the photo back, again returning it to the folder and removing two photos from the second cardboard document wallet. 'What about this pair?'

This time, she held the photos up. They were two more mug shots: one Ben Webb, the other Des Hughes.

'Benjamin and Desmond.' McKenna's response was instant. 'They were both on the same block as myself.'

He took his gaze from the two photos to look directly at Jessica. She put the photos back down on the table and met his eyes. 'Did you associate with them much?'

'They weren't interested in the word of God.'

'That isn't what I asked.'

'No I did not.'

'Do you know all three men are dead?'

'I had been told. I'm sorry to hear that.'

'Really?'

'We are all God's children.'

'Why was your blood found under the fingernails of Craig Millar?'

'I don't know.'

'Why were your hairs found at the scene where Benjamin Webb and Desmond Hughes were killed?'

'I don't know.' Donald McKenna hadn't taken his eyes from Jessica throughout the entire exchange. In their previous meeting she had felt unnerved by his willingness to engage. There was something slightly different about this encounter though. She wouldn't have said she felt intimidated but there was definitely an undertone to his words and his eyes were mesmerising. They were deep and blue, looking straight through her. Jessica paused and the two of them gazed at each other.

The tension was broken by McKenna's solicitor. 'I would like to point out that my client has been cooperative throughout. This morning, for instance, he willingly submitted to a mouth swab despite not being charged with any further crime and having no legal reason to do so.'

Jessica didn't want to break the stare-off with the prisoner but felt obliged to acknowledge the man's legal representative. She looked directly at the suited man, who seemed to shrink under her stare. 'I'm sure the post-office workers he threatened with a shotgun would be delighted to hear what a role model he has become.'

The solicitor motioned as if to answer but, as he had done on the previous visit, McKenna lifted his handcuffed wrists from the table as if to indicate he was fine. 'I regret what I did,' he said solemnly.

Jessica couldn't figure out if he was being genuine or not. She met his eyes again. 'Did you ever fall out with either Mr Webb or Mr Hughes?'

'No.'

'Have you ever fallen out with anyone at this prison?'

'Not recently. In my younger days maybe but not for a while.'

The solicitor was clearly getting frustrated. 'Detective, we're going around in circles here. My client has clearly said he has not had any significant contact with any of the victims. There may be people who might wish him ill will because of his previous misdeeds but he cannot think of anyone specifically. What's more, as if I have to remind you, my client is in prison. If you want to charge him with any crimes, then can I suggest you do so?'

Jessica shifted her gaze from McKenna and looked to his representative. 'Did you rehearse that in bed last night?'

The solicitor shuffled back slightly in his seat and looked back at her with his mouth open. 'Sorry?'

'Was there some legal drama on TV last night that got you all excited? Got you thinking you could end up like some big-shot barrister?'

The man in the suit stared at her, clearly not knowing how he should respond. 'Do you have any further questions to ask my client? If not, can we end this now?'

Jessica turned back to McKenna. She knew she didn't have anywhere to go. The reason she was so annoyed with the solicitor was because he was right. There was no realistic way they could charge his client with anything as there was no chance of any kind of conviction, even if the new forensic samples came back with the same results. He was still their only lead though and was linked to the scenes not only through his DNA but because he had been inside with all three victims at the same time.

'How is your relationship with Warden Morgan?'

For the first time, McKenna stopped looking at her. He glanced at the table, then Rowlands, then back to her. 'He's a fair man.'

'Particularly fair to you though, isn't he?'

McKenna's solicitor went to interrupt but Jessica talked over the top of him, eyes fixed on the prisoner, daring him to look away again. 'Nice room you've got there, perhaps a little small? It could maybe do with a bit of internal decoration and I have no idea what those Feng Shui-types would make of it but it's not bad for this place, is it?'

The man in the suit stopped speaking as McKenna raised his own voice to talk over him. 'I'm not sure what you're getting at?'

'Really? You can't possibly imagine what I might be asking about?'

'No.'

'Well, how about this little scenario. Let's say, for instance, that there's a particular person in charge of a certain set of other people. Now that person in charge is generally a perfectly good man, maybe he's got a long history of honesty. But maybe, just maybe, there's someone in that certain group he's supposed to be looking after that isn't as honest. Maybe he's a bit of a thug, a bit of a bully. He does things like hold shotguns up to innocent people just going about their business . . .'

It felt as if the temperature in the room had dropped by a degree or two. There was absolute silence except for Jessica's voice, as if the other three people present had held their breath and were hanging on what she might say next.

'Now let's say, just for instance, that the previously honest person in charge was swayed by the other man.

Maybe there was some sort of incentive involved? Perhaps some money on offer? Maybe it was more of a stick than a carrot? Perhaps there were threats instead? Promises that loved ones would be harmed? It could be a mixture. Are you still with me, Donald? Now in that hypothetical situation – and bear in mind it is completely fictional – can you perhaps see what I *might* be getting at?'

The prisoner said nothing but looked sideways to his solicitor. Taking the hint, the man in the suit spoke, his voice faltering slightly. 'I think we should end the interview at this point, Sergeant Daniel.'

For the third time that morning, Jessica deliberately switched track. She pushed backwards on the chair, scraping it along the ground. She stood and spoke in her most upbeat voice. 'Good idea.'

She knocked on the door and guards came in to escort McKenna and his solicitor away.

When they had left, Rowlands stopped the recording and picked up the folders from the table. 'Wow,' he said. 'That was good.'

Jessica gave him a small smile. 'He's still got us though. We have nothing to go on.'

'Yeah, but you got him rattled.'

'Hmm, yeah. Do I know what's going to happen next? No. But it could be interesting.'

The constable burst out laughing and Jessica turned to look at him. 'What?'

'You're talking like the DCI now, asking yourself questions and then answering them.'

Jessica grimaced as Rowlands changed his expression. 'What do you reckon?' he asked.

'I think McKenna's lying to us – but I don't believe he was the only one.'

11

Lee Morgan slammed the pint glass down on the bar a little harder than he meant to. He felt the vibration ripple through his hand but luckily it didn't smash. 'Another one of those, love,' he said, pointing at the pump for the local brand of bitter. 'You want one?' he asked the man sitting on a stool next to him.

'Nah, I've probably had one too many already. I still have to drive home tonight.'

'There's a word for people like you – "lightweight".'

Lee Morgan was at the bar in his local pub. When he had first moved into the area twenty or so years ago, he thought this place was magnificent. It was a proper man's pub with smoke drifting around the room, quality booze on offer and barmaids who wore low-cut tops and enjoyed the odd glass of wine themselves, if not a bit more. Over the years, it had gone further and further downhill. The gradual increase in women coming into the place had been the start and then they opened the patio at the back and started letting kids in. After that it was a slippery slope. They shut the members' bar, turned it into a kitchen and started serving food. The smoking ban was the final straw. It had gone from a place to get away from the wife to an establishment that openly courted the business of women and kids.

'This place has become a right dump,' Lee complained

to the man sitting next to him. Even the stools wound him up. Men should stand up to have a pint. It was the way his father had taught him to drink. He said nothing though, he didn't have too many friends – let alone among the people he worked with.

'I've seen worse,' the man said, pointing towards the corner of the room. 'They've got a good TV. It might be worth popping in for a match sometime?'

Lee held his tongue again. He hated football and the big television screens just attracted drunken screeching buffoons, the very type of people they were supposed to spend their days keeping an eye on. He nodded to hide his displeasure. 'What do you reckon about today then?'

The man blew out through his teeth but didn't get a chance to reply before the barmaid put a fresh drink down next to them. 'That's two fifty please,' she said.

'Two pounds fifty?' Lee replied, clearly annoyed.

'That *is* what the last one cost,' the barmaid answered.

'Yeah, but he paid for that,' Lee said, nodding towards his friend and pulling a crumpled five-pound note out of his pocket. 'How much are crisps?'

'Eighty pence.'

'What, even for ready salted? You're having a laugh, love.'

'We don't do ready salted,' the barmaid said. She crouched down to look at the boxes of crisps on the floor. 'We've got chilli twists, then beef and mustard, tomato ketchup and, er, pickled-onion flavour.'

As she stood back up to face them, Lee stared at her, eyebrows raised. 'Nah, forget it, darling. I'll just have the drink.' He looked at the man next to him. 'It used to just be ready salted, cheese and onion and salt and vinegar in my day.'

The barmaid took the note and returned a few seconds later with his change.

'So what do you reckon?' Lee repeated.

'I don't know,' the man said. 'It sounds serious, doesn't it? The guv sounded pissed off at the briefing yesterday and then the coppers didn't even turn up. I could have done without all that tidying up and everything. Then, when they did come around today, they didn't even get round to my area. What did they make of your wing?'

'Not sure. Gallagher took them down there but he didn't say anything to me afterwards. All the prisoners were bundled down into the games room. They were fuming. It was hilarious when they all filed back through. Some of the worst ones had been dumped out in the rec yard just to keep them away in case the Old Bill wanted to talk to any of them.'

The other man laughed nervously. 'No one caused any trouble, did they?'

'No chance. They wouldn't want to risk having their TV taken away for a day or two, would they?'

'What did that woman detective say to you?'

Lee knew his friend was referring to the moment when she had asked him about McKenna. He took a gulp of his drink and shook his head. 'Nothing really. Stuck-up cow probably on her time of the month or something.'

The other man laughed. 'What was it you shouted after her?'

'When?'

'In the monitoring room. She was walking out the door and you called after her?'

'Oh yeah. I don't remember, sorry. Probably something about her arse.'

The other man laughed again. 'Have you heard the rumours?' he said.

'Why, what have you heard?'

'Only bits. It's all about McKenna obviously. They've pulled him off your block twice to talk to him. People have been saying they're trying to get him to confess to other crimes. Someone was going on about some kiddy stuff but others reckon it's some new murder.'

'Nah, I've not heard anything.' Lee was feeling beads of sweat on the palms of his hands.

'What about McKenna though? I don't really know anything about him but you must?'

'Nah. He's just some guy on the block, ain't he? Like all the others. Always banging on about God-this and Jesus-that. It's not done him much good though, has it?'

'Oh right . . . It's just one of the other guys reckoned you got on and that . . .'

Lee spun around quickly, spilling part of his drink over the top of the glass. 'Who said that?'

The other man was clearly taken aback. 'Oh, no one. I don't remember. It was nothing bad or that . . .'

Lee looked at him and then downed the rest of his drink in one go. 'Aye, well, there's a few too many in that place who've got a lot to say.' With the pint finished, Lee put the glass back on the bar, slightly more carefully than the previous one.

'I've gotta go,' the other man said. 'I'm back on earlies tomorrow plus the missus will be wondering where I am.'

'You're not one of *them*, are ya?'

'One of who?'

'Y'know, one of *them* who goes running home when their wife flashes her knickers or gets a strop on.'

The man laughed nervously. 'No, no. It's just late and she's had the wee kids all day.'

'All right, I should probably be off anyway,' Lee replied. 'Mine will probably be snoring by the time I get in.'

The two men said their goodbyes and left the pub together. The other man walked around towards the car park at the back while Lee put his hands in his jacket pockets and started to walk along the thin pavement that ran next to the main road. Aside from the odd passing car, it was a nice quiet journey, exactly what he wanted after the day he'd had.

He was still fuming with the way that female detective had spoken to him. He could remember the day when coppers, prison officers and journalists would mingle together in the local he had just left. They'd drink most of the night, enjoy some cheap imported cigars and then go to work the next day as normal. Women like her wouldn't have even been allowed in the pub back then, let alone the police force.

''kin joke,' he said to no one in particular.

He pulled the collar up on his jacket and turned right to

go along his usual cut-through. It wasn't too cold but the season was definitely beginning to turn.

The main road had been well lit but there were no street lights down this particular path. It only stretched for around forty yards, linking the road to the estate where he lived. There were metal barriers at either end to stop cars using it, with three lines of cracked paving slabs separating two patches of grass on either side. Houses backed onto the grassy areas, the moon casting a shadow from the building on his right across the walkway.

Lee squinted as his eyes adjusted slowly to the gloomier area. He upped his pace ever so slightly. He had never really been a fan of this shortcut but it saved him ten minutes by not having to walk all the way around the front of the estate and then back through again.

His boots echoed as he walked, clipping the hard slabs as he moved. All of a sudden, he thought he saw movement from the right. He didn't want to stop but his eyes flickered sideways and then he saw the shape coming at him. It was dark but he saw a face he recognised in the partial moonlight as the man crashed into him.

He went to shout but felt an enormous burst of pain in the middle of his neck. 'You . . .' was the last word he managed to gurgle as the man hammered the knife straight through his chest.

12

Jessica had been battling with her conscience the day after Lee Morgan had been discovered. As soon as she arrived at the station, she had been told the prison officer's dead body had been found. Emotion flooded through her, as she wondered if the way she had wound up both Donald McKenna and the guard himself had directly led to it.

At first she thought the warden could have committed suicide if he did have something to hide but that was ruled out as soon as she was told his wounds were identical to Craig Millar and Ben Webb's.

After that, her thoughts moved to the prisoner. Had McKenna done something to prove a point to her that no one was untouchable? She didn't even know if the warden had been corrupt. The previous day she had been fishing for information and might have had suspicions but couldn't have expected this. The only thing she felt relatively sure of was that McKenna had to be involved. There was no way it could be a coincidence that Lee Morgan had turned up dead a few hours after she had been to the prison and asked about the potential relationship between the two of them.

After being at the scene in the morning, the body had been taken away for testing and Jessica returned to the station in the afternoon. She went straight up to the first floor to see if Farraday was in his office, assuming he would want to see her anyway. He noticed her walking down the corridor through the windows of his office and waved her in before she had even knocked. He phoned downstairs for Cole and, a minute or so later, the three of them were sitting in his office as they had done a few days previously.

The DCI spoke first. 'Okay, Daniel, while you've been out, the secondary results have come back from the labs for the other bodies. I spoke to the head person there half an hour ago and she told me the new swabs taken confirm Donald McKenna is linked to the three deaths.'

It was exactly what Jessica had been expecting but the confirmation was still a shock. She breathed out loudly. 'What do we do now?'

'Do I think we have a case? Not a chance. What we do now is keep trying to link McKenna to the victims. The DNA evidence is essentially worthless at the moment. I spoke to someone from the CPS briefly and he pretty much laughed down the phone. As we all thought, given our suspect is firmly behind bars, it's unusable in court unless we have some other link between him and the victims. The fact they were all in prison together isn't enough.'

He shuffled through a handful of Post-it notes stuck to his desk, continuing. 'What about this prison guard guy, er, Morgan?'

He turned the Post-it note around that had the prison guard's name written on it as if to remind Jessica who it was. She certainly didn't need her memory refreshing. 'I saw him yesterday. He is the warden responsible for the area where McKenna is housed . . .'

The chief inspector cut straight across her. 'So, some bent warden's turned up dead then. McKenna must be involved somehow.'

Jessica didn't want to sound like she was correcting him but did have to make a point. She wasn't sure why he had jumped to that conclusion. 'We're not sure he's, er, corrupt, Sir.'

Farraday nodded. 'Yeah, yeah, I know. It will be there somewhere, though. What did he say to you yesterday?'

'Well, the governor told me individual head wardens are responsible for cell allocation. Lee Morgan was the warden responsible for McKenna, who was living in a cell on his own. Most prisoners are two to a cell and I just asked him why McKenna instead of one of the other prisoners? He didn't really have an answer.'

Even Cole was nodding now. 'It does sound a little *off*,' he said.

The DCI spoke across them. 'Off? I've seen paper clips less bent than this guy will turn out to be, you mark my words.'

Jessica was feeling increasingly frustrated. It wasn't that she thought the guard was whiter than white, she just wasn't convinced they should be condemning a dead man before they knew the truth. The increasing feeling of guilt that she had accused Lee Morgan of just that, albeit it not directly, was still playing on her mind too.

Neither Jessica nor DI Cole said anything, not really knowing what their boss might say next. Farraday was rocking back and forwards in his chair. 'Right, this is what we're going to do,' he said. 'Daniel, first go see this guy the warden was drinking with last night.'

He was hunting through the Post-it notes again. Jessica had already been given a very brief run-down of the prison officer's movements the night before. She knew he had been walking home from his local pub after stopping out for a drink with one of his work colleagues. The other warden hadn't been a suspect because, at the exact time Lee Morgan was being killed, his friend's car had been pulled over for speeding.

The DCI quickly found the note he was looking for. 'Just see what he's got to say and then go see this warden's wife. Suss her out, that kind of thing. Look around the house, see if there's any expensive jewellery and all that. Cole, you stay here and start sniffing around their bank records. Dodgy deposits, any hidden accounts, all that. I want this guy nailed as soon as possible so we can lump him in with those three other shites who copped it off McKenna. When that's all sorted, we'll get back to connecting him to the victims.'

Jessica wondered what their boss was going to spend the day doing but he didn't take long to tell them. 'I'm going to get the media boys round. Get the cameras in, then shove this vigilante killer thing right up their arses.'

It was the first time any of them had used the word 'vigilante'. In police stations it was almost as dirty a term as 'serial killer'. Generally they didn't like to make assumptions and would hold back with such labels until they were sure. Jessica felt uneasy hearing it. That McKenna, or whoever the killer might be, was tracking down criminals was something obvious to them all. The fact it could be deliberate vigilantism was also a thought that had crossed her mind but it was a big leap from thinking it to feeding it to the press.

'Are you going to tell them about McKenna, Sir?' she asked.

'Do I think it's a good idea to tell them our chief suspect is already in prison? No, Daniel, I don't. For now, we'll just get the victims' names out there and see if anyone can link them together for us. If it brings McKenna into the mix then all the better.'

As uneasy as she felt with the idea, Jessica had to admit it wasn't a bad one. They had tried their usual searches to try to connect the three victims with little luck. Maybe someone who watched the news or read the papers would know something they didn't?

Jessica had first gone to visit Lee Morgan's fellow prison guard, who had been drinking with him in the pub the night before. He had already been visited that morning by officers asking about his movements the night before. He still appeared to be in shock but Jessica had never seen anyone quite so relieved to receive three penalty points on their driving licence. He explained he had only had one drink to make sure he stayed under the drink-drive limit. He was feeling guilty about staying out late, however, and ended up driving at 55 m.p.h. along the 40 m.p.h. main road in a hurry to get home.

At the time, he had been angry and annoyed at being pulled over but when the police officers knocked on the door the next morning with the news of his friend's death – and questions about his own whereabouts – his annoyance had turned to relief that he had an alibi. With his wife in bed when he arrived home and witnesses in the pub quite happy to say they saw the two men leaving together, he knew he could have been in big trouble if he hadn't been stopped.

By the time Jessica arrived, that relief had turned back into shock at his friend's death. He told Jessica he and Lee just made small talk at the pub and that they went out for a quiet drink once a month or so.

'I don't think Lee had many friends,' he said. 'I always felt sorry for the guy. He was a bit of a moaner but harmless enough.' Jessica figured they would find out quite how harmless he was in due course. She asked if he had heard any rumours of malpractice around the prison but he insisted he hadn't.

From there, she drove to Lee Morgan's house. A family liaison officer was already there to support the man's widow. Carla Morgan looked a lot older than her husband had done. Jessica now knew Lee had been fifty-six but his wife looked as if she was in her late sixties. The officer let Jessica into the house and showed her into the living room. Carla had been sitting in a comfy-looking recliner but stood gingerly to greet her.

She apologised needlessly for her lack of mobility. 'Sorry, dear, I had to have my hip replaced six months ago,' she said.

Jessica said it was not a problem and helped the woman back into her seat. Given the marks around her eyes, it was clear Carla had been crying that morning but she now seemed relatively fine. Farraday's suggestion to 'suss' the woman out seemed ridiculous given the state of her. The other officer went to make some tea, leaving Jessica and Carla alone in the living room.

She asked some relatively harmless questions about how the couple had met and how long they had been together. The information wasn't essential but Jessica knew she couldn't dive straight in and ask the woman if she knew whether her husband, who had only been killed the night before, took money on the side or not. She did take those moments to look around the room. Ultimately she knew it was very likely the house would be searched thoroughly by a trained squad in the next day or so anyway – especially if Cole found anything suspicious in the couple's bank records.

The television certainly looked new, large and flat, pinned to the wall and surrounded by large speakers with other media players and a digital box underneath. Jessica had already noticed the black hatchback car parked on the drive. It had a registration plate from the year before and was sparklingly clean. The whole house was incredibly well kept, not something out of the ordinary in itself but perhaps surprising because of Carla's clear difficulties in getting around. It was those types of detail Jessica was trained to spot. She knew the couple had no children, so unless Lee Morgan was an avid tidy-upper after a long day at work, then the pair were likely paying a cleaner.

As the other officer returned with some drinks, Jessica asked where the toilet was. Carla gave her the directions and she made her way out into the hallway then went up the stairs, not looking to go snooping but wanting to get a feel of the house. There were no obvious illustrations of wealth but there were framed photographs on the wall the entire way up the staircase. All of the pictures were of the two Morgans and seemed to be from recent years given the similarity in their appearances. Each one was taken in an exotic location with beaches, attractive-looking palm trees or clear blue ocean in the background.

There wasn't much more for Jessica to see at the top of the stairs but an overall impression was emerging that the couple might not be overtly rich but were certainly comfortable.

Back downstairs, Jessica sat on the sofa close to Carla. The other officer left them alone again. 'It's a nice place you have here, Mrs Morgan,' she said.

The woman nodded. 'Thank you. Lee was always talking about having somewhere nice to retire to. It's taken us a while but we've got the house the way we wanted.'

'I liked the photos on the way upstairs . . .'

The woman smiled sadly. 'Yes. Can you believe I'd never been on a plane until three years ago? Lee had been talking about it for years but we never had the money and I was always a bit scared of flying.'

'Where did you go?'

'We went to Egypt first of all. Lee wanted to go to the Caribbean but I didn't want to go too far. It was nice but a bit too hot. The year after, I let him have his way and we went to Antigua. The island was amazing but I didn't like being on the plane for so long.' She motioned towards her back. 'Last year we just went to France. It was warm but I don't think Lee really took to the food and neither of us could speak the language so it wasn't easy.'

'A new car too . . . ?'

'Yes. Lee always wanted a brand-new vehicle. We always had old ones that kept breaking down. I never learned to drive, so it was all down to him.'

'How did you pay for the car?' Jessica tried to ask the question in as innocuous a way as possible.

'I don't really know. Lee always wanted me to stay at home and he took care of the money.'

'Didn't you ever ask questions?'

Jessica could see that the penny had dropped for Carla. The woman spoke slowly, deliberately choosing her words and shuffling nervously in her chair. 'Why are you asking?'

'Because I have to, Mrs Morgan.'

'Why?'

'Because we are trying to find out why your husband was killed and these things could all be important.'

Jessica knew she had lost the woman. She did ask further questions but everything was met with one- or two-word answers. She wasn't going to get any further worthwhile information and didn't see the point of pushing a clearly upset widow any further. After saying goodbye to Carla and the family liaison officer, Jessica called Cole when she got back into her car.

She asked if he had dug up anything on the family's

finances. 'Sort of,' he said. 'It's not what's in the accounts that's odd, it's what isn't there.'

'How do you mean?'

'Well, you can see Lee Morgan's monthly salary going into his account but the only bits that come out are large things like money for a holiday that was paid off in one go. The items you or I might pay for, groceries, petrol, even things like household bills, there's no sign of that at all.'

'So you think they've been using cash?'

'Yes but there are no actual withdrawals from the account. No credit cards, no loans and no outstanding debts, either. Most people would owe some amount of money but there's nothing. Their current account acts as if it's for savings because, aside from the odd large purchase, the money is rarely touched.'

'No direct debits or standing orders?'

'No but you can pay things like electricity bills in cash at the post office, can't you?'

'I guess . . . How long has that been going on?'

'Maybe three years, perhaps a little less. What did you find?'

Jessica explained about the holiday photos, new car and electronic goods. Cole said he would update Farraday because they would have to apply for a warrant to search the house. It seemed likely there would be cash somewhere but whether it would be kept on the property or in some other location only Lee Morgan knew about was difficult to judge. In some ways Jessica hoped they didn't find anything. She doubted Carla was complicit in whatever

her husband had been involved in, even if she had perhaps turned a blind eye and not asked some of the questions she should have. But it seemed overly harsh to not only have her husband taken from her but also his reputation and possibly any financial security she could hope to have.

She hung up and called Adam. He told her they were yet to find much from the prison officer's body. 'The Scene of Crime officers didn't bring in anything specific and so far we haven't found anything either. I know they've been looking for footprints around the area it all happened in but I haven't heard anything.'

Jessica assured him they were still on for meeting on Sunday, assuming things didn't get too busy for her, and then ended the call. She took special care not to refer to it as a 'date'.

Even if the forensics squad didn't find any specific link to Donald McKenna, it wouldn't mean the killing of the officer wasn't linked to the first three. For one, the obvious connection to the prison was there but so was the similarity in the stab wounds.

Jessica checked the clock on her phone and didn't figure it was worth going back to the station. She had already passed on the information she had to Jack and had again worked comfortably more hours that week than she was required to. She tuned the radio into the local news station. She rarely listened to it, usually preferring a frequency that played rock music. Given Farraday had told her a few hours ago he was going to bring the media in, she felt she should tune in to find out what was being reported.

The station had regular half-hourly updates and Jessica had to listen to an infuriating phone-in show before they finally got to the part she was waiting for. The newsreader's first words were, 'Is there a vigilante on the loose?' with dramatic music in the background. It was sensationalist but the names of Craig Millar, Ben Webb and Des Hughes were all mentioned prominently, which was good. The presenter then gave out a phone number for listeners to call in with information.

But the next few lines were what stood out to Jessica. The reader then mentioned the name 'Lee Morgan' and added that, 'a senior police source told us the officer could have links to corruption within the prison'.

It was clear Farraday believed Lee Morgan had taken back-handers but, having just met the man's widow, Jessica was fuming the woman's husband had been outed with no concrete evidence. If she needed any further proof as to who the 'senior source' was, she got it the next morning. She didn't often buy the *Manchester Morning Herald* but got up early and went to the local shop. She read through their pages at home, half-watching the television news.

The paper's front-page headline was simply 'VIGILANTE'. She didn't recognise the byline on the piece but even she had to admit it was well written if the aim was to sell papers. On pages two and three, they had a profile of the three victims, pointing out in as many words that the streets were safer without them on it. On four and five they laid out in pretty gory detail what had actually happened to the trio and included the force's appeal for information.

It was page six that concerned Jessica. The headline was: 'AS BENT AS A PAPER CLIP', then underneath, 'IS DEAD WARDEN VICTIM NO. 4?'. The chief inspector wasn't named – instead that elusive 'senior source' was quoted – but the exact choice of words left no doubts who it was that had leaked the information.

From listening to the television news and checking a few websites, Jessica could see the story of the prison officer's death was inconsistent between the organisations. Some made the link to the first three bodies, some didn't. It seemed clear to Jessica her boss had given off-the-record briefings to certain journalists in order to muddy the water. If the police found nothing to incriminate Lee Morgan, it didn't matter too much because the damage had already been done to the man's reputation. The DCI could point out he had said nothing formal for the media to quote and the organisations themselves were off the hook because you can't libel the dead.

Jessica felt it was a very sly move that, although making the force look competent and gaining attention for their appeal, would cause maximum harm to Carla, not to mention Craig Millar's mother. It was all right for the chief inspector to play games from his office but she was the one who had to go out and look the victims' families in the eye.

Still angry, she first called Cole, making sure she kept her temper in check. She told him that, given the media attention, she was going to return to visit Denise Millar to make sure she was all right and asked if he could pass that on at the station if anyone asked after her. He told her

that was fine but said she should try not to take too long. The press office had already phoned him at home because the national media had picked up on the local story and they wanted everyone at the station to deal with the attention.

She hung up and made another call but it wasn't to the parent of the first murder victim as she had claimed. Instead, she phoned someone she hadn't spoken to in over a year. After a quick one-sided conversation, she got in her car and drove to the centre of the city, picking up a passenger and then driving back out again and parking in a quiet area at the back of a supermarket car park.

Jessica figured it was best not being seen openly talking to the person she had phoned. She put the handbrake on and switched off the engine, turning to the man sitting next to her. 'So, Garry,' she said. 'How about I tell you what's really going on?'

13

Garry Ashford shuffled nervously in the passenger seat of Jessica's car. 'Hang on a minute, let me get a pen out,' he said.

He lifted himself up, bumping his head on the ceiling of the vehicle with a muffled clang. He rubbed his skull and fumbled in his trouser pockets before rifling through the ones in his jacket. It was a struggle given the lack of space. Jessica avoided his swinging elbow and intervened.

'Y'know, Garry, for a clandestine meeting in the middle of nowhere, you're doing a pretty shoddy job and I've not even started telling you what we're here for yet.'

'Sorry, you didn't give me much notice. I was still in bed.' The man's straggly black hair had grown since the last time Jessica had seen him and was now a little below his shoulders. He was still pasty and scrawny with a questionable taste in clothes. The journalist was wearing brown cord trousers with a navy-blue jacket that looked like it was made of velvet. Jessica had the urge to touch it but held off.

When she had first called him that morning, she had been pretty angry. Given his outfit and the fact he was a journalist who didn't even have anything to write with, that fury had evaporated into comical disbelief. 'Do you want to borrow a pen?' Jessica reached into the storage area on the inside of the driver's door and pulled out a blue biro, holding it out towards her passenger.

'Yeah, that'd be good, thanks.'

'You do have a pad, don't you?'

'Yep, got that.'

Garry took the pen from her and pulled out a notepad from the plastic carrier bag he had brought with him. He tried scribbling with the pen on the front of the notebook, pressing harder and then handing it back to her. 'Er, this one doesn't work.'

'Oh for f— look, do you reckon you can just remember what I tell you?'

'Yes, sorry. Thanks for your call—'

Jessica cut him off. 'Did you go to the press briefing yesterday with all the vigilante stuff?'

'No. We've got this new senior crime reporter guy on the *Herald*. I think he's some relation of the editor. He was only brought in a few months ago but he always gets sent to things like that now.'

'What do you do?'

'Well, since last year, I wasn't able to get many crime beat stories—'

Jessica cut him off again. 'How is Dave Rowlands?'

Garry paused for a moment. 'Who?'

'I know you went to university together. I checked.'

'The name doesn't ring a bell.'

Jessica let it go. 'Okay, so you were struggling with crime stories. What are you working on now?'

'Local government correspondent.'

Jessica didn't mean to but burst out laughing. 'Oh God . . .'

'Yeah, I know. It wasn't my choice.'

'It sounds awful.'

'You don't know the half of it. The reason I was still in bed this morning is that I was at the council chambers until half past eleven last night for some budget vote.'

'You must have *really* annoyed someone?'

'After last year, the stories started to dry up. One of the older guys retired and they moved me over. I get a bit more money but it's not really worth it.'

Rain started to hammer down on the windscreen and Garry jumped slightly. Jessica thought for a moment about turning on the heater in the car but decided against it. For one, it would take the best part of ten minutes to warm up in any case but she also didn't trust the battery to start the car again if she tried to use anything without the engine on. 'You know I shouldn't really be talking to you so no names, okay?'

'Of course.'

'The story you've all got this morning is only half of what's actually going on. The vigilante stuff, that might be true, we don't really know yet. The corrupt prison officer, that might also be true but again we just don't know.'

Garry nodded along as she spoke. He had clearly read or seen the news that morning and knew what she was talking about. 'What you've not been told is that we have DNA matches for the first three victims.'

'You know who did it?'

'Maybe . . . Sort of . . . Well, not really.' Garry had a

puzzled look on his face and was clearly annoyed at himself for not bringing a pen. He still had the notepad on his lap and was running his fingers along the side as Jessica continued speaking. 'The labs have tested and re-tested the samples and each time it comes back as a match for someone who is already in prison.'

'Oh . . . What, like *prison* prison?'

'What other types of prison are there?'

'Er, I don't know.'

Jessica rolled her eyes. 'Yes, *prison* prison. You know that giant great bloody building at Strangeways.'

'Yeah, sorry. Well, what do you think?'

'Honestly? I don't know. We've been to Strangeways and spoken to the people there. The prison guard that was killed was the head warden on the person's wing.'

'Blimey. Is that why you think he was corrupt?'

'We don't know. Perhaps – but the point is all the coverage this morning, it's just not fair. Four people are dead and that's been lost with all this stuff about them somehow deserving it.'

'Do *you* think they deserved it?'

Jessica had been gazing at the windscreen, watching the water run down the outside of the glass, but stopped and looked directly at the person sitting next to her, waiting for him to meet her eyes. 'It doesn't matter what I think.'

Garry nodded as Jessica looked away again, continuing to speak. 'Craig Millar, the first victim, his mother's terrific and he's got a younger brother. Not only have they lost a son and brother but now they've got all you lot calling him a shit on the front page. The guard has a wife, Carla.

Her husband's body hasn't even been released back to her to be buried yet and you are all saying he was bent. It's not right.'

The two of them didn't say anything for a few moments, the only noise the echo of the rain falling on the car's roof and windscreen. Garry broke the silence. 'Why did you call me?'

'Because you're the only reporter I think I can actually trust. I want you to talk to Craig Millar's mother and ask her about her son. Write something to say these victims *are* victims.'

'It's not my department any longer and, even if it was, I don't know if my editor would print it. I'm not sure I should really be taking orders from the police either . . .'

'Fair enough. Look, I'm not trying to tell you what you should and shouldn't do but you do at least know what's going on now.'

'Can you tell me the prisoner's name?'

'He's not been charged with anything so I don't think it's a good idea.'

'Is he going to be?'

'I don't know. I doubt it. If you were on a jury would you find someone locked in a prison cell guilty of a crime on the outside?'

'Good point. So what are you working on now?'

'Blind hope that someone somewhere will call that number in your paper today and fill the gaps in for us. Craig Millar was walking home with two brothers that night but we've ruled them out. We found some drugs when we raided one of their houses. He's been charged but they're terrified they could be next. After them, aside from our guy, we don't really have much. If we can find another link from him to the victims then we could have something to work on. I think the guard could have been that link and maybe that's why he was killed but I guess we'll never know.'

Jessica had told Garry everything she had planned to. The journalist said he would try to speak to the first victim's mother but that there wasn't much he could do with the prison information at that time. 'If you've not released it and I don't have anything else to go on, my editor's going to think I'm crazy if I go in talking about a prisoner being the prime suspect,' he said.

Although she realised he was right, Jessica didn't know what she was hoping to achieve but it was some sort of rebellion against the media campaign her superior had apparently started the previous day. She drove the reporter back to the city centre and dropped him off around the corner from his office.

Over a year ago she had told him not to call her for quotes for his stories any longer but let him know she was lifting the ban. 'You've got my number. Just be discreet if you call, okay?'

Jessica hated driving in the middle of the city on a weekday but the fact it was wet made things even worse. Workers with hoods up and umbrellas being blown from side to side crossed the road with barely a look and the blowers in her car weren't good enough to keep the windscreen clear. She found herself constantly leaning forwards to wipe steam away from the window and it took her nearly forty minutes to make what should have been a fifteen-minute drive back to the station.

As soon as she turned onto the road the station was on she saw the rows of vans with satellite dishes on top lined up, meaning the rolling news stations were there. She pulled into the station and, although she had seen worse media scrums at the entrance, there were a few reporters being shielded under umbrellas doing pieces to camera.

She parked and dashed across the car park through the station's front doors. The television that sat in the reception area was usually turned off but was currently tuned into one of the news channels. Across the bottom of the screen were the words: 'Vigilante: good or bad?'. There seemed to be some sort of debate going on between the host and a couple of guests about whether or not it was ever acceptable to take the law into your own hands. To Jessica it wasn't that much different from the trashy talk shows she pretended she didn't watch – except for the fact this was actually masquerading as something high-brow.

The whole of the entrance was wet where people had walked in dripping from the rain. There was a yellow plastic triangle sign on the ground saying 'caution wet floor'. Considering it was back by the desk, Jessica thought it was probably redundant as you would only have seen it after you had already walked through the puddles. The thought ran through her mind that she could fake a slip and make some spurious no-win no-fee claim about the sign not being in the right place. The few thousand pounds she would hope for could at least tide her over while someone else sorted out this mess.

Dismissing the idea, she nodded to the desk sergeant and made her way through to the main floor, looking for Rowlands. He wasn't at his desk but DC Jones was sitting at hers. Jessica walked over and sat on the corner of the desk. 'Have you seen Dave?'

'I think he's in the canteen.'

Jessica went to stand up but the constable continued speaking. 'Hey, is it true you're off out with some guy from Bradford Park?'

'I really don't know how these things get around.'

Jessica had inadvertently given a half-smile though, which her friend had clearly noticed. 'I hope it goes all right. Are you gonna text me afterwards?'

'I'll think about it.'

Jessica walked out of the room, back towards reception and then along the corridor to the canteen.

She saw Rowlands eating at one of the tables opposite one of the female uniformed officers. She sat next to the woman and coughed, making eye contact with the constable, who took the hint. 'Give us a minute, yeah?' he said to the officer opposite him. The other female stood up and moved to sit a few tables away.

'It's not what you think,' Rowlands said.

'Whatever. Look, Dave, let's just say that hypothetically you had been talking to a certain journalist last year that you shouldn't have been. Let's say that I had put a stop to it even though neither you nor that fictional journalist reckoned you had any knowledge of each other. Well, let's now say that the ban that was in effect has now been lifted.'

Rowlands put down the fork and looked at her. 'I'm not sure I know what you're talking about but, let's say that I did, is there a particular reason why you have changed your mind?'

'That doesn't matter but you should definitely choose what you talk about a little more selectively than last time.'

Rowlands nodded, picking his fork up again and scooping another mouthful.

'You should be careful eating in here,' Jessica added. 'Jason reckons he was once out of action for a week after a dodgy lasagne from this place.'

Rowlands patted his stomach. 'Yeah, but he doesn't have my abs. Body's a temple and all that.'

'Maybe one of those temples that got bombed during the Blitz. What have they got you working on?'

'After the briefing this morning, they put most of us doing shifts on the phones for people calling in. The chief inspector has made us take staggered breaks so we have enough people working. I was on for two hours this morning.'

'Get anything useful?'

'Mainly just people calling in to say we should give the vigilante a job, rather than try to stop him.'

Jessica sighed. 'Typical.'

'There was one woman who asked if we could send whoever the vigilante is round her way to take care of some neighbour causing her problems.'

'Next thing you know we're going to have people dressing up as superheroes and patrolling the streets.'

'As long as it's one of those girls with the big boots and low-cut tops I'm all for it.'

Jessica shook her head and stood up. 'Do you know if the DCI is upstairs?'

'Dunno. He was pretty hyper at the briefing. I've never seen him like that. He was bloody smiling.'

'Christ, the end of the world must really be nigh.'

Jessica left the canteen and went up to Farraday's office. She could see through the windows he was inside but he was on the phone and held his hand up to indicate she should wait. After a few minutes, he put the receiver down and waved her in. 'Daniel. How was your morning out?'

'Okay, Sir. I just thought I should double-check a few things.'

Her superior nodded. 'Good thinking. I take it you saw all the coverage this morning?'

'Yes, Sir. It was pretty hard to miss.'

He grinned unnervingly at her. She had seen him laugh and smile before but it didn't happen often and was particularly out of place considering they had a serious investigation going on. 'We've got a warrant for the bent warden's house and will be going in shortly. Cole is with that team. I spoke to the labs this morning but they've not come up with anything from the body.'

'Have you heard anything from the prison?'

Farraday laughed as loud as she had ever heard. 'I had the super on this morning. The governor called him earlier, furious about the stuff in the papers. Apparently he was going on about how nothing had been proven and that it would undermine his staff. I would have *loved* to have taken that call.'

'What did the super say?'

'Not much, just that we'd have to try to keep the media under wraps.'

'Where do you reckon they got the information about the warden from?' Jessica was careful not to phrase her question in an accusing way.

'No idea. Maybe they're not all completely useless? At least with the information out there we might get a few useful calls in.'

'What would you like me to do now?'

'Not much. Finish up whatever paperwork you have then go home and have a good weekend. Calls have started to come in so it's just a waiting game for now. If this guy's for real we might get lucky and have another piece of shit off the streets by Monday.'

Jessica said nothing but there was something incredibly unsettling about her boss's attitude.

14

Even though they were both scheduled to be off work, Jessica phoned DI Cole the next morning. He was with his kids but did tell her they had found nothing of note at Lee Morgan's house. If the warden had large bundles of cash hidden away somewhere, he had taken the location to the grave. Jessica was glad she hadn't been a part of that raid. Carla had told her how pleased she was with the state of the house and, having just lost her husband, seeing the search team tear her home apart would have been traumatic.

Jessica had bought that morning's *Herald* and there was a small article with Garry Ashford's byline. It was an interview with Denise Millar where she talked about her son and highlighted a few of the good things he had done in the area. Jessica had to admit there wasn't much but he did regularly help out with a local youth group. The story was buried on page eleven, behind ten pages of speculation about the apparent vigilante and more debate as to whether or not people should be taking the law into their own hands.

The coverage was difficult to get away from. It was leading local and national television news bulletins and had a presence on the front of every national newspaper. Well, except one, which instead had a nearly topless photo of a reality TV star Jessica only half-recognised.

Jessica texted Caroline to see how her friend was doing but their back-and-forth messages fizzled out quickly, as they always seemed to now. She spent the weekend doing very little, which was unusual for her. Frequently she would end up going to the station on her days off, if only for a few hours, or arrange to meet up with Carrie for an evening out or in. Given the way things were going, she felt as if she needed a couple of days away from everything work-wise – Farraday in particular.

She did some tidying around her flat, something else that was out of the ordinary and watched hours of bad television. Jessica wasn't particularly in the mood for meeting up with Adam but felt even less like cancelling on him. There was no way she was going to be left on her own waiting for him, so she deliberately caught a slightly later bus on her way into the city centre on the Sunday.

Jessica had texted him the address for where to meet and saw him sitting in the window as she walked from the bus stop. The place they were meeting was a nice cafe Jessica knew next to an independent cinema in an area where mainly students lived. It hadn't been a particularly sunny day but it was at least still daylight as she walked.

Adam seemed a little glum and was staring at his phone pressing buttons as Jessica spotted him. Jessica did that herself when she wanted to look occupied in a public place. As he looked up and saw her through the glass, his expression instantly changed, realising he hadn't been stood up.

Because of her mood, Jessica thought it would be a decent idea to meet up with Adam in the afternoon, rather than the evening. It made it appear more like a 'meeting' than a 'date', ensuring she was unlikely to drink too much wine and end up looking stupid.

Jessica entered the cafe and walked over to the stools where Adam was sitting. 'Hey,' she said.

'Hi, I thought you'd changed your mind or something . . .'

'Nah, just missed the bus.'

'Oh right, okay . . .' Adam still seemed a little nervous about looking her in the eye. He was wearing a pair of jeans with a white T-shirt and black blazer. On his T-shirt was an image of a cartoon Jessica remembered from when she was younger. He had clearly made an effort. The stubble from the first time she had met him had been shaved off and his dark hair was clean. 'Nice place, this,' he added.

'It's not too far from where I lived a while back. I used to come here regularly a few years ago.'

'Oh, you look nice by the way,' Adam blurted out. 'Sorry, I should have said that before . . .'

Jessica struggled not to laugh. The poor guy was clearly so nervous around girls, even the things he obviously planned to say came out at the wrong time. She had made a little effort, with a pair of jeans she still just about fitted in and a black top she'd had since she was sixteen. She had left her hair down too – not having to get dressed up properly was another advantage of meeting in the afternoon.

'Thank you,' Jessica replied, making sure she kept a straight face. 'I was thinking maybe we could have a drink in here and then watch a movie next door? If you're hungry, there are lots of places to eat around here afterwards.'

'Great, yeah, that's great.'

'What kind of movies do you like?'

'Oh, everything really.'

'Even snuff movies and hardcore pornography?'

Adam looked at her, horrified. 'No, God no. Of course not.'

'I'm joking, Adam.'

He laughed nervously. 'Oh yeah, sorry.'

Jessica smiled back at him. 'Look, if we're ever going to, er, meet with each other again, I'm going to have to lay down a few ground rules. Firstly, stop apologising. Second, it's probably fair enough for you to just assume I'm joking about things. Okay?'

'Yeah, sor . . . er, yeah, that's fine.'

The cafe had a rack with flyers advertising the films showing next door. The two went over the list together and decided on a documentary about a photographer. It was not the kind of thing Jessica would have gone out of her way to watch but she didn't fancy a subtitled film. It wasn't that she had anything against foreign movies, just that her faith in her own eyesight was slowly deteriorating. She wasn't ready to admit to herself just yet that she was getting too old to be able to read things correctly from a distance and a subtitled film would probably be pushing things a tad too far.

They had half an hour to wait until their showtime, so made small talk while having their drinks. Jessica found herself relaxing more as Adam finally started to overcome his nervousness. 'Do you go to the cinema much?' he asked.

'Not really. I come here now and then but I can't stand all those big multi-screen places.'

'How come?'

'It takes you a few years to realise but eventually you come to the conclusion that most of the general public are just arses. You want to sit there and watch some nonsense film but if it's not some idiot slurping his drink, then it's some grossly overweight woman troughing a bucket of popcorn.'

Adam laughed, joining in. 'Yeah and you get those teenagers using their phones all the time.'

'Exactly, I once marched up to this lad and hung up his phone for him. He had actually taken a call and was merrily chatting away as if he was in his living room. I had two dozen people giving me an ovation as this little scroat called me every name under the sun. He changed his tune when I pulled out my police ID.'

Adam laughed louder this time. 'What did he do?'

'Well, his little girlfriend didn't seem too pleased when the staff turfed the pair of them out and gave him a bigger mouthful than he'd given me. I left her to sort him out in the end, I think the embarrassment was punishment enough.'

There weren't too many awkward pauses in their conversation and Jessica found herself laughing a lot more than she had done in a long time. When he relaxed and stopped being so nervy, Adam was a fun guy and clearly very clever. Now he wasn't too afraid to look at her, she could see his eyes were as big and brown as she had first thought. Jessica also found out he had a working vocabulary of French, Spanish and Italian, which she found very impressive, if a little intimidating. She wondered if that was why she couldn't place his accent but didn't openly ask him.

The movie was a lot better than she expected and, given it had not long turned dark after they came out, they decided to get something to eat. Jessica told Adam he could choose, seeing as she had picked the initial location. They ended up eating in a small Italian restaurant right next to her bus stop.

Jessica knew the area reasonably well and, for a district where lots of students lived and restaurants were constantly bought and rebranded, this particular place had been ever-present for as long as she could remember.

There was only room for half-a-dozen tables inside and they received a warm welcome as they entered from the man who was presumably the owner. He took Adam's jacket and led them to a table for two in the bay window. 'The most romantic table in the house,' he declared loudly. Jessica and Adam laughed nervously with each other.

The walls were adorned with a mixture of cheesy Italian imagery, such as photos of a man with a moustache, and hanging peppers, chillies and spicy-looking sausages. The smells given off from those and the ones drifting from the kitchen were making Jessica hungry. Despite her earlier pledge not to drink, she ordered a bottle of wine for the two of them to share.

They agreed to split one of the large pizzas but Adam insisted he was allergic to onions, so they opted for a purely meaty one. They had almost finished eating when Jessica asked the question she had wanted to when he had first mentioned it. 'Are you *really* allergic to onions or just a bit funny about them?'

'They give me big stomach cramps.'

'Oh, so it's a fake allergy then?'

'How do you mean?'

'Well, for me, if you're not going to keel over dead, it doesn't really count.'

'So you'd rather I died as opposed to just having a tummy ache?'

'Exactly. If you're going to go around calling something an allergy, I think you've got to be able to back that up.'

Adam laughed and Jessica realised he had finally cottoned on to her sense of humour. 'So where do you live then?' she asked.

'I have a house out Salford way.'

'Do you live alone?'

Adam shuffled in his seat. He finally seemed comfortable with making eye contact but glanced out of the window as he answered. 'No, with my grandma.'

'Oh . . .'

Jessica didn't mean to sound quite so blunt, it just slipped out. She didn't know exactly how old he was but it was certainly somewhere in his late twenties or early thirties. Living with your parents, let alone grandparents, wasn't a great image. It could partially explain his awkwardness around girls. It must be hard getting time alone with the opposite sex if you still lived with your family.

Adam quickly jumped in. 'My parents died when I was a baby and my grandma brought me up. I've been meaning to move out for a long time but . . . well, it's just I don't want her ending up in a home or anything. It wouldn't seem fair to leave her after she took me in.'

'Is it her you get your accent from? It doesn't sound local.'

'She's from the west country somewhere. I guess some of her dialect has rubbed off on me.'

Jessica nodded gently and half-thought about making some sort of cider- or cheese-related joke. Adam had spoken quickly though and there was a strong undercurrent of emotion in his voice. Jessica felt it a little herself. 'That's really nice.'

'No, it's okay. I know it's weird.'

'I think it's nice. What's she like?'

Adam grinned. 'Grandma? She's . . . different. She's got to that point where she just doesn't care what anyone thinks any longer. Whatever's in her head just pops out. I took her to the supermarket the other week and we were behind this woman in the queue. She had these dodgy leggings on that made her look . . . well, y'know?'

Jessica nodded, knowing exactly what he meant. There were some women who, to be polite, didn't have the figure to pull off wearing leggings.

'Most people wouldn't say anything. You might glance, then look away and think, "That doesn't look good" or something like that. But Nan's at the point where she doesn't have any of those social niceties. She just turns to me and goes, "Adam, do you think that woman's got a mirror in her house?"'

'How loud?'

'Really loud. She's a bit deaf too.'

'Oh God . . .' Jessica found herself laughing in a way she hadn't done since before Caroline had moved out, really deep belly laughs. There were tears in her eyes as Adam joined in too.

'Did the woman say anything?' Jessica asked when she managed to calm herself down.

'No but you could see her tense up – she must have heard. Then Nan kept going on about why people dress like that in public. I was trying to change the subject but she was oblivious.'

'Oh, that poor woman.'

'I know! This other time, she scolded a teenage kid in the local shop for wearing his trousers too low. His mates were all there and she goes, "If you don't buck your ideas up, you'll never get yourself a young lady. I didn't see a young man's underpants until I was in my twenties".'

'What did the kid say?'

'Nothing much. What could he say? There was some woman in her eighties talking about his boxer shorts in front of his friends. I think he wanted the ground to open up and swallow him.'

Jessica exploded with laughter again and couldn't stop. On three separate occasions, she thought she had finished but each time, the image of the youth being told off about his underwear by a pensioner popped into her head and set her off again. Even the owner got involved, bringing over a napkin for her to dry her eyes and asking if she was okay.

'She sounds ace,' Jessica finally said when she finished giggling.

'She's all right.'

'I've got to meet her one day.' Jessica had blurted it out before she realised what she had said. It was the equivalent of asking to meet someone's parents.

'We'll see. She's not good with new people. She is always going on about me getting a girlfriend though.'

Adam had clearly said that without thinking too much either as he immediately picked up his glass of wine to stop himself saying any more. For the first time since they sat down to eat, there was an awkward pause between them. Jessica finished her own glass of wine and then broke the silence. 'Can we talk a bit of work for a minute?'

'Okay.' Adam seemed pleased she was changing the subject.

'I know you said before but do you think the blood and hairs could have been planted?'

'I doubt it. It looked too genuine, especially the blood under the nails.'

'What could prove things one way or the other?'

'I guess the only thing for sure would be a fingerprint. It might be unlikely but you could plant blood or something at a scene. Getting someone's fingerprint onto a scene they weren't at would be as close to impossible as you could imagine.'

'Are you going to find anything on Lee Morgan's body?'

'I wouldn't have thought so. We usually find things

pretty early, it just takes time to do the testing afterwards.'

'So what made you want to hang around dead bodies for a living then?'

'I don't know really. I got into it by accident. I always liked science at school and then ended up doing it at university. I didn't want to leave Grandma so went to the local uni and lived at home. I just fell into the job.'

Jessica nodded. 'I pretty much fell into the police stuff too. It wasn't as if I had dreamed of dealing with all this stuff when I was a kid. It just happened.'

'Do you enjoy it?'

It was Jessica's turn to look out the window. She was fine with talking to people about what she did but not so good with her feelings. In truth, she didn't know if she liked her job. She enjoyed some of the people and the teamwork that came with it. She liked it when things went well and bad people were caught. But, overall, she didn't know. It was a question she tried not to ask herself, especially since her friendship with Caroline had deteriorated. They had been best friends since the age of sixteen and then, whether she liked it or not, it had been her job that had split them up.

She looked out across the street where one of the pubs had a bright neon sign that simply said, 'Live football'.

'Do you want a pint?'

It was clearly not the answer to the question Adam had asked. 'Sorry?'

'Do you want a pint? Let's pay up here and go get a proper drink.'

'All right.'

Jessica signalled for the bill. Adam went to pay with a

card but Jessica insisted on giving him half the money back in cash. They stood to leave and, as they were walking out, Adam tripped over the step that led back onto the pavement. Even though he had relaxed, he still had that awkward streak.

'Are you okay?' she asked, again trying not to laugh.

'Yeah, sorry.'

'What did I say about that word?'

They crossed the road and Jessica ordered two pints of lager. They found a round table near the front door where no one else was sitting.

Adam looked at his watch as they sat. 'All right?' Jessica asked.

'It's just Grandma. She tells me not to worry but you still do. I got her a mobile phone so she could call if there was a problem but she doesn't have a clue. I programmed my numbers in for her but she'll only call my work number from the landline. She thinks a mobile can only call another mobile, even though I've told her. Then if she wants me, she'll do this thing where she rings once and quickly hangs up before the call connects. She reckons it costs a fortune to call anyone.'

'Do you want to go after this one then?'

'Yeah, sor . . . I mean, er, I've had a good time . . .'

'Me too.'

'Honestly?'

'Believe me, Adam, if I hadn't, you would be the first person to know about it.'

Jessica felt a little guilty and drank up as quickly as she thought she could without looking like an alcoholic.

Adam followed her lead and they placed their empty glasses on the table and left.

'How are you getting back?' he asked.

'The bus stop over there,' Jessica said, nodding across the road. 'It takes me straight home. What about you?'

'One of the tram routes runs pretty close to my house.'

It was an awkward moment. Adam was looking a little nervous again, so Jessica took the initiative, reaching out and taking his left hand in her right. 'I really have had a good evening,' she said.

'Me too.'

She leant in to kiss him but he seemed surprised by her movement and tilted his head the wrong way. They ended up softly bumping foreheads.

Jessica pulled back but carried on holding his hand. 'You've not done this too much, have you?'

'Not for a while.'

The second time around, Jessica made sure she was in control, kissing him gently and then pulling away. 'We'll do this again. I'll send you a text or something, okay?'

'Great.'

Jessica crossed the road and stood at the bus stop as Adam walked up the main road. The traffic was light but, as she squinted into the distance to see if there was a bus with the number she was waiting for coming towards her, Jessica's thoughts drifted back to the case. She thought about Adam's question she had dodged.

She was lost in her thoughts when the bus eventually pulled in. She paid the fare and took the first seat on the lower level. She hadn't focused on the journey down the main road out of the city but, as they reached the junction where the bus would turn towards her house, Jessica noticed flashing blue lights in the other direction.

Just because she was a police officer, it didn't mean she had to intervene in every incident she ever saw but Jessica had a feeling. The driver had stopped anyway and she asked him to let her out. At first he mumbled something about not being a proper stop but she told him she was a police officer and he opened the doors.

She walked quickly down towards the scene, recognising one of the uniformed officers standing nearby.

'What's going on?' she asked.

The officer looked back at her, clearly not realising who she was at first. He would have only ever seen her in her work suit with her hair tied back.

'Oh, right, sorry,' he said when she stood next to him. 'I didn't recognise you looking like a girl. The call came in half-hour ago – there's another body.'

15

DCI Farraday's words were spiralling around Jessica's head. She remembered them exactly: 'If this guy's for real we might get lucky and have another piece of shit off the streets by Monday'.

She said the first thing that came into her head. 'Who's dead?'

The officer was clearly confused. He pointed towards one of the flats on the opposite side of the road. 'I don't know. One of the people who live there phoned it in. They said they'd heard a disturbance and saw some man running off. I don't think she knows who the body is though. The woman didn't realise someone was dead until after she had called us. She was only reporting a fight.'

Jessica had made a rash assumption that, because the first three bodies had been well known to the police, this one would be too. It dawned on her that this could be nothing to do with the 'vigilante' and instead some disturbance that had got out of hand. 'Where is she?'

'In her flat. Someone's up there talking to her now. She had come down but the Scene of Crime team will be here in a minute and won't want anyone around the body.'

Now she looked properly, Jessica could see there was a small tent-type structure over the top of what was presumably the body. It wasn't a full white one like the SOCO squad would use to walk in and out of, just something temporary to prevent anything being contaminated.

Jessica nodded towards it. 'Can I have a look?'

The officer blew out through his teeth. 'Up to you, I'm not authorising anything.'

Jessica walked over and pulled down the zip to look inside. She instantly looked towards the corpse's neck for a knife wound but there wasn't one. There was a lot of blood though. Glancing back towards the face, Jessica realised she didn't know if the person was male or female. She would have guessed a man but the face was battered and very badly bruised. There was no way she would have been able to recognise who it was, even if they were a well-known local criminal. She zipped the cover back up and checked the number of the witness's flat with the officer before crossing the road.

She was aware she wasn't really dressed for the moment and didn't have her identification but Jessica knocked on the door and was relieved when it was opened by one of the uniformed female officers she knew. 'You were quick,' the officer said, eyeing Jessica's attire.

'Just luck. I was on a bus and saw the lights. How's the witness?'

'Shaken but okay. Do you want to come in?'

The officer led Jessica through to the living room where a woman was sitting with her feet underneath her on a brown leather sofa. She stood as Jessica entered, looking to the officer for assurance.

'This is one of the local sergeants,' the officer said. Jessica introduced herself properly and apologised for her outfit. After deciding she was happy the woman was in a fit state to talk, Jessica asked her what she had seen. At some point a proper witness statement would need to be taken but she was feeling impatient.

'It was pretty dark out and I couldn't see completely because of where the street lights are,' the woman said. 'You could hear some sort of scuffle though and some guy was shouting – that's what made me get up and look.'

'Could you hear what was being shouted?'

'No, I'm not sure they were even proper words, just noises.'

'What happened while you were watching?'

'One man was on top of the other, punching him over and over.'

'Did you see a knife?'

'I don't know, I don't think so.'

'Then what happened?'

'Eventually he stopped and ran off. That was it really. I didn't realise the one on the floor was dead. I phoned you because there was a fight and I thought whoever was on the ground would need an ambulance. I would have gone out but you never know who's out there at night, do you?'

Jessica nodded, trying to look reassuring. 'Are you sure they were both men?'

'Definitely.'

Jessica asked her next question and held her breath. She knew the answer could be crucial. 'Did you get a good look at the man who ran off?'

The woman squinted as if to indicate she was thinking. 'It was dark but he ran straight under that light opposite.

I think I'd recognise him. He wasn't massive, more like one of those rugby players. Do you know what I mean? Kind of thick and strong but not fat. He had dark hair but it was quite short.'

Jessica thought the description sounded a lot like Donald McKenna. She remembered the prison governor telling her they were locked up from eight at night until eight in the morning. She looked over at the clock on the wall; it was almost ten.

'How old would you say he was?'

'That's hard to say. Maybe somewhere in his thirties? I don't know. He had one of those faces, either a younger man who looks older or an older man who looks younger. I've never been that good with guessing people's ages anyway.'

It wasn't an exact description for the man supposed to be locked in Manchester Prison but it wasn't too far away either. Given the darkness and the distance, it could be accurate. Jessica explained they would need her to visit the station and give a formal witness statement and then asked if she would mind doing it that night even though it was late. The woman didn't seem too put out, so Jessica phoned the station and asked the desk sergeant to make sure someone would be on site to sort out a sketch. Not that long ago, it would have been someone with a giant drawing pad and a pencil but most of the profiling was now done through a computer. It could have waited until the next morning but Jessica thought it was best if someone took the description of the assailant while it was fresh.

Back downstairs, the Scene of Crime team had arrived, as had more marked police cars. Jessica arranged for one of the officers to drive the witness to the station.

It was going to be a long night.

The next day, the station was again buzzing with activity and anticipation. The murder had happened too late for the newspapers to get the story but the morning's news broadcasts had led with the e-fit of the killer, as had plenty of news websites. At the start of the main national news bulletin, the newsreader's first words were: 'Is this the face of Manchester's vigilante killer?'

Farraday arrived at the station in the early hours and insisted the photo be released to the media. Jessica had reservations considering there was no formal link to the other killings and she knew they would connect everything regardless of whether it was true. It wasn't her call though and her boss said that even if the cases weren't linked, it would at least get them more attention than they might usually have.

Jessica saw his reasoning but thought the opposite was also true; someone might recognise the picture but not phone in because they didn't think their friend or family member was the so-called vigilante. She had seen the computer sketch and hadn't changed her opinion from the night before. It looked a bit like Donald McKenna but perhaps slightly too young. It certainly wasn't enough to start building a case against him.

She had phoned the prison the night before after

arriving back at the station. It sounded like Dennis who answered on reception but, whoever it was, he didn't hesitate in putting her through to the wing she asked for. She spoke to the warden on duty and asked him to check on Donald McKenna. The warden didn't sound too pleased, especially considering the tension the prison staff must all be feeling after Lee Morgan's death, but did as she asked. He came back to her a few minutes later and assured her the prisoner was in his cell.

Jessica didn't know how many times she was going to have to make a phone call like that. She was already up to two and each one sounded ridiculous. They couldn't request the prisoner be put under constant watch, or placed in an isolation cell which he couldn't walk away from, without actually charging him. But they couldn't charge him unless they had significantly more proof than they did. If the prisoner had somehow committed this new crime, he would have had just enough time to get out and back again given the timings of the incident and her phone call to the jail.

The one piece of good news the next morning was that they had identified the body. The Scene of Crime team found a wallet in the victim's pocket with a provisional driving licence. There was also a mobile phone in his other pocket. The full results wouldn't be back from the labs for a few hours but there was no reason to assume someone would have planted another person's ID on a dead body.

Robert Graves wasn't as well known to the police as the other victims but he did have a record. He was eighteen but had been arrested for shoplifting when he was thirteen. His most recent offence was taking a vehicle without consent and driving without a full licence or insurance. According to his file, it was his mother's car he had taken and she had reported him.

The man's identity clouded Jessica's impression of whether he was linked to the other killings. The fact his wallet and phone had been left was similar to the first victim and showed it wasn't just a mugging that had gone too far but the way he had been killed was different. Even without the full test results, Jessica could see he had been beaten to death, rather than stabbed. There was also something a little different about his criminal record. The prison officer may have been corrupt, while the other three were drug dealers with a history of violence, but Robert Graves was just a pest. There were thefts, muggings and plenty of drink-related incidents, despite his age, but nothing that singled him out as dangerous compared to the others.

Despite that, there was no deterring Farraday from his belief the vigilante killer had returned. He had been in his office the entire morning making phone calls to various people, as Cole was left trying to connect Lee Morgan to the rest of the bodies or Donald McKenna. Jessica's job was to visit Robert Graves's parents.

Their house wasn't too far away from where their son's body had been found the previous evening. Jessica had taken DC Jones with her in a marked police car. The estate they lived on was known for being fairly rough but the Graveses' home was beautifully kept, making it stand out from the rest of the properties. The house next door had various car parts strewn on the front garden but theirs had a lawn mown in immaculate straight lines, with neat trimmed hedges and a well-kept flower bed that ran underneath the front window.

Jessica knew from experience that you could tell a lot about the people you were going to speak to by the first impression you had of where they lived. It didn't always hold true and you had to be careful about the assumptions you made but she felt instantly that the Graveses wouldn't be the stereotypical type of family who lived in this area.

Jones knocked on the front door and a man let them in. He had clearly been crying and led them through to a living room where a family liaison officer was sitting with a woman who also looked as if she had recently been in tears.

Jessica introduced herself and DC Jones. The man said his name was Arthur and his wife was Jackie. Their living room looked as if it had been decorated recently and was as well presented as the outside of the house. Arthur offered to make them all tea but the family liaison officer went to do it instead, leaving the four of them alone. It was always an awkward judgement to make as to whether bereaved relatives were stable enough to talk to you in a situation like this. You had to balance their feelings with the necessity to get the freshest information you could.

'Are you both all right to talk?' Jessica asked. The two parents nodded. They were both somewhere in their early forties but the grief seemed to have aged them, each sporting puffy, swollen eyes. 'Do you know if your son was out with anyone last night?'

Arthur and Jackie looked at each other but it was Jackie who answered. 'We never knew really. He struggled to find a job and seemed to spend all his time out drinking. We knew some of his friends' faces but not names. They weren't the same mates he had back at school.'

'Do you have any other children?'

'No, just Rob. That's why it was so hard when he started getting into trouble . . .' Jackie tailed off into tears and Carrie picked up a box of tissues from a coffee table in the centre of the room and went to sit next to her. Arthur was sitting on the other side and put a hand on his wife's shoulder as she blew her nose.

He picked up the conversation. 'I know you've probably seen the trouble he's been in but he really is a good kid. It's just hard around here with the gangs and so on. He gets easily drawn into things and then he's the one who gets left behind when his mates make a run for it. He's always been like that. We thought that when he left school he would get a job somewhere and sort himself out but there's nothing about. If anything it made it worse because he started drinking. Some of the older lads around here would buy those big bottles of cider and stuff like that. We'd given him the odd glass of wine, like you do, but he wasn't used to it all.'

Jessica nodded along as the man spoke. The story wasn't entirely dissimilar to the tale Craig Millar's mother had told her, albeit Robert sounded like much more of a follower than a leader.

Arthur Graves continued. 'We tried to get him to stop but what can you do? He's eighteen years old, it's not as if you can ground him. He's bigger than both of us anyway. We've been looking to move into a better area for a while but we can't afford somewhere else without selling this one. We've done our best to get everything tidy but potential buyers turn up and see the state of the area and aren't interested. You can't blame them, I guess.'

Jessica didn't know what to say. Robert Graves was no angel but he wasn't a tearaway with an axe to grind against the world because he had a traumatic family life. His parents clearly cared about him.

'Do you know any of the people he regularly hung around with or if he was in a gang? Did he ever bring people over?'

Arthur shook his head. 'I wish I could tell you. I know we should have paid more attention but I don't know. After he took the car, we didn't want to know.'

Jessica had already read about the incident in general but figured she might as well hear it from them. 'What happened exactly?'

Jackie gave another light sob and took a tissue from Carrie. Arthur looked at her and started rubbing her back gently before speaking again. 'We still don't really know. It was stupid because he's never been interested in driving. Most kids get their provisional licence when they're seventeen and can't wait to start learning. We'd pushed him into getting his first licence because we thought it could help him get a job but he was never really interested in driving itself. Then one day, it was about three in the morning and I woke up because I thought I heard the car starting. I went to the window and saw it disappearing off down the road without the lights on. The engine was roaring and it sounded like it was in the wrong gear. Jackie called the police while I ran out of the house to see if I could find out where it had gone.'

'Where was it?'

'It had only gone around the corner at the bottom of the road and then crashed into a hedge. I got there as the police were arriving with their lights going and there was Rob in the driver's seat with some other kid I didn't know next to him. They arrested him on the spot.' He looked at his wife then back at Jessica. 'They came by the house and asked if we had given him permission to drive the car. Obviously you don't want to lie to the police but . . .'

Jackie started speaking over her husband. 'I told them the car was registered to me and that I *hadn't* given him permission to take it. I thought the shock might sort him out but he didn't speak to me for three months.'

Arthur nodded sadly. 'He wouldn't even let his mum go with him to the court. He got a fine but it was added on to the amount he already owes. He doesn't have any money so we've been paying the fiver a week for him.'

Jessica breathed out heavily but tried not to make it sound too much like a sigh. 'Do you know of anyone who might wish to harm your son?'

'I'm sorry, we hardly know anything,' Arthur said. 'If you want to go through his room or anything like that then there might be something but he was out all the time

177

and only slept there. We stayed up last night waiting for him to come in. We were going to phone you to report him missing but I know it's got to be twenty-four hours or something like that and it wouldn't have been the first time he didn't come home all night. Even when I heard the knocking on the door in the early hours of this morning, I thought it was because he'd lost his keys but then it was one of you.'

At that point, Arthur started crying too. Jessica knew there wasn't too much more she could hope to get from Robert's parents. Someone would be sent to search their son's possessions, while the labs already had his mobile phone and could check that for any recent contacts. She offered her thanks for them talking to her and gave them her card.

Arthur led her and Carrie back to the front door. They were about to walk out when he lowered his tone to ensure there was no way he could be heard by anyone other than the two officers. 'Do you think he was killed by the vigilante? I know he'd been in trouble . . .'

They exchanged a look and Jessica answered. 'I'm afraid we don't know that yet, Mr Graves.' The man nodded, trying to hold back more tears.

As they left, Jessica handed the car keys to her junior. 'You drive. I'm not in the mood.'

The journey back to the station was fairly sombre. Both of them had clearly been touched by the interview. Carrie did try to lift the mood while they waited at traffic lights. 'How did you go last night?'

Jessica had almost forgotten about her evening with

Adam given everything that had happened since. 'It was good.'

'What's his name?'

'Adam. But don't tell anyone.'

'You know I won't. Is it true he works in the labs?'

'Yes. He was a bit shy at first but quite fun when you get to know him. How's your bloke?'

'He's all right too. We're still keeping it low-key for now.'

Jessica wasn't in the mood for a talk about relationships and was saved by her phone ringing. It was Adam and she hoped he wasn't calling to talk about the previous night.

'Hello?'

'Hi, Jessica, it's Adam.'

'I know. Are you okay?'

'Yes, look, someone will be calling your station soon anyway but I thought I'd let you know first. I take it you know about the body from last night, Robert Graves?'

'Have you confirmed for sure it's him?'

'Yes, but that's not why I'm calling – we've found something else on the body.'

Jessica felt a tingle down her spine. 'What?'

'We've got a fingerprint.'

16

Jessica could barely get her words out quickly enough. She could feel her heart racing. 'Whose is it?'

'We don't know yet. It's not a full print, so we're having to do some work with it. There's a specialist who works freelance who's on his way in now. If it belongs to someone on file, we should be able to match it this afternoon.'

'Have you got anything else?'

'Bits, it's hard though. There's lots of blood but we haven't found anything that doesn't belong to the victim at the moment.'

'That's brilliant. Will you call me if you get anything else?'

'If I can.'

Jessica hung up. Things had suddenly become interesting. She still didn't know if Robert Graves was connected to the other victims but they might finally be able to build a case if the fingerprint came back as Donald McKenna's.

When they arrived back at the station, things were still frantic. With the e-fit being shown on every news bulletin, calls had been coming in throughout the morning with members of the public suggesting the person's identity. Everyone would have to be checked and eliminated. News had also spread internally about the fingerprint and most of the officers seemed convinced the cracking of the case was just hours away. Jessica hoped so but kept her thoughts to herself.

She went up to DCI Farraday's office to let him know what Robert Graves's parents had said. He had calmed down from when she had seen him earlier that morning but was still convinced everything was linked together. She nodded along as he gave her the official news that a fingerprint had been found, not knowing Adam had told her first.

Jessica took some time to help Rowlands sort through the list of leads that had come from the phone calls. They were stuck between two different types of investigating. On the one hand they were waiting for lab results that could either help or hinder their case but, until those came back, they were using a more traditional method – assessing the phone calls. A couple of specialist officers would also be going to the Graveses' house to look through Robert's possessions, although Jessica wasn't convinced they would find much.

After a while, she left the constable to it and returned to her office. She was desperately hoping her phone would ring with news from Adam but spent her lunchtime skimming through Internet news sites. Some of the coverage was based on fact but a few of the opinion pieces infuriated her. There was one in particular that caught her eye on the *Herald*'s website.

Martin Coleman was a name and face she recognised. He was a local councillor who seemed to have an opinion on everything. Jessica could remember a story recently where he had been campaigning against the implementation of a slower speed limit on a local road. She couldn't remember the exact details but searched his name through the site. It soon became apparent why he was so familiar; he really did get himself around. Over the last couple of years, he had been in the news for everything from backing cuts at the local hospital to explaining why some school fields needed to be sold off.

Jessica had never been interested in politics and figured he was entitled to campaign for whatever he wanted but the comment piece he had his name on that morning really annoyed her. Under the headline 'WHY VIGILANTE HAS THE RIGHT IDEA', he had written hundreds of words about how crime was out of control, eventually reaching a conclusion that said, if not explicitly, that perhaps whoever the killer was had the right idea.

Jessica made a quick phone call and then stormed out of her office. This was one chat she was definitely going to enjoy.

Jessica had deliberately shown her identification as many times as she could in the council chamber's reception area while asking for Martin Coleman. Over the phone, she had established he was in the building but hadn't bothered to actually ask for a meeting. Instead, she turned up, parked the pool car she had taken on double yellow lines outside the building and bounded in asking everyone from the security guard to the receptionists to other people in suits if they knew where she could find the councillor.

She knew full well she could have just asked once at reception but, by flashing her identification around and mentioning his name as often as possible, people would put two and two together and make five. Rumours would be circling around the building in no time about a local detective asking after a prominent councillor.

Jessica figured that if she had tried to make an appointment, she would have had to wait for a few hours, if not days. Within five minutes of her throwing her weight around, Martin Coleman walked forcefully into the reception area. At first he spoke to one of the security guards to ask what was going on. As soon as she spotted him, Jessica made sure she was standing directly in front of the reception desk where there was the maximum number of people within hearing distance.

The councillor's greying hair was swept back tidily. Jessica guessed his suit cost more than her car, although admittedly that wasn't saying much. His shiny expensive-looking shoes echoed on the hard floor as he walked towards her. It was clear to Jessica he was furious but, with council staff and members of the public present, he was desperately trying to hold things together.

'Can I help you with something, Detective?' he said as sweetly as he could, forcing a smile and offering his hand for her to shake.

She ignored it. 'I just need a few minutes of your precious time, Councillor.'

'I'm pretty busy. You could always have made an appointment . . .'

'I'm afraid I'm in the middle of a *multiple murder*

investigation, I didn't really have time to jump through hoops.' Jessica made sure she emphasised the words 'multiple murder', just in case anyone nearby couldn't hear.

The councillor looked quickly from side to side. 'Right, right. I think we should probably do this somewhere more private. Do you want to come with me?' He led Jessica out of the main hallway, up a wide flight of stairs and down a couple of corridors into a wood-panelled room with an enormous ceiling.

He sat behind a large desk and pointed to the seat on the other side of the table. Jessica ignored him, standing next to the chair instead, looking down upon him. 'Why is it so important you had to speak to me now?' he asked.

Jessica walked over to a window and looked out onto the street below. 'Nice view you've got.'

'Sorry?'

'Nice view. Nice office too.' Jessica paced back towards the desk and started fiddling with a lamp, twisting the top part around towards her and then turning it back again.

'Detective?' The man sounded as much confused as he did angry.

Jessica finally stood up straight and looked him directly in the eyes. '"Endemic incompetence",' she said.

'What?'

'"While feral youths run wild on our city's streets, the city's police officers are more focused on prosecuting motorists than catching the real criminals".'

'Oh right, yes, the article.'

'"Policing has been too soft for too long and I for one am sick of it".'

'I'm not sure what you want me to say.'

Jessica could remember perfectly the choice quotes from his article. They had been spinning around her head throughout the drive from the station to the council chambers as she got angrier. '"There's fear on the city's streets tonight but for once it's the right people who are scared".'

'Look—' the councillor started to say but Jessica cut across him.

'Have you ever had to break the news to a parent that their child has been murdered, Councillor Coleman?'

'I don't see what that has—'

'How about identifying a dead body, have you ever done that?'

The man stumbled over his words as Jessica put both palms face down on his desk and leant forwards, daring him to meet her gaze. He looked down at the computer keyboard on his desk and nervously glanced sideways towards the phone.

'"Vandals once wrecked my car but all I got was a token visit from the police. You have to ask yourself in these situations, is this a good enough service?"' Jessica was quoting him again.

'That particular incident is true, Detective—'

She cut him off once more. 'Do you know why you didn't get more than a "token visit", Councillor?'

'What? No—'

'It's because you're a complete arsehole. It's because officers have better things to do than chase around after complete dickheads like you. We don't have the manpower to list the hundreds of people who think you're an idiot, let alone narrow it down to one person who might feel the need to graffiti your car.' The man didn't know whether to be angry or upset. He spluttered words out but there was nothing cohesive and Jessica was on a roll. 'I'll be honest with you, Councillor; I don't care if you slam the police – we're a public service and we don't get everything right – but I do mind when you start telling mothers who've lost their sons that their kids deserved it.'

'I wasn't trying to—'

'Is that what you think about girls who get raped? Do they deserve it for wearing a short skirt too?'

'No, that's not what I . . .'

Jessica narrowed her eyes and leant further across the table. The councillor shuffled slightly but he didn't push backwards hard enough to move the chair and he was stuck trying not to look at her. 'The type of statements you've been making are completely out of order. Do you understand what I'm saying, Councillor?'

The man looked at her, his face red with a mixture of embarrassment and rage. 'You can't just storm in here, you know—'

'I asked you a question. Do. You. Understand. What. I'm. Saying?' Jessica punctuated each word with as much venom as she could manage.

'Yes, fine, whatever. Get out of my office.'

At first Jessica didn't move but then quickly took a step backwards, again standing tall and towering over the seated man. 'If I were you, Mr Coleman, I would hope there's nothing you're trying to keep under wraps. No dodgy deals, no made-up expenses, no secret mistresses hidden away. Believe me, if you even have so much as an out-of-date tax disc, I'll make sure it's on the front page of as many papers as I can leak the story to.'

The man reached for the phone on his desk. 'I'll be contacting your superintendent about this, you know. I play golf with one of the commissioners in this area . . .'

Jessica stomped back over towards the man and he slid his chair backwards, trying to get away from her. She pulled out one of her business cards and slammed it down on the desk. The noise echoed around the room. She pointed to the various lines on the card. 'I don't care if you play golf with the fucking Prime Minister. That's my name, that's my ID number, that's my rank and that's my phone number. Tell them whatever you want.'

She spun around and walked quickly out of the office, slamming the door as hard as she could. Without talking to anyone, she paced back the way she had come and returned to the car. Jessica's anger hadn't gone but she definitely felt better as she drove back to the station. She knew full well there were official ways to go about things. Usually a senior officer would have written a letter back to the newspaper or something similar but she didn't care.

It wasn't that she even disagreed with all of the points Councillor Coleman had made in the article but if he was serious about getting things done, he would have asked questions through the proper channel, especially if he did know the area's commander. As it was, he was simply looking to score cheap political points, not just at their expense but in a way that would cause maximum hurt to people like Arthur and Jackie Graves.

Jessica doubted if the councillor would speak to anyone about her visit. She had no intention of trying to find dirt on him but he didn't know that. She wasn't sure if there was anything he was desperate to hide or not but if there was, the last thing he would want to do would be to draw further attention to himself.

After parking the car at the station and switching the engine off, Jessica sat for a few moments listening to the relative silence. She jumped as her phone rang, picking it up out of the storage well underneath the handbrake.

It was Adam again. 'Hi, Adam, are you okay?'

'Hi, Jess, we've finished working on the fingerprint.'

'Whose is it?'

'Well, we don't know. Whoever it belongs to doesn't have their prints stored in our files.'

'So it's not Donald McKenna?'

'No, definitely not.'

Jessica didn't say anything for a few moments. It wasn't that she had been certain the results were going to come back as a match but the outcome hadn't left them with very much to go on.

'Are you still there?' Adam asked.

'Yes, sorry. Did you find anything else?'

'Maybe. We've got some blood scrapings which don't belong to the victim but we've been working on the fingerprints and it takes time.'

'Have you phoned the station yet?'

'As soon as we've finished talking.'

'Okay, right, I'll leave you to it. Thanks for calling.' Jessica went to add, 'I'll text you about next weekend', but heard the beep to indicate the call had been terminated.

The next two days consisted of one dead end after another. The public responses to the e-fit had dried up and nothing had come from the list of names that had been suggested. Despite not having a match for the fingerprints, they had been anxiously awaiting the results on the blood the forensics team had found.

Jessica and Cole were in their regular morning briefing with Farraday in his office when the bad news arrived. A call was put through to his desk phone and, after a short conversation, he hung up and told them the blood had also come back without a match. Whoever had killed Robert Graves was someone with no criminal record.

The chief inspector sat drumming his fingers on his desk for a short time and then started to speak. 'Do I think we made a mistake with releasing that sketch to the media? Maybe. I think we might have to look at treating this murder separately from the first four victims.'

Jessica was annoyed not only by the way he had asked himself a question and answered it but also by the use of the word 'we'. It certainly wasn't her or Cole who had authorised releasing that photo; it was the DCI alone who had made an enormous error.

The news broadcasters had spent the last few days reporting on the five victims of the so-called vigilante, where they actually only had three for definite and four in all probability. All the while Farraday had let the speculation build and now it was coming back to bite him. He almost shrunk in front of them, sinking further into his chair, before looking at Cole. 'What have we got on the bent prison guard?'

'Nothing, Sir. We've checked his house and his locker at the prison. His wife insists they own no other property and, as far as we can tell, there's nothing else in his name. We've looked into records for things like storage units and allotments that might have a shed or something like that but again there's nothing registered to him. That's not to say he hasn't used a fake name but we don't have anything to go on. Short of digging up the entire garden or ripping up every floorboard I'm not sure there's much else we can do.'

Jessica couldn't remember seeing Cole angry but there was certainly an undertone as he spoke. Their boss simply nodded, his jaw clenched. 'Daniel, what have you got?'

'Not much either I'm afraid, Sir. The search of Robert Graves's room turned up nothing. The labs have been looking at his mobile phone, which was recovered from the scene, but there's nothing from that either. I've been helping with the phone tip-offs. We had been trying to link the suggestions to Donald McKenna but nothing matched up. We've also looked into anyone else who seemed legit separately but there were no obvious hits. We haven't been able to either find a suspect for Robert Graves's murder or link him to the other killings.'

Jessica didn't say it but was pretty sure the reason they hadn't come up with anything was because of her boss's insistence on connecting cases that it now seemed clear had been carried out by different people.

Farraday nodded and continued drumming his fingers on the desk. His calmness was as disconcerting as his enthusiasm from the previous days. Jessica looked at the man and genuinely had no idea what he would do or say next. The rhythmic tapping was the only noise in the room and was almost hypnotic.

Tap-tap-tap-tap.

The noise was broken by a knock on the door. The glass windows ran the length of the wall behind her and Cole. If the chief inspector had seen anyone walking past, he hadn't said anything and the knock made Jessica jump. 'Come in,' Farraday said loudly. His voice boomed around the room. A nervous-looking constable in uniform came through the door.

Jessica recognised most of the faces from around the station but they had recently hired some new recruits and the man in the doorway must be one of them because she didn't know him. 'What is it, erm, Constable?' the DCI asked, clearly not knowing the man's name either.

'Um, I'm not sure, Sir. A man just walked into reception and confessed to being the vigilante killer.'

17

No one said anything for a couple of seconds but it seemed like an age. Farraday had stopped drumming his fingers and they were all waiting for him to speak.

'I'm sorry, what?' he spluttered.

The constable repeated himself but the DCI barely reacted, before eventually replying: 'You two deal with it.'

Jessica didn't think she could have been surprised by anything the chief inspector said given his erratic behaviour recently but his dismissive tone wasn't what she expected at all. A few moments ago he had seemed part-angry and part-upset that the investigation was going nowhere and now someone had walked in and confessed, it was as if he wasn't interested.

Cole stood first, peering towards the constable. 'Where has he been taken?'

'I'm not sure; everyone downstairs was a bit shocked. Someone handcuffed him then they sent me up to tell you.'

Jessica and Cole went down to the reception area where there were far more officers than there might usually be. Word had clearly gone around that something big had happened. Jessica caught the eye of the desk sergeant. 'Where is he?'

'Locked downstairs in the cells. He's refusing to talk to the duty solicitor.'

'Do you know who he is?'

'No idea. He just said he was the vigilante killer and that he wanted to talk to whoever was in charge of the case. He wouldn't give his name.'

Jessica was struggling to hear him over the voices in the area. She moved closer to the desk and spoke louder. 'Does he seem legit?'

'Dunno. He's got the build for it. He seemed quite calm but you never know who's a nutter nowadays, do you?'

They made their way to the interview room and Cole told the uniformed officer outside to bring the prisoner upstairs. It was just the two of them in the room.

'What do you reckon?' Jessica asked.

'It's hard to know.'

'If he is who he says he is then he'll have heard about Donald McKenna's DNA being found at the scene. None of that's been in the papers so if he's just an attention-seeker, that's how we should know.'

'True but if he is for real and wants to confess it doesn't necessarily mean he's going to put everything on a plate for us.'

As the prisoner was brought into the room, Jessica glanced up and quickly did a double-take. The man looked a little like Donald McKenna – he had a similar build and hair that was the same style and colour but facially he was completely different. It was her reaction that really made Jessica start to feel as if the case was getting to her. Perhaps her verbal assault at the council chambers should have been the first indication but she felt as if she was beginning to see Donald McKenna everywhere. First it was in the description of the person who killed Robert Graves and now the person who had confessed. She hadn't spoken to the prisoner in a week but he was still playing on her mind, along with the parents of the victims.

The man in handcuffs was offered the seat across the desk and the uniformed officer looked at them to ask if he should stay or wait outside. Jessica motioned with her head to say he could leave. When it was just the three of them, she asked the man for his name.

'Are you in charge?' he replied, staring directly at Jessica. His voice was higher-pitched than she would have guessed.

'We're both senior detectives,' she replied.

'Perfect.' The man told them his name was Graham Hancock and gave them his date and place of birth, address and, without prompting and for no obvious reason, his national insurance number. Now they knew his name, Cole reminded him he was entitled to a solicitor. The man refused to listen to anything they said, despite being told there was a legal representative on site who would talk with him for free.

With little other option, Jessica formally started the interview. 'What exactly are you confessing to, Mr Hancock?'

He gave the exact date and location of the first murder and then said: 'I stabbed Craig Millar three times, once in the neck and twice in the chest.'

'Why did you do that?'

'I had seen his name in the papers, causing trouble and that. I've just had enough. It's not right, dealing drugs and causing trouble all the time.'

'How did you know where to find him?'

'I checked it all on the computer maps, then went and looked around the area during the day. He wasn't hard to find so I waited for him one night.'

Jessica nodded. 'What else are you saying you've done?'

He again gave the exact date and place and offered the correct details for the murders of Benjamin Webb and Desmond Hughes. He claimed he knew they often played snooker in a certain club through asking around and had simply followed them. He said there had been a struggle but he managed to kill both men as they had been drunk and unable to react. He also knew their exact injuries.

Jessica thought it sounded possible. He made eye contact with both her and Cole throughout, speaking clearly. He obviously knew the areas involved and got the little details right. He stated correctly that one of the men had been stabbed three times like the first victim, while the other one hadn't.

'Anything else?'

'The prison guard, Lee Morgan, I killed him too.'

'Why?'

'I have friends inside and they told me he had been smuggling phones in and giving preferential treatment to certain people in return for money and other favours.'

If true, it was more than they knew.

'Who are your friends?'

'I don't want to say.'

'How did you know where he lived?'

'It's not hard – Internet searches, social networks and so on. They were in the phone book anyway.'

'Anything else?'

'No, that's it.'

It was interesting to Jessica that he hadn't confessed to the killing of Robert Graves. The media had connected all five murders together but he hadn't mentioned the final one.

'Why are you confessing?'

'Because I feel my work is done for now. Others can continue my cause.'

Whether he was genuine or not, the idea of copycats was chilling. It crossed Jessica's mind that perhaps the killing of Robert Graves was done by someone copying what they had read about in the media.

'Do you know we have DNA evidence from the scenes?' Jessica hadn't known whether or not she was going to reveal that but everything he had said so far had been accurate.

She saw his eyes flicker sideways slightly but he stayed calm. 'It's fine, you can test me.' They didn't need his permission to take a mouth swab but the fact he was happy to offer one was confusing. He must know that if he were making it up, he would be found out.

Jessica almost always felt confident in an interview room and trusted her instincts but now she felt lost for words. She wanted to say the name 'Donald McKenna' and ask if it meant anything but, at the same time, the last thing she wanted to do was give the man information he might not know.

Cole must have sensed her unease and spoke next.

'What do you think the DNA test results are going to tell us, Mr Hancock?'

'I know they'll tell you I'm the man you've been looking for.'

'Why are you so sure we haven't already matched it to someone else?' Cole asked.

It was the exact question Jessica should have asked and she didn't know why it hadn't occurred to her. If the man had any doubts, he didn't show them. 'Why are you so sure your results are correct?'

It was a fairly cryptic thing to say. Was he simply feeding from what Cole had said or was he implying that he knew their results had thrown up someone unlikely?

'What do you mean, Mr Hancock?' Cole demanded.

'You tell me.'

The two men stared at each other.

'What type of knife did you use?' Jessica asked, breaking the impasse.

'Just a regular kitchen one. It's still in my house if you want to get it. I had to wash it because I used it to chop some vegetables up yesterday but it's still in the kitchen. It has a metal handle and is at the back of the knife rack next to the draining board. It's not the biggest one, the one next to that. When I came in, they searched me and took everything I brought in. If you go through those things, there's a door key – just take that and let yourselves in. If there are any problems, my next-door neighbour has a key too. I've got his just for emergencies.'

Jessica could feel Cole's eyes on her and turned to look at him. He gave the merest nod to indicate the interview was over and then spoke the formal words for the recording. The officer was called back inside to escort the man back to the cells below the station.

As soon as he was out of the room, Jessica turned to her superior. 'What do you think now?'

Cole shook his head. 'I honestly don't know. He's either for real or someone with a perfect memory who just happens to be one of the best liars I've ever met.'

It was pretty much the only way Jessica could have described him. Almost all of the details he had given them had been released by the media in some form but remembering them all down to the smallest detail took some doing. He had even filled in small gaps, such as the prison warden smuggling in phones, something which had been alluded to but certainly not reported entirely as fact. If he were a fantasist, he was a first-class one.

'What are we going to do?'

'Check with Farraday. Even with this guy's keys and permission we'll still need a warrant to make it legal. If we get his mouth swabs straight off to the labs, they can start their tests while we go check his place out.'

'Have you ever known someone offer you the keys to search their house?'

'Only after we've smashed the door in.'

'How long do you think we've got?'

'We have the usual twenty-four hours without charge but the super will give us an extra twelve if we have to wait for the lab results. If they're not back by then for whatever reason, we can always go to the magistrates for a few more days. It's all going to come down to forensics anyway.'

Cole went to talk with Farraday to make sure a warrant could be quickly put in place as Jessica arranged a team to take to Graham Hancock's property. She and Cole would be going, along with a couple of uniformed officers and some members from the Scene of Crime squad. They would be in charge of collecting anything that could be needed for evidence. It took a couple of hours but every-thing was in place by mid-afternoon and Jessica ended up letting everyone into the house after borrowing the door key from the house next door, exactly as their suspect had suggested. Legally, taking the key that had been con-fiscated from him at the station could cause problems because that property had to be locked away and shouldn't be tampered with.

Jessica knew instantly their job wasn't going to be as simple as she'd hoped. As she opened a door, she took a step back because of the smell, exchanging looks with one of the other officers as if to ask, 'What is that?'

She grimaced but walked across the threshold. The cream wallpaper in the hallway had turned brown at the bottom and was peeling. She couldn't even tell what colour the carpet was as it was barely visible. A bicycle was leant across a door at the opposite end of the hall and various electrical parts and broken plastic toys were left everywhere she could see. She led the way in, stepping over the various items and trying not to trip.

The hallway led into a living room and Jessica gasped as she entered. The curtains were shut and there was minimal light seeping through. She walked over and swished them open, turning around. To her left were row after row of newspapers stacked from the floor to the ceiling. They ran the full width of the room and halfway down the length too. There were thousands of publications. She moved further into the room, allowing others to enter. On her right was a television that looked older than she was. There were dials on the front and a chunky remote control that was connected to the set via a bundled-up wire on the floor in front of it. There was only one chair in the room, a battered brown armchair with light yellow foam spilling out of the side.

The smell was almost overpowering but Jessica blinked through it and walked over to the nearest pile of papers. She took a set of rubber gloves out of her jacket pocket and put them on, turning over the publication on top. It was a national newspaper from the previous day and sat on top of one from the day before that. Jessica put them back down and reached up high to take a paper from the next stack. It had a date from three years ago and the one directly under it was from the day immediately prior.

It seemed clear Graham Hancock had been storing newspapers each day for a very long time. She put the two papers back where she had got them from and then walked over to the very first stack, standing on the tips of her toes to reach two more from the top of the pile. They were both dated from consecutive days twenty-seven years earlier.

She showed them to Cole, shaking her head. 'This is unbelievable.'

Jessica again returned the papers to the stack and walked through to the kitchen. The Scene of Crime officers had already put the knives into evidence bags and were looking through the rest of the drawers.

The smell was certainly stronger in the kitchen and Jessica saw why. Resting against the back door was a pile of rotting food, with maggots and small flies on the top. She quickly turned around and walked back into the living room. Cole was crouched down, unwrapping a balled-up piece of paper that had been left on the floor. 'We'll never get through all of this,' Jessica said. 'This guy hoards everything, be it newspapers or leftover food.'

Cole dropped the paper back on the floor and hunched further over to pick up another ball of paper from the ground. He started to open it out as Jessica continued speaking. 'Unless there's some dead body under the bed upstairs I have no idea what we're going to get from this place. I just hope his DNA comes back as a match for . . . something. God knows how McKenna fits into it all.'

She tailed off as she saw Cole's expression. 'What?' she said. The DI reached back across for the first piece of paper and held both sheets up for her to see. The pages had been torn from a lined notebook and the horizontal guides clashed with the crumples in the paper. On both pages was a beautifully drawn pencil illustration, the likeness terrifyingly perfect.

It was a picture of Jessica.

18

Jessica had gone face-to-face with many characters most people would find intimidating but nothing had ever shocked her quite as much as the images Cole was holding up. She wanted to speak but couldn't even form the words. The pencil drawings were so accurate and it dawned on her she knew exactly which photos they had been copied from.

She looked around the room but couldn't see what she was looking for, so walked back through to the hallway, opening doors in equally cluttered cupboards and then heading quickly but carefully up the stairs. More junk littered the wooden steps and Jessica could hear Cole behind her. 'Jess, are you okay?' In the years she had worked with him, he had called her 'Jessica' less than half-a-dozen times but she could never remember him calling her 'Jess'.

'Jess?'

She carried on walking to the top and kicked a toy car out of the way as she reached the landing. She didn't know where she was going but opened the first door in front of her.

'Whoa,' she said quietly.

Cole arrived just behind her and put his hand on her

shoulder. 'Are you all ri—' he started to say then interrupted himself. 'Whoa.'

Jessica pushed the door all the way open and the pair went inside. In complete contrast to the rest of the house, the room was immaculate. There was a new clean cream carpet on the floor and the only smell was the faint odour of paint. The room was decorated light brown, the only furniture an easel with a stool and a small table facing it directly in the centre. The new-looking curtains were pulled open, letting light spill in. Her eyes took a few seconds to adjust from the gloom of the rest of the house to the brightness of this room. She looked behind her to make sure there was nothing else there but it was completely empty apart from the items in the middle.

Then she saw what she was looking for.

Jessica walked over to the small table and picked up two folded newspapers from underneath. She held the top corner of one, allowing it to flap open for Cole to see.

'Remember this?' she said.

Jessica had been in the news the previous year. On the first occasion she was on the front page of the *Manchester Morning Herald* and they had used an old photo of her taken from the police's website. On the second, Garry Ashford had written a large profile of her. The main photo for each article was an exact match with the drawings Cole still had in his hand.

She no longer felt intimidated, just creeped out. Cole looked at the papers and then the drawings he had. He didn't say anything at first but his expression said it all.

Jessica responded in the only way she could. If she

didn't try to laugh, there was a good chance she would cry.

'If he wanted a date, he could have just asked.'

The formalities had to be gone through but Graham Hancock's mouth swab hadn't matched anything relating to the case they were working on – or anything else on file. The knives had been tested too but there wasn't even a faint trace of blood on any of them. Given his hoarding of the newspapers there was every chance he could have memorised as many details as he felt necessary.

The truth was no one would know anything other than the fact he was a very talented artist. The likeness of her had been unerringly accurate compared to the photos they were based upon.

In subsequent interviews, which Jessica chose not to sit in on, he insisted he was the vigilante killer but refused to speak to anyone except her. Farraday claimed he always suspected the guy was a 'loony-bin nutcase', despite never talking to him but had at least been sympathetic to Jessica and told her to go home for a day.

Aside from knowledge he could have taken from the media, Graham Hancock had no connections to the case whatsoever. He had no criminal record, nothing that linked him forensically and no obvious motive. On advice, they charged him with wasting police time. The maximum sentence would be six months in prison but no one thought he would get that. Cole did try to talk Jessica into applying for a restraining order against the man but she refused. If she ever saw him again, she would want him to approach her, anything that would give her a reason to take matters into her own hands.

Even before his confession, Jessica had been feeling delicate and questioning her own judgement. Everything that happened with him had shaken her more than she was ready to admit. In the old days, she would have put away a couple of bottles of wine with Caroline and got on with things. But Adam's question was haunting her: did she enjoy the job? She hadn't answered because she didn't want to admit what the answer might be.

After Farraday sent her home, Rowlands had tried to cheer her up in his own inimitable style with a text message:

'Some ppl will do anything to get off work. X'

It made her laugh at least and she messaged him back something suitably insulting. He texted back:

'Come to the quiz. Will b a laugh. Carrie's in. X'

Jessica didn't reply and wasn't keen to commit to anything. Carrie called to make sure she was all right and offering to take her out for a drink but Jessica wasn't in the mood. Instead she waited until she knew Adam would be back from the labs and called him.

He answered on the first ring. 'Jessica?'

'Yep, call me "Jess" though.'

Despite going out a few days previously, he hadn't asked what she liked to be called.

'What's up?'

He had obviously guessed something had got to her from the tone of her voice. Jessica had always found something attractive about the impersonal nature of a phone call. She had found it easier to tell her parents awkward things over the phone and, aside from with Caroline, could not really remember opening up too much with anyone in any other way. There was some irony at how she had almost demanded Adam be more confident and direct with her, while now she felt the only way she could talk about anything serious with him was if he wasn't in the room.

Jessica took a deep breath. 'The answer is, "I don't think so".'

'Answer to what?'

'You asked if I enjoy the job.'

'Oh . . .'

Jessica told him everything, about the case with Randall from a year ago, about the way she and Caroline had drifted apart and then about Graham Hancock and the way the overall case was drifting. He listened to everything.

'Are you going to be okay? I'd love to come over but . . .'

Jessica felt better just putting everything into words. 'It's fine. Are we going to do something this weekend?'

'I've got to work Saturday.'

'Sunday?'

'That sounds good.'

Jessica went to speak but Adam quickly cut in. 'Oh no. I promised Nan I'd take her to the seaside if it's dry. I could—'

Jessica interrupted. 'That sounds good if you'll have me?'

'Umm, I don't . . . are you sure?'

'Yeah, you better drive though, I wouldn't trust my car.'

The investigation had again gone nowhere during the rest of the week. The case of Robert Graves had formally been separated from the other four killings and given to DI Cole, with Jessica still trying to connect a jailed man to a case it seemed implausible he was actually involved with. Without Donald McKenna's name they had no other leads. DCI Farraday had barely left his office but had gone quiet on trying to prove Lee Morgan was corrupt and the media had moved on to other stories.

Jessica spent large parts of the rest of the week insisting she was fine. People's concern was satisfying in one way but incredibly annoying in another. She tried to keep her focus on the victims and had another phone conversation with Denise Millar to see how the woman was doing. She was coping but, like the police themselves, had been confused by the conflicting coverage in the media. Jessica reassured her as best she could but the hostility towards Farraday certainly increased.

On Sunday morning, Adam picked her up. His car was only marginally newer than hers but certainly bigger. His grandmother, Pat, was already in the front seat but Jessica didn't mind sitting in the back. The older woman certainly seemed keen on getting to know Jessica. She asked what she did, how old she was, where she came from, what her parents did for a living and everything in between.

Everything took twice as long to explain because, as Adam had said, his nan's hearing wasn't too great.

Even from their car journey, Jessica could tell the woman was a politically incorrect nightmare. After being introduced to each other, Adam had barely reached the end of Jessica's road when his grandmother embarrassed him. 'I thought he was gay all these years,' she said.

Adam coughed and tried to quieten her but she either didn't hear him or didn't care and continued to talk. 'Not that there's anything wrong with all of that. You wouldn't have had it in my day. Well, I guess you probably did but it was all behind closed doors back then. Sometimes you don't know if they're boys or girls nowadays, do you? There's one that works at the local shop. You're afraid to ask, aren't you?'

Jessica didn't really know if you should laugh or be offended but it was clear the woman had no malice.

Adam drove them the two hours or so it took to get to Prestatyn in north Wales. She had never been to the Welsh resort before. It wasn't the best seaside place she had visited but she had definitely seen worse. Adam parked the car and Jessica helped him take a wheelchair out of the boot. They took it in turns to push Pat along the front. It wasn't a particularly warm day but at least it was dry. The woman had an opinion on everything from seagulls to local politics to what was clearly her favourite topic of conversation: 'kids today'.

A car had parked next to Adam's and three children clambered out of the back seat. His grandmother spent fifteen minutes telling Jessica that when she was that age, she would have walked everywhere. She described two lads playing football on the beach as 'hooligans' and thought a young child who dropped an ice lolly was a 'trouble-maker'. Everything was punctuated by her opinion that they would be fine because Jessica was a police officer, as if two lads playing football needed the full force of the law bringing down upon them.

On their stroll down the front, they had been walking behind an older man, likely in his fifties, holding hands with a girl twenty years or so his junior. 'Do you think that's his daughter?' she said plenty loud enough for the couple to hear.

Adam had tried to mumble something about not being sure so, even louder, she asked a second time. 'Bit odd if it is his daughter,' she continued. 'Can't be his wife or anything. Look at them.' If they heard, they didn't react.

Jessica knew she probably shouldn't but she found Pat quite charming. As they reached the end of the front, Adam went into the public toilets and left Jessica sitting on a bench with his grandmother. He had whispered a 'sorry, I can't hold it' in her ear before dashing inside. When they were sitting together, the older woman reached out a hand towards her. 'Jessica?'

'Mrs Compton.'

'Call me Pat.'

'Yes, Pat.'

'I just wanted to say thank you for coming.' The woman was looking directly at Jessica, the wrinkles in her face and lack of hair betraying her age, even though her eyes were full of youth.

'It's not a problem.'

'He's a good lad. I keep telling him I can look after myself but he won't have it.'

'I think it's sweet.'

'Do you know he speaks French? And Spanish or something . . . ?' Jessica went to say that she did know but didn't get a chance. '. . . I don't know where he gets it from. It must be his mother, his dad could barely speak English properly. I don't know why you need it myself.' The woman laughed gently to herself.

Jessica knew Adam's parents had died when he was young. 'How did they die?'

The woman stopped mid-laugh. Her eyes almost transformed, from showing young enjoyment to pure sadness. 'Hasn't he told you?'

'I never asked.'

'I think he would tell you if you did.'

Adam came back from the toilets, shaking his hands to get them dry. They walked back the way they came and his grandmother almost instantly returned to the way she had been, complaining and inadvertently making Jessica laugh.

Clouds had started to gather by the time they arrived at the car and the journey back took longer as Adam drove carefully in the rain. Pat slept for a lot of the trip and Adam asked Jessica if she minded him dropping his grandmother back before her. The two of them helped her back inside and made her a cup of tea as she sat in an armchair watching television.

Adam's house looked as if an old person lived in it.

Jessica could tell it hadn't been redecorated in years but it still had a homeliness to it.

'Sorry about her,' Adam said when they were alone in his kitchen.

'It's all right, she's fun. I'm not sure she should take up after-dinner speaking though.'

'At least she didn't say anything bad to you. When she was going on about me being gay in the car I thought she was going to ask if you were a bloke in drag.'

'Christ, I don't look that bad, do I?'

'No, of course not, I just meant . . .'

'I'm joking, Adam.'

'Oh right, yeah, sor . . . of course.'

'Can I ask you something?'

'Yeah, no worries.'

'How did your parents die?'

Adam gulped and stared at her. It clearly wasn't a question he had been expecting. 'Um . . .'

'You don't have to tell me.'

'No, it's . . . I don't really talk about it. People don't find it easy to deal with . . .'

'It's okay, I don't need to know.'

Adam turned around and picked up the kettle, pouring hot water into a mug. With his back to her, he started to speak. 'When I was a baby, my mum got upset a lot. Nowadays people would call it post-natal depression and be able to help her but back then . . .' Jessica wanted to say something but her mouth had gone dry. She shivered as a tingle went down her back. '. . . She ended up killing herself when I was two. I don't even remember her. Then

Dad, well, I don't know for sure. He killed himself a few months later. No one wanted to tell me about it but I went back and looked in the papers from the time. I think he just wanted my mum, not me.'

Jessica croaked out an 'Oh, Adam . . .' but couldn't stop her voice from cracking.

He still hadn't turned around but had put the kettle down and was stirring the drink. 'It's okay. It was a long time ago. I don't even remember them.'

Jessica urged herself to think of something to say that wouldn't sound pathetic. She felt embarrassed she had told him about her problems that seemed so insignificant in comparison when he had been living with this his entire life.

She reached her arms around his chest and hugged herself into the back of him. Neither of them said anything until Adam released himself. 'I'd better take this through.'

He picked the mug up from the worktop and walked through with it to his grandmother. Jessica followed him into the living room. Pat was slumped to one side of the chair, snoring gently. Adam switched the television off and pulled a blanket from a drawer underneath the sofa and placed it over her.

'She'll sleep all night now,' he said, walking back to the kitchen with Jessica and closing the door quietly behind them. Adam tipped the drink down the sink. 'Thanks for today,' he added.

Jessica could tell he didn't want to say any more about

his parents. 'Not a problem, I had a good time. I'm not going to the bingo next time though.'

Adam laughed. 'She'd never hear any of the numbers anyway and then start shouting at people.'

'What have you got this week?'

He smiled as he spoke. 'Well, now you've stopped firing stuff over to us, we can get through the backlog that's built up.'

'What have you got?'

'All sorts. We've had stuff waiting in the freezers for two weeks relating to those student muggings. Is that one of yours?'

'The guy who shares my office has been following that.'

'We've also got the usual, a few burglaries and whatever comes in this weekend.'

Jessica had switched off for the last few words he said and he had clearly seen her drifting. 'All right? I'm not boring you, am I?'

'No, sorry. It's not that, I just think I've had an idea.'

19

Adam had dropped Jessica back at her flat late the night before but she rushed into work the next morning. She went to her office and signed into the computer system to check the phone logs from the past few nights. All emergency calls were automatically catalogued and she scanned through before finding the item she was looking for. She didn't know for sure there would be a mugging report with the exact details she was after from the past few days but knew there would be something somewhere. She noted down the details and waited for DS Reynolds to arrive.

He looked up as he came into their office, noticing her sitting at her desk. 'Hey, Jess, how was the weekend?'

'All right. Look, can I ask you about this phone report from the other day?'

'Um, yeah, whose is it?' Reynolds hadn't even sat down and clearly wondered why she was in such a rush.

Jessica read him the name as he sat down, adding: 'This is one of yours, isn't it?'

'One of many.'

'Can you talk me through it?'

'Any reason?'

'Can you trust me for now?'

'You tidy up your side of the office and give me back

the ten pounds you still owe me and you've got a deal,' he replied with a big grin.

'How about I think about tidying my side of the office and try to remember to bring your money in?' Jessica was smiling too.

'Fine. Obviously you know I've been working on the student muggings. The difficulty is that things aren't very clear at all.'

'How do you mean?'

'For instance, we charged a lad last week with making up a complaint. He basically wanted a new phone and said he'd been attacked just to get a claim number for his insurance. But there are also real victims we know of who haven't come forward – we've got some of them on CCTV.'

'So you're stuck with some people who have been attacked and won't come forward but then having your time wasted by others trying it on?'

'Exactly and that makes it all the harder.'

'What about the gang initiation thing you had been talking about?'

'The only reason the muggings started to be linked together was because we arrested someone early on. Poor kid was shit-scared, only about fourteen, and said he'd been put up to it by older lads because he wanted to join their group.'

'So did you get any of the other gang members?'

'No chance. It took us long enough to get that out of him, plus he was a youth of course so you can't push it too far. He wouldn't give any names and his mother was having none of it.'

'Have you arrested anyone else?'

'No. With the conflicting descriptions – or muggers wearing hoods – plus the dodgy CCTV and so on, we don't really have anything other than a whole host of scared students. It doesn't help that they go out and get themselves so pissed they can't walk straight but I guess we've all been there.'

'Speak for yourself.'

Reynolds laughed. 'You've not been that drunk? Who are you trying to kid?'

'Oh, I've been that drunk but I can *always* walk straight.'

Reynolds laughed again. 'Why did you want to know then?'

'I need another favour.'

'What?'

Jessica took a deep breath. 'It's a big one.'

'I'm not going to like this, am I?'

'Can you get the fourteen-year-old back in?'

'You are joking? He pleaded guilty to that other mugging and was released. What do you want me to bring him in for?'

Jessica read the name of the mugging victim she had taken from the phone logs. 'Bring him in for that.'

'But there's no reason for us to think it was anything to do with him.'

'We know that but he doesn't. Please, it could help solve two cases.'

Reynolds looked at her. 'What if it doesn't? It could totally stuff mine up. He's a kid too, we'll have to get his mother in and maybe one of the specialist duty solicitors. It's a lot to ask when we don't even think it's him. I don't even know why we would suspect him.'

Jessica read the description of the assailant from the police log.

'That could be anyone,' Reynolds said.

'Exactly, *anyone*. Including some teenager who's got previous for it.'

'Are you going to tell me why you want him in so badly?'

'I don't just want him in, I want to do the interview.'

'Come on, Jess . . .'

'Please.'

'You're going to have to tell me. It's my arse that will be on the line.'

Jessica told him what Adam had said the previous evening that had got her mind whirring then told him how she hoped to solve two cases in one.

Reynolds looked at her when she had finished. 'It's risky. He's still only a kid.'

'He's old enough to threaten someone with a knife.'

'If I didn't know you better I would have said you had logged into those files before I got into the office and already knew all about our young offender. After that, you went through the phone archives to find a mugging description from a victim deliberately vague enough to bring him in on.'

Jessica smiled at him. 'I think you know me well enough . . .'

*

Jessica had a reasonable idea what to expect having read the descriptions but the fourteen-year-old must have grown from the last time he had been in. Now fifteen, he was bigger than plenty of adults she knew. Despite his size, he still shrunk into the interview room's chair like the scared schoolboy he was.

Reynolds and Jessica had done their best to keep her idea under wraps and had certainly kept it away from the ears of Farraday. There was no way they could have gone ahead without an okay from Cole though. He had listened to Jessica's theory, put a few doubts in their minds and then said they could do it anyway.

The boy had promptly been arrested and brought to the station with his mother. He was told he had been arrested in connection with the mugging and cautioned. His mum repeated over and over they had no money for a lawyer, so a specially trained duty solicitor had been brought in, as Reynolds had suspected would need to happen.

The mother was fuming with both the police and her son. In the holding room, Jessica had heard her shouting, 'What have you done now?' at the boy.

Now in the interview, her displeasure was focused on them. Each time Jessica asked a question, the boy would nervously answer and then his mother would jump in; 'See, I told you it weren't him.' She hadn't told them anything of the sort but her anger was clear. Jessica had her secret weapon in an envelope on the table in front of them and was biding her time. They had already gone over the formalities of the mugging, asking where he was, who he hung around with and anything else they would usually include. He hadn't helped himself by not really having an answer for where he was. It had been late on in the evening but, despite his age, he still claimed to be playing football in his local park.

'Were you playing football with other members of the gang you're in?' Jessica asked.

'I ain't in no gang.'

'That's not what I've heard. I read that you robbed your first victim because you wanted to get in with the cool kids.'

'So?'

'So did you get in or not?'

He looked sideways at his mother. 'No.'

'That's not what I've heard.' The boy's solicitor went to step in but Jessica had sewn the doubt in his mind. She showed the boy some photographs of the new victim's injuries, having deliberately picked out the ones that looked the worst. Both the legal representative and his mother objected and she knew she was walking on a tight-rope.

Eventually, she knew she just had to go for it. She opened the envelope on the table, took one final photo-graph out and held it facing her. 'In a moment, I'm going to turn this photo around and I need you to answer one last question. I know your mum is here and you might not want to admit to certain . . . things but this is crucial.' She tapped the top of the photo to emphasise her point that it could be him and then turned it around. The image was of Robert Graves and had been taken post-mortem after he had been cleaned up. When she had first seen his body she hadn't known whether it was male or female but the photo was a lot clearer.

Both the boy and his mother reeled backwards while the solicitor tried to stop the interview. He was outraged but Jessica wouldn't budge. She locked eyes with the boy. 'Was Robert Graves in your gang? Do you know him?'

Amid the noise as Reynolds tried to calm everyone down, Jessica didn't move. She stared at the teenager. She could see the answer in his eyes but needed him to say the words. 'Tell me,' she said.

'Yes.' The answer was quiet and barely audible over the objections from his solicitor.

Jessica put the photograph face down on the table and shushed everyone present, much to their annoyance. 'Please repeat that. Was Robert Graves a member of your gang?'

Finally there was quiet. She hadn't stopped looking at him.

'He wanted to be.'

The teenager had been released without charge but Jessica had got what she wanted. Ultimately he seemed more scared of his mum than he did of them. Reynolds and Jessica had immediately passed the news on to Cole and the three of them were now sitting in DCI Farraday's office listening to him tell them off for not informing him of what was going on.

Jessica was happy to step in and admit it was her fault but Cole didn't give her a chance, instead saying he should be blamed. He said he knew the DCI was busy and that he didn't want to concern him with matters that could come to nothing.

Jessica was grateful for what he had done but also saw it as an indictment of their boss that they had to work behind his back to get things sorted out.

When he had calmed down, Jessica got around to explaining her theory, leaving Adam out of the tale. 'I had been talking to a member of the forensics team at the end of the week and they mentioned they were going to be able to start working on the student mugging cases this week. It got me thinking about Robert Graves's age and the type of kid his parents said he was.' She indicated towards Reynolds sitting next to her. 'Jason has been working on connecting the robberies all together and had mentioned a theory about a gang initiation ritual.'

Farraday nodded along as she spoke, again drumming his fingers on the desk. She tried to block the noise out and keep talking. 'I think we've all got it in our heads now that Robert isn't connected to the other, er, vigilante cases but of course we didn't know why he would have been killed. But now we've been told he wanted to become a member of this gang. So what if he picked on a student who wasn't just some drunk? What if he picked on some-one who fought back too hard?'

The chief inspector stopped tapping his fingers. 'Why wouldn't he have been identified with that sketch if that's the case?'

Jessica knew she had to be careful how she phrased the next part. 'Don't forget the description of the attacker was from a bit of a distance in dim lighting but also . . . we were asking people to look for the wrong thing. We were saying, "This is your vigilante", so people would have been looking at their mates and thinking, "Oh, it can't be him because he was with me the night of the vigilante attacks". But no one would have been reporting their friends for being unaccounted for on just that one evening where Robert Graves was killed.'

'What do you two think?' Farraday looked first at Reynolds, then DI Cole, standing behind the two sergeants. 'Reynolds?'

'I think it's a better theory than anyone else has had.'

'Cole?'

'I think we should go to the local media and the universities themselves. Let's tell them we were wrong and get the description of the person back out there. Let's ask people to think just about the one night Robert Graves was killed instead of asking them to worry about who the vigilante is.' There was a harshness to his tone Jessica had rarely heard.

Before the DCI could respond, Jessica started speaking. 'We have the fingerprint and blood on file. If we get any useful leads, people can easily be ruled out. I know there are thousands of students but there can't be too many who look like that picture.'

'How do you know for sure it's a student?'

Cole spoke. 'We don't, Sir. That's why we would bring the media in too and admit we made a mistake. Either way, it has to be someone relatively local.'

Farraday was back to drumming his fingers and finally

slapped his hand down hard on the wood. 'Right, this is what we're going to do. Reynolds, you get on with the gang stuff. If people are dying, we need to shut them down. Cole, you go to the papers and the university and do whatever you have to. Daniel, if you're so clever you get us a lead on the other killer we have to catch.'

It was basically the same arrangement they already had – except that Jessica had solved at least one case she wasn't directly assigned to and it didn't look as if she was going to get any credit for it. Ultimately it didn't matter as long as they found whoever killed Robert Graves and then, her case or not, she would be visiting his parents.

Jessica went to stand but Cole started speaking. 'I think you should let Jessica close the Graves case, Sir. It was her theory after all.'

Feeling frozen to the spot, she looked from DCI Farraday to DI Cole, who were staring at each other. It was the chief inspector who finally spoke. His tone was steady but had an undercurrent of anger. 'Fine. Sort it out among yourselves but I want some progress on all three cases by the end of the week or I'm going to start kicking some arses around here.'

20

Cole hadn't even let Jessica thank him as they walked back down the stairs to their own offices. As she went to speak, he cut her off. 'Don't worry, you did well today. Now find the killer.'

Jessica went back to her office and immediately called Garry Ashford. Even though Reynolds was in earshot, she thanked the journalist for his article about Craig Millar's mother and then told him the news about the type of person they now suspected had killed Robert Graves. She told him he had a two-hour head start to get a story on his newspaper's website before she called in the local television and radio stations.

She phoned back the witness to the murder and re-checked each detail with her, especially focusing on the time and description of the killer. After that, Jessica went to the press office and told the woman who worked there exactly what she wanted doing. The small team on site were well known for being tetchy with officers in trying to balance the needs of both sides but Jessica didn't make it a negotiation. The press officer was obviously nervous about going to the media and admitting they had made a mistake but Jessica was clear the only way people would pay attention to a new appeal was if they started from scratch.

Jessica sat in their office taking phone calls and giving statements to local radio stations and other newspapers with Farraday reluctantly agreeing to go on camera for that evening's news broadcasts. Officers were brought in to answer the phones and Jessica took Carrie to the main road near the universities later that evening. They had arranged for the press office to print out flyers of the e-fit and handed them out to the young people walking past. Being two youngish women standing on the street, they got a fair amount of attention and inappropriate suggestions but the sight of their respective police identification cards sent people scurrying quick enough.

As the passing foot traffic dried up, with everyone either in or out for the night, Jessica sent Carrie home, telling her to make sure she took the hours back in lieu and then drove herself to the station. Jessica watched the late-evening news on the television in the reception area. It replayed everything that had been on the earlier broadcasts, which was good as their story was still high on the bulletin. She walked through to the incident room where a bank of half-a-dozen phones had been set up at the back. Given the time, the area was fairly empty. Four of the officers were chatting with each other, with two others on calls.

Jessica pulled up a chair and sat behind them. 'How much have you had in?'

'Bits and pieces. Loads earlier but nothing much recently,' one of the officers said.

'Any names being repeated?'

'Two or three.'

Each call would have been logged through the computer system but she had instructed the officers working earlier to make a hard-copy note of any names suggested. The officer used a pencil to point Jessica towards a clipboard at the end of the line. It was about as low-tech as she could have imagined – literally a tally chart. The full length of the page had around twenty-five names listed. Most had just one mark next to the name but three instantly stood out. One had four ticks, another six and one name near the top – Dan Wilkin – had seven. Jessica noticed there was even one for a 'Danny Wilkin' lower down the sheet where someone hadn't realised it was likely the same person. As Jessica was scanning the list, one of the officers who had been on the phone hung up and beckoned for her to hand the list over. She passed them the clipboard and they very deliberately put one more mark next to Dan Wilkin's name.

The next morning, Jessica took DC Jones and four uniformed officers with her to arrest Daniel Wilkin. His name had been added to the tally chart twice more the night before and, from the full call records registered through their computer system, his address had been given too. He lived in a block of privately owned student flats around ten minutes' walk away from where Robert Graves's body had been found.

The building was arranged in a large semicircle with a courtyard at the front. There were half-a-dozen doors, each listing twenty flats inside that particular area. If their suspect was looking to run, he wouldn't have too many options but one of the officers was sent around to the back in case he jumped out of a window.

Inside the main entrance, there were five more doors to choose from, each apparently hosting four flats. One door was on the ground floor, with two on each of the levels above. Jessica and the other officers made their way up to the top floor and knocked on the flat's main door. A man who'd seemingly been asleep in his underwear answered it. Jessica had woken people up many times but couldn't remember anyone looking quite as tired as the young man in front of her. He could barely open his eyes and she wasn't entirely sure how he was standing.

'Is Daniel Wilkin in?'

The person in front of them clearly didn't understand and rocked slightly on the back of his feet. 'What, man? Who's been sick?'

Jessica ignored his ramblings, pushing past him into the flat. One bedroom door was wide open, which she presumed belonged to the man who had let them in, while an opening at the opposite end of the corridor clearly showed a fridge. There were four more doors to choose from. Jessica first tried pushing each of them. The final one on the left swung open to reveal an empty but filthy bathroom.

With only three options, she indicated for Carrie to stand at one door, while one of the officers took another and she took the third. The final two officers stood by the front door. Jessica counted down from three and, on one, they all banged on the remaining bedroom doors. 'Daniel Wilkin,' Jessica shouted loudly.

No one could have slept through the noise. The door in front of Jessica and the uniformed officer opened almost simultaneously. There was a young man wearing only a pair of boxer shorts in front of her. Jessica had her identification in her hand. 'Daniel Wilkin?'

The man was clearly puzzled and tired but pointed to the still-closed door Carrie had been knocking on. 'That one.'

Jessica told him to go back into his room, as well as the man who had answered the main door and then indicated for the officers to clear a bit of space around the remaining bedroom door.

She knocked one final time. 'Daniel, if you're in there open the door now or we will break it down.'

She heard it unlocking and the door was pulled open to reveal a man standing there fully dressed in a pair of jeans, a T-shirt and denim jacket as if he were on his way out. He looked exactly like the e-fit. Jessica didn't know if he had just got dressed because he had heard them or if he had been looking to make a run for it. Ultimately it didn't matter.

Jessica left Daniel Wilkin in the cells under the station talking to a duty solicitor. She checked his name in their records but there was nothing. Being a student it was likely he lived elsewhere but she couldn't find any matches on the national database for anyone with his name and age who had a criminal record.

She asked Cole if he would join her in the interview room and, after getting everything ready, they finally called for the suspect to be brought upstairs. The student confirmed his name, date of birth and address, both his university one and that of his parents, who lived in Portsmouth. Jessica asked him where he was on the night Robert Graves had been killed.

'No comment,' Daniel replied.

'Did Robert try to rob you?'

'No comment.'

'Have you ever seen this man?' Jessica asked, showing a photo of Robert Graves before he had been killed.

'No comment.'

Jessica turned to the duty solicitor. 'Did you tell him to do this?'

The solicitor just shrugged at her. 'You know you can't ask me to disclose what I say to my clients.'

Jessica sighed and looked back at the suspect. 'Look, Daniel, I'll be completely honest with you. We've got fingerprints and we've got DNA. You know that swab you gave us when you were brought in? That's on its way to our labs right now to be tested. I don't know if it's you who did this or not but we *will* know for sure within the next forty-eight hours. No commenting is just going to look bad in court. If you're completely innocent, by all means refuse to answer the questions but if you're not – if I were you – I would go back down to the cells, call your parents and get them to arrange a proper solicitor for you.'

The young man looked to the solicitor next to him and Jessica knew they had their man.

'I want to do what she said.'

Two hours later and they had a full confession. Daniel told them how he had been walking home from the local shops when some guy had jumped out at him and demanded his phone. With all the reports about students being attacked, he acted on instinct and punched the assailant hard in the face. From there, things got out of hand. Before he knew what had happened, the other man had stopped moving.

'It was almost like it was someone else, like a movie or something. I don't know what happened,' he said.

He told them about the nightmares he'd had since and how, because of the e-fit, his mates had joked he was the vigilante. They knew he wasn't of course because he had been out with them on the dates the other victims had been killed. He felt guilty he had got away with it but had kept quiet. Then he had got home from a student bar the previous night and saw his face again on an Internet news site but this time they knew what he had done.

'I wanted to hand myself in,' he added. 'I even went to call the number you put up but I couldn't bring myself to do it. I . . . I've never been in trouble before. I'd not even been in a fight until then.'

Jessica found it hard not to feel sorry for him. He had initially been a victim but had completely overreacted. Jessica thought he would probably end up on a manslaughter charge as opposed to murder but two lives had been ended that night.

He was led back to the cells and would be in front of magistrates in the morning. Jessica was applauded as she walked back onto the main office floor but didn't feel like taking people's praise. Cole told her he would deal with Farraday and that she should enjoy the night. Tomorrow they would both get to work on figuring out who killed Craig Millar, Benjamin Webb, Desmond Hughes and Lee Morgan.

Back in their office, Reynolds gave her a hug and told her he was determined to push on with his case, if only to get a justice of sorts for Robert Graves's parents. 'I'll let you off that tenner too,' he added.

Jessica went back through to the canteen to find DCs Rowlands and Jones. 'Hey, are you two still off to the quiz later?'

'Yep, are you gonna come embarrass yourself?' Rowlands said.

'Yes and I'm going to bring my boyfriend too.' Jessica didn't even wait for any witty comebacks, turning and walking towards her car. She had three phone calls to make.

The first was to Adam to make sure he was interested in going to the pub quiz. Then she phoned Garry and talked him through the day's events. She felt she owed him one if only for listening to her in the supermarket car park and gave him a full exclusive. Other publications would get the standard lines from the press office but he would end up looking the most impressive.

The final call was simply to check if the people she wanted to visit were in. They were and invited her round so she drove the few miles to their house. It was the one job she promised herself she would do without any help.

Arthur Graves answered his front door and invited her in. Jessica knew they would be upset with what she had to tell them but it would be as much closure as they could hope to get.

21

The killer hadn't enjoyed the previous week or so. His project had been going well and then they had started accusing him of murdering someone he didn't know. It was an insult to what he was trying to achieve. Three druggie scumbags and a bent prison warden had been removed from the streets and then they started saying he had taken out some kid who hadn't done any real harm.

Until the newsreader had given the boy's name, the killer hadn't even known who he was. It was a complete disgrace to his legacy and he had stopped working his way through the list in protest. But then, last night, finally the police retracted their accusations, admitting somebody else had killed the boy and leaving him with the credit he deserved.

He didn't know if it was a deliberate game but he had spent the day smiling and trying not to let on to those around him.

That night he could get back to work.

The killer had enjoyed the news bulletins and papers over the past couple of weeks. There were a few people that couldn't get their heads around what he was trying to achieve but a decent amount were willing to give him the benefit of the doubt. They knew there were people who could only act like animals and had to be put down as such.

He looked through the list of names he had made. Three people at the top and one three-quarters of the way down had been crossed out. At first he had thought he would work his way through them in order, from the easiest to the hardest.

Millar had been no problem whatsoever. He was just a big mouth who stayed safe through the number of people he kept around him. Without them, he was always going to be the first to go.

Webb and Hughes had been part-impulse, part-necessity. He had been planning to deal with them one at a time but had then seen them swaying their way down the road and simply acted. If sober they would have been near the bottom of the list given their brutality but, from what he had seen, they were both keen drinkers.

The warden had been a special case. Originally he would have been near the bottom of the list, not because he would be physically hard to despatch, simply because of the attention it would have brought to the mission. Unfortunately certain police officers were getting a little too close for comfort and at least with the warden out of the picture it showed he was willing to go to any lengths.

There were five names left on the killer's list. All of them deserved exactly what was coming to them: drug dealers, rapists, those who were a little too handy with their fists and others who put money above anything else.

The next name would be interesting, although a bit of a challenge. The next victim truly was a wolf in sheep's clothing who couldn't keep his hands to himself.

22

She wouldn't have predicted it beforehand but Jessica was actually looking forward to a night out at the pub quiz Rowlands had invited her to. He lived near the edge of the student area of the city and the pub contained a mix of young professionals like them, students and the locals.

Jessica was always fascinated by the regulars who went to the same pub day after day regardless of who owned it. She would often look for them, either sitting at the bar with a pint of cheap bitter or occasionally feeding pound coins into the fruit machines. She couldn't get her head around how some people's lives literally revolved around getting up, going to the pub, then going home.

The place itself was what she would have expected. The ceilings were low and parts of the floor were sticky from either spilled drinks that hadn't been cleaned up or something she would rather not know about. It reminded Jessica of her younger days when she and Caroline were more interested in the price of a drink than the fancy decor.

Dave was at the pub on his own when Jessica arrived with Adam. After visiting the Graveses, she had gone home to clear her head. She couldn't switch from something so serious into either going back to the station or meeting up with friends. She changed into a clean pair of jeans and one of her favourite going-out tops, which hadn't been worn in well over a year. Adam had caught the train to the station closest to her flat and they had both taken a taxi together to the pub.

When they arrived, Jessica had quickly spotted Rowlands sitting in a booth off to the side, guarding it by stretching himself across the seat in case anyone else tried to sit down. 'Thank God you're here,' he said. 'I've been dying for the toilet but didn't want to lose the seats.'

He stood and offered his hand for Adam to shake. 'You must be Adam. I'm Dave. Apart from your name, which someone else told me, I've heard absolutely nothing about you.'

All three of them laughed together and Dave disappeared towards the back of the pub. Jessica and Adam sat in the booth.

'There's nothing bad about me not talking about you,' Jessica said.

'Sorry?'

'What Dave just said about me not talking about you, it's not because I don't like you. It's just not the type of workplace for that . . .'

Adam smiled. 'You told me to assume everything you said was a joke but when he makes a joke, you take it all seriously. It's okay, I don't mind.'

Jessica didn't get much of an opportunity to feel embarrassed about her moment of insecurity before another familiar face came walking across to them. Carrie had dressed up for the evening, wearing a short blue dress with matching heels. It was definitely a little over the top for the standard of the venue and she was getting plenty of sideways glances from the men. She didn't seem to notice and strolled over to the booth, making Jessica shuffle over so she could sit alongside them.

She initially ignored her friend, leaning right across her to shake hands with the man. 'You must be Adam?'

'Yeah, hi. Are you Carrie?'

'Yeah, you all right? Pleased to meet you at last.' She turned back to Jessica. 'Where's Dave?'

'Gone for a wee and then he's getting the drinks in.'

'Ooh, that's nice of him.'

'He doesn't know yet.'

Jessica turned to Adam, pointing backwards at Carrie. 'Don't mind her accent by the way. She's not got some sort of debilitating brain injury or anything, she's just from Wales.'

'Oi, cheeky,' the constable chirped back.

Conversation flowed easily and, when Dave returned, Jessica told him he could get the drinks in for them all. Adam volunteered to help and, not long after, the four of them were sitting in the booth as the quizmaster read the rules out over a crackly PA system.

'We're still waiting for someone,' Dave said.

'Who else is coming?' Jessica asked.

'You'll see, a mate of yours. That should narrow it down to three or four.' Adam was consistently laughing along with Rowlands's jokes, which was partly pleasing for Jessica as he was fitting in nicely, but somewhat annoying because at least two-thirds of the officer's jokes were at her expense.

'Are you all right by the way?' Rowlands asked the other constable.

'Yeah fine,' Carrie replied.

'Why, what's up?' Jessica asked.

Carrie started to say 'nothing' but Rowlands talked over her. 'I saw Farraday having a go at her earlier near one of the holding rooms.'

Jessica looked from one of them to the other. 'Why, what about?'

'I don't know,' Rowlands said.

'Carrie?'

'Nothing really. It's not important.'

Jessica wanted to push the issue but the quizmaster was starting the first round. As a clearly annoyed Carrie loudly shushed them so she could hear the opening question, Jessica remembered she was well known in the station for being fiendishly competitive.

A couple of years earlier, officers based at Longsight had been part of a charity fun day. The station's police had faced off against the local fire brigade in a sponsored sack race and Carrie had been determined to win. Unfortunately for her, she had hopped a bit too excitedly over the finishing line and wiped out a thirteen-year-old boy who was waving a chequered flag. The poor lad had spent the rest of his summer holiday with a broken leg and she had picked up the unfortunate nickname 'Terminator'. It wasn't used quite so often now but every now and then someone, usually Rowlands, would remind her.

Jessica had a silent giggle to herself remembering the

tangled heap of young teenager, chequered flag, old sack and fully grown woman.

The quizmaster's voice told them the first round was 'geography' as an audible groan rippled around the room before he asked the first question. 'What's the capital of Latvia?'

The three officers looked blankly at each other, as Adam leant in closer to Carrie to whisper: 'It's Riga'.

He also knew the answer to the two questions that followed and they all knew the fiftieth American state. After two rounds of results, they were joint first, mainly due to Adam. The quizmaster stopped for the first drinks break and Adam went to the toilet as the two girls sent Rowlands back to the bar. They had at least given him some money the second time around.

As soon as they had the booth to themselves, Carrie leant in close to Jessica and smiled broadly. 'He's nice.'

'Adam?'

'Of course Adam, I'm not going to be talking about Dave, am I?'

'He's all right.'

'He can take me out if you're being picky.'

'I thought you had a bloke?'

'I did, well maybe still do. I don't know really.'

'Do you want to talk about it?'

'Not now. Let's go out later in the week though? Or come over to mine? I'll tell you all about it then, promise.'

'Okay. Are you all right? You look a little flushed.'

'It's just the alcohol. I've not eaten today.'

Jessica looked up and saw the final person Dave must

have been referring to. She tried not to grin but couldn't stop herself. 'Hugo? I didn't know you were coming.'

'Hugo' was the stage name of a part-time magician she had met through Rowlands the previous year. His real name was Francis and his interest in taxidermy meant his flat was occupied by numerous stuffed animals. She had steadfastly refused to admit he actually helped her on a case but he had made things a bit clearer. From her previous experience, she knew he hugged everyone he met and, as he leant in, she didn't refuse. He then hugged a bemused Carrie, then Adam, then Rowlands. The five of them squeezed into the booth together with Hugo on one end, then Dave, Adam, Jessica and Carrie.

Hugo was wearing a pair of shorts, despite it being pretty cold outside, with a dark T-shirt and a full tuxedo jacket with tails. He was very thin with longish brown hair and, as with the last time Jessica had met him, he was also wearing shoes that didn't match.

Rowlands explained to the rest of the table that he knew Hugo from university and asked his friend if he had any new tricks. Hugo smiled dreamily and said he'd spent much of the last three weeks meditating but did pull a stuffed mouse out of his pocket to show them. Jessica thought he was a very peculiar man.

The interference squeak came over the speakers again as the quizmaster began talking. The next round was quotations. 'Question twenty-one,' the quizmaster said. 'Who said; "Let them eat cake"?'

Dave leant in and whispered loudly, 'Kipling.'

Jessica's eruption of laughter was instant. Carrie didn't

know what was so funny and Rowlands clearly wasn't sure either. Hugo was in a world of his own but Adam's smile told Jessica that he knew what she was laughing at.

Jones had already written a K on the answer sheet and that made Jessica laugh even more. She thought she'd got over the giggles but the quizmaster repeated the question, which set her off again. Jones was getting annoyed because she clearly wanted to win, while the penny had dropped for Rowlands that he was wrong.

Finally Jessica managed to stop herself. 'Kipling's the guy who makes the cakes, you dick. It's Marie Antoinette.'

Adam nodded to indicate the answer was correct and Jessica was really enjoying herself. Hugo began to join in and got a few correct but Adam's knowledge didn't extend to 'sport' or 'the animal kingdom'. Carrie caused a mini scene by shouting at a man for using his phone during the quiz. He insisted he was just texting his girlfriend but she was having none of it. Rowlands calmed the situation by telling the guy not to mess with the 'Terminator', which quietened them both.

In the second drinks break, Hugo finally relented in the face of Dave's pestering, taking a deck of cards from his jacket pocket and handed them to Carrie. He told each of them to choose a card then put them back in the pack while he went to the bar.

When he returned, he took the deck back and worked his way through each person, predicting which card they had opted for.

He got every guess wrong.

Sheepishly, he put the cards into his jacket pocket and

went back to playing with a yo-yo he had taken out of another pocket. Carrie looked at Jessica as if to ask, 'Is he for real?' but Jessica didn't know any better than her friend did.

The next round of the quiz had started when one of the bar staff shouted out, 'Hang on a minute, who's playing silly beggars here?'

Everyone looked around to see what the noise was about except for Hugo. Jessica could see the cash register was open and the barman was standing next to it holding four playing cards in the air. 'Who put these in the till?' he asked loudly.

Hugo didn't react but the other four people around the table stared at him. Jessica stood and walked over to the bar. 'Can I see them, mate?'

'It's not you, is it?'

'I've not even got up until now.'

The man handed over the cards and Jessica could see they were the exact four they had picked out from Adam's deck moments earlier. 'Can I have them?' she asked.

'Whatever, just stop pissing around.'

Jessica went back to the booth and put the cards down one by one on the table in front of them. Carrie gave a small squeal as the final one came down.

'How did you do it?' she asked.

Dave cut across her. 'He can't tell you that.' He then looked at Hugo. 'It was quality though, mate, completely effulgent. How *did* you do it?'

Hugo smiled, picking up the cards, pocketing them,

and returning to his yo-yo. Jessica looked at her colleague. 'Effulgent?'

'What about it?' Dave said.

'You've been using the calendar I got you,' Hugo said out of the blue.

'Calendar?' Jessica repeated.

Rowlands tried to shush his friend but Hugo explained. 'I got him a word-a-day calendar as an early birthday present.'

Jessica looked at Dave with a big smile, glad she had figured out what had been going on. She had no idea why Hugo would have given him a calendar in September as a present when the constable's birthday was actually in November but decided that was a question for another day.

After another round about 'the British Isles', their team had dropped back into second place. Carrie was trying not to be overtly angry and Dave wasn't saying anything unless he was sure of the answer.

The next round was literature and Jessica exploded into laughter again when the first question was, 'Who wrote *The Jungle Book*?' She pointed at Dave and said far too loudly: 'This one's bloody Kipling.'

Carrie shushed her, looking around to see if anyone had overheard.

As the final drinks break arrived, Jones went to the toilets. When she returned, she was looking a little redder than before, carrying her mobile phone in her hand. 'Are you okay?' Jessica asked.

'I'm going to get off. I don't think we're going to win anyway and I'm not feeling too great.'

'Do you want me to come with you?'

'God no, you stay here with Adam.'

Hugo must have heard because he stood up and gave Jones another huge hug. ''Bye, Carrie,' he said. 'It's been really nice meeting you.'

'Um, you too.'

She also made Adam stand up, so she could hug him and then cuddled Jessica. 'Today was brilliant,' she said. 'I'm so pleased it was you who sorted things out.'

'Thanks. It means a lot.'

Dave stood up and held his arms out but Jones blew a raspberry at him. 'You can sod off, Mr Kipling.'

'Look who's talking, sheep-shagger.'

Jones wiggled her little finger at him and winked. 'That's what I've heard.'

Dave looked down at his crotch then back up to see Carrie walking away from him. 'Who told you that?' he shouted after her then, much more quietly as he sat down, 'It's not true, you know. Even if it was, it's all about technique anyway.'

Before the final music round, the quizmaster gave out the scores that had them tied in second place but well behind the leaders. A group of four pot-bellied men who were sitting around a table loaded with empty pint glasses waved their arms about excitedly and Jessica guessed they were the team out in front.

Without Carrie to bully them into silence, some of the fun had definitely been lost. Hugo, who had been relatively quiet throughout the evening, seemed to know far more about recent music than any of them. Adam was good on the rock tracks and Jessica had the Eighties nailed. Her biggest problem, as before, was not shouting out the answers. Adam had taken over the pen duties and even he gave her a mildly annoyed look as she called out 'Bros' far too loudly as one of the answers. He quickly turned his look into a smile though.

With all the scores in, it turned out they had finished third. The team in first place got two free drinks each, while the ones in second got a single drink apiece.

Jessica's team ended with nothing. 'Good job Carrie's gone,' Dave said. 'She wouldn't have been happy with third. She'd have probably tried to break our legs like that kid.'

The quizmaster announced that they were going to do karaoke until closing time and Jessica pulled a face. 'What's up, moody bum?' Dave asked.

'Karaoke's for idiots.'

'You're not getting up then?'

'No chance. Why, you're not having a go, are you?'

'Hell yes, that's why I come.'

'What do you sing?'

'Robbie Williams, "Angels". Pitch perfect.'

'Piss off, is it.'

The first person had started singing. Jessica recognised the opening bars of Elvis's 'Burning Love'. It was one of her dad's favourite tunes and something she could remember dancing around to as a child without having a clue what the song was about.

'Hang on a minute, where's Hugo?' Rowlands said. Just when she thought she couldn't laugh any more for the evening, Jessica was off again. Hugo was stood on the bar, microphone in hand singing along with the karaoke. He was doing all the Elvis moves and getting every word right despite not being anywhere near the screen with the lyrics.

'What's he doing?' Rowlands asked. The servers didn't seem too pleased as Hugo danced in between people's drinks, conducted the crowd for the chorus and then ended with a big jump off the bar.

Jessica didn't think she'd ever stop laughing. Within moments of the song ending, Hugo was sitting back in their booth playing with his yo-yo as if nothing had happened.

'What was *that*?' Rowlands asked.

'What?'

'I didn't even know you sang?'

'Sometimes. I'm still working on the act.'

Jessica exchanged a look with Adam as if to say, 'Don't ask me'.

Rowlands got up to sing his song and, as Jessica had suspected, it was terrible. He closed his eyes for the chorus as if anguished and even sung the final part directly to a table of girls near the bar.

'I think it's time to head off,' Jessica said to Adam. 'You coming, Hugo?'

The magician looked back at them and shrugged. 'I'll wait.' He stood and hugged them both, saying goodbye.

'It's been good meeting you again anyway,' Jessica added.

She waved over to Rowlands, who was finishing the final note and was on his knees by the girls' table. He gave her a small nod to show he had seen her but didn't break from his performance. Jessica and Adam walked out of the pub hand in hand and crossed the road to the small taxi rank next to a row of shops opposite. There was only one vehicle waiting. 'You take this one and I'll get the one after,' Adam said.

Jessica squeezed his hand and pulled him towards her. 'Maybe . . . or you could just stay at mine tonight?'

23

Detective Constable Carrie Jones had quite enjoyed her evening until the flood of text messages towards the end of it. She just wished he would stop playing with her head. She didn't know if she should call him her boyfriend or not. One minute they were on, the next off again. He didn't seem to know what he wanted and the more he messed her around, the more she ran to back him. She hated herself for doing it but couldn't stop.

As she sat in the taxi, her phone beeped again with another message.

'Sorry for earlier. Will make it up to you.'

The woman snapped the phone shut, put it on silent and dropped it back into her bag. The thing that frustrated her most was that today had been one of those days you waited for, the ones where things got figured out and some poor parents, such as Robert Graves's, got their closure. These were the nights you were supposed to go out, have a few drinks and a laugh and forget about the rest of the cases that were going nowhere.

She had really wanted to get Jessica alone for a few moments to say how pleased she was for her. The two had become good friends over the past few months but Carrie could see how badly things had been getting to her superior. In quiet moments she had spoken to Dave about the pressure their friend seemed to be under but, aside from solving the case, neither of them had any firm ideas of how to cheer her up.

Meeting Adam for the first time had been nice. Carrie had never known Jessica to have a boyfriend. Behind her back a few people at the station made cruel jibes about her sexual habits but they soon stopped after Dave had pinned one of the other constables up against the wall by the throat. Adam came across really well though. He was a little quiet but had been meeting them for the first time so was bound to be a bit shy. He was obviously clever and had a sharp sense of humour when he opened up. She hoped Jessica would come over later in the week so they could have a proper chat about Adam ... and her own problems.

The taxi was on the main road a hundred yards or so away from the turn-off to her street and started to slow down. The driver looked over his shoulder and shouted back. 'Do you mind if I pull in here, love? It's one-way down there. I end up having to go half a mile out of my way to get back again.'

'Yeah, no worries.'

The driver pulled over and the constable gave him a ten-pound note, telling him to keep the change. Carrie stepped out onto the pavement and walked a few steps towards her junction but the high blue heels were hurting her feet. They looked great with the dress but weren't that practical for walking in. She sat on a nearby wall and pulled the shoes off, standing up in her bare feet. Her house was a couple of hundred yards away and it wouldn't be the first time she had walked back to the property with no shoes on.

She walked slowly down her road, placing her feet carefully in case of loose stones. As she got towards the end of her pathway, she heard a faint noise coming from further down the street. She squinted into the darkness but couldn't see anything.

Because of the way John Mills, her troublesome neighbour, had converted two properties into one, the blind spot from the street lights coincided with the end of the driveway he had created.

At first it was hard for her to figure out what the noise was but then the constable remembered the smashed-up face of his girlfriend. Even though she had refused to give evidence against him previously, the last thing Carrie wanted was for her to get beaten up again.

She put her bag and shoes down on her pathway and crept forwards into the dark down the pavement towards the noise, crossing onto Mills's front lawn in an effort to track down where the sound was coming from.

The constable was wearing a short dress and no shoes and didn't even have her identification, let alone anything else, so didn't want to be seen walking on his property if it was something innocuous. She felt the dew-soaked grass through her toes and a shiver went down her back. She couldn't make out what the noise was and couldn't see anything. She was standing completely hidden by a shadow when she heard a large shout.

Carrie ran towards the sound. There was a small open-topped van parked on the drive that came into view as she reached the end of the lawn. She ran towards the back of the vehicle and saw two men struggling. They were both silhouettes in the gloom and she shouted towards them. Both men turned to face her but, even in the darkness, she could see that one of them was badly hurt. He had twisted around to face her, screaming in agony as he did so. The shout was muffled, almost as if it were being heard from far further away than it was.

Without thinking, Carrie ran towards them, grabbing for the man still standing. She didn't know if it was John Mills or someone he knew but something serious had happened. She could feel liquid around her toes as she hung on to the man's top. He grunted and tried to bat her away with his forearm. The blow half-caught her across the head but she didn't let go and lashed out with her feet, trying to trip him. She could feel the man on the floor still moving near her other foot but wasn't sure if he was trying to help her.

The man who was standing continued to flail but she managed to duck under his arm and crash her shoulder into him. She might be small but she knew how to look after herself and heard the man exhale loudly and painfully. As he reeled, the constable tried to work her leg behind his to trip him and send him backwards. The man was bigger than she thought though and, as she tried to push, the only noise she heard was her own leg snapping. The pain screamed through her and, as she fell backwards, the last thing she saw was a knife reflecting the moonlight crashing down towards her neck.

24

Jessica couldn't begin to comprehend what DI Cole was trying to tell her on the phone after it had woken both her and Adam up in the early hours. She wasn't good in the mornings at the best of times but the alarm clock showed 4.22 and none of her senses seemed to be working. Adam had groaned and rolled over when the phone had begun to ring but she knew she had to answer it.

She heard the words 'Carrie', 'stabbed', 'infirmary' and finally, 'sorry' but couldn't figure it all out. Cole repeated the sentence four times before the significance finally dawned on her. 'Jessica, I'm at the Royal Infirmary. It's Carrie, she's been stabbed. I'm so sorry.'

It was what he hadn't said that suddenly became clear. He hadn't told Jessica that Carrie was fine. He hadn't said they were waiting for results. He hadn't even called her Detective, or Constable, or Jones.

He had called her Carrie and he had said sorry.

Jessica offered a quick goodbye to Adam and apologised. She told him she didn't know what was going on but that she had to move quickly. She pulled on whatever clothes were closest and drove as fast as she could to the hospital, not caring if someone tried to pull her over for speeding. Given the mood she was in they wouldn't have caught her anyway.

Jessica parked her car in one of the emergency vehicle spaces and ran into the main part of the hospital. She held her identification out in front of her and, without even being given Carrie's name, the receptionist gave her directions.

As she ran down the corridors, Jessica's vision was blurred, a mix of tears and tiredness. She soon reached the correct ward, bursting through a set of double doors into a waiting area that was empty except for Cole. He was sitting looking at the floor but immediately got to his feet as soon as he saw Jessica. It looked as if there had been tears in his eyes at some point recently too. 'Jess . . .'

'Where is she?'

'Jess, stop.'

Jessica was trying to push past him to go through another set of doors but he was holding her back. 'Stop.'

She stopped trying to fight past him and took a step backwards. 'Is she . . . ?'

'Yes.'

'What happened?'

'We don't know. She was found with a stab wound in her neck on the driveway of a property a few doors down from her house.'

'Did Mills do it?'

'Her neighbour? He's been stabbed too but he's alive in intensive care. It was his girlfriend who called us.'

Jessica stared at the inspector, unable to understand what he was saying. 'So they've both been stabbed?'

'Yes.'

'But why would someone hurt Carrie?'

'I don't know.'

A slow realisation came across Jessica and she sank backwards onto a plastic seat, looking down at the floor. 'You don't think . . . this vigilante guy was going after Mills?'

Cole looked back at her. The thought had obviously crossed his mind but he didn't want to say anything. Jessica stood straight back up again. 'Where's Farraday?'

'Pacing around outside of John Mills's intensive care ward at the moment. The last thing I saw he was shouting at the nurse because the victim was in a coma and unable to talk to us.'

'He's already here?'

'Yes, one of the paramedics said he had arrived at the scene as they were leaving and then followed them here. He called me.'

'He was at the scene?'

'Jessica, I don't know. You have to slow down.'

She wasn't listening to him though. 'Which direction is intensive care?'

Cole looked at her with obvious concern. 'I think you should go home. I shouldn't have called you.'

Jessica wasn't ready to listen. She spun around, banged back through the double doors and started reading a sign on the wall opposite. With an arrow giving her a vague direction, Jessica walked as quickly as she could down the corridor. The signs led her up some stairs and down more corridors. Given the time of the morning, there weren't too many other people around the passageways and she quickened her pace.

Farraday's behaviour had been troubling her for a while and Carrie's death had brought everything colliding together. She knew she was feeling emotional but a very clear picture was emerging in her head. Everything that had hindered the case came down to her boss. She was as certain as she could be that it was him who leaked details about the prison warden to the media claiming he was corrupt.

It was him who wrongly put Robert Graves on the list of the vigilante's victims – and allowed the e-fit of Daniel Wilkin to be associated with it. It was even him who let the branding 'vigilante' stick.

He was the one who wanted more 'shits' off the streets, he took Cole off the case, even though he was her superior, and he had been seen arguing with Carrie the afternoon before she had been killed.

Jessica didn't know how he had done it or why. She had no idea what his connection was to Donald McKenna but it was as clear as it could be to her that Farraday was somehow involved in what had been going on. She knew it sounded utterly irrational on the surface but it explained so much. Was the reason he was so desperate to see John Mills because the man in a coma could identify him?

After a few minutes of walking, she pushed her way through another set of double doors into a waiting room. Straight ahead of her was Farraday, pacing the area himself. He stopped and looked at her as the doors banged against their frames. 'Daniel?'

Jessica immediately realised she had no idea what she was doing. She couldn't jump in and accuse him of being a part of what had gone on in recent weeks. She stumbled over what to say. 'Sir . . . I . . .'

His eyes were fuelled with anger but she didn't know who it was aimed at. 'He's still unconscious,' he said.

'Who? Mills?'

'Yes. The doctor says he's stable but they don't know if he'll wake up.'

'Do you know what happened?'

The man was gazing through her. 'How would I know?'

'I don't . . . Jack said you were there?'

Jessica saw his eyes bring her properly into focus. 'Who told . . . ?' He moved quickly from standing on one foot to the other, grunting in frustration before quickly striding past her. As he neared the door, he turned around and shouted over his shoulder. 'I want to know the *second* he wakes up. No one speaks to him before me.'

His reaction confused Jessica even more but, before she could begin to think about things further, she noticed a woman sitting in the corner of the room. Despite the way Farraday had raised his voice the woman seemingly hadn't moved and was sat on a bolted-down chair holding her knees up to her chest, gazing at the floor.

'Hello?' Jessica said, walking towards her.

The woman said nothing. She looked in her early twenties with long shiny black hair tied into a ponytail and would have been very attractive if it hadn't been for the tear-stained black eye she was sporting. 'Are you all right?' Jessica asked.

The woman spoke without looking up from the ground. 'Just leave me alone.'

'Are you John Mills's girlfriend?'

'Are you deaf? I said leave me alone.'

'I'm Jessica.'

'You're a pig is what you are.'

Jessica sat opposite the woman, wriggling into the chair to get comfortable. The row of hardened seats were screwed onto thick metal bars that were bolted into the ground and offered little relief except for thin pads underneath and behind her.

'Whoever stabbed your boyfriend killed my friend.'

The woman said nothing for almost a minute before finally spitting her words out. 'I already spoke to someone at the house and told them everything. I'm not talking to you too.'

Jessica knew she could read the statement when she got back to the station but there was one thing she wanted to ask which definitely wouldn't have been brought up by the officers at the scene. 'Perhaps I've got better questions?'

The woman snorted with mock laughter and finally looked across at Jessica, putting her feet down onto the floor. 'Fine, here you go. No, I didn't *see* anything. No, I didn't *hear* anything until the girl screamed and, by the time I got out there, it was just them. No, I don't know who might want to harm John. No, I don't know why your girl was on our drive and no, I don't know why she had no shoes on. Yes, I called you straight away and, finally, yes, I walked into a door. Now piss off.'

It sounded pathetic but Jessica could only think of one thing.

'She wasn't wearing shoes . . . ?'

Whether it was the tone of her voice, she wasn't sure but Jessica glanced up to see the woman staring directly at her.

She was running her fingers through her long hair and letting it fall back over and over. Her manner had changed again by the time she spoke next. 'I know she was one of yours but I'll always remember the red of the blood and the blue of her dress.' The woman sighed loudly and looked back at the floor. 'Her shoes were on her own pathway with her bag or something like that. I only know because I heard one of them talking. It was dark and then they took me inside to talk.'

Jessica took a deep breath. 'The man who just stormed out of here, was he there?'

'What, afterwards? He was the one directing people.'

'But before that, did you see him?'

The woman looked back at the floor. 'I'm not doing your job for you.'

Jessica could tell straight away the moment was lost. She wasn't sure what she had expected. Cole had told her Farraday was at the incident. It was the first time she had known him go to a crime scene but it was likely he would have been the first call when the dead body's identity was discovered by the paramedics or responding officers.

She wondered if he was already there somewhere, watching and waiting for his phone to ring. Jessica stood and stepped closer to the woman. As she was leaving her flat, her business cards had been next to her identification and she had picked them up just in case. She took one out of her pocket and put it on the seat next to the woman. 'Just in case you do want to talk.'

She turned around and walked back out of the waiting room, heading downstairs towards the room Cole had been outside of. As she approached the double doors, she was almost hit by Cole pushing them out towards her. She stepped backwards quickly to avoid them and he did the exact same thing.

'I was just leaving,' he said. 'They're taking the body back to the labs to do the tests.'

'So was she alive in the ambulance?'

'I guess so; she wouldn't have been brought here otherwise.'

'Sorry, of course. I'm not thinking clearly this morning.'

'I'm going to go home for a bit and then I'll be back at the station in an hour or so. You should go home too.'

'Maybe.'

Jessica had no intention of going anywhere except for the station.

The sun was beginning to come up as Jessica drove along the nearly deserted roads from the hospital to Longsight. She kept to the speed limits for the second journey and felt guilty about her selfishness earlier on. Given her state of mind and the speed she had driven at, she could have ended up causing harm not only to herself but someone else through her recklessness. Her mind was still in overdrive, not knowing if her suspicions of Farraday were irrational and down to shock, or if Carrie's death had instead given her the jolt needed to put the pieces together.

Finding out what had happened the night before would be crucial. DC Jones had been found on John Mills's property so was he the target and the officer had been killed accidentally, or was something else going on? Until Mills woke up, she was unlikely to know.

Although it was early and most officers would still be at home, Jessica could sense the atmosphere of sadness and anger as she walked into the station's reception. The overnight desk sergeant asked if she had any updates on what exactly happened but Jessica shook her head. 'Do you know if we've had a list of things recovered from the scene yet?' she asked.

'No idea. I know Bradford Park have called some of their staff in to start working straight away because they phoned here to check some details. It's still a bit early but it could be on the system.'

Jessica knew the procedure anyway and had only said it to stop the sergeant asking how she was. She nodded and walked towards her office but instead found Rowlands in the corridor. He looked as if he were still in shock. The skin around his eyes was red and, while he was usually smartly groomed, his hair hadn't been spiked and his clothes were creased. 'Jess . . .' he said when he saw her.

'Dave, I should have called you.'

'Do you know what happened? I read the first report through the system but there's pretty much no detail and no one here knows anything other than the fact she's . . .'

Jessica wanted to put an arm around him. She had long

known his outward confidence was the side he showed to everyone else and he was a different type of person when you got to know him. 'No one's really sure yet. I've come from the hospital. Her body has been taken to the labs while her neighbour is unconscious. Both of them had been stabbed.'

'I saw the stuff about John Mills, she was always talking about him. Do you think it's our vigilante?'

'I don't know.' Jessica didn't want to expand on what she had actually been thinking through the morning.

'What's going on now then?' Rowlands asked.

'Jack will be here soon. We need to get people out knocking on the other neighbours' doors to see if they heard anything. I think she took a taxi home last night so we've got to find out who the driver was. The labs are doing their thing and someone's going to have to talk to the media this morning too.'

Rowlands was nodding, clearly wondering what he could do. 'Hey, are you okay?' Jessica added.

'Yeah, I . . .'

'Did you say you'd read the initial reports?'

'There's not much in them, just the emergency call log and a few other bits.'

'Was there a list of evidence recovered?'

'There was something, I don't remember completely.'

'Show me.'

Rowlands and Jessica walked through the hallways to the main floor and his area of the room. He was already logged in to the force's computer system and clicked to bring up the file that had been created just a few hours ago. Jessica asked if she could sit and the constable stood behind her watching as she read the screen. First she scanned through the emergency call details and then looked for the attached information.

Something John Mills's girlfriend said had stuck with Jessica.

Because of the seriousness of the incident, the Scene of Crime officers had taken the evidence from the location. Once they had analysed everything, most, if not all, of the items would be released back to the investigating force to be kept in evidence storage, in the anticipation of a trial. Items could be kept locked away for a long time in case a suspect was found many years down the line. The first thing the SOCO team would do was list everything they had taken and pass it back to the police force – that way officers could start to work on certain aspects of the case even while items were still being examined by forensics.

Jessica wondered if Adam was one of the staff members who had been called in. Someone had already filed a list of evidence recovered and Jessica skimmed through it. As the girlfriend had said, Carrie's abandoned shoes were on the list, as was her bag and a few other objects. They had been picked up from her own pathway, while her body had been found on Mills's driveway half-a-dozen doors down. There was no knife or other type of murder weapon listed and Jessica closed the file.

'She wasn't wearing shoes?' Rowlands said.

'Seems not.'

A new thought entered Jessica's head though and she

quickly reopened the file, checking through the list of items again. 'No phone,' she said.

'Sorry?'

'Her phone isn't on this list. She definitely had it in the pub.'

'Yeah, she was texting all the time.'

'She obviously didn't go into her house else she wouldn't have left her bag and shoes on her pathway. You saw her dress, it's not as if it could be hidden away in a pocket, so if it wasn't found in her bag then where is it?'

Rowlands stepped away from the chair to let Jessica push it back and stand up. 'I'll phone the officers left at the scene to see if they can see it anywhere, then get on to the taxi company to make sure she didn't drop it,' he said.

'Okay, good. I'll be in my office, come let me know.'

Jessica didn't know if it would be significant or not but Carrie had certainly been agitated leaving the quiz the previous evening. She said she was feeling a bit ill but had her phone in her hand as she departed and Jessica felt at the time there was something she wasn't letting on. If someone had called her, the phone's logs could be crucial. Without the device, they could apply to the phone company to release certain records but she couldn't do that without permission from Farraday and probably even the superintendent.

She walked back through the halls of the station towards her office. All of the day-shift workers were now in and the news about Carrie's death had spread, the atmosphere of defiance and anger rising. Jessica had those feelings herself but was trying to bury them and focus on seeing it as a death she should be investigating, not the death of a close friend and colleague.

She walked into her office and Reynolds spun around in his seat. 'Jess,' he said sadly. 'I only heard a few minutes ago. I didn't know if you were in or at the hospital or the scene. I was going to call but didn't want to interrupt anything.'

Jessica hadn't heard what he was saying, staring towards the opposite half of the room where her desk was. 'What's happened in here?' she said, trying not to sound angry but with a clear edge to her voice.

Reynolds was clearly confused. 'Sorry?'

'My things have been moved around.' She walked over towards her side of the room and started picking up papers from the floor, before flicking through a separate pile on her desk.

'Um, I don't know. I mean you're always a bit messy, it looks the same to me.'

'You've not gone through any of this?'

'What? No, I only just got in here ten minutes ago or so. Farraday was walking out and said something about wondering where you were.'

25

Jessica looked across the room at her colleague. 'You actually saw him in here?'

Reynolds seemed a bit confused but pointed over his shoulder towards their office door. 'Sort of, he had just come out of the door as I walked into the corridor. I asked him if he had been talking to you in here but he just mumbled something and walked off. I didn't really catch it but assumed he was looking for you when I saw you weren't around.'

Jessica tried to calm herself and not show Reynolds there was any obvious problem. She wasn't ready to share her ideas with anyone else just yet and still feared she was being paranoid. 'I did tell him I was going to be in my office. Maybe he just knocked something over by accident? It's fine.'

Reynolds looked at her with his head tilted at the angle she hated as it indicated someone was about to ask if she was all right. Before he could speak, she started walking back towards the door. 'I'll check with him now.'

Jessica again didn't know what to think. Her side of the office was always a mess but she knew where everything was and could tell someone had gone through her things. What could Farraday have been looking for?

She headed for reception and then up the stairs. On the

first floor, aside from the chief inspector's office, there were only storage areas and miscellaneous rooms for officers from other districts who were working with them temporarily. If ever the superintendent was at their station for a day he would be given one of the spare rooms to work from. The floor was a lot quieter than the rest of the station and, apart from the DCI himself, very few people spent much time upstairs.

Farraday's office had glass that ran all around it and Jessica could see instantly he wasn't there. She hadn't even known what she was going to say to him but, given Jason had said he was looking for her, it would at least be a start. She stopped and motioned to turn back towards the stairs but then had a thought. Jessica walked towards the door of the office and pushed the handle down. The office would usually be locked overnight but the grip allowed her to open it. She paused at the door knowing she shouldn't go in but the theories in the back of her mind urged her forwards.

She didn't know what she was looking for as she stepped carefully behind his desk. Jessica realised she was on tiptoes even though she had no reason to be creeping; it wasn't as if someone downstairs would hear her. At first she fingered through some papers on the desk and then looked on top of the filing cabinets behind her. There was nothing of any significance but she turned back to the desk and tried the drawers.

The top one was full of pens, rubber bands and paper clips, and she closed it quietly before opening the middle one. There were a few documents inside and Jessica looked through their contents. They related to a separate case that was being worked on but there was nothing untoward in him having them.

Finally, she pulled out the bottom drawer. There was an A4 writing pad on top with two more files underneath. She thumbed through the first one, which had some financial figures relating to their budget, and then picked up the final cardboard wallet at the bottom of the drawer. She opened the front cover and blinked furiously at the top sheet of paper.

It was Detective Constable Carrie Jones's personnel file.

Jessica found it hard to believe what she was holding. She skimmed through the contents and could see all of her friend's personal details. Her full name, date of birth, place of birth, current address and contact numbers were on the top sheet. There were details relating to her parents and education plus underneath were the test results from when she had joined the force. The sheets that had been filled in when she was interviewed were included and so were the results of her physical exams. There was a hard copy of her Criminal Records Bureau check, showing she didn't even have a driving conviction.

She didn't read the contents word for word but everything you could have wanted to know about the constable was present.

Jessica's heart was racing as she returned the contents of the drawer and walked out of the office, closing the door behind her. The personnel department were based on the floor below and, while everyone's records were also stored digitally on the computer system, there were hard copies too. All of the information was supposed to be private and Jessica had no idea how the DCI would have managed to take the file, let alone why he would do so.

Having the file could well be a disciplinary offence but Jessica knew she had to tread carefully. Perhaps he had taken the file after the killing because he was looking for a lead himself? Without talking to Cole or her it would be an odd thing to do but it was possible.

Jessica quickly made her way down the stairs and went to see if Cole had arrived. Despite what she had just seen, she was desperate to act as normal as possible. The whole team would be waiting for the morning briefing and, suspicions or not, she and Cole were going to have to meet with the DCI at some point to get all the details together.

As she was walking towards the offices, Rowlands was coming towards her. 'There you are. Reynolds said you had gone to look for the DCI.' Jessica didn't want to say anything so simply looked at him, asking him with her eyes what he wanted. He took the hint and continued talking. 'I've spoken to one of the officers at the scene and they say there are still Scene of Crime officers at Carrie's house.'

'Did they find her phone?'

'The guy said they'd found her footprints leading towards Mills's house so they know she walked across her neighbour's garden to get there. According to the person he spoke to they didn't find a phone.'

'What about the taxi?'

'It took a few calls but I found the company that operate from the rank by the pub. They checked the records and found the journey from last night. They checked with the driver but he says there was nothing left in the back of his cab. It was his last journey of the night too so it's not as if anyone else could have picked it up.'

Jessica took her phone out of her jacket pocket and pressed a few buttons. 'May as well try it,' she said. The number she called didn't even connect, instead going straight to voicemail. Jessica felt sick as she heard the cheery Welsh voice at the other end.

'Hey, it's Carrie. I'm busy or something, leave a message.'

Jessica hung up, trying to keep her composure. 'It's off.'

Half an hour later, Jessica was sitting back in Farraday's office. She nervously looked at the desk she had searched through not too long ago but, if she had left anything out of place, it hadn't been mentioned. Cole was sitting next to her as Reynolds stood. The chief inspector was drumming his fingers.

'Before we start, I was given some news this morning to pass on to you, Daniel. Graham Hancock has been bailed. You know he pleaded not guilty to wasting our time and had been kept in but some soft-arse magistrates let him out on appeal this morning. Christ knows when he'll be on trial but until then that sicko's free to walk around.'

With everything that had happened during the morning, Jessica had forgotten about the man who had confessed. She didn't feel in danger from him but the idea he could be back on the streets was certainly not what she expected. He had initially been remanded but, because he could only get six months in jail as a maximum punishment, the magistrates had decided he should be let out.

DCI Farraday looked at her but she couldn't read his face. There might have been concern but it could just be annoyance. 'Are you going to be okay with that?' he asked.

'Yes, Sir. It's fine.'

He looked back towards the centre of the room, trying to talk to the three of them at once, without singling any of them out. 'We're all senior detectives here and it's us who have to set the example today. Jones was a colleague to us all and I know you must be feeling angry but we have a job to do.'

Jessica knew he was right but hearing her friend called 'Jones' sounded cold.

'Do I think this is linked to the other deaths? I don't know. We need to start by finding out if this is somehow connected to them and, of course, McKenna. That's going to take time through the labs but, in the meantime, let's start with Mills. Someone needs to go back to talk to the girlfriend and someone else needs to get digging. Talk to the other neighbours too. We know what his record is like but let's really nail him.'

'What about Carrie?' Jessica asked, deliberately using her first name.

The DCI turned around to focus solely on her, his eyes narrowing. 'We all want to push on and find out what happened but we're going to have to wait for the results.'

'Do you know her phone is missing?' Jessica's question

brought an abrupt silence and she could feel the three men looking at her. 'I checked the records,' she continued. 'It wasn't found at the scene, it's not on the body and she didn't lose it in the taxi on the way home.'

Cole and Reynolds turned back to Farraday, who was staring at Jessica. 'Assuming it wasn't accidentally left off the Scene of Crime team's list, she probably dropped it, or it's in her house. I don't see why this matters,' he said.

Jessica met his eyes. 'I think we should talk to the superintendent about asking the phone company to release her call and text records. Maybe the fact it's missing is important.'

Farraday hadn't stopped staring at her, his eyes thin and fixed. 'I've seen that list too, Daniel and, given the fact her purse wasn't taken, I think we can rule out theft as a motive. Her phone isn't a priority and there are too many legal hoops to jump through to get those records released that will take people away from focusing on the real work.'

'If it takes time, surely that's why we should start the process now?'

The chief inspector stopped tapping his fingers on the desk and the room was silent. 'Are you questioning my judgement?'

Jessica was prevented from saying something instinctive as Cole cut in. 'I think we've all had a long night and are feeling a little emotional.'

She said nothing but refused to look away from her boss, daring him to take his eyes away first and wanting him to feel uncomfortable and know she was on to him.

Cole spoke again, trying to defuse the tension. 'What are we going to do about the media?'

It was a question that couldn't be ignored and Farraday finally stopped eyeing Jessica and turned to the inspector. 'The press office have started putting together a statement. At the moment we're going to avoid linking it to the previous cases until the lab results come back. If they put two and two together, there's not much we can do. The office have said that if anyone wants to make a personal tribute or something similar to Jones, then they are compiling a few before putting out a separate statement later.'

He asked if anyone else had any questions but the three detectives stayed silent and the DCI sent them on their way, saying the four of them would give a briefing to the rest of the team in fifteen minutes. On their way down the stairs, Cole said something about staying calm but Jessica wasn't listening. She walked straight out of the station, getting into her car, and calling Garry Ashford.

The journalist answered immediately.

Jessica knew she could have given a statement to the press office that would have been distributed with everyone else's but she wanted to talk to someone she trusted. Garry had already heard about the killing and she told him she couldn't pass on too many specifics about the crime scene. The truth was she didn't trust herself to keep her suspicions about Farraday private. Instead she spoke about how highly she thought of the dead constable. She didn't really know what she was trying to achieve. In one way it was a slight rebellion against the chief inspector by bypassing the press office but it also felt good to talk about Carrie's best qualities. After speaking for ten minutes, she knew she had to be back at the main meeting and told Garry he could call her later if he wanted to.

The team briefing went well. The chief inspector formally told the officers what had happened the night before and said that, for now, they weren't officially linking it to the other deaths at least until the lab results came back. DI Cole let everyone know where they were up to with the investigation, which wasn't far, and handed out the jobs for the day.

Regardless of how she was feeling, Jessica knew Farraday had been right about them setting an example and when it was her turn to talk, she took a deep breath and spoke as calmly as she could manage.

'I know a lot of you are angry and upset and want to get out there and find who did this but we have to work as the trained professionals we are. We need to be calm and level-headed and not make mistakes. If you've been given a job to do, you need to be able to do it to the best of your abilities.'

She paused for a moment to stop her voice from cracking. 'There's no shame in being upset and none of us have a problem if any of you need to speak to the counselling staff. But we need to be able to work on this like any other case and, instead of being consumed by our anger, we must use it to drive us and get things done. We all lost a friend this morning – now let's show everyone what a fantastic team of people Carrie had around her.'

There was complete silence in the room as she finished

talking. She felt a lump in her own throat and could see that a few of the officers in front of her seemingly had something in their eyes that needed wiping away.

Farraday dismissed everyone and Jessica returned to her office with Reynolds. With the door shut behind them, he opened his arms and hugged her tight. At first, she didn't know whether to reciprocate but, despite them being two officers on duty, the moment felt right. After letting her go, he said he had been moved by the way she had talked to the room. It was nice of him to say but didn't help with Jessica's own feelings of anger. She had told the rest of the officers they could speak to the counselling staff if they wanted but knew she needed to above anyone. They were just a phone call away but she couldn't bring herself to dial the number.

Jessica felt in a daze for the rest of the day. She'd had no time to grieve and hardly any sleep but spent the entire time working hard. In the back of her mind was Farraday. She knew it was paranoia but just because she recognised it, that didn't necessarily mean it was misplaced.

The afternoon had been spent talking to Carrie's other neighbours. They all said roughly the same thing; she was a joy to live next to and John Mills was a nightmare. None of them had heard anything the previous night.

After finishing taking the statements, Jessica went back to the station to type them up herself. It wasn't the kind of work she was expected to do but she felt she had to keep going. The rest of the day crew had already gone home by the time she had finished, with some of the night officers openly asking if she wanted them to help her out so she could go. In the end, to get some peace, she closed the door to her office and turned the lights out, with only the glow of the computer monitor stopping the room from being completely dark.

She looked through all the information that had come in that day then re-read everything they already had on file from the previous deaths. Although the killings weren't being officially linked yet, she knew they were, even if the lab results weren't expected for at least another twenty-four hours. She wanted to see something in their records that would either confirm her suspicions about the chief inspector or make her realise she was overreacting.

There was nothing.

Adam had texted her a few times during the day but she had deleted the messages without even reading them. She felt selfish but it was almost if she wanted to punish herself for not preventing what had happened the night before.

As Jessica sat staring at the computer screen, her thoughts drifted to cartoons from her youth for no apparent reason. She considered how simplistic it seemed when Bugs Bunny had a small devil on one shoulder whispering bad thoughts in one ear as a little angel sat on the other telling him the opposite. It sounded stupid but she could almost feel them there behind her, the devil telling her the chief inspector was the one and that she should shout it from the rooftops, the angel reminding her she was just struggling to deal with her friend's death and seeing demons where there were none.

Jessica walked out to her car and got in, looking at the

clock on the dashboard. She realised she had slept for barely four hours in the last day and a half. It felt as if someone else was driving as she pulled onto the road to travel home. Her feet and hands were moving over the pedals, gear stick and steering wheel but Jessica made no real conscious thought to control what she was doing.

Her mind snapped back as a car behind her beeped as she waited at a green traffic light. She wasn't sure if she had fallen asleep for a few moments or simply if she hadn't noticed the colour. She tried to pull forwards but the car lurched over the stop line and stalled. The car behind beeped again, swerving around her and speeding through a light which was now definitely red. Jessica started the engine again and felt that little devil in her ear, whispering mischievous ideas. The next time the light went green, she pulled away quickly and did a U-turn at the junction going back the way she had come.

She wasn't going home.

Jessica couldn't remember the exact directions but knew roughly which area she was going to. She found the estate fairly easily but drove through the maze of roads for fifteen minutes looking for the exact one she wanted. Eventually she parked on the side of the road and turned her headlights off. She had no plan or no real idea what she was going to do but in the darkness she sat and watched DCI Farraday's house.

She had known the rough location because of the party he had thrown when he had first started the job. It was in a fairly affluent area and she knew her car would stand out. Jessica made sure she was stopped between street lights in the shadows and stared at the house. There was a light on downstairs but the rest of the property sat in darkness. Around the house was a mixture of fences and hedges around six feet high or so with an automated gate at the end of the driveway. It was the type where you pressed a button and waited to be buzzed through.

Jessica was thinking as clearly as she had done the whole day. She stepped out of the car and walked quietly up to the gate, making sure to avoid the glow of the street lights. She looked for a security camera but couldn't see one. She first tried opening the gate but it wouldn't budge, so instead she pushed it roughly to see if it was fixed sturdily enough in place to let her climb. It felt as if the bolts fixed into the ground were solid so she squinted into the distance towards the house to see if there were any obvious motion lights that would come on. She couldn't see anything and, after looking both ways to check for approaching cars, Jessica quickly jumped up onto the middle bar of the gate and then flipped herself over the top.

She landed a little awkwardly on her ankle on the other side but gritted her teeth and refused to cry out. She followed the line of the hedge towards the house, stepping carefully in an effort to leave no footprints.

Jessica reached the garage attached to the house. The front door was only a few yards in front of her and a small alley on her right presumably led towards the back of the house.

She jumped as the downstairs light went out and held her breath, ready to duck into the alley if any of the doors opened. She wondered if it had gone out because someone had seen her but she started to breathe again as a light upstairs went on, figuring it was just the occupant going to bed. She gently rattled the garage door to see if it would open but it was locked from the inside.

Jessica realised she had no idea what she was doing. She had acted on impulse but ended up doing exactly what she had told the officers not to do at the briefing; she had let her anger cloud her judgement. She crept backwards but her heel clipped something hard, making it rattle noisily. Jessica quickly ducked, pressing herself towards the hedge. The sound might have seemed louder to her but she again held her breath, waiting for what seemed like an age. She could feel the wind starting to whip around the garden but nobody came.

When she was sure no one was going to discover her, Jessica looked to see what she had bumped into and noticed a black wheelie bin. Her head was telling her to turn and run, to get into her car and drive home to get some sleep but her eyes felt fixed on the plastic container that came up to her chest. She stepped towards it, flipping over the lid. A smell of rotting rubbish hit her but she looked inside anyway. She used the light of her phone's screen to see in the dark but on top was an apple core and two banana skins, plus some sloppy leftover food.

Jessica knew it was time to go and could feel a voice in her head practically screaming at her but, without thinking, she was suddenly digging through the bin. It stank and she didn't want to think about the slime she could feel on her hands but she pulled out small carrier bags full of rubbish, digging her nails in to rip them open and then dumping the contents back into the container as she fingered through whatever was in them.

She took out a supermarket carrier bag, which had been tied at the top, ripping the sides open. Some sort of liquid oozed down her arm as she dropped it back into the bin but, as she did so, something heavier fell out. She used her phone to light up the area and reached in to see what had dropped. In among a small pile of old filtered coffee and drained tea bags, Jessica used her thumb and forefinger to pull out a small plastic object. It was sticky and clearly damaged but Jessica had no doubt what it was and who it belonged to.

It was Carrie's mobile phone.

26

It might have been the wind or the drying dampness stuck to her arms but Jessica felt a chill spiral down her back. She was fixed to the spot, sliding the top part of the phone upwards then downwards and staring into the pile of rubbish. The smell was no longer affecting her, the stinking aroma was nothing compared to the shock she felt at what she was holding. Jessica tried pressing the button to turn it on but then realised there was no back panel and no battery. She used her finger to scratch into the compartment where there should have been a SIM card but it was empty.

She quickly realised her mistake. Her fingerprints would be all over the phone now too. Even if she took it to a superior officer and said she found it in DCI Farraday's bin, all he would have to do was deny it. If he had used gloves to lift it from the scene there would be only her marks on it and who would believe a mad woman who claimed to have found it rooting through other people's rubbish?

Jessica had a connection from Farraday to Carrie's death and John Mills's stabbing. If the lab results came back the way they all expected them to, the latest attacks would also be linked to the killings of Craig Millar, Benjamin Webb, Desmond Hughes and Lee Morgan. That meant she had an indirect link from the DCI to everything that had happened but she couldn't believe her own stupidity. She had blown it and was holding evidence she couldn't use and a theory she would have to keep to herself. The only thing she could console herself with was that her paranoia hadn't been misplaced. It wasn't much of a relief though, given she knew she would have to act on her own.

There were still so many things she would have to figure out, not least how Donald McKenna tied into it all, but at least she knew who she was up against.

Jessica pocketed her own phone and Carrie's, not even being careful to keep the mess that was on her hands from getting on her clothes. She put the lid down on the bin and stepped back towards the hedge line to walk towards the gate. She was almost halfway towards the exit when she froze. A car had turned off the road and its headlights were now shining through the gate. If she had been five yards further ahead, the lamps would have been pointing straight at her.

Jessica quickly walked backwards as she saw a silhouetted figure get out of the car and walk towards the gates. The person stood next to the box that was by the gate, presumably typing in some sort of code as Jessica dashed backwards towards the garage. She didn't want to be caught by the headlights and moved into the alley that ran alongside the house.

There was a large plastic water butt next to a side door. Jessica was beginning to feel the pain in her ankle from where she had landed after jumping the gate. Each time she pressed down, she felt jolts flaming up through the joint. She could hear the car moving down the driveway and risked a look around the corner of the house but saw straight away she had made another error. The bin had initially been in an alcove next to the garage but she had bumped it so it was now partially blocking the door.

She watched as Farraday stepped out of the driver's seat and walked towards the object. Jessica knew she should move backwards so there was no danger of being seen but instead felt transfixed. He pulled the bin backwards and Jessica thought he was going to move it back into place but then felt a twinge in her chest as he flipped the lid over and looked inside. She knew straight away there was something wrong. She had just dumped the torn-open bags on top and, instead of the sealed-up rubbish, he would have seen the unfiltered mess. The car lamps were illuminating the scene for her as she saw him reach in but quickly withdraw his hand, not wanting to touch what was inside. He closed the lid but stood next to the container apparently not knowing what to do.

Jessica crept backwards and hunched behind the water butt, grimacing because of the pain in her ankle and waiting to hear the garage door open or the engine rev again. Instead there was just the sound of the wind and the quiet hum of the car idling in neutral. The size of the water container shielded her from view but she felt watched. She didn't want to risk peering around towards the end of the building. She closed her eyes and held her breath before finally hearing the garage door sliding upwards. She breathed out slowly as the car pulled in and then the door slid shut again. Jessica didn't know if the man would have to come back out of the garage to go into the house or if there was an internal door. During the party they had all been to, she hadn't really left the main living-room area.

Apart from the wind, Jessica couldn't hear anything. She sat and waited, gently rubbing her ankle before eventually stepping back towards the side of the house. She almost expected to see the chief inspector standing beside the garage door as she looked around the corner but there was nothing. Gritting her teeth and ignoring the pain from her leg, Jessica ran as fast as she could to the gate. She could feel her ankle wanting to give way but ignored it, pushing off on her stronger leg and jumping up onto the gate. It had been much easier to get over the first time around but she used her shoulders and upper arms to pull hard on the top of the gate frames and haul herself over, carefully lowering herself down on the other side.

She didn't look back as she half-ran, half-hobbled over to her car. She immediately realised that if Farraday had ever taken notice of the vehicle she drove, there was a good chance he would have seen it parked on the road as he pulled his own car in. But seeing as he didn't seem to know anyone's first name, that was far from a given.

She unlocked the door and slumped into the driver's seat, finally feeling able to breathe properly. Jessica dug the key out of her pocket and realised for the first time just how dirty her hands and arms were. She turned the key and felt the engine roar to life but didn't risk putting the headlights on.

Before she pulled away she looked back at the house

and saw a lone silhouette standing in an upstairs window illuminated by the light from inside.

It took three people to ask if she was all right the next morning before Jessica finally snapped and launched into a barrage of swear words that would have shown them she definitely wasn't.

She had showered when she got in the night before but barely slept, with vivid dreams waking her each time she dropped off. By the time she got to the station, it had almost become a game to add up how little sleep she'd had. She even wrote it down on the notepad she kept on her desk. Her head struggled with the maths but the computer's calculator helped. She didn't feel the same person as she wrote '6/48' on the pad.

She estimated she'd had six hours of sleep in the last forty-eight – and that was being generous, adding up the ten minutes here and the fifteen minutes there from the night before.

For some reason she worked out how many hours that would equate to over a week, writing '21' on the pad. Then she looked on an Internet site and read you were supposed to get eight hours' sleep a night. Again using the calculator to do the maths, she wrote '56'.

You were supposed to sleep for fifty-six hours a week but she was on for twenty-one, not even a full day. Jessica looked at the numbers and let her eyes drift in and out of focus.

Her mobile phone beeped and stunned her out of the

daze. It was another text message from Adam. She had deleted two more the night before but clicked to open the latest one.

'RU OK? Miss U. Worried. Pls call. Ad. X'

She read the words over three times and then deleted the message.

In the hours since finding Carrie's phone, Jessica didn't know if the figure in Farraday's upstairs window had seen her or not. A couple of times when she had woken up in the night she had reached out onto her nightstand to make sure Carrie's phone was still there and that she hadn't dreamed it. When she finally pulled herself out of bed feeling worse than she had when she got into it, she knew she was on her own. Unless DCI Farraday challenged her directly, she would say nothing to him and not risk testing his authority again.

Herself, Reynolds and Cole had their regular briefing with the chief inspector that morning and if he had recognised Jessica the night before, he didn't say anything. The first set of autopsy results were back but all they showed was that DC Jones had bled to death due to the stab wound in her neck. The weapon was consistent with the knife that had been used to kill the other four victims but the lab team still had a lot to do.

John Mills had stabilised in hospital and his life was no longer under threat but the doctors still had no idea if he would regain consciousness. He too had been stabbed in the neck and once in the chest but nothing major had been hit. Jessica thought about the injustice that he could survive while her friend hadn't.

After the briefing, she went back to her office and phoned the labs. Jessica asked the receptionist to put her through to the supervisor directly, knowing there would be no risk of having to talk to Adam.

The lab manager explained that it would be a while until any results would be available because there was such a jumble of blood at the scene. As well as that of DC Jones and Mills, the man's girlfriend had contaminated the scene by touching the bodies before calling the police. There was also diesel on the driveway which had complicated matters and it would take time to separate it all out.

So far, nothing else had been found.

It didn't really matter to Jessica if the results came back with another link to Donald McKenna, her priority was to try to connect the prisoner to Farraday. Given everything she had found, there had to be something. On the surface she was working with the rest of the team in the same way she should be but, when she had time alone, she was hunting for that link.

The obvious theory was that the DCI was somehow planting blood or hair from the inmate at the scenes although, apart from to cover his own tracks, she had no idea why it was McKenna in particular he was using. She knew from Adam how hard that would be but the chief inspector must have seen enough crime scenes over the years to have a pretty good idea how things should look.

She checked to see if McKenna had committed any offences out of the county that the DCI could have been involved with but there was nothing. Without going to the personnel department, she wouldn't be able to find out things like the chief inspector's exact age or place of birth so couldn't tell for sure if there was anything in the past that connected them. She knew they must be roughly the same age and tried using the Internet to see if it threw up any links but there was nothing.

The thought occurred to her that perhaps the warden, Lee Morgan, had helped get the blood and hair samples for Farraday and maybe he had been killed to stop him revealing anything? There was so little she had to go on though. The prison officer had no criminal record and all she had were his basic details. With her boss's personnel file beyond her reach and the Internet offering up nothing to pair him with McKenna, she had nowhere to go.

She thought about approaching Superintendent Aylesbury. The two of them had bonded before he had been promoted but it seemed like such a long time ago and he was always keen on using the correct authority structure. Jessica knew she had no evidence anyway. She couldn't hand over Carrie's phone and the constable's personnel file might well have been returned by now. Even if it was still in the DCI's drawer upstairs it didn't show anything conclusive. The chief inspector being first at the scene could be easily explained by him being called by the desk sergeant as well. It was all circumstantial and proved nothing.

Jessica sat at her desk and leant back in her chair with her eyes shut allowing the exhaustion to grip her. As she drifted off to sleep, she realised she had absolutely no idea what to do next.

27

Jessica spent the next nine days trying to act normally but her nightlife was catching up with her. Each evening she would drive to the estate Farraday lived on, park two streets away and then sit on a low wall opposite his house simply watching. Sometimes she would do it for half an hour but on one occasion she waited until half past five in the morning then went home, had a shower, got changed and drove to the station.

Jessica had no idea what she was hoping to see but justified the way she was acting by the fact no one had been killed since. She knew the chief inspector hadn't left his house overnight and, in her mind, that meant she had prevented anyone else being murdered.

Sitting in on the daily briefings made her feel sick. She had to watch Farraday talk each morning and endure the cold way he said the word 'Jones'. Jessica had hidden the mobile phone she found under her bed but would take it out each morning, sliding the top part up and down over and over.

Her obsession with sleep was consuming her. Each morning she would add to the numbers written on the pad on her desk. Sometimes she felt as if she were deliberately keeping herself awake just to have a little less sleep than the night before.

She felt an arm shaking her gently. 'Jess?'

Jessica jolted awake and could hear the *rat-a-tat-tat* noise of the train she was sitting on speeding along its tracks. 'Are you okay?' the voice asked.

Jessica shook her head and opened her eyes. The flashes of green outside the window were disorientating as she tried to clear her head.

Rat-a-tat-tat.

'Yeah, I just dropped off for a moment.' She blinked a few times and looked across the table to see Rowlands's concerned face. He had that sideways tilt to his head she so hated. 'Where are we?' Jessica asked, pushing herself back into the seat and trying to get comfortable.

'Not sure. Somewhere Welshy.' Rowlands was smiling but Jessica could tell it didn't have the same feeling behind it as it might have done a few weeks ago.

'How long was I asleep?'

'Dunno but you'd started dribbling so I thought I'd wake you.'

Jessica reached up to wipe her chin but it was dry.

Her colleague winked at her. 'Gotcha.'

She forced a smile but there was no sincerity. 'Have you ever been before?'

'Aberystwyth? Nope.'

After over a week of tests, Carrie's body had been released back to her family for the funeral. Jessica was always going to be one of the officers representing the force but Rowlands insisted he wanted to go too. DCI Farraday said he had too much work to do and Jessica knew Cole had a lot on.

'Did you see this?' Rowlands said, holding up a news-paper.

Jessica shook her head but reached out to take it. She read through the front page and then turned inside, skimming through the article. 'Changed their tune, haven't they?'

'Not surprising though, is it?'

'Why did it have to take one of us dying before they finally decided killing people was wrong?'

A few days previously the labs had isolated the various samples taken from Carrie's body and found a single hair that had a DNA match to Donald McKenna. There was a mixture of excitement and disappointment around the station with people not knowing if it was a good thing. Cole had been consistently talking to the CPS about the possibility of a prosecution but there was no way they felt a jury would convict.

The prisoner's DNA was directly connected to four killings and one attempted murder and he was the prime suspect in Lee Morgan's death too but they could do nothing. She and Cole visited the inmate again but hadn't found out anything more than they had managed before. For the first time since they started working together, Jessica told her boss she wanted him to lead the questioning but the prisoner had nothing new to say.

Her own investigations into Farraday weren't going anywhere either. She had even tried staying late on a couple of evenings in case the personnel department left their office unlocked but they were more professional than that. She knew she was clutching at straws but couldn't think of anything better to do.

'Nice piece about Carrie in the *Herald*, wasn't it?' Jessica added as the train continued to thunder along.

'Terrific.'

'Did you tell Garry you liked it?'

Rowlands said nothing, still refusing to acknowledge he knew the journalist. 'Did you see the bit about Daniel Wilkin?' he said instead.

Jessica skimmed through the pages until she saw what he was talking about. Everything that had happened in the past few weeks was blending together for Jessica and had been utterly overshadowed by her growing obsession with Farraday. She remembered the e-fit of the student and read the piece. He had pleaded guilty to a charge of manslaughter and been given bail with very strict conditions to reside at his parents' house with a tagged curfew. From experience, Jessica knew people accused of murder or manslaughter very rarely got bail but Daniel Wilkin really was no threat to anyone.

She looked up to Rowlands. 'I'm glad they gave him bail.'

'He's still going to end up going down.'

Jessica shrugged, knowing the constable was right. She wondered what Arthur and Jackie Graves would consider as justice for their son.

'Have you heard anything from that stalker guy who confessed?' Rowlands added.

'Nothing. He's tagged on a curfew as part of his bail.

I didn't really get the sense he was dangerous anyway, just weird.'

Jessica didn't read the rest of the crime coverage in the newspaper but turned to the gossip and celebrity section. Usually these would be the pages she immediately skimmed past but something about the inanity of it all was reassuring. No matter who had died and how much of a mess the world was in, there was always some orange-skinned semi-naked nobody whining to the papers about her boyfriend.

In recent days, a few of the papers had started to carry angles about the mystery over the DNA evidence. Given the number of bodies and the people who knew within the station, there was always likely to be a leak at some stage. Ultimately, the media didn't know how to report it either. There were a few smaller stories about the bodies being linked to the prison but McKenna wasn't mentioned by name. Another article said there was confusion over the exact nature of the forensic evidence, which was true but not because they didn't know what it was telling them, simply because they didn't know what to do about it.

The train finally pulled into Aberystwyth's train station and they took a taxi to the church. Jessica and Rowlands entered through enormous thick wooden doors at the front and Jessica felt tiny as she peered to either side and saw huge stained-glass windows stretching high towards the ceiling. The roof towered far above them, the soft organ music being played at the front echoing around.

The venue was old and majestic and reminded Jessica of being young when her school would go to the local church once a week. Back then, she was at an age where Jesus was as mystical a figure as Santa Claus and she firmly believed God had created everything around her in seven days. She enjoyed being in the school choir and singing hymns once a week was one of the things she looked forward to most.

Jessica sat next to Rowlands on the hard wooden bench. She was on the end of a row and stretched her ankle out into the aisle, rotating it gently. She wasn't sure if she had sprained it jumping down from the gate but had strapped it tightly each morning to try to stop herself limping. If DCI Farraday had seen her shadow leaving his house he would have seen her hobbling and she didn't want to give him any clues by limping around the station too.

The service was far more positive than Jessica would have expected. One of Carrie's old friends told a story about how she had gone missing for an afternoon when they were still at school. It wasn't like her to miss lessons and no one knew where she was. When people had realised she wasn't at home either, there had been a panic over the missing girl. It turned out she had somehow managed to lock herself in a toilet cubicle and, in an age before mobile phones, hadn't been able to tell anyone. A caretaker found her in tears as the school was being locked up. As the speaker finished the story, there was a mix of tears and laughs, which Jessica felt summed her friend up perfectly.

The woman's mother spoke movingly about her daughter and, along with some readings and hymns, the ceremony engrossed Jessica more than anything had managed to in the last week or so. She didn't even feel tired and had a clearness of thought she'd not felt in a while.

The burial was in the graveyard attached to the church. The casket was closed, which Jessica assumed was because of the work the forensics team had had to do to the body. At the smaller ceremony outside, the vicar said the Joneses were a major part of the local community and that Carrie was being buried next to her grandparents. It was heartbreaking for Jessica to watch the two parents say goodbye to their daughter and, while the mother was holding things together, the father was a mess and couldn't stop himself breaking down.

There was a wake in the church hall a few hundred yards away and Jessica wasn't surprised to see Carrie's father hadn't made it. As soon as they entered the hall, the dead officer's mother sought them out.

'You must be Jessica,' the woman said before turning to Rowlands. 'And David, yes?' Her accent was far stronger than her daughter's but there was a similarity to Carrie's voice that stretched beyond just the accent.

Jessica introduced herself and DC Rowlands properly and the woman gave them both a hug. 'I'm so glad it was you two who came down,' she said. 'Carrie would talk about you all the time. It was always hard for her being away from home but I know she valued the pair of you.'

Jessica felt embarrassed that, despite their friendship, she had never asked the obvious question about why Carrie lived so far away from home. She always assumed her friend had moved north to go to university or something similar but it seemed very selfish she had not been interested enough to find out for sure.

'That's nice of you to say,' Jessica said.

'Are you able to tell me anything about . . . what happened?'

It was the question Jessica was dreading. She stumbled over some vague-sounding, 'We're doing all we can' nonsense, which was exactly the kind of police-speak the general public hated. In truth, she didn't know what else to say. The only other options were either to give the official line, 'No, the man we think did it is locked in prison and we don't have a clue,' or instead tell her, 'I think our chief inspector did it but I made a mess of handling the evidence and have no idea how to fix things'. Neither of those options would be good enough even at the best of times, let alone now.

The woman looked disappointed but nodded sympathetically. 'It's okay, dear, I know you'll be doing all you can.'

Carrie's mother gave Jessica her phone number and both detectives left her a card just in case she wanted to call them. After that, they found a quiet corner and had a drink, trying not to catch anyone else's eye. Jessica felt they had to stay for a while out of respect but she didn't want to get into any further conversations with people.

'That was awkward,' Dave said.

Jessica shrugged at him as if to say, 'What can you do?'

'How's Adam by the way?' he continued. 'He seemed like a really nice guy at the quiz. I know we didn't really get a chance to talk afterwards but I thought he was a right laugh. Hugo was asking after him too.'

'He's all right.'

Jessica hadn't seen Adam since the early hours of the morning after that night and he had stopped contacting her two days ago. She hadn't replied to any of his texts and ignored the messages he had left at the station for her. She couldn't explain the way she was acting but put him out of her mind, hating herself and Farraday for making her waste evenings watching a house instead of spending them with someone she liked.

'The service was nice,' Dave added.

Jessica nodded, not wanting to make small talk and then thought she heard her phone ringing. Because they had drifted off to a corner they had ended up sitting under a speaker and the music drowned out the ringtone. She took the device out of her pocket and realised she had three missed calls from DI Cole. She moved outside, edging into the car park towards the back of the building.

The air was cool and she shivered with the breeze but pressed the buttons to call him back. He answered straight away. 'Jessica?'

'Yes.'

'I've been trying to get hold of you all afternoon. I forgot about the funeral. How did it go?'

'It was good. Carrie's mother asked us to pass on her thanks to everyone.' Cole sounded distracted, which wasn't like him. 'Is everything okay?' Jessica added.

'Are you back tonight?'

'Yes, we've got a train in an hour or so.'

'Good, because you're not going to believe what they've found in Donald McKenna's cell.'

28

'What?' Jessica said.

'They've pulled a mobile phone out of the pipe that connects his sink to the wall. It was wrapped in a plastic bag to stop it getting wet.'

Jessica remembered wobbling that exact pipe when she had been in his cell, not knowing she was millimetres away from something that could have given them a break weeks ago. 'How did they find it?'

'Some routine cell check. It sounds like they surprised him and he didn't have time to put the tubing together again properly. A guard noticed it was a little out of place and they found the phone.'

'What's happening now?'

'The phone is being examined by the labs to see if they can get anything from it. There's a basic call history we've already got but it's just numbers at the moment. Farraday's been going crazy.'

Jessica wondered if the DCI was frantic because he was worried his number was on the list. 'Do we have matches for any of the numbers?' It was almost as if someone was playing a trick as the reception on her phone crackled at that point and she couldn't make out what Cole was saying.

'Sorry? I can't hear you.' Jessica moved quickly around

the car park to see if she could find a better spot and his voice reappeared mid-sentence. 'Can you say that again?' she asked.

'Can you hear me now? I said there are no matches yet. We don't need a warrant to check numbers to names but there were only two people McKenna had called and as far as we can tell they're both unregistered pre-pay numbers.'

It was a long shot and she doubted the DCI was careless enough to let the prisoner have his main number but they finally had a lead. 'What's happening now?'

'McKenna's in isolation at least overnight. He's been charged with unauthorised possession of a wireless communication device.'

'What does that mean?'

'For us directly? Not much – he'll probably get a few months tagged onto his sentence but he's already in for life. I'm guessing he won't have a cell to himself any longer. I've booked us in to go see him tomorrow afternoon. If he's actually been in contact with someone on the outside it gives us a whole new set of questions to ask.'

Jessica was feeling positive about the case for the first time in a while and said she would see him in the morning. If she could just connect one of those pre-pay phone numbers to the chief inspector that would be enough.

She dashed back into the hall and told Rowlands they had to go. They said their goodbyes to Carrie's mother and Jessica promised to call if they had any major breaks.

In the taxi back to the station and on the train journey

home, they talked about the development. Both of them were excited, passing theories back and forth. Jessica kept her thoughts about the DCI to herself but found it nice to chat like friends again.

'Do you think he got the phone from that warden?' Rowlands asked.

'It's hard to tell, but probably. I know we didn't find any hidden bundles of cash but there was definitely something not right about Morgan's bank records. If McKenna was starting to be linked with crimes happening outside of the prison it's no wonder the warden was getting twitchy if he had smuggled a phone in. If he'd said something to the prisoner about it, maybe that was the trigger – McKenna just phoned whoever he knew on the outside and gave the word for the prison officer to be killed.'

'You know how they get phones in, don't you?'

'I don't really want to think about it.'

'I read this article about some guy who was in court for sentencing and knew he was going to get sent down. He bought this phone from the newsagents and got a SIM card off one of his mates. He put it in one of those plastic sandwich bags, then lubed it up and shoved it up his arse.'

'Eew.'

'I know. He only got caught as he'd given the number to the guy who'd given him the SIM card and his mate phoned to ask how he'd got on in court. He hadn't put it on silent and, because his case had been delayed, he was stood in the dock and the bloody thing started ringing.'

'No way . . .'

'Seriously. The judge didn't realise what was going on at first and was telling whoever the phone belonged to they were in contempt, then one of the security guys realised it was the defendant. They checked his pockets and couldn't find it then he told them where it was.'

'Trust you to remember something like that.'

'I've not even told you the best part yet. The ringtone was "The Birdie Song". Stupid bastard was in court with the tune sounding out.' Jessica laughed and, for the first time since Carrie had died, wasn't even faking it.

When she arrived home, there was still a little tickle in the back of her mind telling her she should be watching DCI Farraday's house just in case but, for the first time in days, she ignored it. With McKenna safely in isolation, there was no way any further crimes could be pinned on him and Jessica was confident the chief inspector wouldn't risk anything.

She went into her bedroom planning to take a towel to the bathroom for a shower but her bed suddenly seemed incredibly appealing. Jessica reached under the covers to look for her nightwear but the sheets and duvet itself had an almost hypnotic hold as she breathed in their smell and finally allowed herself to succumb to the tiredness.

Jessica was feeling clear-headed and determined the next day, eager for the afternoon trip to the prison. She had slept through the entire night in her clothes from the day before. An alarm was permanently set on her phone but she hadn't needed it recently. It was her saviour in the morning though, waking her up when she could have dozed through the day.

At the senior officer briefing, Jessica could see something had changed in Farraday's attitude. The week before he had been combative and happy to throw his weight around but now he seemed downbeat. She still followed her earlier pledge to not openly defy him or push issues such as Carrie's phone records but there was something in his demeanour that almost seemed resigned to whatever was going to happen.

She had half-expected him to announce he was going to interview Donald McKenna himself but that would have been hard for him to justify as he hadn't had much to do with things – plus, if the prisoner was looking to admit to anything, it wouldn't have helped the chief inspector's cause to be present.

At the prison, Jessica and Cole were greeted in the reception area by Dennis but she was relieved to see they weren't the only visitors at that time. After they had been scanned, they were left to talk among themselves as the man continued registering the afternoon's other visitors. Instead of the governor meeting them, it was someone Jessica didn't recognise. They introduced themselves as one of the senior wardens and led the officers along the familiar path up to the interview room.

Cole checked the recording equipment and asked Jessica if she wanted to lead the questioning.

'Just try to stop me.'

McKenna was brought in handcuffed alongside his usual solicitor but he was looking far more dishevelled than the previous time they had met. There was a five o'clock shadow on his chin and his dark hair had started to grow out. He was beginning to look his age too, his wrinkles far more defined, but it was his eyes that surprised Jessica the most. The cool confidence he had displayed before had been replaced by the same look of defiance and resignation most prisoners had when you looked them in the eyes.

'How was the isolation cell?' Jessica asked when they were all sitting. The prisoner said nothing and wouldn't look at her directly. 'I've seen those rooms,' she continued. 'Not very nice, are they? One big stone slab on the floor to sleep on, all that noise of the other prisoners screaming through the night. What was the smell like? That's where all the dirty protestors end up, isn't it? Bit of a difference from having a cosy double cell to yourself, I reckon.'

McKenna wasn't reacting and Jessica could sense his solicitor was about to step in. 'So let's talk about the phone, shall we?' The prisoner was staring at his own cuffed hands, refusing to speak or acknowledge he was being asked anything. 'Oh, come on, Donald, you were so keen to engage the last few times we've been in. Aren't we friends any longer? You can't have been that quiet on the phone, well, unless you used it for dirty phone calls. Is that what gets you off, all that heavy breathing?'

'You don't know what you're talking about.'

'So were you just using the phone to play games or something? Maybe you needed the calendar on there to manage your busy diary? What is it? Wake up 7 a.m, breakfast at eight, table tennis at nine, pottery classes at eleven?

I don't think you need a phone to remind you of all that.'

McKenna's solicitor finally interrupted. 'Is there really any need to taunt my client?'

'Oh, I'm sorry. I wouldn't want to hurt his feelings. I know he must be of a delicate persuasion.'

The inmate had clearly had enough and banged his fists on the table. 'Just ask your damn questions.'

'Fine. Question number one: where did you get the phone that was found in your cell?'

'No comment.'

'It wasn't a miracle then? It didn't just materialise out of nowhere?'

'Don't ridicule my beliefs.'

'Faith still strong?'

'I fight temptation every day. Sometimes I don't reach the levels I should.'

Jessica nodded. McKenna still hadn't met her eyes but the final words did actually sound genuine. She had no idea if his religious conversion was genuine or not but pushing him on it wasn't going to get her anywhere. 'Who did you call? We know there were two numbers but who did they belong to?'

'No comment.'

'How long have you had it?'

'No comment.'

Jessica sighed and looked behind her towards Cole, then at the man's solicitor before finally focusing on the prisoner again. 'What are you hoping to achieve by refusing to answer questions?'

'What have I got to gain? I'm probably going to die in here so what do you want me to say? Grasses aren't very popular around these parts.'

'Okay, but if you are a believer and genuinely have no knowledge of everything that has been going on outside of here, then why wouldn't you do everything possible to clear your name?'

'I'm at peace with myself. I know I've done nothing wrong and if you don't believe me then maybe it is part of His plan?'

'So why not tell me about the phone? Tell us who you were talking to and why you had it.'

'No.'

'Did you have Lee Morgan killed because he smuggled you in the mobile and was beginning to ask questions?'

'I don't know what you're talking about.'

'It's how you did it though, isn't it? Is that why you allowed your accomplice to plant your blood and hairs at the scene, so that we'd be looking at you instead of them?'

'No comment.'

'Why won't you give us the name? Is it because you're scared?'

'Mortals don't frighten me. I'm only worried by His judgement when the day of reckoning comes.'

'I thought you said you didn't want to "grass" because of what could happen.' McKenna said nothing. 'If you're so worried about your day of reckoning, wouldn't it be better to tell us everything you know?

The prisoner clearly had no intention of adding anything and his solicitor spoke again. 'Detectives, I've said

305

before, if you want to charge my client with anything then please do so. You can't keep returning here and endlessly ask him the same questions over and over. He has repeatedly told you he knows nothing.'

Jessica looked from the solicitor back to McKenna. She had one final question and wanted to make sure she could see any changes to his expression. 'Final question then, Donald. Is the reason you won't talk to us because there's someone in authority you're worried about? Perhaps a person that's high up in the prison service or a senior police officer?' She felt Cole fidget nervously in the seat next to her but more importantly thought she saw the smallest amount of recognition on the prisoner's face. His top lip and the bottom part of his nose twitched as if he were about to say something but he stayed silent.

'I think we're done here,' Jessica said. She had been thinking of Farraday and wondered if that was what had crossed McKenna's mind when she thought she saw that flicker of movement.

After the prisoner had been escorted out, Jessica and Cole were left in the interview room waiting for someone to take them back to the entrance. 'What was that last question about?' he asked.

'Nothing really, I was just wondering if there's someone else working here who might have something to hide?'

Jessica wasn't sure if her superior was convinced but he didn't follow his question up.

'Didn't get much, did we?' he asked instead.

'I don't think either of us were really expecting to. The problem with the life prisoners is they have nothing to lose by keeping quiet. It's not as if their sentence is going to be overturned. I still don't know if this whole religion thing is a front but either way he doesn't have much to say.'

A minute or two later, a guard knocked on the door and led them back to the front office. Dennis asked them both to sign out and they walked through the main doors towards the car. As they got to the vehicle, Jessica started flicking through the files she was holding. 'I think I might have left something in reception. Can you wait here a minute?' she said.

Cole looked a little confused but shrugged his shoulders and nodded. Jessica walked quickly back to the office. She knew she hadn't left anything but there was one more thing she wanted to do. She beckoned Dennis over towards the door away from any of the other staff in the room. He looked surprised to see her returning but moved over to her.

'Are you okay?' he asked.

'Dennis, how long have you worked here?'

He seemed confused and a little shy given that she was talking to him directly. He stuttered as he replied. 'A few years.'

'Have you always been on reception?'

'Yes but I'm in the training programme so I can move onto the wings.'

'Do all visitors come through here?'

'Yes, this is where the body scanners are. Even the governor and staff have to pass through them each day.'

Jessica reached into one of the envelopes she was

carrying and took out a clipping from the previous week's newspaper. Originally it had been a story about Carrie's death but at the bottom of the page had been a photograph of DCI Farraday that was taken at a press conference. Jessica had cut the photo out without its caption so it wasn't obvious who the image was of. She handed it over to Dennis. 'Do you know if this man has ever visited here? Maybe in the past six months or so?'

Dennis took the picture and looked at it, narrowing his eyes and then pushing out his bottom lip. 'He sort of seems familiar but I wouldn't want to say for sure. I can ask around if you want?'

'That's fine,' she said. 'I'll give you my number.'

She didn't want to give him an official card so instead wrote her mobile number on the back of the picture. 'Can you try to be discreet. Only call me if someone's sure they've seen this person. It doesn't really help if people aren't one hundred per cent certain.'

Dennis nodded nervously at her.

Jessica left the reception for the second time in a few minutes and headed back to the car. She knew it was a gamble but thought of Carrie's mother and the funeral she had been at the previous day. She wanted a result for them. If news did somehow make its way back to the chief inspector she would simply say Dennis had misunderstood what she asked him to do. She doubted the man would end up reporting anything though. Cole had been right on their first visit and the man's nervousness had given him away; he definitely had a thing for her. Jessica hoped he didn't follow it up by calling her for no reason.

As she was approaching her car, Jessica took her phone out to turn the volume back up having muted it for the visit. She had a few unimportant emails but also a missed call and another text message from Adam. She thought about deleting it but out of pure curiosity she clicked to open it.

'Call me pls. Urgent. Not abt us.'

Jessica had reached the car but didn't open the door to get in. She didn't particularly want to talk to him but the way he had worded the message was different to the others he had sent. Jessica ducked to look through the car's window and catch Cole's eye. She pointed to her phone to let him know she had to make a call. He nodded and she turned around, leaning back on the car before dialling Adam's number.

He answered after one ring. 'Hello?'

'Hi, Adam.'

'Oh God, look, um, thanks for calling.' Jessica hoped she hadn't been duped into contacting him for personal reasons. She knew it was all her fault but couldn't face things just yet. He soon told her the reason for calling. 'I've not told my boss yet, Jess, but I think I've got something. I've tested and re-tested all morning. I think Donald McKenna has a sister.'

29

Jessica felt an enormous sense of familiarity as it had only been a day ago she'd had a phone conversation where she couldn't quite take in what she was being told. 'I'm sorry, what?'

'A sister. I know there's nothing in his birth records or anything like that but there's something not right here.'

'Are you at Bradford Park?'

'Yes.'

'We're coming over.' Jessica hung up and quickly got in the car, telling Cole they had to go to the laboratories. When he asked why, she said she wasn't completely sure but something big was happening.

She knew from experience the inspector was a steady driver but tried to stay patient during the journey across the city. Jessica had seen the records herself which all said Donald McKenna was an only child. An officer had even photocopied his birth certificate and related family documents from the local register office and they knew there were no other known relatives. The idea of him having a sister was barely believable.

Eventually they pulled into the labs' car park and Jessica made for reception, Cole lagging behind. Her haste didn't do her any good as they had to wait for someone to lead them through to the lab areas anyway. They were greeted by a woman Jessica didn't know and Adam, who nervously kept his eyes on the floor. She introduced herself as the head scientist for the facility and knew Jessica because they had talked on the phone. She led them into a small office where the four of them sat around a table.

'I know why you're here,' the woman said, 'but I should tell you we don't have one hundred per cent confirmation for you yet. I think Adam should be able to fill you in.'

Adam looked at Cole and his boss but refused to acknowledge Jessica. She didn't blame him but hung on everything he said. 'We had a routine request come in this morning from the Avon and Somerset Police force. They arrested a woman in Bristol last week on suspicion of grievous bodily harm. Because of the severity of the incident she was remanded but in the meantime they logged her swab onto the National DNA Database. That's all completely normal but what happens on the system is that it links together family members.'

His boss cut in. 'The reason it does that is if we go to a scene and get a blood sample or something like that, we might not find an exact match for it in the database because the person has no criminal record. But we could end up with something like a fifty per cent match which would indicate the culprit was a parent or sibling of someone we already had registered.'

'That's pretty clever,' Cole said. 'So even if you don't have the person on your system you can tell if they're related?'

'Right,' said the woman. 'Sorry, Adam, you tell them.'

Jessica said nothing, eagerly waiting to hear what they had found.

'After they logged the DNA, it gave them a quarter match to Donald McKenna, which might mean this woman was his half-sister or aunt or niece or something like that. Because Mr McKenna has no known relatives, they called this morning to say it looked like there might be a mistake on the system. It wouldn't usually happen but an error like that would be so rare the guy down there thought he would check.'

The female scientist cut in again. 'With the notoriety of McKenna at the moment, Adam did a full retest on the sample and passed it back through to the Bristol labs where they confirmed it. This woman is definitely related to him.'

'Do we know how?' Jessica asked.

'I don't want to baffle you all with science but we check something called "mitochondrial DNA",' the woman said. 'This is only inherited from your mother and is how you can follow a family line backwards. Through looking at that, we know McKenna and the woman in Bristol are half-siblings and have the same mother but different fathers.'

'Does that mean this woman could be responsible for the murders up here?' Jessica asked.

'No, it's not as simple as that,' the lab manager answered. 'We know this woman is related but, at the same time, her sample is still different to her half-brother's. It's only a partial match.'

'Has anyone told this woman or asked her if she knows McKenna?' Cole asked.

'I can't tell you if she already knows but, from our end, the only people aware are us and the Bristol lab.'

'Good work,' Jessica said.

'It's Adam you should thank,' his boss replied. 'He was the one who spotted it. We have one final round of testing to do but you'll have confirmation one way or the other by the end of the day.'

Adam kept his head down as Cole congratulated him and Jessica made sure she spoke at the exact same time as her boss so her words would be drowned out.

'While we're here,' Jessica said, 'is this where McKenna's phone was brought?'

'Yes and no,' replied the female scientist. 'It is this building but on a different floor. I can take you up if you want?'

Jessica was relieved that Adam stayed behind as the woman led them upstairs towards a department that worked with electronics. They didn't get anything new from the people who had been testing the phone though. The expert said they had only been able to extract the numbers that had been stored in the phone book, which they already had. As far as they could tell it had never called a different number, had never received a call and no text messages had either been sent or opened.

Pretty much the only thing it did tell them was that, whatever was happening, it was likely McKenna was calling the shots in one way or another as people weren't calling him, he was phoning them.

Back at the station, Jessica was looking forward to telling Farraday what had happened. Cole did the speaking but Jessica didn't take her eyes from the DCI. She wondered if he already knew about McKenna's sister and if she was somehow connected to everything that was going on. If he did know, or if he was surprised, he showed no emotion at all.

Having already spent large parts of one day on a train to Wales that week, Jessica had another journey to Bristol, this time with Cole. Neither of them were big on small talk and Jessica spent the trip flicking through a magazine and reading Internet sites on her phone. She had half-expected either Adam or Dennis to message her the night before but there had been no contact. For the second evening running she felt confident enough not to watch the chief inspector's house and had another uninterrupted night of sleep.

After their train arrived at the station, they caught a taxi from the rank outside but the driver didn't know where he was going. Jessica checked the papers she had printed out the night before and told him the prison they were looking for was next to a village called 'Falfield' north of the city.

Eastwood Park Prison was about as different to Manchester's as Jessica could have imagined. The one in the north handled 1,300 of the most serious male offenders with the one McKenna's half-sister was at holding 350 lower-risk females. Strangeways was full of heavy metal doors and cells that stretched three storeys high but the building Jessica and Cole were shown into had a mixture of one- and two-storey rooms and everything was decorated in more delicate cream and red colours.

Back at Manchester, even when the wing had been cleared for her to look at McKenna's cell, Jessica had felt an air of menace that wasn't present at the women's prison. She didn't doubt there were still plenty of unsavoury things that went on behind closed doors but thought the atmosphere was more geared towards education and rehabilitation than it was where McKenna was based.

The governor greeted them both at the entrance of the prison and was far cheerier than the one at Strangeways. The previous evening, Cole had established the prisoner's name was Mary O'Connor and spoke to the governor, assuring him the woman wasn't suspected of any further crime but that they wanted to speak to her as a potential witness.

On arrival, they first went to the governor's office where they explained to him their situation and said there was a good chance Mary might not know she had a brother. It was good practice given as the man's staff would have to deal with the prisoner once they had left.

He led them through to an empty visiting room and Mary O'Connor was brought through uncuffed and sat opposite them. Two prison guards stood close enough to act if there were any problems but far enough away so they weren't in earshot. Jessica introduced herself and DI Cole and explained they had travelled down from Manchester to see her.

The woman had long black hair with grey strands around her ears. Facially she wasn't similar to McKenna but Jessica could see her light blue eyes were identical; they must have inherited them from their mother. The colour seemed familiar to Jessica in another way too but she couldn't place them.

Jessica checked the woman's name and then her age. 'What I've got to say may or may not come as a shock to you, Mary,' Jessica said. 'But do you know you have a brother?'

The woman smiled at them. 'Not me, you must be thinking of another Mary O'Connor. I was brought up on my own and my ma and dad died years ago.'

'I'm sorry, Mary, but we're not telling you this because of your name, it's because of the mouth swab you gave when you were arrested. I don't want to make it too complicated but basically that sample was matched to someone else in prison and it shows you're related as you have the same mother.'

Mary's smile had begun to slip as Jessica spoke and her expression was now a look of pure puzzlement. She had an accent that was hard to place. There was definitely a twinge of Irish but something from the local area too. 'Is he younger or older than me?'

'Younger by a couple of years.'

'See, that's why it must be a mistake. My ma couldn't have children after me. She always told me they wanted to have a big family but there was some medical problem so I ended up on my own.'

'I can't tell you whether what you were told was right or not, Mary, but these tests aren't wrong. I know it's a bit scientific but we brought these papers down for you.'

Jessica reached into an envelope and pushed some sheets across the table. She had looked over them herself on the train. The language wasn't the clearest but even from the graphics you could see that whatever it was displaying matched the other part. 'I'm sorry, I don't read well,' the woman said. Jessica told Mary the man's name was Donald McKenna and did her best to show her the parts of the chart she should be looking at but felt hampered as she wasn't completely certain either.

The woman rubbed her head and grimaced. 'If this is right, what are you saying? That my mum is his mum?'

'Well, that's partly why we're here, we don't know. We have a copy of Mr McKenna's birth certificate and wondered if we could compare it to yours?'

'You'll do well, I've never had one.'

Jessica looked to Cole and back again. 'How is that possible?'

'My ma and dad were travellers and we moved around a lot. There was always some kind of work. Usually you'd get married in the community but they died before I was an adult and it wasn't the life for me. I ended up settling around this area.'

'But how did you get work, a passport or driving licence?'

'Never had a passport or driving licence but I did get a national insurance number. I don't know if it's easier now but I got passed from agency to agency back then. Eventually someone was given my case and sorted it out. They told me it's not completely uncommon for traveller children to be unregistered and reckoned they get three or four every year. It didn't stop them arsing me about for a couple of years but I ended up with a number that lets me work. I still don't have a birth certificate though.'

Mary looked as if it was a story she was familiar with telling. Given the employers, councils and other organisations that would have asked the question over the years, it wasn't surprising.

'That's mad,' Jessica said.

'You're telling me. I've had to put up with this all my life.'

A possibility was occurring to Jessica. 'Mary, can I ask you something personal?'

The woman looked back at her. 'I think you're going to ask me something I've had in the back of my mind for the past fifty-odd years.'

'Do you think there's a chance your parents weren't actually *your* parents?'

Tears suddenly formed in the prisoner's eyes and Jessica felt guilty for asking it. Given she was locked up, Mary was about as calm an inmate as Jessica had ever met. She found herself wondering how on earth this mild person in front of her had assaulted someone seriously enough to end up here. Jessica motioned for one of the guards, who picked up some tissues from one of the other tables and brought them over. Mary took one and blew her nose. 'I guess it would answer a lot of questions,' she finally said through the tears.

'The problem is, Mary, that Mr McKenna's mother has also passed away and there's no father listed on his birth certificate. Without your parents, the way I understand it is that we have no way of knowing whether you and he shared "your" mother or "his" mother. All we know is that you definitely had different fathers. Your dad could well still be your own.'

'So you're saying that, one way or the other, either my ma or my dad was definitely not mine? Either my dad went with his ma or my ma went with someone else?'

Jessica took a deep breath, trying not to look confused. 'I think so, yes. I'm sorry.'

The woman had tears in her eyes again. 'Does my brother know?'

'Not yet, no.'

'Why is he in prison?'

'An armed robbery. He's serving life.'

Mary looked down at herself and flung her arm into the air. 'I guess we have something in common straight away. It must run in the family.' Jessica said nothing. The woman carried on sniffing. 'Do you think there's any way they would let us meet?'

Jessica felt out of her depth, not knowing the answer. 'I don't know how these things work. You're on remand here, I guess some of it depends on what happens at your trial.'

The woman leant back on her seat, wiping away more tears. 'Not gonna be a trial, m'dear. I'm pleading guilty.'

With little more they could get from the woman, they said their goodbyes and one of the prison officers gave them a lift back to the train station.

When they were back on the train, they sat opposite each other, speaking quietly to avoid being overheard, aware it was unlikely to do any harm but feeling concerned for the woman's privacy.

'What do you reckon?' Cole asked.

'It seems plausible. I don't think she was faking it about not knowing McKenna.'

'Me either. We can check all the national insurance number stuff anyway so there'd be no point in making it up. She seemed keen to meet him too.'

'She must have had some life, with people at every corner asking her to prove who she is.'

'Still, it gives us something huge to work on now.'

Jessica didn't get his point. 'How do you mean, the lab guys said her DNA couldn't be a match to what was found at the scenes.'

'True, but if McKenna's got a long-lost sister who doesn't have a birth certificate then who's to say he doesn't have a long-lost identical twin that was never registered?'

30

Jessica knew instantly he was right but tried not to look surprised or sound as if the idea hadn't occurred to her. 'We could get a photo out to the media and see if anyone recognises him,' she said. 'The papers don't need to know it's a picture of Donald McKenna they're printing, just that we are after someone who looks like that.'

'Exactly, good thinking. We'll get plenty of people calling to say it's Donald McKenna but maybe we'll get a few other names suggested too? We'll have to talk to the chief inspector in the morning.'

Jessica had almost forgotten about Farraday and was trying to figure out how he could be involved. He didn't particularly look like McKenna, although they had a similar physique. She remembered her first meeting with Adam when he told them matching DNA could come only from an identical sibling. The DCI had to be involved somehow though, with the way he had held up the investigation and then the fact he had taken Carrie's phone to cover his tracks. The idea of McKenna having a brother could still be a red herring too.

'I think we should phone it in now,' Jessica said. 'If we can get McKenna's photo on tonight's news, in tomorrow's papers and on the Internet, it gives us a bit of a head start.'

She checked the clock on her phone. They didn't have

much time and couldn't do anything themselves from the train so Cole called the chief inspector. Jessica could hear only one side of the conversation but it didn't sound good. When he had hung up, Jessica asked the obvious question. 'What did he say?'

'He said we should wait until tomorrow and that he wants to talk to us both first. I think he's worried we're going to make another mistake by putting the wrong photo out there.'

'It wasn't *our* mistake last time.'

'I know but he's probably right. If we make sure all the paperwork from the labs is correct first, we can hammer the media with it tomorrow. We'll still hit all the TV broadcasts and get it on the Internet, we'll just miss the papers.'

Jessica thought Farraday might well have a different reason for wanting to hold things up – he wanted to give himself a few more hours to cover whatever tracks he might have left.

'We still don't know what's going on, do we?' she said.

'Not really. After all this, it could be McKenna is actually nothing to do with any of it. If there is a twin he could be acting alone safe in the knowledge any crime he commits will get blamed on his brother who's already locked up. Maybe the phone was left in the cell by whoever was in there before McKenna? If there is a twin, perhaps he never realised he had a brother and the coverage could be news to him too? Then again, we could have been right the first time and it is somebody on the outside working with McKenna. There are so many permutations, even if we get the guy we might never know.'

He looked up to make sure he caught Jessica's eye and winked at her. 'There could still be a secret tunnel out of the prison too, remember.'

The thought hadn't occurred to Jessica that McKenna could be completely innocent in it all. She had spent so long trying to think of ways to connect him to the crimes and then to Farraday that it hadn't even crossed her mind the prisoner could now be exonerated.

'If you're right then I guess the phone isn't necessarily relevant to the case either. You're always hearing stories about people smuggling things into jails.' A second thought then popped into her head. 'Hang on though, if McKenna is nothing to do with it, that doesn't explain what happened with the warden Lee Morgan. I know nothing has been proven against him but he must have been killed for a reason.'

'True, but he was the one where no DNA was found so they could be separate cases.'

'Same stab wounds but I guess it could be a copycat thing to puzzle us.'

Cole rubbed his head. 'This is all getting confusing.'

'You're telling me. We have Craig Millar, Benjamin Webb, Desmond Hughes and Carrie who were all definitely killed by either Donald McKenna, someone who planted his DNA or his twin . . .'

'. . . and if there is a twin, either, neither or both brothers may or may not know he has a relation.'

'Er, right.'

'Then there's John Mills, who is still unconscious, and Lee Morgan – who may or may not be connected to all of this as well as McKenna separately.'

The two detectives looked at each other and broke out into grins at the same time. It wasn't meant as anything disrespectful to the victims, more as a way of coping with the complex nature of everything. 'I think we should write this down before trying to explain it to anyone else,' Jessica said.

Cole laughed and said he would while Jessica leant back and closed her eyes. The inspector might think it was intricate but he didn't know the half of it considering what she knew about Farraday as well. At first she pretended to be asleep but, when she felt Cole tapping her forearm and telling her they were back, she realised she actually had dropped off.

It was early evening and beginning to get dark as they walked out of the train station and caught another taxi back to Longsight. Jessica knew the chief inspector would have left early in order to not have to make any decisions about what they were bringing back but wasn't too bothered. With everything that had happened in the past couple of days, she felt as if something had lifted from her and knew she wouldn't be sitting on the wall opposite Farraday's house that night hoping for who knows what.

Jessica drove home and parked in one of the designated spaces at her flat. She switched off the engine and headlights and took her phone out without moving from the driver's seat. It was gloomy outside and the street lamps were just beginning to come on. She thumbed through her contacts and stared at Adam's name.

After a couple of days of proper sleep and the way she finally felt she was coming to terms with Carrie's death, Jessica could see how badly she had treated him. She felt terrible watching him in the office the previous day knowing he had done some really good work but not having the guts to tell him so. Jessica was fully aware he had done nothing wrong and that she should tell him so – but the thought of calling him up and admitting it was all her fault wasn't something she knew if she could do.

It almost felt as if she needed someone like Carrie or Caroline to give her a kick and tell her she was being stupid. She closed her eyes and could almost hear the Welsh officer's accent in her head. 'Stop mucking around and just call him. You obviously like him, y'daft sod.'

What would Jessica say to him though? 'Hey, just calling to say sorry I was a bitch, fancy a pint?' Would he understand she just hadn't known how to react to Carrie's death? Could she tell him about everything that had happened with Farraday? Or about the phone under her bed which belonged to the dead officer and where she'd found it? She didn't know what to do and felt it would be hard to tell him why she had blanked him without explaining everything she knew about the chief inspector.

Jessica sat looking at her phone, watching the screen turn itself off to save the battery and then pressing a button herself to make it come back to life.

'Adam Compton', the name read at the top.

Her thumb hovered over the 'Call Mobile' button and

then the device started ringing before she could make up her mind. It was a number she didn't recognise but she immediately pressed to answer.

'Hello?'

The voice on the other end stuttered and was clearly nervous. 'Um, hello. Is that Detective, erm, Daniel?'

'Yes, who's this?'

'It's Dennis from the prison. You gave me your number. How are you?'

Jessica's heart immediately sank. She had known it was a mistake to pass on her details and felt sure he would end up phoning her at some point. The last thing she wanted was a social call from him. 'I'm fine but a little busy at the moment.'

'Oh, um, I was wondering if you were free this evening? If maybe you wanted a drink or something?'

Jessica had half a mind to tell him to get lost but she forced herself to be polite. 'I don't think that's a good idea. I only gave you my number in case someone recognised the picture.'

'Oh yes, sorry, that's why I'm calling. It's about the picture. Can we meet?'

Jessica didn't know if he was being genuine or not. Something in his voice didn't sound quite right but it could just be his nervousness. 'We can meet in town but I don't really have time for a drink or anything. Does that sound okay?'

Jessica thought that, if he was trying it on, he would change his mind but instead he said 'yes' and asked for an address. She named a pub in the middle of the city, not wanting to be openly seen with him for either professional or personal reasons. At the same time, she didn't feel quite right having the type of illicit meeting she'd had with Garry Ashford in a supermarket car park. Jessica knew the pub wasn't one of the busy ones and should be fairly quiet on a weeknight. She hoped she wasn't wasting her time but turned her engine and headlights back on and reversed out of her space.

As Jessica walked into the pub, she looked around hoping Dennis would already be there so she could make it quick; the last thing she needed was to be left sitting at a table on her own as if she'd been stood up. There was a raised seating area that ran around the whole of the pub, with a wooden banister separating it from the bar and tall tables with stools. Jessica put one hand on the rail and started walking around in a circle to see if she could see him.

The pub was as empty as she could have wished. Aside from a couple of people serving at the bar and a few customers watching football on the other side, there wasn't anyone else present. It was the type of place that had been done up nicely around a decade ago but hadn't had anything renovated since. A thin layer of dust came off on her hands from the rail as she continued walking and she wiped it on her trousers until she finally saw Dennis sitting in a booth at the very back of the pub. He was cradling a pint of bitter and stood as he spotted her.

Jessica walked up the three steps to the raised area and slid herself into the booth opposite him. He followed her lead and sat back down. She had only ever seen him before in the standard uniform of heavy boots, dark trousers and a navy-blue jumper but he definitely must have thought she'd consented to some sort of date given the way he was dressed. As he sat down, the lights caught his black shoes which were either brand new or had been recently shined. He was wearing dark suit-type trousers with a light blue shirt, with the top few buttons undone.

Jessica felt slightly sick at the amount of wiry greying chest hair that was poking out of the top. She tried not to look but the way the hairs spiralled was almost hypnotic. 'I've got to be quick, Dennis,' Jessica said. 'I've got quite a lot on at the moment so only have a few minutes.'

'Are you sure you don't want a drink?'

'Sorry, I'm driving. I never drink on duty anyway.'

It was a little white lie. She didn't drink when she was driving but pretty much every officer she had ever met wasn't averse to a quiet drink, even if their shift wasn't quite over. Dennis's face fell slightly and his scar seemed even more prominent, illuminated by the small spotlights overhead. It really did run the entire length of his face from his mouth to the bottom part of his ear. She almost wanted to ask where he got it but the idea of getting into a full conversation wasn't too appealing.

'Are you sure you don't fancy a soft drink?' he asked.

'Sorry, I'm really in a rush. You said you had some news about the photo?'

Dennis dug into his trouser pocket and took out the newspaper clipping she had given him. Jessica could see instantly it was slightly torn and a lot grubbier than when she had handed it over. He put the photo on the table between them and pushed it towards her. 'Who is this guy anyway?'

Jessica had known it was a gamble to pass on a photo from a newspaper because it would indicate it was of someone semi-important. Aside from printing out something from the force's website where Farraday would have been in uniform, she had no other option. She didn't know if either Dennis or someone else he showed it to would have recognised the image as being of her boss – he was involved in TV appeals – but, at the same time, if you didn't know what you were looking for, he was just another face.

'I can't really tell you that, Dennis.'

The man shuffled in his seat. 'I thought he looked familiar but didn't recognise him directly. I showed him to a couple of the other office guys but they had no idea. One of the late girls reckons he was definitely a regular visitor a few months back.'

From being sceptical about why he had asked to meet, Jessica was suddenly hanging on Dennis's every word. 'What do you mean by "late girls"?'

'Oh, right. Nothing really, just that she does the late shift which is why I don't always see her. I waited around especially though because you asked me . . .'

He was waiting for a compliment but Jessica was feeling too impatient to indulge him. 'What did she say?'

'She used to work on days up until about three or four months back. Everyone's shifts got bumped around and I moved from earlies to days and she moved from days to nights. But she reckoned, when she was on days, he was a regular visitor. She said he looked a bit different, like he had a beard or something, but that he used to come all the time.'

'Why haven't you seen him then?'

'She reckons he just stopped suddenly. He went from visiting a couple of times a week to not coming at all. Not long after that we all swapped shifts which is why I didn't know him.'

'Doesn't everyone have to sign in with ID when they come to the prison?'

'Yeah, if you don't have your driving licence or whatever, you're not allowed through reception.'

'Did you ask her if she remembered the name?'

'Funny you should say that. I never remember anyone but, as soon as she saw the picture, she knew exactly who it was.'

Jessica could feel her heart pounding in her chest, knowing all the paranoia she had shown was about to be proved correct, that all the sleepless nights weren't in vain. 'What was his name?'

'Somebody Farraday.'

31

Jessica had to fight showing any emotion. She wanted to yell out, 'I was right' as vindication for all the things she had found herself doing over the past couple of weeks. She knew she couldn't do any of that in front of Dennis though.

She pulled the scrap towards her and pocketed it, desperately trying not to react to what he had said. 'You've been really helpful, Dennis, thank you.'

'No worries, shame you couldn't stay longer. Still I've got your number, maybe we can try another night?' She gave him a half-smile and said something utterly non-committal, walking out of the pub before he could say any more.

Jessica couldn't sum up the way she was feeling. There was some sort of elation that she hadn't just been paranoid, but sadness she hadn't figured any of it out before Carrie had died. Then there was the realisation she still didn't have the proof she needed. She had a broken phone under her bed and the second-hand word of someone who worked at the prison. She still had to figure out how it happened too. Farraday could have met Donald McKenna in prison and somehow smuggled blood and hairs back out again but it wouldn't have been easy.

Then another idea struck her, something she should

have thought about when she was on the train earlier. Adam told her a twin had to be identical to share DNA but what if one of them changed their appearance? Could it be possible that somewhere along the line her boss and McKenna were direct relations but one of them had altered the way he looked? It was unlikely but surely more of a possibility than tunnelling out of a maximum-security prison? The more Jessica thought about it, the more she was convinced. They were around the same age, same height and same build. As she reached her car, she took out the piece of newspaper from her pocket and stopped under a nearby street light to look at the photo of the DCI. She tried to remember what McKenna looked like. Surely it was like this? Surely?

She could feel the itch in the back of her head again.

'It's him. You're right. You were always right.'

Jessica knew she wasn't heading home. She drove to the estate Farraday lived on and parked where she had done in the previous days, a couple of streets away. She hadn't changed her clothes all day and was still wearing the suit she'd had on at the women's prison and for the train journeys. The nights were beginning to get cooler but Jessica didn't want to miss anything, shivering as she got out of the car and walking the short distance to sit on the wall opposite the chief inspector's house. Behind the low row of bricks was a large hedge which meant no one from the house behind could see her and she could push back into the greenery to avoid being seen easily from the front. On a night like this, it also offered a small amount of protection from the cold.

She sat on the wall, leaning backwards, eyes fixed on the house in front of her. She eyed the gate she had jumped over and hurt her ankle. It was as imposing as ever and, as she squinted into the darkness, Jessica could see a car parked on the driveway. She let her mind run away with her.

'The garage is being used for something sinister. Just go and look.'

There were lights on downstairs and Jessica fixed her eyes on the illuminated rooms, looking for silhouettes or clues of anything that might be untoward.

How could she prove it was him?

A light breeze whipped across her and Jessica edged backwards into the shrub. She could feel its spiky branches pushing into her back but it was more appealing than the cold. An owl hooted somewhere nearby and Jessica found herself looking around for the source of the noise before cursing herself for taking her focus away from the house.

'Don't look away, you'll miss something.'

She flicked her eyes back towards the building and tried to see if anything had changed, remembering the spot-the-difference puzzles she used to do as a kid. The car hadn't moved and the light was still on in the same downstairs room but had someone moved a curtain? She blinked to test that her eyes were working fine. It wasn't that late but Jessica knew she couldn't risk moving. With her watching the house, the chief inspector couldn't leave and no one else could be killed.

As she moved her focus towards the gate, Jessica felt the

blinks lasting longer until, finally, she could resist them no more.

Jessica jumped as the sound of a car's engine roared past. She went to move her arms but one of them was full of pins and needles, the other wedged tight. Opening her eyes to see a tangle of leaves and branches, Jessica jolted upwards, knowing where she was but not quite believing she had let it happen. It was light and cool so she knew it must be morning. She had somehow slept for the whole night in the small gap between the wall and hedge opposite DCI Farraday's house.

She squeezed her way up and looked over the top of the wall. The chief inspector's gates were still shut but there was no car in the drive. Jessica banged her hand on the edge of the bricks to try to get some feeling back into it before pulling out her phone and checking the time: 07.41.

Jessica could feel the pain had returned to her ankle and grimaced as she put her weight on it, hauling herself back onto the pavement. She tried to run but could only hobble back to her car. In her mind she knew she had let another victim down; she had fallen asleep and that meant the DCI had been free to leave the house the night before. She was trying to calm the panic rising in her as she reached her car, fumbling in her jacket pocket for the keys. Her hands were grubby and she could see dirt stains on her trousers but there was something far more important than all of that.

She unlocked the car door and threw herself into the driver's seat, starting the engine and tuning the radio to the local talk station. If there had been another killing the night before, it would definitely be a big story. She knew she hadn't missed any calls but maybe it was because they were waiting for her to get into the station?

Jessica crunched the car into first gear and turned around in the road, heading towards the station. The two radio presenters were joking about something irrelevant and she swore at them to get to the news. Eventually, when she was just a few minutes from Longsight, the jingle kicked in and the newsreader started to speak. Jessica turned the volume up but they were talking about football. She took a hand from the steering wheel to rub her head. Something wasn't right but maybe they just hadn't been given the story yet? That made sense.

She pulled into the station and parked at an angle in one of the bays but didn't want to waste time straightening out. She hurried through the front entrance, heading to the front desk.

'Are you all right?' the desk sergeant asked.

'Yeah, yeah. What happened overnight?'

The man looked confused. 'Um, nothing in particular – a domestic violence call-out, a bit of vandalism. The usual. What are you looking for?'

It was Jessica's turn to be puzzled. 'That's all?'

'Yes . . . are you sure you're okay? You look a bit, um . . .'

Jessica ignored him, moving quickly around the counter towards the female toilets. She pushed through the door and went quickly to the sinks, putting together the pieces of what had happened in the past few hours. It barely seemed believable but, after hearing Farraday's name, she had driven to his house, sat on the wall opposite watching him, slept in a hedge and then, for some reason, convinced herself someone else had been killed in the meantime.

Were those the actions of someone thinking clearly?

Jessica looked at herself in the mirror, staring into her own eyes and wondering what was happening in her head. There was a scuff of dirt on her right cheek and, as she reached up to wipe it away, she saw just how filthy both of her hands were. As she looked closer, Jessica could see there were a couple of small twigs lodged in her hair and one was stuck to her suit jacket.

She took deep breaths as she cleaned her hands and face, trying to get as much soil from her suit as possible. All she could think of was DCI Farraday. He must have left all the clues because he knew whoever found them wouldn't be able to prove anything.

'He's playing a game with you.'

Or was she seeing something that wasn't there? Jessica looked under the cubicle doors to make sure there was no one else in the room and then took out her phone. This time she didn't hesitate in calling Adam.

'Jess?'

'Yes, Adam, look, can you do something for me?'

'Um, I guess. I mean you didn't call and then . . .'

'You'll have to do the testing quietly though?'

'Testing?'

'Yes, at your labs.'

'Oh, right. I didn't realise that's what you meant. I can't do that, everything we test has to be logged and then they can check it all back through the computer system.'

'Forget that. Say I wanted to bring some skin samples or saliva in for you to test, what would you need? Like a fork or something the person had touched?'

'I can't do that, Jess.'

'Okay, but say you could, what would you need?'

'Um, look, it's not as easy as that. DNA isn't just an object you can pick up, it's why we're so careful at crime scenes. The second you touch something, you contaminate it. It's not like just picking up some cutlery and then running it through a scanner. We even use sterile storage bags to put things in, so the material can't pollute the object either. Plus it's why we use swabs because saliva is much purer – either that or blood. Even with hairs, if you touch them then your signature is on it. But I can't do anything like that anyway, I could lose my job.'

'Can we meet tonight?'

'Jess . . .'

'Please, Adam. I'm asking you if we can meet up.'

'I . . . well, yes. I've wanted to see you ever since the quiz but . . .'

'Brilliant. How about that pub we were in before opposite that Italian place. Around eight?'

'Um, yes, I guess but . . .'

Jessica hung up, not waiting to hear if he had anything else to say. She had a plan that would hopefully prove once and for all she was right.

She knew she first had to keep up appearances. If things were going to work, she couldn't seem to be acting erratically. She found Cole in his office and they both went up to DCI Farraday's floor for their morning briefing. Jessica let the inspector do the talking and didn't push her own views. Eventually the chief inspector consented to let a picture of Donald McKenna be released to the media – without a name – and ask the public for information.

Jessica wanted to grin, knowing she was already on to him, but kept a straight face. She looked at the picture they were sending out of McKenna and could see Farraday completely. The eyes weren't quite the same, the hairline was completely off and there was definitely a different shape to the face but there was unquestionably something similar only she could see. Maybe it was the ears? Perhaps the chin?

In the meeting, they agreed to keep details about McKenna's sister from him. With nothing else formally to go on, they were edging towards a secret twin and didn't want to risk letting the prisoner know they were on to him. Instead, the three were going to spend the day working with the media, either directly or behind the scenes, to get the photo as widely circulated as possible. If papers or TV stations wanted interviews, one of them would be on hand to peddle the line that this person was someone they wanted to speak to. They would give no extra details and no names. Meanwhile, more officers were being brought in to take the phone calls. Anyone who suggested McKenna as the identity would be instantly discounted and there would be a secondary team of officers ready to start looking into the backgrounds of any other names suggested who had a similar date of birth to McKenna – or better yet no trace of a birth certificate.

Jessica nodded along and spoke when she was supposed to, silently thinking her own plan through. The way the day was going to work out should go in her favour. The three of them would be operating closely together, which would give her a better chance.

After the meeting, she went to the storage room to ask for some evidence bags. It wasn't unusual for officers to be asking so she wasn't giving anything away. Jessica then returned to her car and hunted around in the door wells. She knew there was a nail file in there somewhere but hadn't used it for years. She found it in the passenger door and started chiselling one of the nails on her right hand, knowing she had to get it exactly right and that she would only have one chance. Finally, she looked through the first-aid kit in her boot, taking out a fine piece of gauze and handling it as gently as she possibly could by the corners.

With everything in place, she went back into the station and entered the Pad – which was the ridiculous name that had been given to their media briefing room. DI Cole and DCI Farraday were already in there along with the press office staff. They worked on a statement together, reiterating they were appealing for help with the identity of the man, and then it was faxed and emailed to the various media organisations along with the photo of McKenna. With that done, the three detectives put in follow-up calls to various newsdesks to give them any additional quotes they might want. They first started off with the local media as the press officer contacted a few national broadcasters and the wire services.

Jessica got through the morning looking for an opening that never came. As lunchtime approached, she was beginning to feel pangs of anxiety about whether she could pull off what she hoped for. She could also sense grumblings in her stomach and realised she hadn't eaten since breakfast the previous day. She hadn't wanted to risk train food and then simply forgot to eat.

They were working on a large desk, each with a different phone and their own laptop just in case they needed to either type anything or use the Internet.

With none of them on a call, Jessica stood and caught Cole's eye across the table. 'I'm going to nip to the canteen and get something to eat. Do you want anything bringing back?'

He pushed out his bottom lip and breathed through his teeth. 'Why not? Just a sandwich or something. Nothing with egg though.'

Jessica walked around her chair towards Farraday. 'How about you, Sir? Do you want me to bring you through some lunch?'

The DCI looked quizzically at her. 'I suppose. A sandwich is fine for me too.'

Jessica took another step towards him. 'No worries, I'll be back in a . . . I think you've got something stuck to your cheek, Sir.'

The man used his hands to brush at his face but Jessica leant in. 'No, you're missing it, it's just . . .' She quickly flashed her palm across his cheek using the nail she had sharpened to deliberately nick his skin.

Blood instantly ran down his face as he jumped back. Jessica held the hand she had caught him with to her side, using the other to take some tissues out of her pocket. 'Oh God, I'm so sorry. I keep meaning to sort my nails. Shit, you're bleeding. Here, take these.'

The chief inspector stared at her, his eyes wide as he took the tissues. 'Are you okay?' Cole asked from the other side.

Jessica continued to apologise as the DCI dabbed at his face. 'It's not deep. Those are some sharp nails you've got there, Daniel.'

'I know. Sorry, Sir. I'll go sort them, then go to the canteen.'

Jessica turned around, moving as quickly as she could towards the door without making anyone even more suspicious. She took the gauze from her pocket and wiped all of the blood she could onto it, placing it carefully into the evidence bag. Jessica strode out to her car and un-locked it before putting the bag under the driver's seat. The day was cool and she figured that, although it wasn't a freezer, it was the best she could manage.

Despite rarely being on time, let alone early, Jessica got to the pub twenty minutes early to wait for Adam. She hid herself away on a table out of sight from the bar so no one would question why she was hovering there without a drink. At eight o'clock exactly, she saw Adam walk through the front doors. She didn't want to out herself to the bar staff so waited for him to find her.

He looked good and was wearing casual jeans, another T-shirt based on a cartoon she knew, a thin jacket and canvas trainers. 'Do you want something to drink?' he asked, approaching the table.

'No, I'm not feeling too great.'

Adam looked a little disappointed and sat on the stool opposite her. 'Oh right, I was hoping we were going to talk about . . .'

'I need you to do something for me.'

Adam sighed and looked away from her. 'I knew I shouldn't have come.'

'Please, Adam. It's just one thing.'

'Jess . . . I'm not very good with this type of thing. You didn't contact me for all that time. I called and sent you texts and left you messages. I know you were ignoring me and I figured "fair enough". I mean, I was upset and all because I thought we got on great but I'm not a stalker or anything and figured that if you didn't want to see me, it was up to you.'

He sighed and ran his hand through his hair, rubbing his eyes. 'Look, I know your friend from the quiz was killed that night and it's all right if you were upset and everything. I understand that and thought I'd give you space but I don't know what you want from me.'

Jessica breathed out heavily. 'I need you to do one thing for me and then we can try again.'

Adam kept looking at the table and wiped his eyes a second time. 'What?'

Jessica reached into the handbag she'd brought with her and took out the transparent wallet that had the bloodied gauze on it. She put it on the table so he could see. 'Please can you test this for me against Donald Mc-Kenna? I couldn't freeze it but I kept it as cool as I could. I touched it too but I can give you a sample so you can eliminate me. I got these . . .'

She reached into her bag again and took out a clean mouth swab she had taken from the station and another clear packet. 'If I give you a swab, you can separate any traces of me, yes? I was careful when I picked it all up anyway so you might not have to.'

Adam shook his head but still didn't look up. 'It's not that simple but I can't do it anyway, Jess. You can't ask me to. When you log into the database it all gets stored. If anyone ever checked, I'd have no answer and would lose my job. They could even prosecute me.'

'They don't just check as a matter of course though, do they? It's unlikely they'd find out.'

'That's not the point. It's illegal.'

'Can you do it for me?'

Jessica had never seen Adam lose his temper before but he banged his fist on the table and looked through teary eyes straight at her, his voice full of anger. 'How dare you. I've waited all these days to get any kind of reply from you. Anything to say "hi" or "sorry for not getting back to you". Anything. You ignore me completely and then, when you want something, you get me out here and ask me to break the law for you.'

'Adam, I'm sorry, I . . .'

'I *told* you about my parents. I don't tell anyone but I *told* you.' Jessica simply stared at the man in front of her, with no idea what to say. He wasn't making any effort to control his tears any longer.

When it was clear she wasn't going to add anything, Adam looked away again and picked up the small bag with the blood-soaked gauze. 'Jess, look, I like you. I *really* like you. I know we only went out a few times but I had some of the most fun I've ever had. If you want me to test these, just swab your mouth and say the word and I'll do it. *For you.* But after that, I don't want to ever see you again unless you absolutely have to come to my work. Even then, I want you to ask for someone else. But if you enjoyed those moments as much as me, please don't ask me to do this.'

Jessica looked at the tears running down his face and the redness around his eyes then picked up the mouth swab, ran it around the inside of her cheek and put it in the evidence bag.

'Just test it.'

32

In the two days since seeing Adam, Jessica jumped every time her phone went off. Whenever it rang or sounded the familiar text-message tone, she would snatch it from her pocket and look to see if it was Adam contacting her. She had spent two more nights outside of DCI Farraday's house but had been careful not to fall asleep. She took a thicker jacket each evening to guard against the cold and waited until three in the morning before driving home and trying to sleep for a short while before heading to the station.

She had managed four hours' sleep in two days and had barely eaten, having just picked at a couple of pasta dishes for lunch from the station's canteen. She could feel her body craving rest and food but fought to keep going, telling herself that as soon as Adam got back to her it would all be worth it. Jessica was struggling with her conscience to justify the way she had treated him. It was as if a coldness had taken her over in the pub, pushing her to act in a way she wouldn't normally.

Whether it was at briefings with others or in the quietness of her own office, she found her mind wandering frequently and could still hear the voices in her head telling her she was right.

'*The end justifies the means.*'

The media appeal using Donald McKenna's photograph

hadn't gone well at all. On the first evening, they fielded a very irate call from the prison's governor asking what they were playing at. Farraday also told them he'd had to deal with an incensed superintendent who had been contacted by the governor wanting answers.

None of that would have mattered if any of the calls had been useful but almost every person who phoned had pointed out the picture was McKenna. There was a small number of other names put forwards but nothing that fitted their criteria. The positivity that had gripped the team in the previous days now felt distant and everyone was back to hoping for a lead rather than being able to push for one.

Jessica was sure one call from Adam could change all of that. When she got her match she knew she'd still have no admissible evidence, given the way she had taken the chief inspector's blood, but at least she would know for sure he was the twin and either he or McKenna had somehow changed their appearance.

After an unproductive day, Farraday asked Jessica if she could hang around at the station to finish off the paperwork relating to the phone campaign. She didn't know why he wanted her specifically but she gave it twenty minutes before passing it on to another officer. She was planning to go home and change before heading off to wait outside his house for the evening.

The nights were drawing in and there was only an hour of daylight left as Jessica drove out of the station. The rain had begun earlier in the day and not relented and her car's heater was again struggling to keep the steam from the windscreen. As she reached forwards to wipe away the mist, she heard her phone ringing. Knowing she shouldn't, she took the device out of her pocket and glanced away from the road down at the screen.

'Adam Compton' the screen read. Jessica pulled over to the side of the road, only realising after she'd stopped that she hadn't indicated. The driver of the car behind beeped their horn in annoyance as they swerved around her but Jessica wasn't bothered. She quickly pressed the screen to answer the call. 'Adam, have you done the test?'

The man on the other end was clearly a little shocked at her directness. 'Yes.'

'What did it say?'

'I don't know what you were expecting but there was nothing. No match to Donald McKenna, no match to anyone.'

Jessica was silent for a moment, stunned by what he had said. 'It's not?'

'No.'

'I didn't contaminate it or anything, did I? It's definitely right?'

'I know how to do my job.'

'Of course, I know. I didn't mean that. You're not going to get in trouble, are you?'

'I don't know.'

'I'm so sorry, Adam.'

'I'm sorry too.'

Jessica paused for a moment before continuing. 'It's just . . . I've fucked everything up. I didn't know how to cope after Carrie died. There's so much that's happened.

I've not slept, I can't eat. I thought I knew what I was doing but now I'm worried I was wrong all along.'

She felt a lump in her throat and struggled to finish her sentence. 'I think . . . I might have had a breakdown or something.'

Jessica felt tears in her eyes but didn't fight them. 'Adam?' She took the phone away from her ear and looked down at a blank screen.

He must have hung up after saying he was sorry but she hadn't heard the noise.

Her car was stopped by the side of the road with the headlights still shining forwards. Vehicles squeezed around her as rain smashed onto the roof and windscreen. As the front wipers thundered back and forth, squeaking their way across the glass, Jessica couldn't hold back any longer and let the tears engulf her.

She realised there was so little rationality to what she had been doing. Most of what she thought she had on Farraday was circumstantial but there was still Carrie's phone under her bed. It was an object she could hold in her hands, found in a place that couldn't be explained. Not being able to figure out why it was there was the thing really haunting her.

It took what seemed like hours for Jessica to calm herself but it was likely just minutes. Cars continued to manoeuvre around her, some tooting their horns, as the rain eased off slightly. Jessica settled back into the driver's seat and indicated to pull away.

She felt as lonely as she ever had on the journey back to her house.

Her relationship with Caroline hadn't been the same for over a year, Carrie was gone and she had destroyed things with Adam. Her parents had recently retired from running a post office in Cumbria but this wasn't the type of thing she would ever share with them and she felt she had no one to talk to.

She drove much slower than she usually would, taking her time and forcing herself to concentrate on the road. It was almost dusk as she pulled into her parking space. She didn't know if she was going to go to Farraday's house that evening any longer, thoughts swirling in her head about what she should do next. She switched the engine off and got out, slamming the door behind her and walking to the entrance to her building. Jessica reached into her pockets to find her keys but her eyes were drawn to a movement over to her right. She stopped and squinted at the bushes that surrounded that side of the property and thought she could see a figure.

Jessica stepped onto the grass towards them but, as soon as she did, whoever it was bolted backwards. The light was dim with the street lights just beginning to come on as the sun set but something about the person's build and the way they moved seemed familiar. Jessica started running after them without thinking, ignoring the pain she was still feeling in her ankle from jumping over Farraday's gate.

The figure had turned and run around the hedges and Jessica followed about thirty yards behind. They dashed towards the woodlands that backed onto her housing development and jumped a small chain-link fence that separated the two areas. Wincing as she did the same, Jessica tried to avoid landing on her ankle but wasn't able to manage it.

The rain had slowed to a light drizzle but the ground was soaking and her feet slid around the moss and overgrown grass. The person in front was struggling to keep their balance too and, after first looking as if they were going to head towards the trees, veered back left towards the fence. They used one hand on the barrier to help keep their balance, moving as quickly as they could along its length.

Jessica followed and knew she would usually be faster if it wasn't for her ankle. She was also struggling to keep her grip because the path had already been churned up by the person ahead. As she gained a few yards, Jessica knew for sure it was a man. He was around six feet tall and his height should have given it away in the first place but her mind wasn't feeling sharp. A mixture of the lack of sleep and minimal food was beginning to hurt. She tried shouting 'hey' but felt exhausted.

The man ahead kept to the fence line and then used both hands to propel himself back onto the other side, landing in a car park that served a block of flats next to where Jessica lived. As he landed, Jessica watched him look around, not knowing where he was, before heading towards where she knew there was a dead end.

Jessica jumped the fence herself and landed awkwardly on her ankle, involuntarily yelling out in pain. She looked up and the man glanced backwards but the near-darkness meant she couldn't see his features clearly. She forced herself back to her feet and drove forwards following the person, knowing he could only run for another hundred yards or so before reaching an enclosed area where the complex's giant metal bins were kept. She stumbled forwards, letting his lead increase, and entered the wide alley behind him.

Slowing to a walk, Jessica moved further down the opening. There was an orange security light on the left but otherwise the area was dark. Jessica edged forwards looking from side to side but then stepped backwards as the man took a pace out from the shadows of the trash containers.

The light wasn't brilliant but there was no doubt about the identity of the person stood in front of her. 'Good evening, Daniel.'

Jessica stared. When she had started chasing, she hadn't been completely sure about who she was pursuing or why she was running but something instinctively told her to act. She realised she had no plan, no weapon and, given the pain in her ankle, no way to turn and make a bolt for it. In a period of time defined by bad decisions, she had just run into a dead end and was now facing the imposing figure of DCI Farraday towering over her.

'What are you doing at my house?' Jessica asked, trying to sound confident.

'Is that really the question you want to ask me?'

He took another step forwards, his face now clearly lit. He was still dressed in his work clothes and it now seemed obvious why he had asked her to stay late – he was planning to search her house the way he'd hunted around her office. She moved her weight from her sore leg to the other, desperately trying not to show she was in pain, and took a deep breath.

Jessica knew he was right, there was only one question she wanted to ask. 'Why did you have Carrie's phone?'

The chief inspector looked directly at her, his eyes narrow. 'You really shouldn't have gone looking for it.'

33

Jessica felt frozen to the spot, droplets of rain dribbling from her nose. She gave a slight shiver as Farraday took another step towards her. She felt ready for whatever was going to happen, her mind tormented by everything that had occurred. As Jessica looked back up at her boss, she wasn't prepared for the scene in front of her.

He had started to cry, his large frame bobbing up and down with each sob as he wiped his eyes. Jessica could see the small cut on his face where she had nicked him. It had largely healed but there was still a slight red mark.

His voice was shaky as he tried to speak. 'It's not that you shouldn't, I guess. I knew someone had found it but I didn't know who it was. I wanted someone to come and ask me about it but no one did and then I was stuck because I couldn't admit where it had gone.'

Jessica didn't understand what he was trying to say. He wiped his eyes and coughed loudly into his sleeve. 'I don't . . .' Jessica started.

'I thought it could have been you because you asked me about the phone records but then you never followed it up so I went back to not knowing what had happened. It could have been some kid who'd broken in, though who knows why they'd go through my bins.'

'Sir, I have no idea what you're talking about.'

Farraday peered up at her, pushing his dripping hair away from his face. 'Detective Constable Jones . . . Carrie . . . and I were having an affair, Daniel. When I got to the scene that night, I didn't know what to do. I was distraught but trying to stay professional, then I saw her shoes and bag on the pathway of her house. Her phone was on top and I realised that if anyone started looking into things, it would all be found out. I know it was selfish but I love my wife and I didn't want to lose my job. So I took it.'

Jessica stared at him. 'You didn't kill her?'

The man snorted in surprise, water spraying from his nose and mouth. 'Is that what you thought?'

'I . . . I don't know. There were other things. I've not been sleeping.'

They looked straight at each other and Jessica saw the chief inspector's head tilt to the side in the way she hated. He was about to ask if she was all right. 'Can we go inside and talk about this? It's always bloody raining here and we're both soaked,' he said.

Jessica turned and started walking back through the maze of the estate where she lived, still not really understanding everything that had happened. It was no wonder Carrie wasn't willing to talk about her boyfriend if he was not only a married man but their boss too.

She led Farraday into her block and then walked up the stairs to her flat, unlocking the door and pointing the DCI towards her kitchen. 'I'll get us some towels,' she said.

Jessica rarely used her own kitchen, except for warming up frozen meals in the microwave. It was always the coldest room in the flat and the dull light-blue walls made it feel worse. There was a small cheap wood and plastic dining table with two low-backed stools around it. Jessica re-entered the room, handing a towel to Farraday, who started rubbing his head. As she dried her own face, she thought her boss's hair seemed greyer than it had done a few weeks ago.

'I think I should start at the beginning,' he said with a sigh. 'When I arrived here, I tried to fit in but it was a bit of a shock for all of us. All the jokes were fine but it was tough for me to try to play along and be one of the team while at the same time having to be everyone's boss. Meanwhile my wife hadn't enjoyed the move. I don't really know how it happened but, before I knew what was happening, Carrie and myself had started seeing each other a couple of times a week. Usually it was just hotel rooms but once or twice it would be her house or mine.'

Jessica sat opposite him listening, letting the pieces fall into place in her head and realising how badly she had judged things. 'She wanted me to leave my wife but . . . Have you ever been in love, Dan . . . Jessica?'

She was slightly taken aback by the question and it must have showed on her face because her boss spoke again. 'Sorry, that's a really unfair question.'

Jessica cut in to answer it anyway. 'I don't know, Sir.'

'Please, I think you should call me John for now.'

'Okay.'

'Well, if you ever thought being in love could be complicated, then having those feelings for two people is overwhelming, especially when you see one of them every day at work and the other every morning and evening at home. I could feel it beginning to affect my work and tried to put an end to it with Carrie but it's hard when you see each other all the time. We argued on the afternoon she died. It was at the station, which was unprofessional.'

He picked up the towel again and Jessica wasn't sure if he was using it to wipe away more of the rain or a few tears. The description of the argument at least explained why Rowlands had seen them having a row.

'What happened on the night she died?' Jessica asked.

The chief inspector said nothing for a few moments, composing himself, and then spoke in a broken voice. 'I got the call from the station that said one of our officers had been badly injured. When they told me the name, I was straight out of the door. I got there and she was being taken away. The paramedics said they had to get her to the hospital to have any hope of her surviving. I was going to follow them and it was then I noticed her things on the path. I saw the phone and took it without thinking. I know it was selfish, thinking about my own preservation, but it wasn't really a conscious decision.'

He took a deep breath before continuing. 'Of course, once I had it, I didn't know what to do with it. I didn't want to risk dumping it, just in case it was found, so buried it in my own bin thinking it would be emptied and end up in a landfill where no one would find it. Then I came home that night and saw someone had gone through our rubbish and had no idea what to think. I didn't know if someone was on to me, or trying to frame me or what. So I waited but no one ever mentioned it.

I saw someone running off my driveway that night but had no idea who it was because it was so dark. They were hobbling but I looked around the station the next day just in case and everyone was walking normally. I didn't know if it was someone I knew, or just a person looking to rob us.'

Jessica gave a small laugh. 'I think we were trying to be too clever for our own good. My ankle was killing me, it still is. But I've kept it strapped tight.' She bent down and took her shoe and sock off before lifting her foot up for her boss to see. The ankle was purple and yellow with bruising and the swelling had reappeared.

'You thought I killed her?' he said softly.

'I thought you killed them all. I didn't know what to think when I found that phone.'

'But . . . how would I have even done that? With McKenna and all?'

'I . . . don't know. After we found his sister, I'd got it into my head you were his twin and one of you had changed your appearance or something. I've not been thinking straight.'

'Twin? I look nothing like him.'

'I know . . . but I'd convinced myself. I even had you tested . . .'

Farraday reached up to his cheek where the small cut was still visible. 'Oh . . .'

'I know. Stupid, wasn't it?'

Jessica stood and told him she'd be back in a moment. She returned shortly afterwards and put Carrie's phone down on the table in front of them. The man shook his head as he gazed at it. 'Why did you come to look for it in the first place? You couldn't have known it was there.'

'I didn't. It was instinct and a bit of an accident. It was just all the things that had gone wrong, I thought they were your fault.' The chief inspector slumped slightly as Jessica continued. 'Sorry, but it was your decision to get all that stuff into the papers about Lee Morgan being corrupt and then you were so sure Robert Graves was one of the killer's victims. We put the wrong mug shot into the press and I don't think we recovered from that.'

The man closed his eyes and shook his head. 'You're right but that's why I told Carrie we had to call things off. The relationship was affecting my judgement.'

'Then you kept talking about being grateful for these people being killed.'

'Do I wish they were still around? Well, I'm not going to say I'm sorry they're gone.'

'They were still people though.'

The man nodded. 'Maybe I was a little unprofessional in expressing my personal views.'

'There's more though. You had been in my office the day after Carrie was killed. Things had been moved around.'

'That's true. I knew Carrie was good friends with you. She said she hadn't told anyone about our relationship but I figured if she'd told anyone, it would have been you. It was an odd morning and I was a wreck because she'd just died but I couldn't tell anyone. I didn't know if you were in your office but it's so bloody messy in there I ended up sending all sorts of files flying. I thought I'd put them back but then sent another load tumbling.'

Jessica giggled gently. 'Jason keeps telling me I should tidy my side.'

'Is there anything else?'

'You had her personnel file.'

'You checked my desk?'

'Um . . . yes. It was after I thought you'd gone through my things. I had gone up to your office but it was empty and, before I knew what I was doing, I'd gone through your files.'

'I guess I shouldn't really be talking about correct protocol. I'd had that file for a while. Maybe it was a little paranoia on my part but she'd been talking about me leaving my wife. I didn't know if I wanted to and I just did something stupid by checking up on her. With the kind of things you read in the papers, there's always that nagging thought in the back of your head that someone's after your money or whatever. I mean, look at her and look at me. She could have been my daughter.'

Jessica nodded but felt close to tears as the image of her friend's face drifted into her head. 'Why were you here?' she said.

'Paranoia, pure and simple. Ever since I saw someone had gone through my bins, I've been waiting for some sort of blackmail note or even someone to simply ask about it but it never came. Like I said, if anyone knew about our relationship, I figured it would be you but you hadn't said anything. You had asked about her phone records, then nothing. But you've not been yourself the past few days, maybe longer. I thought I had seen your car around our estate once or twice. I'd convinced myself you were on to me and were going to try to expose the relationship to destroy my career. I didn't even know what I thought I was going to do here, it's not as if I was going to break in or anything. I guess I just wanted to see where you lived.'

'So we've both been suspicious of each other this whole time?'

Farraday laughed this time, although it didn't sound completely convincing. 'Sounds like it.' Jessica tried to smile but couldn't force it. 'Are you okay?' her boss added. 'I'm not trying to speak out of turn but . . . you look awful.'

'I've been sitting outside your house almost every night since she died.'

'You've what? Why?'

'I'd wait on the wall of that house opposite yours, watching the lights and your gates. I don't know why . . . I thought it was you. I guess I reckoned that if you weren't leaving your house then no one else would get hurt.'

He shook his head, seemingly not quite able to grasp what she was saying. 'I don't even know what to say . . . I wish we had talked to each other.'

'I know. I'm just so tired.'

Farraday pointed to the phone on the table. 'I think I should leave now and maybe we'll talk more tomorrow? If you want to hand that in and say where you found it, I won't deny anything. Just get some sleep and come in when you're ready. I'll tell people you're doing some work for me.'

Jessica wanted to say no but knew the one thing she needed above anything else was rest. 'Will you call me if anything happens?'

'Yes.'

She picked up the phone from the table and started playing with the sliding mechanism. 'I'm not going to tell anyone about this but I don't think I'm ready to let it go either.'

The chief inspector stood and put the towel back down on the table. 'Get some sleep, Jessica, I'll see you tomorrow.'

She showed her boss to the door and locked it behind him before walking into her bedroom. She took off her clothes and climbed under the covers. Jessica let her eyes close but couldn't help but feel she'd forgotten something.

34

Jessica tried to look at the clock by the side of her bed but her eyes had a hazy greyness around them and she struggled to focus. Her arms were cocooned in the duvet cover and she twisted one way then the other to free herself, sitting up in the bed. The time soon came into focus.

1.43.

She rubbed her eyes and wondered why there was a faint light drifting through her curtains if it was the early hours of the morning before realising it was the afternoon and that she had slept for around sixteen hours. Jessica instantly snatched for her phone, hoping Adam had texted her. He had drifted into her dreams during the night but she had no idea how to fix things.

There were no text messages but there was an alert saying she had missed an alarm, which seemed pretty obvious. There were three missed calls, one from Farraday and two from Cole. She sat on the edge of her bed and dialled the inspector, who answered straight away. 'Jess, are you okay?'

'Yeah, fine. I've just had some bits to do. Were you after me?'

'Farraday was. He told me to keep calling you and to get you to meet him when you answered.'

'Why? Where is he?'

'He's at the hospital. John Mills came out of his coma yesterday evening and his doctors say he should be able to talk to us at some point today.'

Jessica could barely move quickly enough, grabbing some clean clothes from her wardrobe, dressing and driving to the hospital. As she parked in a proper bay, she thought it seemed like such a long time ago she had charged into reception after hearing Carrie had been hurt. So much had happened since then.

She tried to stay calm and followed the receptionist's directions. As she kept an eye on the coloured lines on the floor and the signs on the wall, it occurred to her that a hospital always appeared far bigger on the inside than the out. One corridor led into other identical-looking corridors and eventually, after asking for directions from two other people, she found her way to a small ward that seemed miles away from where she had started.

There was a row of four seats outside a single door and Farraday was sitting on his own. He looked up as she approached. 'Daniel . . . Jessica . . . how are you feeling?'

'Good, I've slept all the way through from last night.'

'You look better.'

'What's going on?'

'He woke up late yesterday afternoon but the doctors had to do their tests and he needed more rest than you did. They're shocked by how alert he is. Usually they'd make us wait but apparently he's been asking for us.'

'Really?'

'That's what the nurse said. They're forcing him to take

it easy for obvious reasons. His girlfriend was with him for a bit this morning so they said we couldn't talk to him until this afternoon.'

'He doesn't come across as the type who usually talks freely to the police.'

'No, but I presume no one's tried to kill him before. Is everything okay after last night?'

'I think so. It's just going to take time to clear in my head. I've spent so long looking at you as the enemy.'

'I'm sorry. I know I haven't helped.'

'I keep thinking I've forgotten something too. Something . . . important.'

'About me?'

'I don't know.'

Their conversation was interrupted by a nurse walking through the door. She told them they could go through to speak to the patient but that they would have fifteen minutes and no more and shouldn't push him on anything. Farraday assured her they weren't going to be grilling the patient and would let him do the talking.

John Mills had a private ward to himself. As they walked in, he was sitting up on a bed in the middle of the room. An empty gurney was next to him but they were separated by some equipment that was monitoring the patient. Jessica thought that the room, like the rest of the hospital, looked far larger than it actually was. The bright white walls reflected the overhead fluorescent strip lights, helping the illusion.

Jessica thought Mills must have had a shaven head when he was stabbed but there were now tufts of dark hair growing. He would have been fairly muscular at some point too but his body looked slightly out of proportion given the weight he must have lost in the past few weeks. As they entered, he shuffled further in his bed so he was fully sitting up.

'Are you okay, Mr Mills?' Farraday asked, taking a seat next to the bed. Jessica sat next to him.

'Dunno, mate. Feel all right but I didn't think there'd ever come a day when I was inviting you lot in for a cosy chat.'

'You don't have to talk to us, Mr Mills. We're here because you asked for us.'

'Yeah, I know. I guess things change when some mad twat tries to knife you, don't they?'

'What do you remember about that night?' Jessica asked.

Mills shifted his eyes to look from the DCI to her. He seemed annoyed she had spoken but glanced back to the chief inspector to answer. 'Which one of you is in charge?'

'I'm not sure why that matters,' Farraday said.

Mills bobbed his head from side to side. 'Yeah, whatever.'

Jessica wondered if it was her specifically he had a problem with, or women in general. It would explain his girlfriend's black eye if he simply didn't like females.

The patient carried on looking at the chief inspector as he spoke. 'Well, boss, I'd just got home and parked my truck on the drive. I've got this American-style open-backed thing. Absolute beauty. Anyway, I'd gone around to the back of it because I'd been out on, er, business.'

'Did you regularly get home at that time from *business*?' The DCI coughed as he spoke the last word and Jessica fought to stifle a smile.

'Sometimes, yeah. Maybe a couple of times a week? It all depends what's going on that particular week. I'd gone around to the back and thought I heard a noise behind me. As soon as I turned I felt someone coming at me. It was pretty dark and he was just a shadow at first.'

'Was it definitely a man?' Jessica asked.

The man laughed. 'Fuck me, love, do you think I'd let some bird do this to me?' He pointed towards the mark on his neck and shook his head dismissively.

'Okay, Mr Mills, what happened?' Farraday said and Jessica could tell he was trying to keep his tone steady.

'Right, well, this chancer came flying at me and nailed me in the neck as I turned. He must have been waiting or something. One on one and he wouldn't have stood a chance but cowards use weapons, don't they?'

Jessica wondered if he thought really brave men used their fists to beat up their girlfriends but said nothing.

'Anyway,' Mills continued, 'he pulled back to do me again but I smacked him straight on the jaw and he went down. I was trying to get to my feet but couldn't breathe properly. Before I knew it, that bird from down the street . . .'

'Carrie,' Jessica interrupted. 'Detective Constable Carrie Jones.'

The man looked sideways at Jessica. 'Yeah, her. She came out of nowhere and tried to get involved. I'll give her credit, considering she's a girl, she was fearless.'

'What do you remember after that?' Farraday asked.

'Not much. A bit of the ambulance, then waking up here.'

'Do you know she was killed saving your life?' Jessica snapped.

Mills looked straight at her but this time genuinely did seem surprised. 'No . . . I . . . no one said anything. I figured she scared him off or whatever.'

'She was stabbed three times and died that night.' Jessica was struggling to control the anger and emotion in her voice. 'Do you remember the girl you bullied, the one you'd watch and intimidate because she was a police officer and you're such a big *fucking* man? Remember her? She died and you're here.'

The man in the bed struggled to pull himself up further in the bed. 'I didn't know . . . '

Farraday spoke next, defusing some of the tension. 'I guess all we have left to ask is if you would recognise the man who stabbed you?'

Mills's tone had changed and he spoke far more softly. 'Yeah, I mean it was dark but you don't forget a face like that.'

Jessica blinked back tears but listened to the description of the killer. She remembered the crucial question she had forgotten to ask the chief inspector the previous evening and knew instantly who they were looking for.

35

The killer knew he'd blown it. He hadn't meant to harm the female police officer but, when she'd come at him, he had no other option. With all the noise, he hadn't even risked finishing off that animal Mills. He had been worried about how the papers would talk about him after such a mistake. He'd hoped they would understand the woman was an accident, collateral damage, as part of a wider project.

Instead they hadn't, they changed their minds and decided he was the problem. He hadn't known if he could continue working through his list and thought it would be a good idea to keep his head down for a little while and then maybe make a comeback when people had begun to forget about him.

Things had been confusing though. That photo of Donald McKenna had ended up on television and in the papers. He didn't know how they could have figured it out but waited to see if anyone came for him. The killer wasn't quite sure if he understood all of it himself when it came to McKenna. He had tried not to think about it but it was something niggling away at the back of his mind. Either way, when they hadn't come for him, he realised he might be in the clear after all. Perhaps if he just dealt with the next person on his list, the people that wrote their columns would realise he wasn't the bad guy after all?

He began to start planning exactly what he would need to do next. Obviously he didn't want to get caught and most of the people he went after were bigger or stronger than him. It was all about biding his time and looking for a routine.

But then the woman had come to him. It was strange but, after talking with her, he knew he had to change his plans and go for a different target. He wasn't sure if she knew about his project or not but, even if she didn't, it didn't matter. She hadn't told him specifically this man should be targeted but her careless talk had given him enough to go on. Maybe he would tell her afterwards that he had done it for her? Maybe she would guess?

In any case, after watching the person for two nights, it was clear the new target had a very simple routine to follow – this would be the easiest one yet.

He was grateful for the darker evenings as it meant he could comfortably get into place in time. He pressed himself into the bush and watched as the car pulled forwards towards the garage. As with the last few nights when he had simply been an observer, he knew the vehicle would stop and the man would get out to open the garage door. That was when he would strike.

The headlights illuminated the chipped paintwork of the garage door and the killer heard the car slide into neutral.

Just a few more seconds.

He stepped forwards out of the hedge, crouched and moved silently towards the driveway. He heard the car door open and saw the person he was waiting for stand

and start towards the garage door. The man had his back to him and the killer moved quickly as the wide door started to slide upwards.

The killer took his hand out of his pocket, holding the knife tightly ready to strike but, as he pulled back, the target suddenly dropped to his knees and rolled backwards.

The man with the knife stopped and looked sideways but the other man on the ground was looking directly at him.

How could he know?

The killer motioned to turn and run but the man spoke loudly and clearly. 'Game's over, Dennis.'

Dennis Doherty panicked and looked to his right but saw officers swarming out from under the garage doors. He spun and ran as fast as he could towards the gate. As he got nearer it started to open and he wondered if somehow he had a guardian angel who was setting him free – but more officers poured through the gate towards him. He looked backwards but was surrounded and walking at the front of the officers was the woman.

The penny suddenly dropped – the one he thought might be on his side had set him up.

'Drop the knife, Dennis,' she said.

He did as he was told, the weapon falling to the floor with a clang which echoed around on the breeze. The woman didn't stop walking though. He put his hands out, waiting to be cuffed and knowing it was over. Instead of reaching for his wrists, she launched forwards and hammered her fist into the lower part of his nose.

He felt the liquid explode around his face, pain lurching through his body as he tried to shove her away. He couldn't move his arms, as someone else pulled them behind him, wrenching them into handcuffs. Dennis looked up to see the woman inches from his face. 'That was for Carrie,' she said, rubbing the blood from her knuckles.

Jessica looked at Farraday standing next to her by John Mills's hospital bed, trying to catch her boss's attention. Mills noticed her expression first. 'Hey, do you know who it is?' Jessica said nothing but told the chief inspector with her eyes they had to leave.

The two detectives stood but the patient raised his voice. 'Oi, I have a right to know. Tell me who it was. Hey.'

Jessica and Farraday headed out of the ward together with the man shouting after them. The nurse outside muttered something about not getting the patient excited and dashed in behind them but Jessica and the DCI were already walking quickly away.

'What is it?' Farraday said.

'Outside.'

The two of them hurried out to the car park and Jessica strode towards an empty bench. They both sat down and she kicked away the smattering of cigarette ash that was next to her foot.

'Do you know who it is?' the DCI asked.

'Yes but I don't think we have anything to arrest him for. Mills's description wouldn't be enough.'

'Tell me.'

'When you left last night there was one thing I couldn't

quite recall, something that felt on the tip of my tongue. I remembered it when we were in there.'

'What?'

'Well, the other reason I was so sure it was you was because of one of the front-office guys at the prison.' Farraday was looking confused. 'You have to understand, I was so convinced, I was really sure. I thought you were either related to McKenna or had somehow smuggled his blood or something out.'

'What did you do?'

'I took in a picture of you and asked this guy on reception if he'd ever seen you. He came back to me a few days later and said one of the other women who worked there had. He knew your name.'

'I've never been to the prison. Lots of people would know my name from the picture, especially if they were following the case.'

'I know that now but he had me convinced. I didn't think it through, I was sure it all made sense that you had been there and it didn't even cross my mind I could be wrong. That's why I wanted to get your blood tested, I thought you were related or something. I know it sounds crazy now but I'd put all the pieces together and . . .'

'. . . It does sound pretty crazy,' DCI Farraday interrupted, smiling softly.

'I'm sorry, Sir.'

'There's time for that later. What are you saying? That it's this prison reception guy?'

'Mills said the guy had bright blue eyes and a scar on his face. The guy at the jail is called Dennis, you can't miss his scar but the eyes too. I was so obsessed before I didn't even see it. McKenna, his sister Mary, and Dennis all have those same light blue eyes. They almost look through you with them.'

'You think they're all related?'

'I don't know, I have no idea but why would Dennis say he'd seen you when you've never been near the place?'

'We can't arrest him because he has a scar that's a little bit similar and blue eyes. We'd have thousands of people to bring in if that were the case.'

'I think I know how we can find out for sure, Sir.'

'We can't just take hairs from him or take blood to check him and we can't swab him without arresting him for something. Any evidence would be inadmissible.'

Farraday scratched at the mark on his face, an unconscious movement at the place where Jessica had cut him.

'I know but if we catch him in the act . . .'

'We still can't entrap someone.'

'Maybe not but say we had an anonymous tip telling us someone's life was in danger. We could watch that person and if someone did try to attack that person, there would be no problem arresting them then, would there? Then we get a swab and, if it just happens to match the ones we had before, we'd know for sure if this person was our killer or not. Even if there was any confusion with his DNA matching someone else's, we would have caught him in the act.'

'Are you still talking about this Dennis character?'

'Yes.'

'How would you know who he was going after next?'

'Say I gave him a push in the right direction? Maybe dropped a few hints that someone in authority was a little corrupt? That must be why the warden Lee Morgan was killed. I think there's a good chance he would go after someone else.'

'Why would he listen to you?'

'He may not but I have a little feeling he might.'

'It still sounds like entrapment.'

'Maybe we can cross that bridge if it all works?'

'Who are you intending on putting in the firing line?'

'There's already one person I've asked him to look at the picture of. All I would have to do was tell him I was asking about that man because they were possibly on the take.'

DCI Farraday puffed out his cheeks, blowing through his teeth and rubbing his head. 'I'm not going to like the sound of this, am I?'

36

Jessica, Cole and Reynolds were sitting in Farraday's office. The chief inspector put the phone down and glanced between the three of them. 'The superintendent doesn't have a solution,' he said.

'How long has Doherty been in custody?' Reynolds asked.

'Almost two days. I went to the magistrates earlier and we've got two days more maximum, then it's charge or release.'

Jessica swore loudly. 'We got him red-handed though.'

The DCI looked across his desk at her. 'How's the fist?'

'Fine.'

'It's a good job twenty-three officers saw him slip and fall on his face, isn't it?'

'I said I was sorry.'

'Are you?'

'No.'

DCI Farraday said nothing. He couldn't be seen to endorse violence from his officers. 'I know we got him red-handed but the problem is, at best, we could only charge him with attempted murder. At worst, trespassing.'

'What about the knife?'

'What about it? He's no-commenting and his solicitor could just say he found it on my property.'

Cole spoke next. 'Surely the fact his DNA is a complete match for everything we've found is enough?'

The DCI answered again. 'I thought so too. I've been talking to the super and he's been going back and forth with the CPS. Basically, no one knows because the situation is so unusual. Normally when you find DNA at a scene and pair it to someone, that's the end of it. The problem is it's also a direct match for McKenna.'

Jessica cut in. 'But we know they're twins now, so what?'

'Identical twins who aren't, well, identical. Look at it from a jury's point of view. You have one scientist who gets up and tells you the DNA is a definite one-hundred-per-cent match to Dennis Doherty – the defendant – but that it's also a complete match for someone else too. It's hardly "beyond reasonable doubt", is it?'

'Yeah, but that other guy is in prison,' Jessica said, exasperated.

'Doesn't matter though, does it? There's still doubt and it could go either way. All it takes is a clever barrister who has a different expert witness banging on about planting evidence and some dopes on the jury let him walk.'

'John Mills is an eyewitness. He saw the guy.'

'He saw someone with a bit of a scar after he had already been stabbed. Besides, all it would take is a witness to his bad character and he'd be laughed out of court. If the other side had any sense they'd use a female barrister and the misogynistic prick would blow his top anyway.'

Jessica nodded in agreement but still tried to force the point. 'We *know* it's Doherty though.'

'What are we sure of?' Reynolds asked.

The chief inspector spoke. 'Not enough. There's no doubt they are twins. Their DNA matches for a start and we've got both birth certificates – they have the exact same birthday and birthplace. McKenna has a mother listed but no father, Doherty has a *different* mother listed and a father. Just to confuse matters more, their half-sister, Mary O'Connor, doesn't have a birth certificate.'

DI Cole sighed before he spoke. 'We know Mary said she was born to travellers and certainly the area McKenna and Doherty were born in was home to traveller families. Is there any chance the mother could have given away a daughter and then, a couple of years later, split up twins because she couldn't cope?'

Farraday looked across at the three of them. 'I'm not sure we'll ever know that. You don't have to have a baby in a hospital and although the parents should legally register a birth, we know from Mary's experiences it doesn't always happen. None of their parents are alive and it would have happened before any of them were old enough to know any better. I think the only thing we can ask is if either McKenna or Doherty – or both – have realised since they were related. It would help if we knew why they looked different too. With Doherty no-commenting, we may never know.'

'Did you get much from McKenna at the prison?' Jessica asked, turning to Cole.

'A long stream of "no comment"s.'

The four detectives looked at each other, as if hoping for inspiration. 'What do you reckon?' Jessica asked the DCI.

'I think the CPS could possibly charge him with the murders and then hope we actually dig something up before the pre-trial hearing. Otherwise, everyone's screwed.'

'Can I talk to him?' Jessica said.

The chief inspector looked at her. 'You know why I've kept you out. For one, you can't just assault someone, even if he did "slip". Secondly, if he brought up the fact you dropped him my name, we could end up with nothing. Frankly, I don't know why he hasn't done it already.'

'Do we know why he's giving us no comment?' she asked.

The DCI gazed at her quizzically. 'Same reason they all do, so they don't give anything away.'

'But he's not just our standard killer, is he? If he wanted to cause a fuss, he would have told his lawyer about me already but he hasn't. Don't forget, he went after specific people because he thought they deserved it. I don't think he's afraid of facing up to his crimes – you might even find he wants to go to prison because he'll have better access to the people he's targeting.'

'If that was true, why wouldn't he just confess?'

'Maybe he needs an incentive?'

'Like what?'

'Let me talk to him.'

'No. Tell me your idea and one of us will try it.'

'I think it has to be me.'

Cole spoke next. 'He was somewhat smitten with Jessica at the prison, Sir.'

'You don't think he's going to confess to everything just because he has a bit of a crush?'

'No, Sir,' Jessica said. 'I think he's going to confess because we know something he doesn't.'

Jessica was sitting in the interview room as Cole set up the recording device. 'Are you sure you're going to be okay?' he asked.

'Yeah, I'm fine.'

'You can't do anything . . . *silly*.'

'You know me.'

'Yes I do and that's my point.' Jessica said nothing as the heavy door clanged open and Dennis Doherty was led into the room handcuffed with his solicitor just behind him.

The lawyer was someone Jessica recognised from one of the local firms, convincing her even more the suspect wasn't too bothered whether or not he got off. If he was really desperate, he would have either hired one of the better-known defence solicitors himself or waited for the ones who were desperate to get their faces in the papers to come along. Jessica knew she was playing a dangerous game and that if Dennis really did want to be acquitted, he would bring up their various meetings. The possible entrapment would muddy the waters further for a jury when it came to trial if a solicitor mentioned it.

'I'm just wondering if we can have a bit of a chat, Dennis?' she said.

He said nothing, staring at his own hands. His nose still had flecks of dried blood around it and was flattened to one side. Jessica thought she should probably feel guilty for doing it but there was no remorse.

She wanted to stare into the blue eyes of the man who had killed her friend but he wouldn't look up. 'You and I both know you did this but I don't think anyone else in this room understands why you did it. You see, I think you worked on the front gate for all those years and you saw people coming in and out and in again and you got sick of it all.'

No response.

'First there was Craig Millar. He was a bit of an unsavoury guy, wasn't he? Drugs, intimidation, all sorts. Bit unimpressive though, wasn't he? On his own I bet he was a pushover?'

Dennis didn't acknowledge her, still staring at his own wrists.

'Then it was the big two, Webb and Hughes. I wondered if you planned to hit the two of those together. Still, it worked out all right, didn't it? What about the prison guard, Lee Morgan? It must have driven you crazy seeing him walk in and out of work each morning knowing what he was up to on the side?'

'No comment.'

'Is that all you've got to say? Here's my point, if you wanted to deal with those people, why wouldn't you want to be inside with them? Couldn't you operate better from the inside?'

The man shuffled slightly in his seat and Jessica wondered if he was understanding what she was trying to say. She pointed towards the solicitor. 'This man in the suit who's been telling you to not say anything, you don't think he's interested in your work, do you? He's the exact kind of person who gets all these criminals off. All those ones you hear about on the news, all those people you see walking in and out of the prison, they're all represented by people like him.'

The lawyer leant in across the table. 'You're out of line – and the actions of other people have got nothing to do with my client.'

'Do you hear that, Dennis? You're his "client". Does that sound like someone who's remotely interested in what your reasons were?'

Dennis again fidgeted nervously in his chair but didn't say anything.

'Obviously you know you have a brother in prison. All the coverage through the papers would have told you if you didn't already know. Now I'll be honest with you – we don't know whether you were working with your brother or not. We have no idea. But isn't it strange that you want to get these types of people off the streets and yet one of them is your brother?'

'No comment.'

'Here's my second point, Dennis. Does it strike you that maybe this kind of thing runs in the family?'

Dennis was clearly getting agitated. He raised his cuffed hands to scratch at his head.

'And then your sister's in prison too . . .'

He moved in his chair, shuffling backwards and then looking up at her. His solicitor went to cut in but the prisoner spoke over the top of him. 'I don't have a sister.'

'Did you always know you had a brother?'

'You're making it up.'

'I'm not. All three of you have the same eyes.' Jessica opened an envelope that was on the table between them but didn't take any of the contents out. 'Can you see the irony, Dennis? I know you're someone who's very intelligent. You want to cleanse the streets but at the same time you, your brother and sister are all criminals yourselves.'

The solicitor stood and physically tried to pick his client up by the arm. 'No chance, you're not doing this,' he said angrily. 'This is over. You can't blackmail a confession out of someone by holding back knowledge of a relative.'

Dennis rose too and his lawyer started bundling him towards the door but then the prisoner pushed his solicitor back before he could be taken out of the room. The man in the suit looked at his client, weighing up whether he should try moving him again. He clearly didn't fancy his chances.

The suspect looked at Jessica and his head sank. He started to speak in a quiet, more solemn tone. 'I was in a bad car accident when I was younger.' Everyone in the room froze. Dennis's lawyer looked panicked while Jessica said nothing, giving the prisoner space to talk. 'That's why we look different.' He lifted his cuffed hands to his face and ran them along the length of his scar. 'That's how I got this. I didn't really have much of a face left.'

He slumped to the floor as Jessica rose from her seat, crouching near to him. He spoke in a broken voice. 'I didn't know I had a brother, let alone a twin. He's been in and out over the years and, on the few times we've seen each other, there has always been this sort of familiarity. But if you were brought up as an only child, you wouldn't necessarily assume you had some long-lost brother just because someone looked a little like you, would you?'

He indicated his scar again. 'Have you ever seen a person on the street or on TV and someone says you look a bit like them? Because of this I didn't even know if that's what I should look like anyway. I just kind of saw him and forgot.'

The lawyer sat back at the table, defeated. Cole was opposite him, with Jessica settling cross-legged on the floor across from Dennis.

'When did you find out?' she asked.

'Officially? In the last couple of days with all the questioning and everything. Obviously it got around the prison after you had been to talk to McKenna because you had matched him to the crimes. I suspected then of course. I checked his birthday on our system and saw it was identical to mine. It's not like I could have just asked him though.'

'Do you know you have the same mother?'

'No. Is it true we have a sister?'

'Yes.'

'What's her name?'

'Mary.'

'And she's in prison too?'

'Yes.'

Dennis sniffed away a tear. 'I spent all my life thinking I was on my own then it takes all of this to find out I actually have a twin brother and a sister.'

'Do you know anything about your parents, Dennis, or why you might have been separated?'

'No. We travelled around a lot when I was a kid then ended up back here. They were getting on a bit in years and said they were to ready to settle. I knew I'd been born here but didn't know anything specific.'

'We know you and Donald McKenna have different mothers on your birth certificates but I don't think we'll ever be able to tell you who your parent actually was.'

The man shrugged. 'I don't think it really matters any more. Whoever it was would probably be ashamed of us.'

'Why did you kill them, Dennis?'

The man shrugged again. Jessica had been annoyed at herself for beginning to feel a little sympathy but the casual way he moved his shoulders showed he had no real regret. 'I just got sick of it. The same faces doing the same things over and over and no one does anything about it.'

'You must have known you'd get caught?'

'Maybe but I planned carefully and watched everyone so I knew their routines. I knew I wasn't on any databases or anything because I'd never been arrested. Even if I left some traces at the scene I didn't see any way you could ever link it back to me.'

Jessica could see he was right. If it wasn't for the link to McKenna, they would have just had some random DNA without knowing whose it was. 'What about the police officer?'

'Your friend?'

'Yes, my friend.'

'I didn't hear her. She had nothing on her feet and was on me before I could think. I didn't mean to but she was really strong. You were the last people I would have targeted.'

Jessica wasn't going to push her luck by mentioning the fact he'd gone after Farraday a few nights previously. She asked Dennis if he could sit back at the table and give them the full details they would need. Facially he barely reacted but he did what she asked, resigned to whatever was going to happen to him.

When he had finished speaking, he was taken back to the cells as Jessica passed the details of the man's sister to his solicitor. She didn't know if there would be any co-operation between the prisons to allow people to meet and, given everything that had happened, didn't really care.

37

Jessica walked along the gravel path and listened. The few birds that hadn't yet flown south were chirping noisily but, aside from that, she couldn't hear anything other than the scrunching of her own footsteps. She realised the quiet was almost more deafening than the noise she was so used to. Living in a city, even on the outskirts, you grew accustomed to the low hum of traffic and people and it became the norm. She didn't know if the tranquillity was better or worse. In some ways the constant clamour she was so familiar with was reassuring.

She followed the trail around the church and then moved onto the grass, walking carefully in between the gravestones to find the one she was looking for. There had been dew earlier in the morning and the ground felt soft underfoot. Jessica looked from side to side, taking in the names and wondering how everyone came to be there. Most of the dates on the stones would have meant it was simply old age but, every now and then, there were names of people who died young. She found it humbling, seeing the details of people born after her but who were already buried beneath her feet.

The graveyard was bigger than she remembered but Jessica eventually saw the stone she was looking for. The whole area was a mix of old weathered monuments and new chiselled markers. Carrie Jones's stood out as the wisps of morning sunlight reflected off its surface. Jessica crossed towards it and placed the flowers she had been carrying next to the fresh ones already there. She stood looking down at the engravings, with Carrie's name, date of birth and death, and a simple message.

'Always in our hearts.'

Jessica sat between the plot and the one adjacent to it, leaning gently on the gravestone. For a while she listened to the breeze and the birds and then she smiled. 'I can see why you left this place,' she said with a small giggle. 'Bit quiet, ain't it?'

The ground was wet underneath her and she could feel the dampness seeping through her jeans but it was already too late to do much about it. 'Your mum's a character, I can see where you got the laugh from now. I don't know how you stayed so thin though, all she wanted to do last night was feed me. She's doing all right, looking after your dad and shouting at the rugby players on the TV. I'm not sure if she shouts louder when they're winning or losing.'

She moved her head to the side so it was resting on the stone. 'Everyone keeps telling me I did a good job for figuring things out and getting Dennis to talk but no one wants to tell me the truth. Maybe if I'd been a better mate we would have been able to talk about your bloke and things would have happened differently? I've not told anyone about things but Farraday – your John – quit last week. He called me into his office to tell me first and then announced it officially to everyone else. I think he felt guilty.'

Jessica was wearing a thick jacket but felt a chill go through her as the breeze picked up. 'I think I lost it for a while somewhere along the line. I was seeing things that weren't there and acting without thinking things through. I look at it now and it doesn't even seem like me, it's as if I was watching someone else doing those things.'

She tried to suppress a shiver as she continued talking gently to the stone. 'I spoke to Denise Millar a few days ago. She's keeping everything together for Jamie and says he's got a job now. I think catching the person that killed her other son has helped her come to terms with it all.'

She stood and wiped as much of the dampness from her trousers as she could, peering back at the stone. 'I'm just here to say goodbye and thanks for being a mate when I needed one.'

Jessica turned and walked briskly away back to the cemetery's entrance. There was a wide wooden gate which she unclasped and moved through before shunting it back into position. She leant back onto it and took out her phone, skimming through the first couple of contacts. She highlighted Adam Compton's name and typed out a simple text message.

'I'm sorry. J'

She pressed the button to send and walked quickly out towards the waiting taxi on the main road before getting into the back seat. 'You all right, love?' the driver asked.

'Yeah, can you take me to the train station now?'

The driver pulled away as Jessica leant back into the seat and closed her eyes. She felt her mind beginning to drift but was snapped back to the present as her phone beeped to say she had a new message.

Notes and Acknowledgements

As with *Locked In*, I will fully admit to taking a few liberties with the length of time certain scientific processes take. This has only been done in order to keep the story moving even though, in theory, I guess they could be called 'mistakes'.

This book is a lot more science-based than the first one for obvious reasons if you have reached this bit without just skipping to the back first (tsk, tsk if you have). I'm not a very scientific person myself but, as far as I can check and tell – and according to the people I've spoken to – everything in the story should be correct.

As for the police work itself, my aim wasn't to create something one hundred per cent accurate in terms of procedure as I'm not really sure how much enjoyment people would take from reading numerous chapters about filling in paperwork. These books are meant to sit close to reality. Many of the places are real but locations such as Longsight Police Station aren't really as I've described them, certainly in terms of the interior.

The people who have helped me with the editing and research for the book know who they are and I can only thank them all yet again.

Thanks for your comments and questions. Feel free to contact me through my website http://kerrywilkinson.com

THE WOMAN IN BLACK

Jessica Daniel Book 3

Severed body parts. A woman in shadows.
These are the only clues.

Someone has left a severed hand in the centre of Manchester and the only clue Detective Sergeant Jessica Daniel has to go on is CCTV footage of a woman in a long black robe placing it carefully on the ground.

With a lengthy missing persons list and frantic families wondering if the body part could belong to their absent loved ones, she has plenty to deal with – and that's before a detached finger arrives for her in the post.

By the time a second hand is found and a local MP's wife goes missing, Jessica is left struggling to find out who the appendages belong to, how they are connected and just what the mysterious woman in black has to do with it all.

An extract follows here . . .

ISBN 978-1-4472-2567-6

1

Detective Sergeant Jessica Daniel swept the strand of long dark blonde hair away from her face and looked down at the object in front of her before saying the only thing that came to mind. 'Well, it's definitely a hand.'

The man standing next to her nodded in agreement. 'Blimey, nothing gets past you, does it?'

Jessica laughed. 'Oi. It's just you never know what you're going to get, do you? When I was in uniform I got sent out because there were reports of a dead animal blocking a road and it was only someone's coat. For all we knew, this "severed hand" could have been part of a kid's doll.'

Detective Inspector Jason Reynolds looked at the scene in front of them, nodding. 'You're right but this ain't a kid's toy.'

The appendage was greying in colour and blended with the patch of concrete it had been left on. Jessica thought it looked fairly hardened, as if the fingers would be stiff and awkward to move, even though the digits were splayed and it was flat to the ground. Given the clean-looking cut where it would have once been connected to someone's wrist, Jessica was surprised there was no blood. She didn't want to touch it but stepped closer and crouched, peering towards the small stump where the person's ring finger had been neatly sliced off. It looked as if the area had been burned after the amputation to stop any infection and she wondered if the finger had been removed before or after the rest of the hand.

Jessica stood and stepped backwards out of the small white tent into the heat of the morning sunshine with Reynolds just behind her. The inspector was a tall black officer who had an outwardly friendly demeanour but, when he wanted to be, was as tough as anyone she knew. She walked towards the edge of the police tape surrounding the scene, stopping before she got too close to the nearby uniformed officer who was preventing passers-by from getting too good a look. 'What do you reckon happened to the missing finger?' she asked.

'Who knows? It looks as if it was cut off as cleanly as the hand itself,' the inspector replied.

'Do you think the person it's from is dead?'

Reynolds blew out through his teeth as he squinted into the sun. 'Probably. We'll have to check the records to see if there have been any remains found in the past year or two that are missing a hand. There's nothing to say it would definitely be from a body from our area, so we'll have a bit of work to do. The way it's been preserved, it could be an old victim or someone brand new. Whoever left it has been very careful.'

'Not much to go on, was there?' Jessica said. 'No tattoos or anything.'

'I know. Given its shape with the wider fingers I'd bet it was a man's hand but that could just be minor decomposition. It looks as if whoever cut it off has kept it carefully.

We're going to have to wait for the forensics team to see if they can find anything.'

'Yeah, you've got to *hand* it to the lab boys, they do a top job.'

Reynolds looked at Jessica, eyebrows raised. 'I really don't think stand-up comedy is the career for you.'

Jessica grinned back. 'Oh come on. Just because you've been promoted, it doesn't mean you have to stop laughing at my jokes.'

'I don't remember ever laughing at your jokes.'

'All right, fine, be grumpy. What are we going to do next?'

Reynolds looked around at the buildings surrounding them. 'The thing is, this is the centre of Manchester, the second or third biggest city in the country. Just look at the cameras.' He pointed out the CCTV units mounted high on the shops, hotels and flats nearby. 'This is Piccadilly Gardens. You couldn't have picked a more public spot if you tried. Whoever left this wanted it to be found.' He paused, as if pondering what he wanted to do. 'If you take a constable and look through the footage from last night, I'll start working through any missing persons reports to see if there have been any bodies found without a hand nationwide. By the time we've gone through all that, we might have some test results back to give us a gender and age for the victim.'

Jessica looked to the areas the inspector had pointed out. Piccadilly Gardens was one of the main meeting points in the centre of Manchester. The middle part was a mixture of grassy park areas surrounded by benches and fountains, along with concreted and paved sections for people to walk. One side was dominated by a bus and tram station, another lined by a wide walkway and shops. Looming over the top of the area was a hotel and a road with more shops edged along the final side.

Jessica looked back towards the area the hand had been found in, just underneath one of the fountains next to a bench. Unless someone had dropped it, which made some very odd assumptions about the types of thing people carried around with them, it seemed clear the hand had been left purposely.

Jessica could see at least seven security cameras scanning the area, one of which was swivelling high on a pole around fifty feet away from where she was standing. Three other similar cameras were placed around the square. She knew they were linked into a set of other CCTV cameras throughout the city, the images feeding back to a central security point that was manned twenty-four hours a day. Most people thought the cameras were constantly watched by police officers but the operators were a private security firm paid for by the council.

As she scanned around, she could see two other cameras attached to the hotel and a further one high above a shop front. She figured footage from those would be kept somewhere on their respective sites.

Jessica felt the warmth of the June sun on her arms and thought about spending the rest of the day indoors watching camera footage from the night before. 'Whoever left it could have at least picked a rainy day,' she said to no one in particular.

Jessica slumped back into her chair and sighed. The office she was sitting in belonged to the private security firm who monitored the city's cameras. It felt small, lit only by a fluorescent strip on the ceiling above her and the bank of monitors she was facing. She leant forward to press a button on a control panel, stopping the video images she had been watching, then pushing back in her seat again and peering at the woman next to her. 'Bored of being in CID yet?'

The female officer slouched back in her own chair and laughed. 'We've only been looking through the tapes for an hour.'

'Exactly, an hour; we could have been out doing all sorts. Someone with a name like yours shouldn't be stuck inside on a day like this. You should be in a rock band or something.'

'"Isobel" isn't that strange a name.'

Jessica nodded. 'Maybe not but "Izzy" sounds cool. Especially "Izzy Diamond". It's too good a name to be wasted on the Greater Manchester Police force.'

'It wasn't so "cool" when I was at school. "Dizzy Izzy", "Isobel-End", "Izzy A Bloke?" and all that.'

'That's quite original bullying,' Jessica said, trying not to sound too impressed. 'At my school, I just got called "Dan the Man" for ten years.'

Detective Constable Izzy Diamond had only joined

Manchester Metropolitan's Criminal Investigation Department six weeks before. The division's detective chief inspector, John Farraday, had given up his job almost seven months ago but stayed on for a short while to help guide his successor into the post. The new incumbent, Jack Cole, had previously been a DI and, with his promotion, Jason Reynolds had been elevated from detective sergeant to inspector. Jessica had previously spent just over two years sharing an office with the then DS Reynolds and the pair's relationship hadn't altered much despite his change in job.

Because of the reshuffle and the fact one of their colleagues, DC Carrie Jones, had been killed the previous year, two new constables had been hired. DC Diamond was one of the fresh faces and Jessica had chosen to take the new girl under her wing. There was very little between them in terms of age, with Jessica in her early thirties and the constable less than a year younger.

Jessica glanced away from the monitors to look at the officer. 'Did you have that colour hair when you were at school?'

Izzy ran her hands through her long bright red mane seemingly without thinking about it. She let it drop to her shoulders then tied it into a ponytail with a band she'd had around her wrist. 'Nope, it was a type of browny dark colour then. I've only been red like this for the past year, since I got married. I fancied a change after we got back from honeymoon.'

Jessica nodded. 'I think it's pretty cool.'

'It scares off the older guys at the station so that's a

bonus. I think most of them think I'm a vampire or something.'

'What's it like?'

The constable grinned and had a twinkle in her blue eyes. 'What, being a vampire?'

Jessica laughed. 'No, being married.'

Izzy bit her bottom lip. 'Marriage is fine. My husband, Mal, would like to start trying for kids but I want to do this for a few more years at least before I think about that. I'd rather try the vampirism.'

Jessica looked back towards the monitors and pressed the button that started the footage at double speed. She kept her eyes on the screen, continuing to talk. 'Is Mal short for Malcolm?'

'Malachi.'

'Wow, you two have the best names ever. You did marry him just for the last name though, didn't you?'

Izzy laughed. 'Of course. Who could resist "Diamond" as a surname? I used to be "Isobel Smith", which was way more boring.'

Jessica had worked on a few minor things with the constable since she had been appointed but the mystery over the severed hand was by far the most serious case Izzy had been involved with. Jessica hadn't been told by anyone she had to go out of her way to work closely with any of the new recruits but had done so anyway. It felt strange because she was Izzy's supervisor but, in some respects, she felt inferior to her. Jessica lived in a flat on her own, the constable was married and owned a house. It wasn't that Jessica was desperate to have a boyfriend or settle down but they were roughly the same age and Izzy seemed like the proper grown-up to her. While the constable would do a full day at work and talk about hosting dinner parties and the like, Jessica would spend her evenings either in front of the television or on the Internet while eating microwaved food. The fact the woman next to her could even contemplate having children nailed her down as a genuine adult. Jessica couldn't stand other people's kids – let alone think about having any of her own.

'My mate's getting married,' Jessica said.

'Someone from the station?'

'I do have other friends too!'

'Sorry, I didn't mean . . .'

'It's all right. She's my oldest friend actually, Caroline. We lived together for ages but grew apart. We've only been back in regular contact for the last couple of months or so.'

'Let me guess, the job came between you?' From her tone, it sounded as if Izzy spoke from experience.

'You don't know the half of it . . .'

Two years previously, Jessica had been trying to find a serial killer. The trail ultimately led her to Caroline's boy-friend Randall, who tried to kill her. He was currently in a secure hospital and, as far as Jessica knew, hadn't spoken to anyone since his arrest. After that things hadn't quite been the same between the pair.

'Is it something you want to talk about?' Izzy asked, apparently sensing Jessica's discomfort.

'Not really. She phoned and asked if I'd be a bridesmaid for her.'

'Are you doing it?'

'Of course. We didn't fall out and I'd still call her my best friend. I'm glad she asked but I'm not so sure about the whole big event thing. I don't really do dressing up and all that.'

Izzy peered down at the light brown trouser suit she was wearing, fingering the thin lapel on her jacket. 'Don't you ever get bored of these suits every day?'

Jessica glanced away from the screens at her own grey suit. 'I used to, maybe a couple of years ago. I don't really think about it now. She's not picked the dresses yet. I'm worried it will be some sort of pink or yellow monstrosity and I'll be left living with those horrific photos until the end of time. If anyone from the station sees them . . .' She drifted off, contemplating how she would struggle to live down those potential images.

The constable laughed, glancing up at the screen Jessica was watching. 'I think my bridesmaids were worried about the same thing. We all chose together and went for something relatively plain and cream.'

'Caroline's favourite colour is purple, so I'm hoping she's kind.'

There was a short pause as they both watched the monitor. There wasn't much to see but every now and then a person or two would walk across the shot. After a period of silence, Izzy leant forward. 'Do we have any idea what time this hand would have been left?'

Jessica slowed the footage so it was playing at one and a half times the regular speed. 'Presumably after it went dark. It was found a little before eight this morning, so sometime between half-ten last night and then.' She pointed at the screen. 'There's a blind spot during this night footage because of where the street lights are.'

'What do you reckon's going on with the hand?'

Jessica made a humming noise. 'I don't know. Jason thinks whoever left it wanted it to be found.'

'You don't sound so sure.'

'I agree with him actually but I'm always worried by people who go out of their way to get attention. Most people we deal with don't want to be caught and do every-thing they can to avoid it. A handful are genuinely sorry and admit to what they've done in order to clear their conscience. Then you get a very tiny minority who want to show off. They're the ones who are unpredictable but know what they're doing. Maybe they want to be caught at some stage but not before they've made their point.'

'I'd never thought of it like that.'

'You don't until you find yourself in the middle of things.' Jessica reached forward and set the speed back to double. They sat in silence watching the images slowly lighten in front of them as the sun began to come up.

'Not bad quality, is it?' Izzy said.

'Most of the CCTV you go through isn't this good. Half the shops with cameras only have these grainy setups where you can't figure out who someone is even if they're looking directly at the camera,' Jessica replied.

'I've had a couple of those when I was back in uniform. It's ridiculous when you put the pictures out in the papers and you can't even tell if it's a man or woman.'

Jessica reached out and paused the footage, putting her

finger on the screen in front of them. 'What's that?' she said.

The constable turned to face her as Jessica scrolled the action back a few seconds and let it play at regular speed. The light was still dim but the video clearly showed the back of a figure wearing a long black robe walking across the paved walkway in between the fountains. The figure in itself wouldn't have necessarily been out of place but, aside from someone sleeping on one of the benches, they were the only person in shot. As the shape moved out of the frame, Jessica flicked the controls to change the angle to one of the other central cameras.

'Is it someone wearing one of those religious robes? A burqa or niqab?' Izzy said.

Jessica's fingers flicked across the controls as she spoke. 'I don't think so. Look.' She pointed towards the new screen that had appeared. 'There's no facial cover, it's just a robe, like a dressing gown. Let's see if we can zoom in.' She ran her hand over a dial and the images refocused closer in.

'Is it a man or a woman?' Izzy asked.

'Probably a woman. You can see she's wearing low heels and has that way of walking as if she's comfortable in them. It's the way she's moving too.'

Izzy clearly agreed. 'I doubt there are many men out there who can walk so comfortably in heels. I'm not great myself.'

'There are no clear images of the person's face. You can just about tell they're white but nothing more. She knows where the cameras are.'

Jessica pressed buttons to cut from one camera perspective to a second, then a third, before continuing. 'Look at the angle of her face. She's deliberately looking down and across because she knows there won't be a clear view of her.' She scrolled backwards through the footage to reinforce her point. 'She's turning ever so slightly as she walks to keep the angle and is wearing gloves too. This person knows what she's doing.'

Jessica moved the footage forward, switching between cameras until the hooded figure neared the base of the fountain where the hand had been found. Jessica slowed the stream down to regular speed, watching as the cloaked figure stopped by the edge of the fountain and crouched. She reached across herself, stretching into an inner pocket of the robe and taking out an object that had to be the hand, before placing it on the ground. It seemed as if the figure was deliberately spreading the fingers into the correct position, before nudging it towards a nook between the bench and fountain. Then they stood, walking back the way they came.

Jessica started to ask a question but Izzy got there first. 'Who the hell is that?'

extracts reading groups
competitions books new events reading groups
discounts extracts extracts discounts
competitions extracts
books new events
events books extracts
extracts new reading groups
interviews
events extracts events events books
discounts interviews new books
new books events events new books extracts
events new
discounts extracts discounts

www.panmacmillan.com

extracts events reading groups books
competitions books extracts new